TIMING IS
EVERYTHING

TIMING IS
EVERYTHING

Sabra Brown Steinsiek

Enjoy!

Sabra Brown Steinsiek

Writers Club Press
San Jose New York Lincoln Shanghai

Timimg Is Everything

Writers Club Press
an imprint of iUniverse.com, Inc.

For information address:
iUniverse.com, Inc.
620 North 48th Street, Suite 201
Lincoln, NE 68504-3467
www.iuniverse.com

ISBN: 0-595-12656-1

Printed in the United States of America

For my husband and research partner, Will, who has always believed I could, and should, do anything I put my mind to.

To every thing there is a season, and a time to every purpose under the heaven…A time to be born and a time to die…a time to weep and a time to laugh…a time to get and a time to lose…a time to love…

Ecclesiastes 3

ACKNOWLEDGEMENTS

A book is never written by just one person. In my case, it took almost a whole army. I could not have done it without—

—my Mother, Mary Louise O'Hearn Brown, who gave me the love of books at an early age.

—my husband, Will, and my son, Jared, the computer gurus that made the physical writing process possible and who never once complained because dinner was late…again.

—the "editors" who bravely volunteered to read the early version without even knowing if I could write. Elodie, Cindy, Frances, Nancy, Roberta, and Beth. Thanks, too, to all the others who read it at varying stages, Barb, Carol, Carolyn, Deb, Gen, Heidi, Jude, Kathy C., Kathy P., Maggie, Marsha, Mary, Pat, and my sisters, Eileen and Shannon.

—the *real* Beth, who never let me give up, and Nancy, my partner on this journey through the publishing jungle. You never stopped believing in me.

—Carla Aragon and Jim Belshaw who gave me insight into the news business, both television and print.

and

—Michael, who inspired me to create Taylor.

PROLOGUE

As Nancy Morgan pulled into the driveway she saw her husband, Jay, coming out of the house. It was late and, as usual, he had been watching for them to come home. She reached across and unlocked the passenger door for him. Jay picked up their sleeping son, carrying him into the house and up the stairs to bed. Nancy followed them and kissed the sleeping boy goodnight as she pulled the blankets up around his small shoulders. The dim light of the hall caught his reddish-brown curls and she couldn't resist touching them. Sleepily, the boy roused and murmured, "'Night" before falling soundly asleep.

As Nancy pulled the door closed, Jay asked, "So, how was the show?"

"It was wonderful, Jay. I wish you had come with us."

"No, I would have spoiled it for both of you. I can't sit still that long." He put his arm around her as they walked down the hall to their bedroom. "How did Taylor like it?"

Nancy slipped off her shoes and turned so he could unzip her dress for her. "He loved it. I expected he would, but he said something on the way home that surprised me."

"Taylor has a talent for doing that," his father acknowledged with a smile.

"He does," Nancy agreed, "but this was different."

Seven-year-old Taylor had been uncharacteristically quiet after the performance of *Phantom of the Opera*. This was the first "grown-up" show she had taken him to see and she had been a little concerned that it had been too much for him. It hadn't been until they were out on the highway beginning the hour-long drive home that he spoke.

"Mom?"

"Yes, Taylor?"

"I know what I want to do now."

"Now, Taylor? It's a little late…"

"No, Mom, what I want to do when I grow up. I want to do what he did—the Phantom."

Nancy was a little startled that her son wanted to grow up to be a disfigured, manipulative misfit but was willing to hear him out. "The Phantom, Taylor? You know he's just a fictional character."

Taylor sighed, "I know that, Mom. I meant I want to be an actor and a singer. I want to be able to make people feel the way he made me feel tonight."

"It's a good dream, Taylor, but you know it doesn't just happen. You'd have to work very hard."

"I know and I will. Someday, Mom, that's going to be me. Can we listen to the music again?"

Nancy reached out and started the tape player and the rich sounds of the *Phantom* overture filled the car. In a few minutes, Taylor was fast asleep leaving his mother to think about his announcement.

"Nancy, you know Taylor. Last week it was paleontology, this week it's theatre. Taylor changes his career goals to match his current interest!"

Nancy brushed her hair slowly, stopping to look at her husband, "I know that, Jay. But this announcement was different. I think I'm going to see if there are any children's theatre classes scheduled for this summer."

Jay took the brush out of his wife's hand. "Fine, Nancy. Let him try. Right now, it's late and I want to make love to my wife before we both fall asleep."

Laughing, Nancy put her arms around him and kissed him, the matter of their son's future forgotten for the moment.

I

"You're kidding! Right, Robert?" Laura Collins looked up from the assignment sheet the city editor had just thrown on her desk.

"Nope. He's all yours, Laura," the man said with an evil grin. "There are people on this staff who would kill for the chance I'm giving you."

"Then let them kill me and take it! You know I hate doing these celebrity stories." Laura pushed her fingers through her long, copper-colored hair. "Why can't Heidi do it? She loves this stuff."

"Heidi has the flu; so does half of the staff, Laura. In fact, you're going to have to run without a photographer, too. We'll just use the publicity shot that came with the press packet. Taylor Morgan is yours, like it or not. Your appointment is at eleven. Don't be late."

"Great. Just great," Laura muttered under her breath as she watched her boss walk away. She glanced at her watch, then down at the jeans and cotton shirt she was wearing. She hadn't dressed for an interview, especially not one with a major celebrity. If she hurried, she could look over the background file and still make it home in time to change before she had to be downtown for the interview. As she picked up her purse and notebook, she glared at the office where Robert was now closeted with Henry Alaniz, the paper's editor.

As she headed out the door she heard someone call out, "Laura!" She turned to see her best friend, Beth, hurrying to catch up with her. "Laura! Did you forget we were doing lunch?"

"I'm sorry, Beth, I did forget. Robert just assigned me an interview, and I have to get home to change."

"Change? Must be a pretty important interview."

"I have to interview that singer who's performing here tomorrow. Taylor Morgan, God's gift to the musical theatre and women everywhere." She rolled her eyes as she saw the look on Beth's face. "Not you, too!"

"Yes, me, too! Have you heard him sing? Or taken a look at that gorgeous face?" Beth knew Laura's taste in music ran more to classic rock and that it was unlikely she had ever paid much attention to Taylor Morgan. "If you need an assistant, I'll volunteer!"

"I'd give you the whole assignment if I could! I was planning on using today to finish up my research on that story about the governor's stand on drug use. I don't have time to waste on fluff!"

"Collins!" She looked up as her boss shouted her name across the busy newsroom. "Are you planning on making it to that interview today?"

She waved at him as she headed for the door. "We'll have to do lunch tomorrow, Beth. Sorry!"

"I'm going to want details!" Beth called after her. But Laura was already out the door and running down the stairs, too impatient to wait for the elevator.

*   *   *

Laura pulled her ancient Opel GT into a parking spot at the Hyatt Regency's garage with fifteen minutes to spare. She took ten minutes to review the file Robert had handed her. It was the usual bio stuff. Small town boy. Only child. Parents dead. Overnight sensation. Broadway's golden boy. She was impressed to see that he had channeled the considerable energy and resources of his fan club into raising funds for the children's charity he sponsored. Albuquerque, like many of the stops on his concert tour, had been chosen because of their Shelter for Children house. A fund-raiser reception was scheduled after the concert tomorrow night.

She glanced at the black and white glossy photo that was included in the packet. He was good looking with a boy-next-door kind of style. (Not that the boy next door to her had ever looked so good!) Nice smile. Thick, wavy hair. Maybe this wouldn't be so bad after all.

*   *   *

Laura mentally ran over her background notes about Morgan as the elevator ascended. A discreet chime signaled her arrival. As the doors opened, she was a little surprised to be met by two security guards who politely asked for her credentials. Sure, he was famous, but this was Albuquerque! After checking her name against a list, one of the men went to the door of the suite across from the elevator, received approval, then came back and escorted her to the door.

A very pretty young woman greeted her. "Ms. Collins, I'm Taylor's assistant, Christine Spencer. He'll be along in a moment. Could I get you some coffee or tea while you're waiting?"

"Thanks, but no. I'm fine. Where would you like me to set up?"

Christine showed her to a sunny window where a small table and two chairs had been placed. There was a superb view of the city and the Sandia Mountains to the east. "This will be fine, thanks. Have you been Mr. Morgan's assistant for long?"

Christine smiled, "A couple of years now."

"It must be interesting traveling all over the place," Laura commented as she got out a pad and pencil and placed them on the table.

"Interesting and a little wearing," she replied. "We're on the end of this leg of the tour, and I'll be glad to get home."

"I envy you. I've never traveled much, but I hope to someday." Laura took out a small tape recorder. "Do you know if Mr. Morgan will be agreeable to my using this?"

"I think we can work something out," said a deep voice behind her. Laura turned to find the most beautiful man she had ever seen smiling at her. The black and white press kit photo had not prepared her for his charisma and it had given no hint of the unique turquoise of his eyes; eyes that were now looking at her with a touch of amusement.

"You must be Laura Collins." He held out his hand and, for a split second, she nearly forgot to shake it. "From the *Herald*?" he prompted as her hand finally met his.

Laura had never had this kind of reaction to anyone before. She had to look away from him before she could focus on what she should be saying. Suddenly aware that she was still holding his hand, she took a deep breath as she released it, then said, "Yes, the *Albuquerque Herald*. It's very nice to meet you, Mr. Morgan." There was a security in saying all the right things that allowed her to regain her self-control. "Thank you for taking the time for this interview. I know our readers will be interested in your latest projects."

"First, Ms. Collins, I hate being called Mr. Morgan. That was my father. He was the school principal, and being called into Mr. Morgan's office was not a good thing. So, it's Taylor, please."

Laura laughed. "Then please call me Laura."

"I left some letters in the other room, Chris; I think they're ready for you." Christine put a pitcher of water and two glasses on the table, then left the room. Taylor indicated the chairs and waited until Laura was seated before he took his.

"Did Albuquerque arrange this beautiful weather just for my visit?" Taylor liked to take the lead in these interviews. If he could just develop some rapport with the interviewer, the whole experience was a lot less tedious.

Laura glanced out the window before answering. "I wish I could say that we did. Might keep some of those Easterners from moving here if we could say it was horrible all the time. See those patches of yellow on the mountain? Those are the aspens that have changed color, but you won't see many other signs of the changing season. Fall in New Mexico isn't like it is anywhere else. It comes on a little slower with less fanfare. Usually it's summer one day and winter the next. Sometimes it feels like we skip fall and spring altogether."

Taylor found her honesty a refreshing change from the people he usually dealt with. "I imagine that your newspaper doesn't agree with your views."

"No, and my editor would probably kill me if he knew what I said. I was born here and I wish, in some ways, that we weren't growing so quickly. But, then as a small town, we wouldn't be attracting someone like you." Laura deftly turned the conversation back to interview mode. "Tell me a little about how you got started in show business."

"I had a mother who was interested in theatre and music. My father, however, was tone-deaf and hated sitting still for very long. He was happy to hand off the escort duties to me as soon as I was old enough to be a companion instead of a responsibility. She and I went to every show or concert that came anywhere near us, and there were quite a few that came to Sacramento. It was only an hour away from Woodland where I grew up."

"You were pretty young when you left California for New York, weren't you?"

"Nineteen and sure I could conquer the world. I'd already been accepted to an outstanding drama program with a full scholarship, but I decided to go ahead and give it a go in New York."

"Nineteen? I can't imagine your parents were thrilled with the decision."

He laughed. "Not hardly! My parents and I had a really good relationship, and that was the first time I'd ever actually defied them. They finally gave in when they saw how determined I was. They gave me one year to make it. If I didn't, I would come back and go to school on the deferred scholarship."

"But you never had to go back?"

"It came close to happening. I'd had a couple of parts in shows that flopped, and I was living off my salary as a part-time bookstore clerk. I only had a month left on our agreement when I got my first big part. After that, everything just clicked into place, and I never looked back."

"So it took you a year to become an overnight sensation?"

"I was lucky. There are people out there much more talented than I am who are still waiting tables and working nights to keep their days open for auditions."

"And now it's concerts?"

"Before I left New York, I was onstage for eight years, in a combination of several shows. I'd had the chance to record a couple of CDs that sold fairly well. Then, I was approached a year ago to do this concert tour—tours, really, since we'll pick up again after the first of the year."

"When did you get involved with Shelter for Children?"

"I had a pretty idyllic childhood, not that I realized it at the time," he said with an engaging grin that almost cost Laura her hard-won poise. "My last year on Broadway, I was asked to perform in a benefit concert for Shelter. I met some of the kids, heard some of the horror stories. I couldn't forget them. I have an eleven-year-old goddaughter who could have easily ended up like one of them. So, I began to help in whatever way I could. Now I'm 'president' of the organization. Mostly it just means I lend my name for fund-raising, but I spend time with the kids when I can."

As Laura glanced down at her notes, Taylor was grateful for the break. There was something about Laura Collins that he found disturbing. She had a way of really listening to his answers, and he realized he had been telling her more than he had ever let out in an interview before. He would have to be careful that he didn't reveal too much. When she raised her head and her deep green eyes met his, he forgot all about being on his guard.

Laura smiled at him. "How does it feel to be the 'Sexiest Man Alive'?" she asked as she pulled out a copy of *People Magazine* that had been published a few weeks ago.

"Embarrassing, if you want to know the truth."

"Does this have anything to do with those guards outside your door?"

Taylor was silent for a moment before he answered. "I guess it does in some ways. I've got a pretty large fan base, and not all of them are stable. There have been a couple of incidents that have made security a necessity."

Laura said, "What about family, friends? What do you do in your free time, Taylor?"

"My best friend and her daughter, my goddaughter, live near me. I spend a lot of time with them when I'm home. I do a lot of in-line skating and reading, too."

A woman? His best friend was a woman? An unexpected bolt of pure jealousy ran through Laura before she continued.

"What about on the road? You do a tremendous amount of traveling. Do you ever get to really see any of the places you visit?"

"Not often. There's rarely time, always somewhere else to be. I wish I could spend more time. For example here—Albuquerque. It would be great to really take some time and explore it, share it with someone." His eyes softened as he looked out the window, like a child forced to do piano practice when others were outside playing.

Laura heard a note of melancholy in his voice, and she found herself unexpectedly filled with compassion for this man whose life was not really his own. She had never felt this way about any other interviewee, and she found it disconcerting. She changed the subject back to the concert and the plans for the post-concert charity benefit.

Finally, closing her notebook and turning off the recorder, she said, "Thanks for your time, Taylor. It's been a great interview. I hope you'll be pleased with what we publish."

He stood and watched as she gathered up her recorder and notebook. More than once during the interview, he had been distracted by her beauty. But, it was more than that. He felt a kinship with her, a connection he couldn't really pin down. All he *was* sure of was that he wanted to spend more time with her. Quickly, before he could reason himself out of it, he said, "Laura? Would you like to come to rehearsal tonight? And have dinner with me afterward?"

Laura was surprised and more than a little wary. This was not the first time she had been hit on by an interview subject, but it was the first time she had ever been tempted to say "yes." Something in his eyes told her that this was not the usual come-on and she said, "Taylor, I'd love to. Should I meet you back here before you go to the theatre?"

"That would be great; around six?"

"I'll be here." Laura picked up her things and headed for the door.

As he opened the door for her, he told the security guards, "Ms. Collins will be back tonight to go to the theatre with me."

"I'll see you then, Taylor," she said as she entered the elevator.

He turned and reentered the suite, closing the door behind him. Walking to the window, he stared out toward the mountains, his hands unconsciously caressing the back of the chair where she had been.

2

Beth was waiting at her desk. "Laura, how did the interview go? Is he really as sexy as people say?"

"If I tell you no, you won't believe me anyway, so, yes, he is definitely as sexy as they say he is."

Beth moaned. "Why did I decide to go into graphics? You reporters get all the good stuff!"

"Sure we do. Following the mayor around is so exciting." Laura logged on to her terminal and opened her notebook, ready to enter her notes. She had a four o'clock deadline to meet if this was going to run tomorrow. That would give her barely enough time to get home and change before she was supposed to meet Taylor.

"Oh, Laura," Beth said, reminding Laura that she was still standing there. "Cary called. He said to tell you that he would pick you up at seven."

"Who?" Laura looked at Beth as the message got through to her. "Oh, no! I forgot!"

"So, now you remember. What's the problem?"

"The problem is," Laura hissed at her, "I told Taylor I'd go to rehearsal and dinner with him tonight. I completely forgot about Cary."

"What?" Beth's voice startled most of the newsroom.

"Hush!" Laura shook her head. "Beth, I don't really want this to get around."

"Good Lord, why not? Everyone will die of envy."

"Except for Robert and Henry. I don't think the editors are going to be pleased that I'm dating one of my interview subjects."

"Dating? You mean this isn't business?"

"No...yes...Beth, I don't know what it is! He kind of blurted it out at the last second and I decided to say 'yes'. And, if you don't leave me alone, I won't get my article done and I won't get home in time to change and I will have nothing to report so that you can have a vicarious life. Go away!"

Beth said, "Fine, I'm going. But you will owe me details, girl, lots of them. Call me when you get home no matter how late it is." Beth paused, then grinned as she continued, "Of course, if you don't call, I will assume...."

Laura glared at her, then waved Beth away as she picked up her phone to dial Cary's number. They'd been planning dinner for between the early and late news broadcasts, so he should be at the television station by now. He wasn't going to be happy.

"Cary Edwards." As usual, Cary didn't waste time on everyday pleasantries when he answered the phone.

"Hi, it's Laura."

"You got my message? Seven should work out about right."

"Not for me, Cary. I have to work."

She could hear the disbelief in his voice as he answered, "Work?"

"You television people aren't the only ones to keep late hours. The flu has half the newsroom out sick, so I've got to cover for someone. It'll be late before I'm done, so we'll have to take a raincheck on this evening."

"Sure, Laura. Just let me know when." His words were reasonable, but his tone made it clear he was annoyed. Cary Edwards was not used to being stood up.

"I've got a deadline to meet, Cary. Can we set a new time later?"

"I'll talk to you later, then."

He hung up without waiting for her to respond, but Laura didn't have time to think about it—she had a deadline to meet.

*   *   *

Cary Edwards was a reporter for a local television station. Tall and slender, he had black hair and dark blue eyes. The camera loved him, and most of the women around him had the same reaction—at first. He took full advantage of the benefits his looks and high-profile job brought, and he was never with any one woman for very long. He preferred to "love 'em and leave 'em." The chase was a game; bedding a woman was the prize. Once he'd had someone, the fun was over and he began looking for his next conquest.

Cary had met Laura a few weeks ago at a party, and he'd been immediately attracted to her. While she didn't mean any more to him than the rest of the women in his past, she was proving difficult to get close to; that only made the game more interesting. Cary had no doubt he would win in the end, but his tentative job offer from The News Channel—TNC—narrowed the time he had to make the conquest.

"Cary!"

He looked up to find the assignment editor at his desk. "Sorry to do this to you," he said as he tossed a folder onto Cary's desk. "I need to you to do a stand-up tonight. Here are the details. Jon's on camera. We want it for ten and will probably run it again tomorrow. Try to get a few words with him," he said, heading back to his desk without waiting for Cary's response.

Cary didn't really mind working late. A last-minute gig like this always got his adrenaline going. He opened the folder, then stared in disbelief at the picture inside.

*   *   *

Taylor wondered what had possessed him to ask Laura to the rehearsal; it was something he never did. He preferred to have only those necessary around while he prepared. He had never invited anyone, let alone a reporter, to a rehearsal. And dinner? He rarely ate much after a rehearsal; he was usually too tired and keyed up to eat.

There had been a progression of women over the years, even a brief engagement, but Taylor tended to be a loner for the most part. He avoided the party scene and preferred staying in when he wasn't on the road. If he was alone, it was by choice, not from lack of opportunity.

So, why now? Why this woman he knew nothing about? For all he knew, she had accepted just to get some kind of exclusive story. Briefly, he considered calling and canceling or having Christine do it for him. But the look he had seen in her eyes when he talked about sharing with someone kept coming back to him. There had been something more than a reporter's curiosity in her eyes. "One night," he thought. "How bad could it be?"

*   *   *

"My God, what was I thinking?" Laura stood in front of her closet trying to decide what to wear for an evening with a superstar. "He's probably a Lothario with a girl in every town, and I'm it for Albuquerque." She added another shirt to the pile of rejects on her bed. "Why am I so wound up over this? He just wants some company and my question put it into his head. Rehearsal and dinner, that's all it is. He didn't ask you to run away with him!" Her image in the mirror shook its head. "Oh, great! Now I'm talking to myself. That's not a good sign!"

She turned back to the closet and pulled out a deep green silk shirt and black leggings. Quickly, she dressed and stepped into a pair of green suede shoes. Glancing at the clock, she realized that she had better leave if she didn't want to be late. Taking a matching scarf from the rack on the wall, she pulled her copper-hued hair back into a simple ponytail, picked up her purse, and headed out the door.

3

As it happened, she got caught in one of the city's nightly traffic jams and barely made it to the parking garage before six. Consequently, she was a bit breathless as she stepped out of the elevator just as the door to the suite was opened.

"Taylor! I'm sorry I'm late." Laura launched into an explanation without giving him time to say anything. "There was another traffic jam; they happen all the time, and I got caught in this one. I really hope I haven't held you up."

"Laura! Slow down. They can't start the rehearsal without me, and we have plenty of time." He was laughing as he took her arm and led her into the suite. "Come in and catch your breath."

"I'm babbling, aren't I?" Laura returned his laughter. "I do that when I get in a hurry, especially if I'm violating some time frame I've set for myself. I promise, I'll stop."

Taylor found himself laughing with her. She was so different from all the others who treated him as something special, someone to be set apart. She was treating him as if he was…well, as if he was a friend. It had been a long time since he'd had that feeling with anyone.

"Come sit down for a minute. Let me get you something to drink."

"Just water, Taylor. I don't think I could handle anything else right now."

She watched him as he moved to the bar of the suite and opened a bottle of water. He was wearing a black T-shirt with black jeans and loafers. The color intensified the red highlights of his hair and the unique, brilliant turquoise of his eyes. There was a natural grace to his movements, and he didn't seem to be uncomfortable under her gaze. In fact, just as she realized that she was staring, he looked at her and grinned; "Well, do I pass inspection?"

Laura blushed. "Sorry…but you are rather easy to look at."

Taylor burst into laughter. "Well, you're honest, I'll give you that." He handed her a glass and sat down on the other end of the sofa. "What else are you, Laura? You already know everything there is to know about me. I think it's my turn to do the interviewing. Tell me about yourself."

"Me? There's nothing exciting about my life."

"So, bore me then. Turnabout is fair play."

"Alright, but remember you asked for it. I was born here in Albuquerque and have never lived anywhere else. I went to school at the University of New Mexico, then went to work for the *Herald*. That's about it."

"You were serious…your life is dull!" Laura was startled by his comment until she saw the teasing look in his eyes.

"So, where do you want me to start?"

"Tell me about your family."

"My parents are both professors here at the university. Dad teaches European history, and Mom teaches women's studies. I get my coloring from Dad's side of the family, the Irish. My mother's family, the Armijos, received one of the original Spanish land grants, and they helped settle this part of the country. Her name was María Consuela Bernadette Genevieve Armijo. You can imagine the fuss when she fell in love with her penniless Irish professor! But, they've always said it was love at first sight, and they were married six months after they met."

"Are you an 'only', too?"

"Only? Oh! No, I had one brother, but Tomás died of cancer two years ago. I miss him terribly." She could feel her throat tighten as it always did when she talked about Tomás, and she was grateful that

Christine chose that moment to come into the room to remind them it was time to leave.

*   *   *

A limousine waited downstairs to take them to Popejoy Hall on the University of New Mexico campus. Laura was a bit intimidated; the only other time she had ridden in a limousine was for her senior prom, and that had been with a whole group of friends. Taylor waited until she and Christine were seated, then got in beside Laura, perfectly at ease in an environment he was used to. For Laura, it was a perfect example of how far her world was from Taylor's.

On the short ride from downtown Albuquerque to the university, Laura played tour guide to cover up her nervousness. The love she felt for her city clearly showed and, for the first time in a long time, Taylor felt a wave of homesickness for the place where he had grown. He had never gone back to California after his parents' funeral. The house had been sold, what few things he had chosen to keep had been put into storage, and the memories locked safely away.

The limo turned off of Central Avenue and onto the campus. The concert was scheduled at Popejoy Hall, the only indoor performance venue of any size in Albuquerque. "Unless you count the Pit, Taylor."

"The *pit?*" His face clearly showed his amusement at the name. "People actually perform at someplace known as 'the pit'?"

"Sounds pretty awful, doesn't it? It's really the university basketball arena. Not too conducive to an intimate concert, but it does okay for the more raucous stuff and high school graduations."

Taylor and Christine were still laughing as the limousine pulled up to the rear entrance of the theatre. Laura was surprised at the number of people waiting. "Is it always like this, Taylor?"

"It has been the last few years. That's one of the reasons why I have so much security. Sometimes these people tend to forget that they don't own me. A few have even been threatening, and there was a stalker last year. For the most part, though, they seem to genuinely care about my well-being. Still, it gets a bit much to have to deal with it all the time. Are you ready to run the gauntlet?" he asked as the chauffeur came around to open the door. "I didn't think about this when I asked you to come with me. Some of those people are your peers, other news people. Would you rather wait in the car until the worst of it clears?"

"I'm fine, Taylor. Maybe my being with you will keep some of my fellow jackals in line."

As the driver opened the door and Taylor emerged, Laura was overwhelmed by the wave of sound that engulfed them. Fans were waving flowers or begging for an autograph; reporters were yelling questions; photographers shouted for him to look this way or that. Laura was embarrassed to realize that she could be as bad as any of them out there when it came to getting her story. Taylor waved to the crowd, then turned and helped Christine, then Laura, out of the car. The intensity of the crowd was frightening when seen from this perspective, and Laura was grateful for Taylor's security people who sheltered them to the door. She and Christine were escorted inside as Taylor turned to speak to the crowd.

*   *   *

"There's Taylor Morgan's car now," Cary said with a brilliant smile. "He obviously has a lot of fans who will be attending tomorrow night's benefit concert and reception for Shelter for Children." The camera cut away from Cary and came in close on the limo as Taylor exited and waved to the crowd. Cary turned to watch, keeping a running voice-over going as Taylor helped a pretty woman from the car. Cary noted to himself that Taylor evidently still had a taste for blondes, then found himself momentarily speechless as Taylor held his hand out to another woman, a redhead, who was emerging from the car. Laura? What the hell was *Laura* doing with Taylor Morgan?

His cameraman elbowed him. "You gonna try for that soundbite, Cary?" Cary glared at him, then headed to the door where Taylor had turned to address the crowd. Usually he was pushing his way forward to get the quote he needed, but tonight, he surprised his cameraman by blending in at the back of the crowd, making no attempt to ask a question. It was almost as if Cary were trying to hide.

*   *   *

As chaotic as the backstage bustle was, it was still calmer than the scene outside. Since Laura had never been involved in the production side of theatre, she was surprised to find the number of people it appeared to take to put on a simple concert. Christine had disappeared, but Laura waited until Taylor came inside.

Taylor deftly made his way through the bustle. Laura followed as closely as she could, afraid of getting lost in all the activity. When they finally emerged onstage, she stopped, overwhelmed by this view of the theatre. It was huge, and as she imagined it filled with people, she realized what stage fright must be like.

"Laura?" Taylor walked back to her. "Are you all right?"

"Good Lord, Taylor, how do you do it? How do you walk out here with all those seats filled, all those eyes staring, all those people...*wanting!*"

Taylor laughed. "It's what I eat, drink, and breathe, Laura. I couldn't survive without it."

He took her hand and led her to the steps of the auditorium where he hesitated. "Look, Laura, I didn't give you much choice in this. It could be pretty boring for you. If you'd like, I'll have the driver take you back to the hotel."

"Trying to get rid of me, Taylor?"

"No, it's just that...well, I never invite anyone to rehearsal. Let alone anyone who happens to be a reporter. There are times that things don't always go right and, when they don't, I don't stop to think about my image."

Laura realized that he was afraid she would write something about tonight, something detrimental. It bothered her that he could think such a thing, and for a moment, she could feel her temper rising. Then she realized that he had no reason to trust her and had undoubtedly been burned in the past.

"Taylor, I'm not here tonight to report on this. I thought it was a chance to get to know you better. But, if it really makes you this uncomfortable, then I'll leave—no hard feelings."

"Laura, I...please stay. But, if it gets too awful for you, just let my driver know and he'll take you back to the hotel."

"Go practice, Taylor. I'm fine."

She watched him walk across the stage, then made her way into the auditorium. She deliberately chose a seat just outside the range of the stage lights so that she was in shadow. Tonight promised to be interesting to say the least.

*   *   *

The rehearsal was as chaotic as Taylor had promised, but it was obvious he had quickly forgotten she was in the auditorium. He had everything under control, managing all the details of the production as well as his own performance. By the time the rehearsal was over, Laura was impressed with the range of his talents.

Christine had been in the front row taking notes for Taylor. As he went over a few things with his back-up singers, Laura moved forward to sit beside her.

Christine smiled at her. "Still here, Laura? These rehearsals can get tedious."

"I found it pretty interesting. I guess I've never given any thought to what goes on behind the scenes. Is Taylor always this involved?"

"Absolutely! He really is a bit of a perfectionist and knows all the technical stuff. He would be a great director if he ever gives up singing."

"Give up singing?" The two women looked up to find Taylor looking down at them from the stage apron. "Wishful thinking, Chris?"

"I can always dream, Taylor!" she said with a laugh. It was obvious they shared a comfortable relationship, and Laura wondered if there was more than work they had in common.

As the two women joined him on stage, Christine said, "If you don't need me later, Taylor, I thought I might go out with the crew for awhile. Everything should be ready for you."

"Go ahead, Chris. Have fun. And tell them I said thanks for all the hard work this evening."

"I'll see you in the morning, then. 'Night, Laura!"

*   *   *

As they exited the theatre, the earlier scene was repeated on a smaller scale. Laura recognized many of the same people who had been waiting for him to come back out. The news crews were long gone; their deadlines already passed. Without the cries of the reporters and photographers, things were almost calm and Taylor stopped to speak with a few of his fans.

Finally, back in the waiting limousine, Laura looked at Taylor with a new respect.

He held her gaze for a moment, then asked, "What?"

"Taylor, I have to tell you, this assignment to interview you was last-minute. I didn't have time to do much homework beyond your usual press release. I had heard of you, of course, but I had no idea who you were. I have to tell you, I am amazed and impressed."

"No wonder you didn't seem to be intimidated by meeting me!" Taylor laughed. "I know it's late, but are you still up for dinner?"

"Sure, I never turn down food. Offer me chocolate and I'll follow you anywhere. But, Taylor, I don't think I can face your fans again, so where do you propose we go?"

"Laura, I'd already thought of that. Please, don't take this wrong, but I thought we'd go back to the hotel suite. It will be quiet there and we can talk."

Laura was touched by the sincere concern she saw in his eyes. "It sounds perfect, Taylor. But I have to warn you, I turn into a pumpkin at midnight!"

4

The quiet of the suite was soothing after the chaos of the evening. The table where she had interviewed him had been ~~had been~~ set for two. Smoked salmon, cheese, crackers, and fruit waited along with a chilled bottle of champagne and a plate of chocolate truffles. Taylor opened the bottle, then filled and handed her a crystal glass. "To new friends, Laura," he said, and she smiled as she met his glass with hers.

"This looks wonderful, Taylor."

"But way too formal. What do you say we move it all over to the coffee table?"

"Great, but I have dibs on the sofa!"

They quickly moved everything to the coffee table. Laura took off her shoes and sank onto the sofa, her legs curled beneath her. Taylor took an overstuffed armchair facing her, then said, "So, tell me more about Laura Collins, the half-Irish, half-Spanish reporter. Which are you more? Irish or Spanish?"

"I don't think I know. Both cultures were—are such a part of my life. You'd like my parents, Taylor. They're special people. They've been married for thirty years, and they are still deeply in love. There were times when we were growing up that Tomás and I felt like we were intruding. I remember it being really embarrassing when I was a teenager and caught them kissing. Yech!" Taylor laughed as Laura wrinkled her nose.

"I think I would like them. They sound a lot like my parents. Dad had no interest in the arts, but he made sure Mom had tickets to everything she wanted. He teased her about it, but there was such love in that teasing."

"Your bio said that they're gone, Taylor. How long?"

"Almost twelve years...it seems like yesterday. They were on their way to New York to see me in my first big role. Mom was afraid to fly, so they took the train; it derailed in Arizona and they were both killed."

"You were so young!"

"I'd just turned twenty. It was as if I had lost my whole world. But the worst part of it was that my mother died without seeing me on Broadway. She had been so proud...."

His voice trailed off as he was lost in memory. Laura sat silent, unsure of what to say or do. If it had been Beth or another friend, she would have moved to embrace them but she hadn't known Taylor long enough to have that right.

"Sorry, Laura," he said.

"Nothing to apologize for, Taylor. I've been there."

"Your brother. You mentioned him this afternoon."

"Tomás. He was four years older than me, but we were always very close. It took two years for him to lose his battle with cancer. I don't know which is worse; to watch someone you love struggle or to lose them suddenly like you did."

There was a silence as they both tried to figure out where the conversation should go from there. Then they both spoke at once and the spell was broken by their laughter.

They chatted easily for awhile before Laura asked, "You said this afternoon that your best friend was a woman?" She hoped the question sounded casual.

"Did I? I don't remember, but it's true. Annie and I met in New York just before my time limit was up. We attended the same casting call and literally ran into each other waiting in line. I dropped something, and we both went to get it and ended up banging our heads together." Taylor smiled at the memory. "We were friends right away, and have managed to stay friends through everything since then."

"And your goddaughter?"

"Megan. She's eleven now and the love of my life. Her father abandoned Annie before Meg was born. Annie stayed with me until after Meg came, then moved to Tampa. She owns a dance studio there. I finally bought a place there to be closer to them when I'm not on the road."

Laura had the feeling that there was more there than he was telling but couldn't figure out a way to pry further. She glanced at the clock on the suite's VCR. "Taylor! Look at the time. I have to be at work at eight! I have to go."

Taylor, too, was surprised at the amount of time that had passed. "Laura, I've really enjoyed tonight. Thank you. Are you still coming to the concert tomorrow now that you've heard me?" His grin was teasing, but his eyes still held a vulnerability that touched her.

"Actually, it's today and yes, I'm still coming. I have the tickets the newspaper gave me. I'm expected to write a follow-up article, but don't worry, none of this will be in it."

"I know. I trust you. But those press seats are awful. There are always a couple of seats held for me to give away. Front row center. Think you could stand it? And there's the charity reception afterwards...would you go with me?"

Laura looked at him for a long moment. "Taylor, what's happening here? I don't want you to get any ideas that there's something more going on than there really is."

"It's been a long time since I sat and talked with someone like this. I enjoyed it, and I'd like to see you again. No strings, Laura."

"Good. As long as we understand each other, I'd love to go."

"I'll have Christine send the ticket over to the *Herald* tomor...today, I mean. I try to spend concert days in total silence to save my voice, so I'll see you afterwards. Christine will bring you backstage."

He walked her to the door of the suite. "Eddie? Please make sure Ms. Collins gets to her car safely. Laura, I'll see you tomorrow. Sleep well."

*   *   *

Cary slammed down the receiver. He'd just phoned Laura's apartment again. He had started calling when he got home at eleven. It was now midnight, and she still wasn't home. He knew she didn't like late nights, especially when she had to work the next morning. The difference in their schedules was one of the reasons Cary hadn't made more progress with her.

There could only be one reason she wasn't there. Taylor Morgan! He hadn't changed much, Cary thought. Still good-looking and attracting the crowds. Still after someone else's woman.

*   *   *

When Laura got back to her apartment, the answering machine had no fewer than a dozen messages. Apparently, Beth had been calling every fifteen minutes since ten o'clock. Knowing Beth was perfectly capable of calling all night, Laura knew she'd better check in.

"Laura?"

"Yes, Beth, it's me. Who else would be calling you at one-thirty in the morning?"

"So, tell! And don't leave anything out."

"We had a wonderful time, he was a perfect gentleman, and I'm going to bed now, Beth. Talk to you tomorrow." Gently she hung up the phone in the middle of Beth's protest.

As she got ready for bed, Laura thought back over the evening. Taylor had been a perfect gentleman—and a great companion. As much as she loved Beth and her other female friends, she still missed the companionship she had shared with Tomás. There wasn't a day that went by that she didn't think about calling and telling him something that had happened or seeking his advice. His death had left a dreadful hole in her life.

Taylor reminded her of Tomás. Not physically, but on a deeper level…something indefinable. There was so much more to find out about Taylor, and she regretted that she would never get the chance to know him better.

＊   ＊   ＊

Taylor stayed awake for a long time after Laura left. He wanted to call Annie and talk to her, but it was after three in Tampa. What could he tell her anyway? That he'd met someone, and after only a few hours with her, he was in love? He wasn't ready to hear Annie's opinion about that!

Taylor poured the last of the champagne and sank back into the chair, staring into space. He hadn't told Laura the whole truth about Annie. They'd been much more than friends. They had been lovers for almost a year after they'd met, until the pressures of being in different shows on different time schedules had finally pulled them apart. But they had parted friends and had worked at staying friends despite the best efforts of her husband. He had done everything he could to keep Annie out of Taylor's life.

It had almost worked, but Taylor wasn't ready to give up his friend. He went to her apartment unannounced one afternoon and had been shocked at the Annie who had answered the door. She looked old and tired, and there were fading bruises on her arms and a fresh one on her cheekbone. When Annie begged Taylor to leave, he had tried to get her to come with him. She refused, and Taylor had to be content with her promise to come to him if she needed help. That had been the last time he'd seen her for several months.

Then, his phone rang late one night. Annie was in the lobby of his building, running from the man she'd married. The bastard had taken it out on her because he had lost out on a promotion. The fact that she was pregnant hadn't made any difference to him.

Taylor had taken her to the hospital. The baby was fine; Annie less so. A broken arm and multiple bruises would mend, but Taylor wasn't sure her broken spirit would.

When Annie's husband showed up at Taylor's two days later, drunk and spoiling for a fight, Taylor was happy to oblige him. He would have killed him if Annie had not intervened.

She had stayed with Taylor until after Meg was born. He'd asked her to stay permanently—to marry him—but she had refused. She wanted no more of the New York theatre life and decided to settle someplace where she could start over. She settled on Florida to be near her parents, and Taylor had eventually made that his base to be near to her and Meg.

He drained the glass, then set it on the table. He would talk to Annie when he got back…if there was still anything to tell.

5

The alarm rang at six. "Four hours of sleep." Never a morning person, Laura groaned out loud. "I'm not going to make it through the day and tonight's concert." Mentally, she checked her calendar and finally decided she could afford to take the afternoon off. A nap today was not going to be a luxury but a necessity she didn't dare miss.

*   *   *

When Laura got to work, Beth was waiting at her desk. "Well, it's about time you got here!" she exclaimed as she elaborately looked at her watch.

Laura glanced at the clock that was just ticking over to eight. "Good morning to you, too, Beth. It's wonderful to start my day with the Inquisition." Laura gently pushed her friend out of the chair and collapsed into it. "Now, go away like a good girl. I have work to do."

"Uh-uh! No way! Not after you hung up on me last night. You owe me something for not calling you back."

"Beth, we cannot talk about it here. Let's do coffee at 9:30. I have a meeting in a few minutes."

Grumbling good-naturedly, Beth left for the art department, and Laura pulled up her schedule for the day. Just as she had thought, it was light. Her follow-up article on Taylor wasn't due until tomorrow. The related research piece she was doing on children's charities could wait a day. She picked up her copy of the day's edition of the *Herald* and read her article to make sure there were no mistakes. When the phone rang she answered it automatically, "Laura Collins."

"Laura?"

She dropped the paper and knocked over her soda. "Taylor! I thought you maintained silence for the day." She dabbed ineffectually at her jeans, much to the amusement of the reporter who sat across from her.

"I know, but it's early enough I think I can risk it." She could hear the smile in his voice. "I just wanted to thank you for last night. I..." his voice trailed off.

"Taylor?"

"I don't know why I'm calling, Laura. I just felt like it, I guess."

"Well, friends don't always have to have a reason to call. Although it would probably make my life more peaceful sometimes."

"Christine will send the ticket over this morning. Are you sure you won't be too tired tonight?"

"No, I'll probably just nap during the concert if you don't sing enough rousing pieces to keep me awake," Laura laughed. "I'm kidding, Taylor. I already planned to take this afternoon off and take a nap; I'm looking forward to this evening."

"So am I. Let me send the car for you tonight. I'll be going to the theatre early; then my driver can pick you up. I really should have thought of that last night. My dad always taught me to see a lady to her door."

"Fine, Taylor. That would be easier. Parking on the campus is a major problem. Do you want the address now, or should I call Christine?"

"She just walked in, so you can give it to her now. I'll see you tonight, Laura."

After Laura gave her address and fixed a time with Christine, she hung up and turned to her research on the charities story. It was time to organize some of her notes so she could see where the gaps were. Resolutely, she put the coming evening out of her mind and got to work.

*   *   *

The editorial meeting seemed to drag on forever. Robert wanted her to do both a follow-up and a review of the evening's concert. Her charity story was being expanded and moved to next Sunday's edition to capitalize on the current interest brought about by Taylor's concert. "And, Laura, see if you can do some more personal stuff on the guy. Today's article had that quality. Do it again. Now get to work, all of you."

Laura glanced at the clock. 9:30. Time to meet with Beth. Just what was she going to tell her, anyway?

*   *   *

"So, tell me all of it," Beth demanded. "Do not leave out one single thing, missy."

"Beth, there's not that much to tell. I sat in Popejoy for two hours watching him rehearse; then we went back to the hotel and had dinner and talked."

"Talked? You were with the sexiest man alive and you talked? Laura, I raised you better than that!"

Laura laughed. It was almost true; she and Beth had been friends since they were thirteen years old. They had practically raised each other, through first dates and makeup and prom and broken hearts. There was nothing they did not know about each other. Except for the marked differences in their appearance, people would have thought they were sisters, but tall, copper-haired Laura was so different from petite, blonde Beth that it was obvious that it was heart, not blood, which bound them to each other.

"Beth, we talked. About everything and nothing. It was…well, it was like being with Tomás again. Talking with Taylor felt a lot the same way, like I had known him forever and he had always been a part of my life. Tonight I'm going to the concert, then to the reception with him. Tomorrow he'll leave and go back to his life. I'll go on with mine. Nothing to get excited about. Now, I have to get some work done. I want to take this afternoon to go home and sleep. You know that I can't take two late nights in a row."

"I'll let you off the hook—for now. Lunch tomorrow with all the details?"

"You are relentless, Beth. Fine, lunch tomorrow."

*   *   *

Cary got to the station at noon. Since he was scheduled to co-anchor tonight, there were no pressing assignments for him. He decided to try Laura again. She had been in a meeting when he'd called earlier, and he had been at the gym since then. He listened as her voice mail picked up before slamming down the receiver.

Where was she? And why had she been with Morgan last night?

Carla James, the regular co-anchor, stopped by his desk to remind him that they needed to tape the newsbrief spots. He nodded and waved her away as he picked up the phone again.

Carla shook her head as she walked away. At least he hadn't hit on her this time. Maybe he had finally gotten the message that she wasn't interested…nor were most of the other women at the station who had seen him in action. If it was female and attractive, Cary presented himself as God's Gift. It didn't take long to figure out that there was nothing giving about Cary. Somebody needed to tell Laura Collins that.

*   *   *

Laura woke from her nap with plenty of time to get ready for the concert. Savoring the quiet for a few moments, her thoughts turned to Taylor Morgan. She hadn't exactly told Beth the whole truth. She did find Taylor attractive, and she allowed herself to fantasize about what it would be like to kiss him…and more.

Still, she wasn't willing to set herself up to be a one-night stand in his road show, so they would be friends tonight, and then he would be gone. She could tell her grandchildren about it someday and listen to them say, "Who? Taylor Morgan? Who was he?" Laura laughed as she got up to get ready.

*　　　　*　　　　*

Taylor had spent the day reading, with a short nap in the afternoon, followed by his daily vocal exercises. Now, in his dressing room at Popejoy Hall, he finished tying the bow tie that went with his tux.

"A man should be able to tie his own bow tie, Taylor." His mother stood behind him, watching in the mirror as a teen-age Taylor struggled to tie his. "There's a lot of truth when they say 'clothes make the man.'" She smiled as he turned to her, the tie conquered and in place.

There was a knock at the door, drawing Taylor back to the present, his mother's smile still playing in his memory. Christine poked her head through the doorway. "Five minutes, Taylor. Need anything?"

"No, thanks, Chris. Wait, did Laura get here all right?"

"Front row center, Taylor, just as you ordered. I'm on my way out front to join her. Any messages?"

"Tell her I hope she can manage to stay awake."

Christine shook her head and left the room. Taylor was usually so concentrated on the coming performance that nothing else entered his mind. Laura Collins had certainly made an impression on him.

*　　　　*　　　　*

"Taylor said to tell you he hoped you could stay awake." Laura laughed as Christine delivered his message.

"If I hadn't taken the afternoon off to take a nap, I wouldn't have. My friends are all amazed that I am planning two late nights in a row. I'm not exactly known for being a party animal."

"Neither is Taylor. On those rare nights he has off, he tends to retreat with a book, or he logs on to the computer. He has a pretty broad range of friends on the Internet."

"Really? He's not besieged by fans?"

"He logs on under another name. No one knows who it is." She lowered her voice so only Laura could hear. "He's even a member on his own fan list. Usually, I monitor it for him, but he likes to browse through it when he has time."

"Hmm…might be an interesting story," Laura murmured, then saw the look on Christine's face. "Oh, sorry! Not Taylor incognito, but his fan list. Can you put me in touch with his fan club?"

"Sure; I'll send you the address before we leave town in the morning. I'll give you my address, too. I'd like to see the article when you get it done."

The two women fell silent as the pianist entered and quietly took his seat. The stage was bare except for the highly polished black grand piano. Soft lights fell on the scrim behind it, and the audience quieted as the pianist began to play. Before he could be seen, Taylor's voice was heard from offstage, and a short spattering of applause greeted his appearance when he entered and stood next to the piano. Laura caught her breath at the sheer beauty of the man and the voice that was even richer than the night before.

*   *   *

After two encores and a number of curtain calls, Taylor finally made his exit. The audience was in high spirits even though some of his songs had left them in tears. His ability to communicate a range of emotions in his music was phenomenal. Laura had not been prepared for the emotional rollercoaster his concert had turned out to be.

"Come on, Laura. Taylor gave me orders that you were to be brought backstage right away. We'll go through here," Christine said as she led Laura through a door near the stage to the dressing room door. Taylor's security man was waiting outside the door. He knocked, then opened the door for them, giving Laura a wink as she went past him.

The room was quiet after the crush outside. Taylor was nowhere to be seen, but Christine indicated a closed door. "He's probably changing clothes. He won't wear the tux to the reception." She raised her voice, "Taylor? Laura's here. I'm going to go check on the arrangements, and I'll be back in a few minutes." She seemed satisfied with the mumble that came through the door. "Make yourself at home, Laura. He'll be out soon."

Laura looked around the dressing room. There were small touches here and there that said something about the occupant. A number of cards and packages, teddy bears and flowers were stacked to one side of the room, gifts from his admirers. Laura smiled at a few of the more exotic offerings. Two pictures on the make-up table caught her eye. She picked up the first silver frame and recognized a younger Taylor with two people she assumed were his parents. He bore a marked resemblance to his father, but his smile had clearly been inherited from his mother. The second picture was of a petite, blonde woman with a dark-haired little girl; she assumed they were Annie and Megan. She didn't have long to study it before she heard Taylor ask, "So, did you stay awake?"

Laura replaced the picture and turned to look at him. "I had no choice! Your fans kept waking me up." She smiled at him, and he laughed.

"They can be pretty enthusiastic. But I couldn't do what I do without them."

"It was wonderful, Taylor. Thank you."

He looked at her for a moment, then simply said, "You're welcome." He reached for a jacket hanging on the clothes rack. He had changed into dark slacks and a turquoise, banded collar shirt with a silver button closing the collar. With the black jacket he was putting on, he looked elegantly casual.

"Nice look, Taylor. Are you dressing this way for us Westerners or is it your own look?"

"What? Oh, the turquoise. No, I just happen to like the color. And I hate wearing the tux anytime I'm not performing. Think people will freak out at the party?"

"No. If anything, you'll probably still be overdressed. We do tend to be a bit casual even on dressy occasions."

"You look pretty elegant." Taylor took in the copper-colored silk broomstick skirt and matching velvet shirt. Her hair was piled on top of her head in unruly curls and she wore simple gold earrings and no other jewelry.

"Ah, but that's the difference, Taylor. Women like to get dressed up no matter where they live. Men take every chance possible to dress down."

Their sartorial argument was interrupted as Christine came back in. "Ready, Taylor?"

He made a face at her and held his hand out to Laura. "Ready as I'll ever be. Let's go see if we can impress them."

*   *   *

Taylor was greeted with applause as he entered the crowded reception hall. The movers and shakers of Albuquerque and Santa Fe were all in attendance, not so much because they believed in the charity but more because they believed in being seen. The local charity director immediately drew Taylor away to introduce him to the mayor, the governor, and the other politicos in attendance. Laura spotted her paper's editor across the room and decided to try to be invisible for a few minutes longer. Taking a glass of champagne from a passing waiter, she moved across the room to the windows that overlooked the city.

Taylor watched her as he made small talk with the governor and his wife. Laura was a beautiful woman, and his eyes were not the only ones drawn to her. He realized he would have been attracted to her for her looks alone, but now that he was beginning to know who she was, he was even more drawn to her. And there was only tonight to find out more. He excused himself and made his way to the window where she stood.

*   *   *

Cary arrived late to the reception. The production meeting after the ten o'clock news had run long as they discussed some technical glitches. Cary had waited impatiently, almost bolting from the room when the meeting had finally ended. He hadn't been able to reach Laura all afternoon, and he had a suspicion that she would be with Morgan again tonight. He had just located her when he saw Taylor excuse himself from the group he was with and head straight for her. Cary took a glass of champagne from a passing server and watched as she turned to smile at Morgan.

*   *   *

"Penny for your thoughts," Laura turned when Taylor spoke.

"They're probably not worth that much," she laughed. "Truth is, I'm hiding from my editor, but I'm not doing a very good job of it because here he comes."

Taylor turned just as Alaniz reached them.

"Taylor, this is our editor, Henry Alaniz."

"Nice concert, Mr. Morgan. My wife and I enjoyed it." Without waiting for comment, Alaniz continued. "Are you on my time or yours tonight, Laura?"

Laura replied, "My time tonight, Henry. But it should be good for another article."

"Glad to hear it. Glad you could make a stop here, Morgan." As Alaniz turned and left them, Taylor asked, "Is he always that abrupt?"

"Henry? That's just Henry. You get used to it. He's got the proverbial heart of gold under that gruff exterior. If we checked the list of contributors for the charity tonight, Henry A. Alaniz would be up at the top."

The charity director came to claim Taylor again, taking him off for photos with the bigwigs. Laura joined some friends, and they were separated for the rest of the evening.

*   *   *

Cary stayed out of Laura's sight, chatting with people he knew, always keeping an eye on her. He didn't want to talk to her. He just wanted to see what would happen next.

As the reception started to break up, Taylor saw a chance to leave. He thanked the charity director again, then claimed Laura. "Let's get out of here," he said as he took her hand.

Cary watched as they left together. Not again, he thought. Morgan would not win this time. He waited a few minutes, then left the party. He would call her when he got home, and she had better be there tonight!

*   *   *

"What a zoo," Taylor said with a smile as he removed the silver collar button. "Don't misunderstand. They're all very nice and I appreciate their contributions to the charity, but I get tired of the same questions over and over again."

"I can imagine. How many more of these do you have?"

"We're on for the next ten days with only one day off. We'll end up at the Tampa Performing Arts Center, and then this leg of the tour will be done."

"Then what? Where does Taylor Morgan go when he's not onstage?"

"Good question. Actually, we scheduled this leg of the tour to end in Tampa since I have a place there. It's quiet and warm, and I'll be able to celebrate the holidays with Annie and Meg."

"Tampa's home, then?"

"Home? No, not really. Home is a place that doesn't really exist for me anymore. I wander here and there, a typical theatre gypsy."

The limo pulled up in front of Laura's apartment complex. As the driver opened the door, Taylor got out and then helped Laura before walking her to the security gate.

"Thanks for making this stop a lot more interesting, Laura. I've really enjoyed it."

"Me, too, Taylor. It was a fascinating glimpse into another world for me. I don't know how you do it."

"Laura, would you mind if I called you sometime? Just to talk?"

"I'd enjoy it, Taylor. Christine told me you spend a lot of time on the Internet. So do I." She pulled one of her cards from her purse and handed it to him. "This has my e-mail address and the work phone. Wait," she said as she took it back from him and wrote on the back, "that's my home phone. Call anytime."

He took the card and put it in the pocket of his jacket. "I guess the only thing left to say is good-bye. Take care of yourself, Laura." He took her hand, gazing into her eyes. Laura's heart beat a little faster as he leaned toward her, but he only kissed her cheek before turning back to the limo. He turned and waved before he disappeared into the limo.

*   *   *

The phone was ringing as she entered the apartment. She picked up the phone and said, "I just walked in Beth. Give me a break!"

"It's not Beth, Laura. It's Cary."

"Cary? Why are you calling so late?"

"Actually, I've been calling all day. You were never in."

Laura sat down and kicked off her shoes. "It was one of those days, Cary. You know how it goes."

Turning on the charm, Cary said, "I guess I got a little worried when you weren't home this evening. I know you're not crazy about late nights."

"I was working again. A follow-up to the story I was working on last night."

"Must have been important."

"Important might not be the right word, but it was pretty interesting."

"Any hints, or do I have to read about it in the paper?"

Laura laughed. "You probably wouldn't bother. Just a concert review. Cary, I'm beat. Was there something you wanted?"

"Just wanted to set up another dinner date. It can wait."

"Goodnight then. I'll call you tomorrow."

She hung up the phone and shivered a little. Something had made her keep Taylor out of the picture. He would be gone tomorrow. Cary would still be here, and nothing had happened that he needed to know about.

It took Laura a long time to go to sleep. Bits and pieces of the concert and the party kept playing in her head, especially that moment when Taylor admitted he had no "home." She could not imagine it. She had always lived here in Albuquerque. The idea of wandering like that was unsettling to her. As she remembered the look in his eyes, she had the feeling that Taylor felt the same way.

She resented that he was being removed from her life after being so briefly a part of it. She wondered if he would ever get in touch or if this would only be some vague memory for him. It was early morning before she fell asleep with the memory of Taylor's voice singing in her head.

*   *   *

Taylor didn't fare much better. He always had trouble sleeping after a concert. Tonight, though, it was more than the concert keeping him awake. He was amazed at how quickly he had connected with Laura. There had been other women he had met on tours, but none of them had ever had this kind of impact on him. It was not just the physical attraction, although that was certainly there. There was something about Laura that spoke to his soul. As he stared out the window at the lights of

Albuquerque, he found himself wishing that he could cancel the next stop on the tour and stay here with Laura for just a little while longer.

*   *   *

Laura finally woke up midmorning, grateful that she had arranged to go in late to work. As she opened the curtains on another beautiful New Mexico day, a plane flew overhead and her thoughts turned to Taylor, who was long gone by now. Determined to get on with her life, she called Beth and arranged to meet her for lunch at the Pyramid before she officially came into work.

*   *   ·   *

Beth could tell that something had happened to Laura. They had been friends too long for her to miss the subtle change.

"So, how was last night?"

"Can't I even order lunch first?"

"Nope, already ordered for you. I thought it would give you more time to tell me the details."

"Thanks," she laughed as the waitress placed a bowl of her favorite green chile chicken soup in front of her, "but I think we have to quit spending so much time together!"

"Too late for that. Now, eat so you can tell me what happened."

For a few minutes the two women ate in silence. Finally, Laura put down her spoon and picked up her soda.

"There's nothing to tell." At her friend's raised eyebrows, Laura continued, "I swear, it's true!"

As Laura described the concert to her, Beth noticed a light in her eyes as she talked about Taylor. This was serious. In all their years as friends, she had never seen Laura look like this when talking about anyone.

"Then he walked me to the door, took my phone number and e-mail address, and left. That was it, Beth, nothing more. And this morning he headed out for the next stop on the tour. I'll just be a memory of 'that strange reporter in New Mexico.' Right now, I have a story to file. Let's get back to the paper."

6

A week later, Laura found her desk almost obscured by a crystal vase of red roses; her first thought was that they were from Taylor. She hadn't heard from him since his Albuquerque concert. She had checked her e-mail regularly and stayed home in the evenings, hoping he would call. She was disappointed when she opened the card and read:

> Dinner Friday?
> I miss you.
>
> Cary

"Pretty impressive." Beth's voice came from behind her.

"Overwhelming, actually. They're too big for my desk. I can't even see my computer!" Laura tried to keep the disappointment from her voice. She had been such an idiot, thinking that someone like Taylor Morgan could care about a nobody like her.

"Laura Elizabeth Collins, anyone but you would be thrilled to get flowers like these!" Beth leaned closer and whispered, "Are they from Taylor?"

"No, they're from Cary. We're still trying to find a time to get together for dinner."

"*These* are a dinner invitation? I don't think so, Laura. Looks to me like Cary wants a lot more than dinner. When do I get to meet this guy?"

"Eventually, Beth." Laura tucked the card back in the envelope and put it in her desk drawer. "I'll talk to you later. Right now I have to see what Robert wants."

Beth knew Laura had been hoping the flowers were from Taylor; Beth had been hoping they were, too. She hadn't mentioned him, but Beth knew that Laura had been well on her way to being in love with Taylor Morgan. Since Tomás had died, Laura had withdrawn; she hadn't dated anyone for two years. When Cary came into the picture, Beth had hoped things would change. Laura had gone out with him a couple of times, but when Taylor came into—then left—the picture, she had reverted back to her solitude.

*   *   *

Laura knew that it made no sense to be this disappointed about the flowers. Wishing they were from Taylor was stupid! She hadn't heard from him since he left and probably never would. It was time to get on with her life. She shook off her mood as she opened the door to Robert's office. She would call Cary as soon as this meeting was over and tell him 'yes' to dinner for Friday.

*   *   *

When Laura opened the door on Friday night, she found Cary—and another dozen roses. As he handed them to her, she laughed and said, "Thanks, Cary, but they weren't really necessary."

"Maybe not," he said with a grin, "but it's easier than coming to the door empty-handed."

"Come in while I find a vase for these. There's wine on the table if you'd like to pour it."

Cary poured the wine, then turned to survey her apartment. It was the first time he had been there. For the few dates they had had, she had preferred to meet him at the restaurant. The apartment was small, but a comfortable size for one person. There were bookshelves everywhere. He glanced over the eclectic collection of titles that included everything from children's literature to philosophy. What spaces weren't filled with books held pictures or knick-knacks. He was looking at a framed photo when she came back into the room.

"That's my family," she said as she placed the roses in the middle of the table.

"The young man?" There was a faintly suspicious tone to his question.

"My brother, Tomás. He died two years ago."

"I'm sorry. That must have been rough. Gang-related?"

Laura stopped and looked at him, appalled at his question. "What would make you ask that?"

"Well, that seems to be the number one cause of young Hispanic male deaths here."

"Cary, are you always this judgmental?" Laura was suddenly furious. "My brother was at the top of his medical school class and expected to do great things. He fought for two years before the cancer finally killed him."

"Wait, Laura. I'm sorry. I didn't really think. I've been working on this series on the gang problems, and it's coloring everything for me right now. You've been on stories like that, right? I really did not mean it to come out the way it did."

Laura's face was flushed with the anger she was trying to control. Cary was tempted to tell her she was beautiful when she was angry, but he decided that might not be a good move even if it were true. He decided to try another route.

"Laura, I can see I've really spoiled the evening. I should probably go ahead and leave. Maybe when you've had some time, we can try this again." He put down his wineglass and headed for the door. It was a gamble he had tried with other women before. It usually worked.

"Cary, wait." Before turning around, he allowed himself a small smile of satisfaction. It hadn't failed this time, either. He turned to face her, one hand on the door handle. "Cary, I'm sorry. I overreacted. It really angers me when people make that kind of assumption about a local kid. If you're willing to forget it, so am I. I've really been looking forward to this evening."

He gave her a slow smile and said, "Thanks, Laura. I've been looking forward to it, too. Shall we go?"

7

Two weeks later, Laura finally heard from Taylor. Logging on to check her e-mail, there had been the usual notes from cyber-friends and a deluge of messages from the lists she belonged to, including Taylor's. As she scrolled through, looking for messages she should handle immediately, she saw an address she didn't recognize. Barnum@eaglenet.com. The subject was simply, "Hi, Laura!" Her curiosity piqued, she had opened the message to read:

Hi, Laura-

It's me—Taylor, as in Phineas Taylor Barnum, the circus guy. Since he and I share a name and my life often feels like a circus, I figured it would be an appropriate alias.

We're in Tampa now. It's nice to be coming back to familiar surroundings every night. I didn't realize how tired I was of hotel rooms.

I'm sorry it's taken so long to get in touch. I really enjoyed spending time with you in Albuquerque. I'd like to come back and visit when I actually have some time to enjoy it—especially if I can count on you to play friendly native guide?

Taylor

Laura stared at the screen. She had quit waiting for him to get in touch and put him out of her mind. Now, here he was, again and she wasn't sure how she felt about him, about the possibility of a long-distance relationship. She was even less sure he was offering anything more than friendship. Complicating things further, Cary was now very much a part of the picture. They had been dating steadily for the last couple of weeks and seemed to be building what could become a lasting relationship.

Suddenly, she became aware of someone reading over her shoulder. "Beth! Do you mind?"

Her friend shook her head and sat in the chair beside the desk. "No, I don't mind at all! I just wanted to see what had the great Laura Collins so riveted."

"So, did you?"

"What?"

"Did you see?"

"Looked like a cyber mash-note. Anyone I know?"

"Stop it, Beth. You know good and well who it is."

"Um-hmm. So, are you going to let Taylor come over to play?"

"I don't know, Beth. I…I don't know that I want to get involved with him…."

"Really? I must have missed that part. What I saw wasn't asking for anything but to see you if he ever got back this way."

"So, you think I'm reading too much into this?"

"Hey, you're the one who met him, not me. But it sounds like he enjoyed your company, liked Albuquerque, and would like to come back to visit sometime. No big thing."

Laura sighed. "You're right—as usual. I'm overreacting."

"Are you going to tell him 'yes'?"

"Probably. And maybe, if you really behave yourself, if it ever happens, I'll even introduce you."

The two women laughed, and Beth returned to her work area. Laura decided to wait until evening to respond. Besides having more privacy at home, it would give her time to decide what she wanted to say.

*   *   *

Taylor paced around the spacious living room of his Florida condo. It was dominated by a grand piano that sat at one end of the room in front of floor-to-ceiling windows overlooking Tampa Bay. Now that he had finally gotten up the nerve to send Laura a message, he was second-guessing the wisdom of doing it.

His computer was on in the corner, the blank screen seeming to taunt him with the lack of response. He glanced at his watch and realized he had wasted an hour waiting for a message that probably wasn't coming. This was crazy! He logged out and turned off the computer, then picked up his in-line skates and headed out the door. He had to work this off somehow and exercise seemed to be the answer.

He headed for the paved walk along Bayshore Drive. It drove his agent crazy that Taylor risked appearing in public without any protection, but Taylor refused to have security when he wasn't on the road. When no expected to see him, Taylor had an uncanny way of blending into a crowd and going unrecognized. Taylor knew some of the people he encountered knew who he was—he had seen the startled looks on their faces—but no one had ever bothered him as he skated along Bayshore. It was as if the people out there saw him as one of their own and were willing to give him the space he needed. That was why he kept coming back here, he supposed. It wasn't "home" in the way Laura had meant, but it was as close as he was going to get.

Taylor returned to find that he still faced a blank computer screen; well, empty, at least, of the one message that he wanted to see. He mentally kicked himself for even sending it. Laura had a life of her own—why would she want to pursue a long-distance relationship?

Picking up the phone, he dialed Annie's number. When she answered, he said, "Hey, it's me! Want to meet me for dinner at The Colonnade?" When they had set a time, Taylor hung up the phone and ran up the stairs to shower.

8

When Taylor got to the restaurant, Annie was waiting. She still looked and moved like a dancer, fine-boned and graceful. She had cut her sun-bleached blonde hair very short while he had been on tour, and she didn't look a whole lot older than her eleven-year-old daughter, Meg.

"Hello, Taylor," she said as she stood on tiptoe to kiss his cheek. "It's about time you called me. You've been back for days."

"You saw me after the concert the other night."

"Along with about five million other people!"

Their banter was interrupted as they were seated and gave the waiter their order for the Colonnade's famous pecan-crusted shrimp. Taylor selected a wine to go with dinner, and they settled in to catch up with each other.

"So, how did the rest of the tour go, Taylor? See anything interesting? Meet anyone? Actually have a life?"

"Oh, yeah, Annie. There's so much possibility of a life when you sleep until noon, rehearse, perform, and travel on."

"My point exactly. Why do you think I left?"

"It's different for me, Annie. You know that. I would die without it."

Contrite at teasing him, she reached out and took his hand, "I know, Taylor. I would just like to see you have a little more."

"How is Meg?" he asked, changing the subject.

"She's a totally spoiled brat, thanks in large part to you, Taylor!"

"She's my goddaughter. I have a responsibility to spoil her. And she's not a brat—which is more than I can say for her mother!"

"Okay, so she's not a brat all the time, but she is eleven going on thirty, and she's driving me crazy. She was not happy that I didn't bring her tonight."

"You could have, you know."

"I know, but tomorrow is a school day. There has to be one grown-up in this threesome, Taylor. I wish you would get married and have one of your own, then maybe you'd be more sympathetic."

Taylor didn't respond right away, staring out over the bay as if seeing something else. When his silence stretched out, Annie finally called him back to the present. "Taylor? What's up?"

"Sorry, I must still be tired," he replied.

"Don't bullshit me, Taylor Morgan! There's something up with you. If you don't want to talk about it, fine; but don't lie to me."

"You're right. There is something. I'm not ready to talk about it yet, but when I am, you'll be the first to know, I promise." He gave her a smile before they were interrupted by the waiter with their food.

*   *   *

Laura had trouble writing her article for tomorrow's paper. Taylor's e-mail had been in the back of her mind, and it had been a lot more interesting than writing a column about the new mayor and his entirely unoriginal plans for change at city hall. She was grateful she had voted for his opponent so she didn't have to take any responsibility for his election.

She had picked up dinner on the way home—more fast food. She really needed to visit her folks' this weekend. Mom would see that she ate some real food for a change. After pouring a glass of wine, she changed into shorts and a T-shirt, pinned her hair on top of her head, and ate her solitary meal while she watched "Jeopardy!".

At 7:00 she logged on; opening her e-mail account, she quickly read through her messages, answering some, deleting others, saving those she would have to deal with later. Finally, the only current message left was that from Taylor. Hitting the reply key, she began to compose an answer.

Hi, Taylor-

Barnum? And no one has figured it out yet? Your fans must be as dense as Lois Lane was with Clark Kent's glasses.

Actually, I'm kidding. It fooled me and seems a pretty good alias.

It must be nice to be back on solid ground, so to speak. I hope you're getting some rest; from what I saw while you were here, you must need it by now.

So, what does Taylor Morgan do with his days when he's not on tour? Tell me what Florida's like. I've never been there.

Laura

She read back over what she had written and decided it would have to do. After all, what could she say? Hitting the "send" key, Laura shut down the computer and took her wine out to the small balcony of her apartment.

She wasn't sure how she felt about Taylor. His message today had really had an impact she had not been expecting. Until she had seen it there in her file, she hadn't realized that she had still been looking for it every day. She hadn't given him much thought since Cary had entered the picture—at least not that she would admit to.

Now that he had gotten in touch, she realized how much she had been hoping he would. There had been something between them, some...*spark*, although that had a connotation she wasn't willing to accept. Connection was a better word. There had been a connection that was almost instantaneous. She had to admit that she didn't have the same kind of rapport with Cary. Spending time with him certainly beat sitting home alone every night.

Now, Taylor was back in her life, or would be if she let him. She had no idea what he felt, what *she* felt. She had no idea where this was going, if it was going anywhere at all. Draining her glass, Laura returned to the living room. She was very tempted to open her e-mail file again, but instead, picked up the new novel she was reading and headed for bed.

*   *   *

After dinner, Taylor asked Annie if she wanted to take a walk, but she turned him down. "I need to get home and get Meg to bed. Come out for brunch on Sunday, Taylor. She misses you."

After giving her a hug and promising to be there on Sunday, he headed home. It would be nice to drive out to Annie's. He would kidnap Meg, and they would head to the beach. It would give him some time with Meg and give Annie a little time to herself. He worried about her; she worked so hard at the dance studio and still managed to always be there for all of Meg's school functions. She was looking tired, he realized, something unusual for Annie with her seemingly boundless energy.

As he opened the door to the condo, Taylor was struck by how empty it was. He was on the road too much to keep a pet, although the house had been full of them when he was growing up. There were no house-plants, either, since no one was there to water them. In fact, except for some family photos, it looked more like a layout for some architectural magazine than a place someone lived.

He opened a new bottle of wine and went out onto the deck. The sun had already set; the empty blackness of the bay stretched out before him. A few lights from ships dotted it here and there, but it was mostly deserted. The gated community was quiet, too. Usually, solitude didn't bother him but tonight the silence seemed oppressive.

Coming back inside, he turned on the computer and started the auto log-on. After pouring another glass of wine and starting a Yo-Yo Ma cello concerto in the CD player, he went back to the computer.

He looked over the list of mail in his box and read the messages from his agent and a couple of theatre friends. He skimmed over the others, deleting most of them until, toward the end of the list, he saw the one he had been looking for—an answer from Laura. He hadn't realized until then that he had been almost holding his breath hoping it was there. Relaxing for the first time all evening, he began to read her answer.

*   *   *

Laura read several chapters of her book. Normally, reading was her great escape, her recreation. Tonight she realized that she had managed to read for an hour and had no idea what Dirk Pitt had been up to. For all she knew, he and Giordano had finally confessed their love for each other and come out of the closet. She wondered what Cussler, Pitt's author, would think of *that* scenario!

Restlessly, she wandered into the kitchen and took a couple of cookies before heading for the computer. It was not unusual for her to check e-mail when she couldn't sleep, but she knew that wasn't the reason now.

Logging on, she skimmed down the short list of messages. Some in-house mail from the paper, one from an old college friend who lived in California now, but nothing from Taylor. Sighing, she answered her friend, then started to log off; just as she hit the quit key, the computer beeped with new mail. She quickly logged back on and found an answer from Taylor.

Laura-

> Great to hear from you! I was out to dinner with Annie and just got home.

> Yes, I have been resting quite a bit. Long walks along the bay, a little skating, sleeping late, being lazy. It's been nice.

I start work on some new music next week to add to the
next leg of the tour. I'll be seeing Annie and Meg on
Sunday. Meg and I will probably head to the beach for
awhile to give Annie a break.

That's it. The exciting life of a superstar. I'm sure yours
must be considerably more interesting.

Taylor

Laura debated with herself as to whether she should answer right
away. She didn't want him to think she had been glued to the computer
waiting to hear from him, but he was probably still logged on if the lag
time tonight wasn't too bad. Finally, she pushed the reply key.

*   *   *

Annie drove home through the soft, tropical evening. It might be
autumn in the rest of the world, but Florida didn't believe in seasons.
That was one of the reasons she loved it here.

Taylor had been strange tonight. He had been brooding over something, and she had a suspicion he had met someone he was attracted to.
Please, God, not someone like Janis—that barracuda he had gotten
himself engaged to. She had been so wrong for him.

Janis had been the closest they had come to losing their friendship.
Annie had tried to tell him how wrong Janis was for him, but he had
been furious, reminding her that he hadn't tried to keep her from marrying "that cretin," and he had stomped out after telling her he was marrying Janis no matter what she thought.

They had not spoken for two weeks.

Finally, late one night, the phone rang. When she answered, Taylor
had said, "You were right." His voice was flat.

"About Janis? What happened, Taylor?"

He and Janis had been at a charity function benefiting Shelter for Children. She had been perfect and beautiful until one of the children had brought her flowers. Accepting them, she smiled, then perfunctorily, handed them off to someone. Taylor had been down on the little girl's level, talking with her, when she had reached out one sticky hand and touched the bright blue silk of Janis' dress. Janis had been livid, causing a scene and claiming her dress was ruined. The child was in tears, Janis in hysterics, Taylor embarrassed. They had left quickly, and when they got to the hotel, they had a horrendous fight. Janis had demanded he give up the charities, give up being accessible to his fans, give up touring, and concentrate on recording and living the fashionable life she wanted. He had broken off their engagement then, finally seeing what Annie had seen all along.

They had picked up their friendship as if there had never been a rift. In the five years since, they had never seriously quarreled. Their few disagreements had been over his outrageous spoiling of Meg, but as he had pointed out, that was his job as her godfather; as the only kind of father she had ever known.

Pulling into the driveway, Annie could see the dark head of her daughter silhouetted in the window. Meg did this to make her feel guilty for leaving her. This was her bereft, lonely, orphan routine, and it was working. Maybe she should have taken her along. Giving herself a mental shake, Annie went into the house where Megan was studiously ignoring her.

"Hi, kid." There was no answer. "You should be in bed. I'll tell Susan goodbye while you get ready. Then I'll be in to tuck you in. Go on—scoot."

At this point, ignoring Meg was the only way to handle her. When Annie returned, she found that Meg had actually gotten ready for bed. In fact, she was so ready, she was already under the covers, with her back turned to the door.

"Well, Miss Megan, I guess you don't want to hear that Taylor will be out to brunch on Sunday."

The transformation was instantaneous. Meg sat up, her eyes glowing, and said, "He will? For the day?"

"He didn't say, but he probably will. He usually does."

"This is great, Mom! I have so much to tell him. He's been gone so long this time."

Looking at her daughter, Annie found it hard to believe that this leggy child was hers. Meg had inherited her father's dark coloring, but not his temperament, thank heavens. She was a sunny child, incapable of deliberately hurting anyone.

"I know you've missed him, darling. He missed you, too. He was a little annoyed that I didn't bring you with me, but how could I have talked about *you* if I did?"

"Mother!"

Annie laughed and hugged her. "Go to sleep, Meg. Sweet dreams."

"'Night, Mom." Meg slid back under the blanket as Annie went to the door. She turned out the light and started out when Meg said, "Love you, Mom."

"Love you, too, Meg," she said as she gently closed the door behind her.

     *   *   *

Annie went to her desk in the family room and opened her account books. The studio was doing well, but expenses were going up; rent had nearly doubled in the last three years. Keeping Meg in private school was beginning to be a struggle. It looked like she would have to raise her rates again, although she wasn't sure how much that would help. Whenever she did, someone dropped out, and she felt terrible for causing some child to lose her dream of becoming a dancer. She was never sure the increased rates compensated for the dropouts.

She knew she could go to Taylor for help. He had been trying for years to get her to let him pay Meg's tuition. But, damn it, he *wasn't* her father even if he tried to be. She just couldn't bring herself to ask him for help.

Feeling an increasingly familiar tightness behind her eyes, she closed the books and put her head down. The tightness intensified to a pain that built, then subsided, leaving her a little breathless and with a dull headache. This wasn't the first time it had happened. She supposed she should make an appointment with the doctor, but what could she tell him? Besides, she thought, as she wearily stood to go to her room, it would just be another expense that she could ill-afford right now.

9

Taylor woke late on Sunday. He had been up late "talking" to Laura by e-mail. They had been writing every day this week and seemed to never run out of things to talk about. Most of the time it was little everyday stuff, but he had begun to hear details of her life and was sharing small details of his with her. Until now, Annie had been the only one in his life that he had opened up to. Even Janis had never known the real Taylor, not that she had really wanted to.

Looking at the time, he knew he should get up and get moving. Meg was not the most patient of people, he acknowledged with a smile. She would be driving Annie crazy about when he was supposed to be there.

After showering, he dressed in khaki shorts, a cream-colored linen shirt, and put on a pair of sandals. He started out the door, then turned back to check the computer. Nothing from Laura. He wasn't surprised; it was still early there, and she had said last night that she planned on spending the day with her parents.

He logged off and left the condo, carrying flowers for Annie and a new book for Meg. She loved to read, and he paid attention to what was new in children's literature so that he could keep her up on all the newest books. He had read it himself, as he did all of the books he gave to her, so that they could discuss them when she had finished. Obviously, having a librarian for a mother had marked him for life!

*　　　　　　*　　　　　　*

It was midmorning when Laura woke. Talking with Taylor last night had been fun. She tried to remember all that they had discussed, but there had been so much. He had told her about the condo and the bay, the area where he went on his in-line skates, little details of his everyday life. She had told him about Beth and the paper and started trying to educate him about life in the land of *"mañana"*—tomorrow—which was when she would mention Cary since she had somehow never gotten around to it this week!

It had been late when they had logged off, and she had fallen asleep almost as soon as her head hit the pillow. Now she needed to get up. Mom was making green chile chicken enchiladas for her. Real food for a change, and before the end of the day, she hoped to find time to talk to her mother about this abundance of men in her life. Maybe Mom could help her sort out her feelings.

                    *   *   *

Taylor arrived at Annie's house a little after ten. As he got out of the car, a small figure exploded from the door and launched herself into his arms.

"Taylor! I thought you would never get here."

Taylor whirled her around in a circle before he set her back on her feet. "Hello, Meg! I've missed you!"

"I missed you, too, Taylor," she said, suddenly solemn as she stared at him. "I wish you didn't have to be gone so long."

"I know, Meg, but it's my job. C'mon now. Let's go find your mother."

He took her small hand in his, and they went into the house. Annie was in the kitchen, cutting up fruit for a salad. Taylor gave her a kiss before reaching into the cupboard for a vase.

"You didn't have to bring flowers, Taylor," she said as she washed her hands.

"Maybe they're not for you, Annie," he teased. "Maybe the flowers are for Meg, and this book is for you."

Meg giggled. "You are both so silly. What's the book, Taylor?"

"A new one by Robin McKinley. I've read it already. I think you'll like it."

Meg was already looking through the book as Taylor and Annie exchanged a look over her head. "Megan? Isn't there something you need to tell Taylor?" Annie chided her gently.

"What?" Meg was already lost in the first paragraph of the book. "Oh…thank you, Taylor."

"You're welcome. Why don't you go start that while I help your mom with lunch?"

Meg wandered off to the family room while Taylor began to get down plates and glasses to set the table. "Inside or out, Annie?"

"Outside, I think. It's a beautiful day." She pulled a quiche from the oven as Taylor opened the patio doors. "There's a tablecloth there by the door."

They had played this scene so many times before. He was comfortable in Annie's house, probably more comfortable there than in his own. He knew where to find everything and soon had the table ready for them. As he turned to come back into the kitchen, he saw Annie staring out of the window over the sink. She seemed to be miles away in her thoughts, and Taylor noticed that the shadows under her eyes, shadows that had been slight only a few days ago at dinner, had grown larger and darker.

"Annie?" Taylor's voice was filled with concern. "Is everything alright?"

"Everything's fine, Taylor." Annie picked up the bowl of fruit, handed it to him, then picked up the quiche. "Megan! Lunch!" she called as she moved past him through the door.

He couldn't question her with Megan there and had to put his concern aside until later. He would find time to talk to her before he left today. Something was up with Annie, and he knew that it was probably money. She was too stubborn to turn to him for help despite the fact that he had offered repeatedly. It was probably time for their annual argument over Meg's tuition, anyway.

*   *   *

Laura pulled into the driveway that approached her parents' house. Built on a cliff on the West side of the Rio Grande, it faced East overlooking the river and the city with its backdrop of the Sandia and Manzano Mountains. It had been pretty unremarkable when they moved here, but Dad had put in a lot of work on it over the years, including installing an indoor pool and atrium. He and Tomás had done most of the work themselves, allowing Laura and her mother to do some of the more mundane things like painting. It wasn't that Dad was a chauvinist, it was simply his time with Tomás. He had made other time to be with her, and she had never felt slighted. She pushed open the heavy wooden door and followed the tiled entry as it sloped down into the living room. Her mother was in the kitchen and looked up at the sound of Laura's footsteps.

"Hello, darling," she said as she came out of the kitchen, wiping her hands on an apron. She was a small woman with beautiful dark hair still unmarked by gray. She looked very little different from the pictures Laura had seen of her as a young bride.

"Hi, Mom," she said as she bent down to give her a kiss. "It smells wonderful. I'm starving!"

Her mother laughed. "You're always starving, Laura. I don't know how you stay so slim. It's a good thing you inherited your father's genes instead of mine."

Laura's father came in at that moment. "Which genes would those be, Maria?" he asked as he hugged Laura. He was tall and slim, with the same coppery red hair as Laura's.

"The ones that allow her to eat anything and still stay so thin, Sean. It's a good thing she inherited her figure from you and not from me."

Her father gave her mother a frankly appraising look and dryly said, "Well, there are certain things I think she inherited from you, my love. And a damn good thing, too." He leaned down and gave her a lingering kiss.

"Excuse me?" Laura laughed. "Maybe I should go somewhere so you two can be alone?"

"Why?" her father countered. "We never let your presence stop us before!"

Her mother blushed, the color staining her olive cheeks and making her look even younger. "Sean Patrick Collins, behave yourself," she said as she turned back to the kitchen. "Laura, help your father set the table. I think we'll eat out on the patio today."

While they carried plates and glasses outside, her father asked her about her work. She mentioned her opinion of the new mayor, and they were off into a political argument. It wasn't that they really disagreed, it was more that they both enjoyed the mental exercise. They were interrupted by Maria bringing out a salad and sending Sean after the hot dish of enchiladas.

*   *   *

Taylor and Meg cleaned up the kitchen after lunch. Taylor had poured a glass of wine for Annie and insisted she put her feet up and let them do the cleaning. She hadn't argued and had moved to the chaise lounge on the patio. She could hear them now through the open doorway, Meg prattling about the important doings in her eleven-year-old world, Taylor giving her his full attention and responding to her with respect. They were very good together, those two.

"Annie?"

She opened her eyes to find Taylor standing beside her, Megan close behind him. "So, how many dishes did I lose this time?" she teased them.

"None, thank you!" Taylor said in mock indignation. "Well, Meg, it looks like we're not appreciated. What do you say we run away to the beach for the afternoon?"

"Yes!" Meg turned and ran back into the house to get ready, leaving Taylor and Annie laughing. Taylor sat on the edge of the chaise and said, "I probably should have asked you first, but I didn't think you would mind. You look like you could use a quiet afternoon."

"I probably could," she admitted. "Just not too late, Taylor. She has school tomorrow and she needs to be home in time to wind down a little."

"I promise, Annie. No later than six."

"Have a good time, then."

"You, too. Enjoy the quiet." He leaned forward and kissed her forehead. "I meant what I said, Annie. Try to get some rest; and I want to talk to you when I get back." He went into the house before she could argue.

*　　　*　　　*

Lunch over, Laura and her mother cleaned up the kitchen. They worked in silence, listening to the faint sounds of the television in the living room where Sean had settled in to watch the game. At least that's what he always said he was going to do; he really slept through the whole thing. It had been a Sunday afternoon tradition as long as Laura could remember.

"Feel like taking a walk, Mom?"

Maria had been aware all during lunch that there was something bothering Laura. They had always been close. Laura hadn't been a rebellious teenager and had usually brought all her troubles to her mother to talk over. Maria was aware of how lucky she was, and was grateful that little had changed. Laura still brought her troubles home to talk through.

"Of course, *mi 'jita*. Let me change my shoes."

Stopping long enough to tell Sean their plans, the two women headed out the back of the house and down a path that went along the river. Sean watched them until the bright head and the dark one had disappeared from view. He, too, had noticed a restlessness about Laura and was glad she was going off with her mother. They would work it out, whatever it was. They always had.

It was cool along the riverbank. The noise of the city was far removed, and there was a peacefulness that Laura let sink into her heart. They didn't talk as they went along until they came to a favorite spot along a curve in the river. A large boulder jutted out into the water; it had always been Laura's favorite thinking place. The two women climbed up and sat on top of it, enjoying the warmth of the sun, the light on the river. As Maria waited for Laura to begin, her personal serenity began to enfold her daughter.

"Mom? How did you know that Dad was the one?"

So, that was it. Her Laura had met someone. Maria was pleased. It wasn't that she minded her independent daughter being unmarried or even uninvolved, she just wanted Laura to have the same kind of closeness that she shared with Sean.

"That's not an easy question, 'jita. I think that it's something you just know. There's someone?"

"Sí, Mamá." Laura easily slipped back into the soft Spanish of her childhood. "Do you remember the singer who was here awhile back? Taylor Morgan? I told you about him."

"I remember. You seemed very taken with him at the time."

"I was, I guess. He was very to talk to, Mamá, and he reminded me of the way Tomás and I used to talk. But it wasn't just that, he's very attractive, Mom." Laura blushed as she told her, keeping her eyes on the river, avoiding looking into her mother's eyes. "And now, he's gotten back in touch by e-mail. I heard from him earlier this week and we were up late last night 'talking.'"

"It doesn't sound like much of a problem, Laura."

"But, it is, Mamá. He's famous. He's been everywhere, done everything. He's fascinating, and I want to keep him as a friend, but I don't know why he'd be interested in me."

"It sounds like friendship isn't the only thing you want from this man."

"Oh, Mom," Laura sighed. "I don't know what I want, where I want this to go. And now there's Cary, too. I like him a lot, and he's here, not halfway across the country. How am I supposed to figure out what I want—and who?"

"Laura…" Her mother reached out and turned Laura's chin so that she was facing her. "You can't plan this one out, *'jita*. You want to organize everything and friendship—or love—can't be organized. It has to just happen. I think all you can do is let this take its course and see where it goes. Your heart will tell you what you need to know."

I O

Taylor and Meg headed to the beaches in St. Petersburg. She loved his convertible, a Jaguar XJ8, and always wanted the top down even though it tangled her hair. Taylor was always happy to oblige. After all, that was why he had bought a convertible in the first place.

Arriving at their favorite beach, within sight of the venerable Don Cesar Hotel, they carried a blanket and towels to the sand. Taylor watched as she ran out into the warm green waters of the Gulf. Meg was like a fish—or a mermaid; she had loved the water since she was a baby, learning to swim before she could walk. Taylor preferred to do his swimming in a pool, but was happy to sit in the sun and watch her as she played.

The green of the water reminded him of Laura's eyes. Not that they were even remotely the same shade, he acknowledged. Right now, it seemed that everything reminded him of Laura. He had been telling her about Tampa all week and wanted to show it to her in person. He was anxious to see her again, and wondered if it was too soon to invite her to visit.

"Taylor!" He could hear the exasperation in Meg's voice. "I've been standing here forever. What *are* you thinking about?" she said in a voice uncannily like her mother's.

"Not thinking, Meg, just dreaming. What have you found?" She handed him a perfectly formed seashell. "A perfect one, Meg! Good job. We'll add it to the others." They had started a collection years before which was kept on the wide windowsill in the living room of his condo. When they started, Meg had insisted that the shells would miss the ocean and had decided they would be "happiest" on his windowsill where they could still see the water.

She flopped down on the blanket beside him, and he handed her a towel. "What's up with you, Meg?"

She gave a world-weary sigh then said, tragically, "School..." her voice trailing off in despair. Taylor had to fight the urge to smile. Meg had always been dramatic, and Annie blamed it on his influence.

"School? Care to be a little more specific?"

"It's that stupid private school Mom makes me go to. I hate the uniforms, I hate the campus, I hate the rules!"

"Megan, that's not true. I know it and you know it. You love it there, or at least you did. You're on the swim team, you're starting drama and chorus; so what's got you so upset?"

"Just stuff, Taylor."

"Megan Elizabeth Miller, out with it."

"There's a dinner coming up. The chorus will be performing."

"So? That doesn't sound like a problem, Meg."

"It's a father-daughter dinner," she said practically in a whisper. "And some of the girls say I can't come since I don't have a father." She sat very still, staring straight ahead.

"They're wrong, Meg. You have me."

"*Would* you come with me, Taylor?" She looked at him with her heart in her eyes.

"Of course, just let me know when so I can put it on my calendar," he said gently, taking her hand in his. He wanted to storm into the school and ask them what the hell they thought they were doing with such a stupid idea, wanted to find the little brats who had hurt her. Instead, he continued, "You'll have to let me know what color your dress is, Meg. And if it's strapless or not so I know what kind of corsage I should buy. And will I need to rent a tux?"

She giggled and said, "Taylor! You are so silly!" She stood up and turned to run back into the water then stopped and came back. Throwing her arms around his neck she whispered, "Thank you, Taylor — I love you." Holding her tightly, he whispered back, "I love you, too, Meg," before he released her.

*   *   *

On the way back to the house, Taylor stopped at a deli and picked things up for sandwiches. They would be back a little earlier than Annie expected, and he didn't want her worrying about dinner. When they got there, he sent Meg off to shower and change while he fixed a tray and told Annie what had happened.

"I can't tell you how angry I was, Annie! Doesn't that school know that there are a lot of little girls out there with absentee fathers?"

"I know, Taylor, but it's a traditional thing. They'll give it up eventually. Right now, I have to thank you for being there for her. It's a big deal, unfortunately."

"Well, it's a stupid idea, but I'll be there for her. Just give me the date." He poured a glass of wine and joined Annie at the table. "And as long as we're on the subject of school...."

"No, Taylor."

"No what, Annie?'

"No, Taylor, you are not paying her tuition."

"Annie, we have this argument every year. Don't you think it's my turn to win? God knows I can afford it. I just put it in her trust fund when you turn me down."

"Then you can do it again this year, Taylor. She's my responsibility, not yours." Annie stood and walked out of the kitchen.

After a moment, Taylor followed her. She was staring out the window of the family room, tension in every line of her body. Taylor came up behind her and put his arms around her. "Annie?" He turned her to face him, and he was surprised to find her crying. Gently he brushed a tear from her cheek. "Annie, what's going on?"

"I'm just tired, Taylor. And this with the school is too much. I just want her to be happy; is that so much to ask?"

Taylor pulled her into his arms and held her. Annie rarely cried. He knew now that there was something wrong, but he would have to wait until she was ready to tell him.

11

Taylor left Annie's house early in the evening. She had stopped crying when they had heard Meg coming. He had headed Meg off to help him in the kitchen, giving Annie a few minutes to pull herself together. After they had eaten, Taylor had kissed them both goodbye, reminded Meg to let him know about her dress, then headed for home. He chose to take the long way rather than going straight home. He found that driving sometimes helped him clarify his thoughts...and he certainly had enough to think about tonight.

*   *   *

After Taylor left, Annie and Meg watched a television program together; Meg curled up in her mother's arms. Annie saw little of the program, but enjoyed the feel of snuggling with Megan. She had chattered for awhile about her day with Taylor, but had quieted for the program and now was almost asleep.

Today was not the first time that Meg had had to deal with the fact that she was fatherless. It had happened before, times that Taylor knew nothing about. Annie had handled it in the best way she could, and it somehow worked out all right. Still, she was grateful that Taylor would be there to help Meg through this one. He was gone so much, though,

70

that she couldn't let Meg count on him. It was a fact of life that Meg would have to learn to live with, no matter how difficult that was.

*   *   *

Laura arrived home laden with food her mother had insisted she take. She hadn't had to argue very hard. Cooking was not one of the things Laura enjoyed, and she tended to eat fast food instead. Having leftovers to look forward to was a nice change.

She hit the message button on the answering machine while she put things away. There was a message from Beth about dinner tomorrow with the girls, then a message from Cary.

"Laura? I must have missed you. I wondered if you wanted to go for a drive this afternoon, but I guess that's out. Can we have dinner one night this week? Give me a call."

She put the last of the containers in the refrigerator, then hit the erase button on the machine. Checking her calendar, she called Cary, only to get his answering machine. She left a message that dinner Thursday or Friday would be good or lunch any other day if he could get away. Hanging up, she turned on the computer and started the log-on sequence while she changed clothes.

*   *   *

By the time Taylor arrived home, he had put his worries about Annie aside. He had known her long enough to know that she wouldn't talk to him until she was ready. No amount of worrying on his part would change that. He wished she would let him help, but she had been determined from the beginning that she would make it on her own, without help from him or anyone.

When he let himself into the condo, he immediately noticed the message light blinking on the answering machine. Few people had his direct number, and it was always a surprise to find a message from one of them.

"Taylor? It's Christine. Give me a call when you can. I have some news for you."

Christine, his assistant, was supposed to be on vacation. She had been with him the whole tour and had been indispensable as usual. When they weren't traveling, she kept track of his mail, sorting it and keeping him on top of what he needed to respond to. She was very good about giving him his privacy and would only call if it were truly necessary. As he dialed her number, he wondered what her news could be.

*   *   *

Laura put one of Taylor's CD's in the player before opening her e-mail file. Skimming her messages for one from Taylor, she was disappointed to find there wasn't one. He had said he would be spending the day with Annie, but it was getting late there now. Shrugging mentally, she began to compose a note to him.

Hi, Taylor-

> Hope your day was as pleasant as mine. Mom spoiled me, as usual, with my favorite green chile chicken enchiladas. Yum! I wish I'd inherited her cooking talents instead of Dad's hair!
>
> Mom and I went for a walk along the river after lunch. It was a beautiful day, great to be outdoors.
>
> Then we came back and totally humiliated my father by beating him at Scrabble. Well, technically Mom was the one who won, but my score was higher than his was, too. He doesn't like losing and has sworn revenge.
>
> I'll be checking back in a little later. Hope to talk to you then.

> Laura

She sent the message, then turned to reading and answering her other mail, hoping he would log on while she was still connected.

The doorbell startled her. She wasn't expecting anyone, and it was nearly nine. Cautiously looking out the peephole, she was surprised to see Cary standing there. She quickly ran her fingers through her hair before she opened the door to him.

"Cary? What are you doing here? I wasn't expecting you."

"Well, you might have been if I'd been able to get through. The phone's been busy for the last hour." He tried to sound like he was teasing her, but his impatience showed through.

"Sorry, I was online. In fact, I'm still connected, let me log off."

She turned to the computer and Cary admired the way she looked in the leggings and sweater she was wearing. They were dating steadily now, but he hadn't been able to get past her reserve for more than some heavy petting. He wasn't used to this kind of cool treatment from a woman. Usually, they were all over him. Her hands-off attitude both annoyed and excited him.

He became aware of a voice singing in the background that sounded vaguely familiar. Since Laura was still occupied with the computer, he picked up the CD case.

"Taylor Morgan?" he asked, holding out the CD case as she turned.

"Yes, he was here a few weeks ago. I interviewed him and went to the concert. I like his voice and his style."

"Well, his style must have changed, then."

"What are you talking about, Cary?"

"I knew him in New York, back when he was just getting started. Remember I told you about my having the theatre beat? I covered several of his early failures. My ex-wife was in his big show, the one about Italy."

Even as she supplied the name of the show, Laura's mind was reeling. An ex-wife? Cary had never mentioned that before, and she listened as he went on.

"He was quite the big deal then. Had women falling at his feet. He took them up on all their offers from what I understood. Unfortunately, one of them was my ex-wife, which is *why* she's my ex. She had been carrying on with him before we got married and saw no need to stop. He evidently had no problem with sleeping with a married woman."

Laura found all of this hard to believe. It sounded so unlike the Taylor Morgan that she had met; of course, that had to have been more than ten years ago.

"Cary, you never mentioned you had been married," Laura said casually.

"I'm sorry, Laura." Cary came over to stand where he could look into her eyes. "I wasn't trying to hide it. It was all a long time ago. We were young, and I was pretty naïve, still a small-town Ohio boy. She just turned out to be very different from the girl I had thought I was marrying. It's not important to me anymore. The marriage only lasted a few months." He gave her a rueful smile before he continued, "But, you can see why I'm not too happy to find Taylor Morgan in your apartment, can't you?

"Cary, you never did say why you came over."

"Because I missed you, Laura. It's been days since I've seen you." He reached behind himself and turned off the CD player even as he lowered his mouth to hers, kissing her lightly, then more insistently until they both forgot about Taylor Morgan.

*   *   *

Taylor hung up the phone. His conversation with Christine had been a real surprise. She was getting married in February and wanted to give him her resignation. She and her husband were going to be starting their own small business and it would take all of her time. She had said all the right things, how sorry she was, how she would help train her replacement, but he really didn't want to go through all that again. He was happy for Christine, but he was going to miss her terribly.

At least he had until after the first of the year to find a replacement; maybe a little longer depending on his schedule. Right now, he just didn't want to think about it. It had been far from the relaxing day he had anticipated.

He thought about logging on to see if he had heard from Laura, but realized he wasn't in a mood to chat with her or anyone. Instead, he picked up a book and went to bed to read, to escape from the reality that seemed overwhelming today.

*   *   *

It was late when Cary finally left. They had spent the last couple of hours watching a video. At least that was what the official story was. They had really spent a lot more time *not* watching while paying close attention to each other.

As Laura closed the door behind him, after a final lingering kiss, she tried to clear her head. She knew that Cary had been expecting more from this evening; he had even been a little too aggressive tonight until she had made it clear that she wanted him to back off. It wasn't that she didn't find him attractive; far from it. He had the ability to make her pulse race, but it was too soon. Laura had no intention of going to bed with him until she felt the time was right, and she wasn't sure that he was willing to wait until she was ready.

Laura had never been one to give her affections lightly. There had been a serious boyfriend in college. For awhile they considered getting married, but despite the fact that they had a great sex life, there wasn't enough there to build a life on. They had broken it off just before graduation with no hurt feelings on either side. She still ran into him occasionally and considered him a friend. She hadn't been attracted enough

to anyone since then to consider going to bed with him, so she had settled into her solitary lifestyle.

She thought about checking her e-mail since she had told Taylor she
would be back online later, but it was so late now, he must have given up
on her long ago, if he had been there at all. Considering Cary's revelation
tonight, it was a good thing she hadn't told Taylor about him after all.

As she changed for bed, she thought about what Cary had said about
Taylor. The man he had described seemed to be so different from the
Taylor she was getting to know. But, she admitted to herself, she really did-
n't know much about Taylor at all. For that matter, she didn't know much
about Cary either. She certainly hadn't known he had been married!

Wearily, she went to bed and turned out the light, her mind filled
with conflicting thoughts and questions.

*   *   *

As Cary drove home, he had trouble controlling his frustration.
Laura was turning out to be a real challenge, and Cary had never been
one to turn down a challenge. He was determined to take her to bed
before he left Albuquerque and he was willing to use any tactic to reach
that goal. The time frame had tightened this week. The tentative job
offer from TNC was beginning to look like it was a done deal, so he
would be out of here before too much longer.

Since all was fair in love and war, he felt no guilt for turning the story
of his marriage into a sermon against the great Taylor Morgan. Most of
it had been true, although he had certainly embellished it freely enough.
It was Laura's voice that had been the giveaway. She had tried to be
casual when he'd asked about Taylor, but he had heard the careful control in her voice and seen the light blush that had colored her face. He
would be damned if he would lose another woman to Morgan!

12

Taylor handed a glass of wine to Laura as she looked out at the sunset from the deck of his condo. The sun glinted off her copper-colored hair and delicately tinted her face. As she turned to thank him, he took the glass he had just given her and set it on the railing next to his. Burying his hands in the mass of her hair, he pulled her close, kissing her deeply. She returned his kiss with an equal fervor and let her hands explore the contours of his back. He was the first to pull away, but only long enough to look deep into her eyes, gauging her feelings. She reached up one hand to trace the outline of his mouth, then caressed his cheek before she pulled his face down to hers in another soul-searing kiss.

Somehow, they were in the bedroom, and his hands were unbuttoning her blouse, her hands sliding beneath his shirt, eager to touch him. He slid the blouse off of her shoulders and let it fall to the floor. He traced the curve of her breast above her bra, then gently brushed his thumbs across the nipples underneath the delicate fabric. He caught her as her knees grew weak, and she nearly lost her balance from the sensations racing through her body. Laughing softly, he drew her into his arms and swept her off her feet to carry her to his bed.

Lying beside her, he feasted his eyes on her as he undid the catch of her bra, freeing her breasts to be captured by his hands. Then, gently, he pulled her skirt down and tossed it away and allowed his hands to caress her body, letting his mouth follow the lines his hands traced.

Laura, with trembling hands, began to unbutton his shirt until it, too, was tossed away. Standing by the bed, he quickly stripped off the rest of his clothes before returning to lie with her and continue his exploration of her body.

Her hands began an exploration of their own, tracing the curve of his hip, the muscles of his stomach and chest. She kissed his nipples, teasing them to hardness with her tongue, smiling in pleasure at the low moan that escaped his lips as she touched him.

Quickly, he stripped off her panties, sliding his fingers between her legs as he covered her breasts with kisses, smiling as she almost purred with the pleasure of the moment.

She pushed him away from her, onto his back, as she came above him, straddling his body with hers, ready to take him inside of her. A persistent noise distracted her, and she looked away...

...and woke to find the alarm clock buzzing across the room, her bedroom filled with early morning light, and the dream dissolving into scattered memories in her head.

It had been one hell of a dream, Laura thought, as she forced herself to get out of bed. Shutting off the alarm, she came very close to hurling the clock across the room in frustration as if she could blame it for her feelings.

She walked into the kitchen and got a soda from the refrigerator. She had started drinking caffeinated soda in college as a substitute for the coffee she disliked and as the only possible way to stay awake during an eight o'clock class. Now it was essential to her mornings. As she drank it, she turned on the computer to check her e-mail. Nothing from Taylor. She was disappointed, more disappointed than was reasonable, she realized. Taylor had a life of his own just as she did. Still, she had enjoyed their daily contact and felt as if something was missing from her life without it.

Trying to put the dream out of her head, she turned on the television to Cary's station as she got ready to face her day.

*   *   *

Taylor had had a restless night. He had read until the early morning hours, then tossed and turned until the sun began to fill his bedroom with light. Giving up on sleeping, he got up, put on his skates, and headed toward Bayshore Drive. He hoped some exercise would clear his head.

*   *   *

Meg was overtired, cranky, and at her most difficult as her mother tried to get her ready for school. Once she got her there and headed off for the studio, Annie realized she had another headache. She would have given anything to have gone home and crawled into bed for the day. That was the problem with being her own boss; there was no one she could call to tell she was sick and not coming in. She had a class to teach as soon as she got in. Thank heavens it was ballet this morning and not tap or jazz. Her head couldn't have taken the noise.

*   *   *

Cary was due at the station by five every morning this week. Filling in for the early morning anchor, he had to deliver the news every fifteen minutes, make small talk with the traffic reporter, and do local human-interest interviews. He hated it! While it gave him the on-air time he craved, it was so small time. He wanted to be traveling the world reporting on big stories, not showing off prize-winning vegetables and interviewing their owners who were only marginally more interesting.

The morning crew quickly found out that approaching Cary in the morning was a risky proposition, so most of them left him alone. By the time he was on camera, he had undergone a total transformation to the

sincere, bright, witty anchor that had already caused their ratings to go
up ten points. And, once Cary was "on" he was "on" for the day.

*   *   *

After Taylor returned from skating, he showered and dressed, then
had fruit and juice on the deck. It was going to be a beautiful day, and he
had absolutely no plans for how he would like to spend it. He was supposed to be vacationing, recuperating after the tour. But, everyone he
knew was working. He certainly wasn't up for more traveling and had
no time for hobbies, so he was faced with a large amount of free time.

He carried the dishes back into the kitchen, and rinsed and added
them to the dishwasher before he turned on the computer and discovered Laura's message from the day before. His spirits lifted just seeing it
there in the list of incoming mail.

*   *   *

Laura watched Cary's on-the-hour news segment. She smiled as she
remembered the evening before. It didn't seem possible, but Cary was
even more attractive on the screen. Idly, she wondered how much
longer it would be before she gave in and slept with him. The problem
was, she couldn't even imagine Cary making love to her. Taylor, on the
other hand—well, if last night's dream had been any indication, imagining Taylor was not going to be a problem!

She was disgusted with herself for being so confused about all of this.
Laura was used to organizing and compartmentalizing her life. This
business of being torn because of her feelings for two men just wouldn't
be nicely packaged and put away. Shaking off her mood, Laura picked
up her briefcase and purse and headed out the door.

13

After reading through his mail, Taylor sent a reply to Laura and then logged off the computer, still with a whole day to face. He decided to check on Annie at the studio and see if he could take her to lunch. If Annie didn't have a class scheduled it could be possible.

    *   *   *

Through the studio window he could see a line of preschoolers trying very hard to master a few basic ballet steps. Annie was working with them, adjusting an arm here or a foot there as she worked her way down the line. She had infinite patience with these children, and Taylor loved watching her with them. As he stepped inside and stood with the audience of watching parents, Annie clapped her hands and praised the children for their hard work before she dismissed her class. She received a number of hugs as they scattered. Taylor waited while she talked to some parents; then finally, they were all gone and the studio was silent.

As Taylor walked across the studio to Annie, he noticed that the circles under her eyes were as dark as they had been last night. Maybe he could get her to open up to him at lunch.

"Morning, Annie," he said as he gave her a kiss.

"Hello, Taylor. What's up?"

"I just thought I'd see if you were available for lunch."

Annie looked at him, then said, "I am, Taylor—if you promise we're not going to argue about Meg's tuition again."

"I promise. Just lunch, and we don't even have to talk if you don't want to."

Annie laughed and said, "That'll be the day! Let me put a sign on the door and I'll be ready."

*   *   *

Over lunch, Annie and Taylor talked about everything except Meg's tuition and what it was that was bothering Annie. She had made it very clear that she wouldn't discuss whatever it was yet, and Taylor had to accept it.

"Sure you don't want to change jobs, Annie? You could take Christine's job, and I wouldn't have to worry about hiring or training someone. You already know me."

"Which is precisely why I would never take the job, Taylor! Because I do know you, and I'm not crazy enough to try to work for you!"

"Remind me not to use you for a reference!" he said, laughing with her. The sparkle was back in her eyes, Taylor noticed. Maybe whatever this was that was spooking Annie really was nothing. He didn't really believe that so much as he wanted to believe it.

"Thanksgiving's coming, Taylor. Will you be in town?"

"Have I ever missed it, Annie? There's no place I'd rather be."

"Good. I thought I'd invite Jane and her husband and Susan this year."

"Sounds perfect. I assume I'm delegated the mashed potatoes again this year?"

"It's a tradition, Taylor!" Annie widened her eyes, feigning innocence. "Besides, I hate peeling potatoes and even you can't ruin something that simple."

"I swear, Annie, someday I'm going to surprise you by fixing you a gourmet meal. Then you'll have to take back all these cruel things you've said about my cooking."

"I won't hold my breath, Taylor. Right now, you had better get me back to the studio; my jazz class will be arriving soon." Annie was relieved she wouldn't be facing it with the headache that had finally eased off during lunch.

Taylor paid the check, and the two of them walked out of the restaurant, Taylor's arm draped over Annie's shoulders as if to shelter her from whatever was bothering her.

        *   *   *

It had been a busy day at the paper. Robert wanted a draft of her feature article that was scheduled to run in the Sunday paper in two weeks. She had been too busy all day to check her mail, and now that she was home, too tired. Still, she knew herself well enough to know that she was still obsessing on getting a message from Taylor. If she didn't check, she would never be able to relax. She turned on the computer and skimmed the message list. There it was, sent this morning, probably right after she had left for work. She opened the file and began to read:

Morning, Laura-

> Sorry I didn't log on last night. I got home later than I expected.
>
> Sounds like you had a wonderful day with your folks. The bright spot of my day is that I managed to come home with a 'date' for next week.

Laura's heart sank when she read those words. A date. He was seeing someone, getting involved with someone. Never mind that she was dating Cary.

Actually it's a date with Meg. Seems her stupid private school is having a father-daughter dinner. Since her father abandoned her before she was born, she asked if I would go with her, and of course, I said I would.

Laura breathed a sigh of relief. It was just Meg, not a serious rival.

So I will be escorting Meg to her dinner—where I hope I don't run into the little brats that told her she couldn't come because she didn't have a father!

Believe it or not, my day went downhill from there. Remember Christine? My assistant? Well, actually, it's good news for her. She's getting married in February. It's bad news for me since it means hiring and training someone new. I know I sound like a whiny kid, but I really don't look forward to trying to find someone as reliable as Chris. Luckily, for me, my schedule is pretty clear until after the first of the year. So that means I don't have to handle this right away.

Sorry, Laura. I'm usually not this much of a grump. But I guess I needed to talk about it some. I'll try hard to be a lot more cheerful in the next message.

Thanks for listening.

Taylor

She wanted to think about his message before she answered it, so she saved it, then logged off. She still wasn't sure what really existed between Annie and Taylor, but she was certain there was more than he had told her. It was clear that he cared deeply for Annie and Meg, had cared about them for a long time, and would continue to do so. Any woman who came into his life would have to be able to deal with that.

Until now, Laura had never had any trouble believing that a man and a woman could just be friends. She had male friends, for heaven's sake! But the thought of Annie with Taylor…Laura never knew she could feel so jealous of anyone, and she didn't particularly like the feeling.

The phone interrupted her thoughts. She considered letting the answering machine pick up, but decided to answer and was glad she did when she heard her mother's voice.

"I wanted to check with you about Thanksgiving, Laura. You don't have to work, do you?"

"Thanksgiving? It's next week, isn't it? I completely forgot! No, I'm not working. Shall I come out early to help?"

"Help? Well, I'm sure I can find *something* for you to do. I wondered if you would like to invite your reporter friend. He's not from around here, is he? Maybe he would like some family for the holiday."

Laura felt guilty for not thinking of it first. "What a good idea, Mom. I'll call and ask him and let you know. Thanks for thinking of it."

"You know your friends are always welcome. I'll talk to you soon. Love you."

"Love you, too, Mom."

As Laura hung up the phone, she realized that Taylor would probably be spending the holiday with Annie and Meg. She was glad he wouldn't be alone, but even as she dialed Cary's number, she found herself wishing it were Taylor she was inviting instead.

*   *   *

Cary hung up after talking to Laura. This was a good sign—she was inviting him to meet her parents. Normally, he would have made some excuse. Being taken home to meet the family was more commitment than Cary was willing to give. If his instincts were right about Laura, this would be an important test he would have to pass.

He remembered the family holidays when he was growing up. More food than anyone could possibly eat, too many aunts and uncles and cousins, and weeks of leftovers. For a brief moment he wondered about his ex-wife and the baby who was what now? Ten? Eleven? He dismissed them from his thoughts as he picked up the phone to cancel his Taos ski trip reservations. He could always catch a couple of days skiing on Sandia Peak, and he already had Taos booked for Christmas—even though he planned on being long gone from Albuquerque by then.

*   *   *

Laura logged back on and began an answer to Taylor's message.

Hi, Taylor-

> I see you're into dating younger women.
>
> It's really good of you to be there for Meg. It must be very hard for her sometimes. I can't even imagine what it would have been like without my father.
>
> It sounds like you and Annie have a special relationship. You're both lucky to have each other. It's terribly important to have someone you can talk to about anything and everything.
>
> That's the kind of relationship I had with Tomás and that I have with Beth. She's been my best friend since we were 13 years old. I'd be lost without her.
>
> Sounds like you're going to be pretty lost without Christine, too. I liked her. She seemed to really understand all the demands you have to handle. Training someone else will be difficult, and it's obvious you have to find someone you have some rapport with. I don't envy you the search.
>
> My mother just called to remind me that Thanksgiving is next week. Will you be with Annie and

Meg? I'll be with my folks, Beth and her family will be there. The two families have been celebrating together for years. It wouldn't be T-giving if the Collins and Wilkins families didn't get together!

Taylor, please feel free to "grump" at me anytime. I can always hit the delete key.

Seriously, it helps to have someone to talk with, and I'll be glad to listen.

Laura

I 4

Thanksgiving Day dawned clear and bright in New Mexico, not that Laura was awake to see the dawn. She took advantage of the day off to sleep in a little before she went out to help with dinner. Cary would join them a little later. She hadn't wanted to subject him to all day with the mob—at least that was what she had told herself.

*   *   *

Taylor was awake early on Thanksgiving morning. After taking a morning run, he showered and dressed and headed for Annie's. He wanted to help her as much as possible since she still seemed so tired. He hadn't seen her since lunch last week but had talked to her a couple of times. She just didn't sound right. He couldn't explain what it was, but he knew that something was wrong. Today probably wasn't the time, but he was really getting worried and he would make her tell him soon.

*   *   *

Beth and her parents had arrived by the time Laura made it out to her parents'. The house was already beginning to fill with the smell of turkey roasting. Posole bubbled on the stove, pumpkin pies were cooling, and the table had been extended to its full length.

"It's about time you got here," Beth said as she peeled potatoes. "This is your job, not mine."

"Why do you think I was late?" Laura laughed as she hugged her mother, then turned to hug Beth's mother. "How are the Moms this morning?"

Beth's mother responded, "We're fine, Laura. Where's this young man of yours?"

"Why don't you ask Beth? She seems to know everything about my life."

Beth said primly, as she handed the potato peeler to Laura, "He will be here later, just before dinner. Laura was afraid that we would be too much for him to deal with all day."

"Not the rest of you, just her!" Laura said as she took her place at the sink.

The four women kept up a lively conversation as they prepared the trimmings that would complete the feast. The fathers wandered in after awhile to see what samples they could sneak, and there was so much teasing laughter that they almost didn't hear the doorbell.

"Oh, that must be Cary!" Laura said as she looked around for a towel to dry her hands.

"Never mind. I'll let him in," Beth said, exiting the kitchen before Laura could protest.

*   *   *

Cary was a little startled when a petite blonde answered the door. For a moment, he thought he had the wrong house until she said, "You're Cary. I recognize you from the news. I'm Beth, Laura's best friend. Come in."

Cary came through the door, carrying flowers and a bottle of wine. "Thanks. It's nice to finally meet you. Laura talks about you a lot."

"Well, she hasn't told me much about you, so I guess I'll just have to find it out for myself today." She grinned at him, but he was pretty sure she wasn't joking. She was making him a bit uncomfortable, and he had the feeling she knew it. When he added her resemblance to his ex-wife, Cary was pretty sure he wasn't going to like this pushy little friend of Laura's. But he put on his best television "mask" and laughed with her.

"Cary!" Laura had come to rescue him.

"Hello, darling," he said as he kissed her. Beth shut the door behind her and followed them down the entryway to where the rest of the families were waiting.

Beth was doing an assessment of her own. Cary was a little too polished to suit her. She had seen the annoyance in his eyes when she had teased him, before he had hidden behind that professional smile. She didn't want to make a snap judgment, but she had a feeling that Cary could only mean trouble for Laura.

"Cary, these are my parents, Sean and Maria."

"Thank you for inviting me," he said as he handed the flowers to Laura's mother. "Laura said there was nothing I could bring, but maybe you can use this for another occasion," he said, handing the bottle of wine to her father.

"I think this is enough of an occasion to justify opening this with dinner," Sean said, shifting the bottle to one hand so he could shake Cary's hand with the other. "Welcome to our home."

Laura watched as her parents introduced the Wilkins to Cary. He was gracious and charming to them all, and she felt like things were going all right.

"How do you feel about football, Cary?" Sean asked.

"Depends on who's playing but I enjoy watching a good game."

"I don't know how good it is, but men are banished from the kitchen until dinner so you might as well come join us."

Cary looked at Laura. "He's right, Cary. Go watch the game. Dinner will be ready soon."

She watched as he followed her father up the steps to the living room that overlooked the city. He really was good-looking, she thought, as she admired the way his jeans fit. She was startled when Beth said softly, "Not bad if you like the smooth, polished, suave, and debonair type."

"I take it you approve?"

"I didn't say that. He still has to pass a few 'Beth tests' before I give you my blessing. Right now, girlfriend, you have a date with some potatoes."

*   *   *

When Taylor arrived at Annie's, the turkey was already cooking. She had Meg busy scrubbing vegetables and most everything else ready to start. True to her word, however, she had left the potatoes for him.

"You have work to do, Taylor Morgan," she said, laughing as she handed him a potato peeler. He snapped off a salute to her and clicked his heels together, which caused Meg to go off into uncontrollable giggles. Taylor picked up a potato and looked at it so woefully that Annie started giggling, too. He tried to maintain the somber face, but their laughter was too much, and he gave in and joined them before finally turning to his assigned task.

As he worked, listening to Meg's chatter, he was happy. He liked working with the two of them, being with them. The three of them were a family, maybe not in the traditional sense, but probably closer than many conventional ones.

Taylor watched Annie as she moved around the kitchen. She looked better this morning. The circles under her eyes had faded, and she moved with more of her customary energy. Whatever had been bothering her seemed to be over, and Taylor was relieved.

*   *   *

The long Spanish-Colonial style table was picture perfect, Laura thought, as she added the last napkin. Beth was at the other end of the table, filling water glasses when Cary came down the steps.

"Anything I can help with?" he asked.

"Thanks, but no. We're nearly ready," Laura said, smiling at him.

"It smells wonderful. Reminds me of Ohio."

"What about your family, Cary?" Beth asked.

"Actually, there's no one left. My parents were both only children and died several years ago. I was an only child so that was it for family."

Laura placed a hand on his arm in sympathy. "I'm sorry, Cary. Holidays must be lonely for you."

"Not this year," he said, deftly changing the subject. Laura didn't notice, but Beth did. That answer about his family had been pretty unemotional, as practiced and polished as the man who delivered it. She didn't know why, but Cary set off every warning alarm she possessed.

*   *   *

Dinner, at both locations, was a noisy event. There were several different conversations going on at once, lots of good food and friends.

In Florida, Meg's babysitter, Susan, and Annie's assistant, Jane, with her husband, completed the guest list. Taylor asked a blessing as "family" and friends joined hands around the table. Unsaid, but heartfelt, was his private prayer that Annie was really all right. The wishbone was claimed by Meg who cleaned it and hung it to dry as she already planned what she would wish for. Annie relaxed, enjoying the company of her friends, and pushed her troubles away for the moment. Taylor caught her eye, and she raised her glass to him in a silent toast to their friendship.

In New Mexico, the whole event reminded Cary of another reason he had hated the holidays when he was growing up. Even then he had wanted to be the center of attention, but there were always too many people around. He didn't miss it, hadn't spoken to his parents since he left. For all he knew, his story about them being dead was true. Now, even as he smiled and laughed, he was wishing he had stuck with his plans to ski. He would have given anything to be out on the slopes—alone!

15

When dinner in Florida was over, the dishes done, and leftovers put away, everyone lazily retired to the family room. The television was tuned to the football game, but no one was watching it very closely. Taylor and Meg were having their traditional Monopoly battle, fought every year on Thanksgiving. Meg was getting pretty good; Taylor was having trouble defending his properties against her. The rest of the adults chatted, Taylor joining in when he could afford to take his eyes off of Meg.

Both games ended at about the same time. After dessert and coffee, the other guests left for home. Meg was tired enough that, after a bath, she was willing to head for bed early. Taylor took care of tucking her in, then met Annie in the family room.

"I think she was asleep before her head hit the pillow," Taylor said with an indulgent smile.

"Thanks, Taylor. It's been a nice day, hasn't it?"

"It has, Annie, but you don't look a whole lot more awake than Meg. I'll head for home so you can get some rest."

Annie watched Taylor from the doorway and waved as he drove off. As she closed the door, she offered up a silent "thank you" to whatever power had helped her get through today without one of her headaches. With any luck, they were gone for good.

✶   ✶   ✶

After dinner in Albuquerque, the men did the dishes. Cary wasn't treated like a guest. Instead, he was handed a dishtowel so he could dry while Sean washed. There was no graceful way out of it, and Cary silently seethed as water dripped on his expensive suede loafers.

When they joined the women in the sunroom by the pool, Cary sat next to Laura and took her hand in his, giving her a fond smile. He could feel Beth's eyes on him as they had been during most of the day. It was like having a gargoyle watching him, and he decided he really didn't like this friend of Laura's. Thank heaven he wouldn't have to put up with her much longer.

Laura could tell that Cary was growing restless. Being around a bunch of strangers, no matter how nice they were, could be wearing. She decided to give it another half-hour, then she would leave with Cary. Mom could bring her car tomorrow when they were scheduled to go shopping together.

*   *   *

When Cary took her home, Laura invited him in. He watched silently as she put away the leftovers her mother had sent home with her. When she had finished, she poured two glasses of wine and handed him one. After pausing just long enough to kiss him lightly, she moved to the couch and sat in one corner, facing him as he sat at the other end.

"It was nice having you there today, Cary."

"I'd forgotten what family holidays were like," Cary responded, truthfully for a change.

"What will you do for Christmas?"

"Actually," he said, putting down his wineglass and taking her hands in his, "I wanted to talk to you about that. I've made reservations to go skiing in Taos the week before Christmas, through the holiday. I was hoping you would come with me."

"I can't, Cary. I have to work, and that week is a big thing for my family. We participate in *Las Posadas*. The procession is always held in our neighborhood on the 23rd. And it's our turn this year to hold the party. I can't possibly go off and abandon Mom to all that work."

"I've just found it easier to be gone over that week. That way people don't have to feel awkward because I'm alone."

Laura said softly, "You don't have to be alone, Cary. You would be welcome to celebrate Christmas with us."

He smiled and reached out to caress her cheek. "Thanks, Laura. I think I had better stick with my plans. I'm not very good at holidays anyway." Then he smiled at her and continued, "But that doesn't mean we can't celebrate together before I leave, does it?" And he drew her into his arms and kissed her.

*   *   *

It had been a nice day, Laura thought as she closed the door behind Cary. She was pleasantly exhausted, but couldn't resist turning on the computer to check for messages. She smiled as she saw "Barnum" in the message list that appeared on the screen.

Hi, Laura-

> Hope your day was as nice as ours. I still have some trouble with Thanksgiving falling on such a tropical day. It was in the 70's here. Even in California, when I was growing up, the day was usually a little cool, and it was always downright freezing in New York!

> Meg and I had our annual Monopoly game. We started when she was really little, probably 5 or so, and she's gotten good enough at it that I have to really watch what she's doing if I want to retain my championship title. I barely managed to keep it this year.

I'll be picking her up tomorrow to take her shopping for Annie's Christmas gift. That's been a tradition, too. We make a day of it with lunch and a movie if we've found what we're looking for. I'll let you know how it goes.

Taylor

Christmas! It seemed so far away, but she'd be spending tomorrow shopping with her mother. Cary wouldn't be here over the holidays—almost without thinking, she began to type a reply.

Hi, Taylor –

You must be a pretty poor Monopoly player if Meg is beating you already! I'll have to see how you do at Scrabble sometime.

We had a great day. The Moms (mine and Beth's) always cook enough food for an army—and expect us to eat it all! You should have heard them worrying about us when we were teenagers convinced that if we ate a bite of stuffing we'd gain ten pounds. Luckily, we outgrew that phase!

We'll be preparing now for Las Posadas. It's a Mexican tradition that's migrated here. In Mexico, it begins on Dec.16th as Mary and Joseph search for a place, an inn (posada), for the birth of the Holy Child. It goes on for nine nights as they knock on doors and are turned away until Christmas Eve, when the family is welcomed at the final house. Neighbors follow along and sing the traditional songs of the story.

Here we do it all in one night. Local people, mostly the kids, are chosen to play the parts of Mary and Joseph. Believe it or not, they chose me when I was 17. But I had to give up the part because my legs were too long for me to ride the little donkey that was available that year. And to make it worse, Beth took my place. I'm not sure I've ever forgiven her!

Anyway, we do it on the 23rd so that the families can spend Christmas Eve together. The final house this year is ours. Everyone will bring food for the celebration, and we'll have a piñata. It's a wonderful time.

Why don't you join us? I'm sure you want to spend Christmas with Annie and Meg, but you could fly back on Christmas Eve morning. I'll stay with Mom and Dad, and you can use my apartment. There are so many lovely things about Christmas in New Mexico. I'd love to share them with you.

Laura

Laura reread the message she'd typed. Should she send it? She hadn't planned on inviting him when she started. For some reason, Cary's insistence on spending the holidays alone had made her think of Taylor. And, finding out that Cary would be gone had opened the door to inviting Taylor.

Taking a deep breath, she gave the command that sent the message. It was done; there was no turning back. She logged off and got ready for bed. Lying in the dark, she found herself hoping he would say "yes."

*　　　　　*　　　　　*

Taylor was surprised when he read Laura's message. They had been corresponding almost daily now for a little less than two months. He felt like they had become friends, but he certainly hadn't anticipated her invitation. On a computer screen it was easier to not think about the way he had felt about her when they met. It might be impossible to ignore that attraction if he saw her again.

She had never mentioned dating or a boyfriend in any of her e-mail. He felt sure that she had to be seeing someone even if it wasn't serious. If he went, he might have to deal with that. Still, he realized, he wanted to see her again, so he began composing an answer.

Hi, Laura-

> Are you serious about Christmas? It sounds wonderful, and I would love to see more of Albuquerque, especially with you. If you're really sure, send me more details and we can make plans.
>
> My shopping trip with Meg was a great success. Of course, I'm not sure what Annie's going to think of purple hippopotamus slippers, but Meg insisted she needed them. It's my job to take her shopping, not to censor her purchases, but they will match the purple robe that I bought for Annie.
>
> You were a girl once—well, you still are, I guess! Any suggestions for a perfectly precocious eleven-year-old?
>
> Taylor

Laura had a moment of panic when she read his answer. He said "yes!" She had never thought beyond the invitation to what would happen if he took her up on it! Then panic was replaced by excitement, and she realized how much she had been hoping he would say "yes." Cary would be gone after the twentieth, so if Taylor came out then, she wouldn't have to worry about them meeting. Maybe she could talk Robert into letting her have another day off if she got her articles in early.

Hi, Taylor-

> Purple hippos? Are you sure they were completely Meg's idea? Why do I have the feeling that you were egging her on?
>
> Of course, I was serious about Christmas; it will be great to have you here! I have to work, but can probably

sneak off early any afternoon that week. You're welcome to come anytime after the 20th if you don't mind exploring on your own during the day. Just let me know when to pick you up at the airport.

I do hope you own a coat. You'll need it, and gloves and a hat for the procession. It can get pretty cold. Don't worry if you don't. You can always borrow some from Dad.

Oh! I just realized all that cold wouldn't be good for your voice. If you want to skip the procession, we can wait with Mom and Dad for the finale.

I'll give some thought to something for Meg, but I'm sure you don't really need my help. I think you have her pretty well figured out.

Laura

16

Hi, Laura-

I just got home from Meg's concert and father/daughter dinner. It was almost a disaster—was a disaster as far as I'm concerned.

The dinner was fine, if you overlooked the music teacher fawning all over me. The woman is a total twit. Luckily, Meg's friends were less impressed since I've met most of them at one time or another. The fathers didn't care who I was.

After the girls went to get ready for the concert portion, I realized that Meg had forgotten the stole that goes over her choir robe. I went to take it to her and came upon a group of girls in the hall...

...They hadn't seen him as he walked toward them. Only Meg was facing him, and he could see the pain in her eyes before he heard what they were saying.

"Are you trying to impress us with your famous friend? If you are, it's not working, Megan Miller. He is not your father, and you shouldn't have come." The tallest of the girls was leading the attack, but the four or five others around her were nodding in agreement. Taylor could see that Meg was close to tears.

They jumped like startled cats when Taylor spoke, "Actually, you're wrong. I am Meg's father—her godfather. And that's even more important because I got asked if I'd like to do it and I said "yes." I *chose* Meg." He walked around the small knot of girls. "You forgot your stole, Meg," he said as he handed it to her. His back was to the others, and he winked at her, coaxing a small smile to her face and drying up the tears that threatened to spill over. Knowing that making too much of a fuss would embarrass her, he turned and said, "Nice meeting you, ladies" before he walked away…

…Laura, leaving her there with those little beasts was hard. But when they filed out on stage a little later, Meg winked at me and smiled, so I knew she was all right.

After the concert, we met up with the ringleader again in the parking lot. She seemed pretty impressed when we took my Jag that she had been eyeing. Meg waved at her like a princess acknowledging a subject as we drove away.

I worry about Meg a lot. This fatherless stuff is hard on her. Annie's never lied to her. She's told her that her father left before she was born, and Meg's always seemed fine with it, but someday she's going to want to find him, and I know she'll be hurt when she does.

Enough of that. I promise I'll be more cheerful when I see you next week. I'm really looking forward to it.

Taylor

* * *

For some reason he couldn't explain even to himself, Taylor still had not told Annie about Laura. He remembered Annie's opinion of Janis and the fight they'd had. Annie had been right, and a part of him was afraid that Annie wouldn't like Laura. She fussed at him often enough about finding someone, and now maybe he had. It was that "maybe" that was stopping him.

Since he would be going to New Mexico this week, it was time to tell Annie. He couldn't put it off any longer. He just wished he knew what he was going to say! He tried to compose his thoughts as he drove to Annie's for Sunday brunch. Meg was having a friend over and would be occupied. He would talk to Annie after they ate.

*   *   *

Laura hadn't told anyone, even Beth, that Taylor was coming. She would need to soon, but she didn't want it to get back to Cary. Considering his history with Taylor, it wouldn't be a good idea to let either of them know she knew the other.

She and Cary were going out tonight to "have an early Christmas." Cary had planned all of it; dinner at the Hyatt, dancing, then…it was what she was sure he was expecting afterwards that was making her nervous. He had become more overt about his expectations lately, his embraces a little rougher, his kisses more aggressive. She had begun to think seriously about breaking if off with him, and she probably would after the holidays. It just seemed unnecessarily cruel to do it when the whole world was wrapped in happiness.

*   *   *

Hi, Taylor-

    I can't believe that it will be Christmas this week. The year seems to have rushed by.

    I'm glad Meg survived the father-daughter dinner. Being different is always hard. While it's not on the same scale, of course, I was always singled out because of my height. I wanted desperately to be shorter.

Meg will remember someday what you did for her at that dinner. Right now she's probably gone on to the next thing, to excitement about Christmas. But a memory like that doesn't disappear. It stays hidden in your mind until it's needed. I'm sure it's going to help her through more than one rough spot in the future. She's very lucky to have you in her life, Taylor.

See you in a few days.

Laura

*   *   *

After brunch, Meg and her friend went out to skate around the quiet neighborhood. Annie made sure they were helmeted and padded before she let them out the door with an admonition to check in every thirty minutes. The house was amazingly quiet without them.

Taylor handed Annie a glass of wine as they went out to the patio, where they took chairs facing each other.

"OK, Taylor. Out with it."

"Out with what, Annie?"

"Whatever it is that's bothering you. You've been nervous all morning. So, tell me already."

"Annie, how do you do that? How do you *always* know?" he asked.

She just grinned at him and answered, "That is something you'll never find out, Taylor."

"I'm going to be gone for a couple of days this week, Annie. I'm flying to New Mexico on the twenty-second, but I'll be home in plenty of time for Christmas Eve. We won't have to change any plans," he was quick to reassure her.

"New Mexico? I know you stopped there on the tour...."

"Annie, I met someone there. Her name is Laura Collins. She was the reporter who had been assigned to write about the concert."

As Taylor told her about that short time with Laura, Annie studied his face. Taylor was very attracted to this girl, but there was something else, too. He was already half in love with this Laura Collins, she was sure of it. Thankfully, Laura sounded a million miles away from what Janis had been.

"It sounds like you'll have fun, Taylor. I'm glad you're going."

"I'm looking forward to it, Annie. I think you'll like Laura. She's nothing like Janis, I promise."

Annie's eyes darkened as she told him, completely seriously, "She had better not be, Taylor."

*   *   *

Cary arrived at her door, promptly at 6:30 with a dozen roses, a bottle of champagne, and a package wrapped in silver paper and tied with gold ribbons. He had told her he expected her to dress up, but she was surprised he was wearing a tux. She commented on it as she took the roses, and he replied, "It's a special evening, Laura—at least, I hope it will be." He looked with approval at her long, deep blue velvet dress. Her hair had been pinned up with unruly curls escaping here and there. If all went well tonight, he looked forward to removing those pins—and the dress.

When she finished putting the roses in water, he handed her the package. "Go ahead and open it, Laura."

She undid the ribbons and carefully opened the box to find a pair of heavy crystal champagne flutes. She lifted one and held it as the light caught and reflected in the carved facets. "They're beautiful, Cary."

"Not as beautiful as you," he said as he popped the cork on the champagne and filled the glasses. He lifted his and proposed a toast, "To Christmas wishes, Laura" and gently tapped his glass against hers.

"Thank you. They really are wonderful. It makes the champagne seem even more special."

He kissed her lightly, then finished his champagne. "Ready?" he said as he set the glass on the table and corked the champagne. "We can finish this later."

Cary put the champagne in the refrigerator, then helped Laura with her coat, his hands lingering on her shoulders as he dropped a kiss on the back of her neck. He assumed it was a shiver of pleasure that ran through her at his touch.

*　　　*　　　*

It had been a nice evening. Cary could be a wonderful companion, charming and funny, if he just wasn't so insistent on a more intimate physical relationship. As he opened the car door for her at her apartment complex, she felt herself losing the relaxed feeling of the evening and beginning to tense at the confrontation she was sure was coming.

At her door, he took the key from her and opened it. Following her in and closing the door behind him, he kissed her as he pushed her coat from her shoulders. Pulling her into his arms, he whispered, "I think I'm falling in love with you, Laura Collins." She was spared having to answer as he kissed her again.

Gently, she pushed him away from her and said, "We have a bottle of champagne to finish, and unlike certain people who start a vacation tomorrow, I have to be at work in the morning."

Still confident that he could change her mind, Cary took no offense at her implied end of the evening. He was sure that she wouldn't be able to resist him, especially after another glass or two of champagne. He smiled at the thought of lying next to her as she called in sick in the morning, ready to spend the day in bed with him.

He took the glass of champagne she handed him. "Thanks for a wonderful evening, Cary."

He took a sip of champagne before he answered her, "It doesn't have to be over, Laura."

She laughed and said, "But it does, Cary. I need to get some sleep."

She started to move past him, towards the door, when he caught her and turned her to face him. He took her glass and put it on the table. "You could call in sick tomorrow, darling," he said quietly as he pulled her into his arms. When she brought her hands up to push him away, he caught her wrists and held them as he kissed her.

"Cary, stop. You're hurting me," she said as she twisted her face away from his. He released her wrists, sliding his hands along the velvet sleeves of her dress, finally taking her face between his palms.

"I never want to hurt you, Laura. But, I do want to make love to you, and I think you want it, too."

Laura stepped back from him. "No, Cary. You're wrong," she said, her voice shaking. "Please, leave now."

He was genuinely shocked. He had been sure that the romance of the evening and his confession that he was falling in love with her would be the final keys that would gain him access to her bed.

"Laura…"

"No, Cary. I want you to leave, now."

He was suddenly filled with rage. Taking two swift steps toward her, he caught her by the shoulders. "Damn it, Laura, you can't toy with me this way."

He was surprised when she slapped him. "Get out, Cary. Now." She pulled away from him and opened the door, her eyes blazing with anger.

Reaching deep inside himself, he presented a calm front as he straightened his jacket and tie before he walked to the door. Stopping in front of her, he looked into her eyes and whispered with bitter irony, "Merry Christmas, Laura," before he walked away without a backwards glance.

Laura closed the door behind him and locked it before she collapsed, trembling, on the couch. She had never expected the evening to end this way, but at least now she didn't have to worry about breaking up with him. Slowly, she stood and took the crystal to the kitchen where she poured the remaining champagne down the sink and washed the glasses before she went to bed.

17

Waiting at the airport for Taylor's plane to arrive, Laura finally had some time to think about what had happened with Cary. She had been so busy this week trying to get things done before Taylor arrived that she had refused to let herself think about it until now.

When she had arrived at work the next morning, a single white rose had been waiting on her desk, a letter propped up against the vase. She knew it was from Cary and considered just trashing the letter, but her own curiosity wouldn't let her, and she had opened it to read:

Darling Laura,

I was a hopeless jerk last night. I'd like to be able to blame it all on the champagne and the intoxicating effect you have on me, but I'd be compounding my already poor behavior with a lie.

I let my own wants override your needs. I'm ashamed of my behavior and realize you probably never want to see me again. I can't blame you.

Still, I find myself hoping that you can forgive me. I'll call you after Christmas to see if there's any chance.

Penitently,
Cary

She hadn't decided what she was going to do. Albuquerque was really still a small town at heart. The media community often had to work together. She was bound to run into him again, and it would be easier if they could declare some kind of truce.

The announcement of the arrival of Taylor's flight caused all thoughts of Cary to vanish. It was finally happening. He was here, and she was scared to death. What if this was a disaster?

Then she saw him as he raised his hand to wave at her. She waved back and waited for him to make his way to her through the crowds. They made an awkward scene in the midst of the joyful reunions around them, neither of them quite sure what to say or how to act. Their eyes met, and they both burst out laughing at the mutual panic they saw in each other's eyes.

"Welcome back, Taylor."

"Thanks, Laura. I've been really looking forward to this."

"Me too—let's get out of this madhouse." She led him down the busy concourse. Since he had brought what he needed in a carry-on bag, they didn't have to stop for luggage, and proceeded to the garage. Taylor stopped at the sight of Laura's car, an ancient, bright yellow Opel GT.

"I'm sure it's not as impressive as your convertible, but I love it." Laura said as she opened the door.

"Actually, it's great. When I was in high school, I had a teacher who had a car like this. We all thought it was the coolest thing we had ever seen, which made him the coolest teacher. Where did you find it?" He ran his fingers across the line of the roof, and Laura had a momentary image of his hands caressing her in the same reverential way.

"Actually, it belonged to my brother, Tomás. He bought it in high school and spent hours restoring it. It was his baby. He was so full of instructions about how I was to care for it that it might as well have been a real baby. It's like having a part of him still around."

"Well, I would trade you my Jag for it in a heartbeat."

"Watch it, Taylor. The next time this breaks down and I have to hunt all over for parts, I might take you up on it!"

As they exited the airport, Laura said, "I thought we would take your stuff back to the apartment before we set out exploring. Is there anything special you'd like to see?"

"I have no idea, Laura. I'm completely at your mercy."

Laura maneuvered the sports car through the Albuquerque traffic and the ever-present road construction, pointing out landmarks on the way. The first one she showed him was a sculpture called *San Mateo Cruising I.* "Locally, it's known as the 'Chevy on a Stick.' The artist, Barbara Grygutis, put a real Chevy on the arch and tiled the whole thing. It has two companion pieces down that way—a tiled table and a tiled chair. They cost the city a small fortune, and people either love them or hate them; there's no half-way."

Taylor watched her as she talked. Laura was a person of strong opinions, and she wasn't afraid to express them. He hadn't told her that he had been accessing the *Herald* on the web and reading her articles. He admired the stand she had taken on some issues and her ability to get to the heart of the matter. Now he was forcibly reminded of the beauty that went with the brain, a beauty that was distracting him from her words.

She pulled the car into a parking space in front of her apartment complex in the foothills of the Sandia Mountains, and led the way up the stairs to her apartment. "I should warn you," she said as she unlocked the door, "I am not the best housekeeper in the world. It's hard to clean around the clutter I keep."

Laura's apartment was the opposite of his sparsely decorated condo. It was obvious that someone lived here. The bookcases overflowed with books and keepsakes, punctuated here and there with photos. Her computer was in one corner with a bulletin board over it that displayed a large calendar. Bits and pieces of paper were pinned to the board and overflowed from the file folders on her desk.

"I'm sure it can't compare with the view from your condo," she said as she opened the drapes to the small balcony, "but I have a great view of the city, which is the main reason I took the place. It's not convenient to anywhere, but I think it's worth the commute."

She led the way into the bedroom and showed him where his towels were, leaving him to freshen up while she checked her messages. She looked up as he came back into the living room.

"Since you haven't given me a clue to what we're doing, I had to guess at what to wear," he said. "I hope this is all right."

It was more than all right. Wearing a beige sweater and jeans, he looked even more handsome than she had remembered. "Sorry, Taylor, I should have said something. That's fine, since I thought we'd play tourist today. You'll want to bring your coat for later, though. Tonight I have to be out at my folks to help make *tamales* for tomorrow. You can come along if you'd like or avoid the crowd 'til tomorrow if you'd prefer."

"If you think I won't be in the way, I'd like to come along."

A vision of Cary drying dishes with ill-hidden resentment crossed her mind so she warned him, "You'll probably be put to work."

"I don't mind—as long as it's not peeling potatoes." Laura's startled look made him explain. "It's just that Annie is convinced I can't cook, so I always get the job of peeling the potatoes."

Laura laughed. "Taylor, that's so funny! I have the same job here for the same reason."

Their laughter eased any awkwardness between them, and they left the apartment, both of them feeling like this visit just might work.

18

Laura's fervent pleas to the weather gods had been answered—it was a beautiful day. As often happens in a New Mexico winter, the weather was mild so they could get by with just a sweater.

Old Town was already dressed for Christmas. As they wandered around the central Plaza, Taylor asked her about the paper sacks set up all around the square. "Those are the *farolitos* to light the way for the Christ Child. Some places they're called *luminarias*. Rudolfo Anaya has a good book about them that you might want to take to Meg." She watched as he leaned down to inspect one. "They're pretty simple, really, just a little sand and a candle in a brown paper sack, but they're magical. You'll see them tomorrow night. The whole neighborhood will be wearing them. In fact, we get to spend most of tomorrow helping to set them up."

In one of the shops, Taylor was fascinated by a display of storyteller figurines, finally choosing one to take home.

"Why that one, Taylor?"

"I don't know, really. It was just the right one."

"Good," she said with a smile that caused his heart to skip a beat, "a storyteller should speak to the heart of its listener." She put her arm through his as they left the store and said, "Now it's time to introduce you to green chile!"

She explained to him on their way to downtown Albuquerque that New Mexico actually had a "state question," voted on and passed by the legislature. "Red or green?" she asked.

"Red or green?" he said, puzzled. "Is this a Christmas question?"

She laughed. "Well, in a way it is. The question is about red or green chile. There are die-hard fans of red chile and those of us who think green is the only way to go. And Christmas? Christmas is both!"

She took him to McGilvray's at Central and Sixth for a lunch of green chile chicken soup. Even Laura admitted it was a pretty hot batch, but Taylor gamely struggled through most of it.

"You eat this stuff all the time? Voluntarily?" he gasped after the first bite.

"Here, try a bite of tortilla. It will help," Laura said, trying hard not to laugh at him. "Maybe not everyday, but most days. I'd die without it."

"Well, I may die from it!" he said as he tried another spoonful. This one went down easier, and he began to taste the subtle flavor of the chile hiding behind the heat. It was good, but he wasn't sure he would ever develop a permanent taste for it.

"But that's the secret, Taylor. Chile, red or green, is addicting. Once you've had it, you'll want more. This way I make sure you come back again."

After lunch, she took him down the street to Maisel's for Indian jewelry and art. He found a turquoise bracelet and earrings for Meg, and Laura helped him choose a pair of earrings for Annie. They walked across the Fourth Street Mall and came out in front of the Hyatt where he had stayed when he had been in town for the concert.

"I don't know that you got to see this when you were here," she said as she led him to a group of bronze statues on the corner. "It's my favorite piece of public sculpture. It's called *Sidewalk Society*. The artist is Glenna Goodacre. I interviewed her when she created the Vietnam Women's Memorial. I love all of her work." Taylor was fascinated by the slightly larger-than-life-sized bronze figures that included a construction worker, a mother and child, and a teenage boy on a skateboard. He was surprised when Laura took a stick of gum out of her purse and put it on the outstretched hand of the teenager.

Laughing, he asked, "What *are* you doing, Laura?"

She looked a little embarrassed, then laughed with him. "OK, so I know it's silly. But you can rarely come down here and not find something on his hand. I always hate it when there's nothing there."

Taylor thought she looked beautiful, the winter sunlight on her bright hair, her face glowing with laughter. He was falling in love with Albuquerque and green chile—and, most of all, Laura.

She had arranged the day so they ended up at the Sandia Peak Tramway just before sunset. The mile-long tram to the top of Sandia Peak offered a perfect view of the city and the spectacular New Mexico sunset as they went up. It was bitterly cold at the top of the tram, and he was surprised at the tremendous temperature difference. They hurried to the High Finance Restaurant where they enjoyed the view and a margarita, as the sunset put on its multi-colored display. The city had changed to a jewel-strewn blanket of lights by the time they came back down.

As they got back into the car, Laura asked, "Have I worn you out, Taylor?"

"Not a chance. It's been a great day. I can see why you love it here."

"Well then, are you ready to face my family and friends?"

"*That* I'm not so sure about," he said only partially in jest. "But let's do it anyway."

Laura's parents lived literally on the other side of town. Even in normal traffic on the freeway, it took close to half an hour to drive from the foothills and across the Rio Grande. Laura and Taylor shared a comfortable silence on the way. Laura stole a glance at him now and then. He seemed to really be enjoying himself, but she was still afraid all of this was boring him.

Taylor couldn't remember the last time he had felt so completely at peace. It was as if he'd come home to someplace he never knew he had missed.

Laura pulled into a graveled driveway that curved down and around to reveal the house that seemed to have grown from the hillside. A cluster of dried red chiles, a *"ristra"* Laura called it, hung next to the door. She opened the door to release a burst of voices and delicious smells before she turned to smile at him. "Ready, Taylor?" As he followed her into the house, he was suddenly terrified of meeting her parents, something he hadn't felt since his date for the junior prom.

19

The kitchen was full of people involved in a number of mysterious tasks. Taylor watched as Laura leaned down to kiss a small woman and bring her to him.

"Taylor, this is my mother, Maria Consuela Bernadette Genevieve Armijo Collins," she said, the soft, musical sounds of the Spanish names coming naturally to her.

"Laura!" her mother chided gently. "Welcome to our home, Taylor. *Feliz Navidad.*"

Taylor shook her hand and said, "Thank you for letting me share your Christmas—and your daughter."

A tall, red-haired man materialized from out of the crowd. "What's this about sharing my daughter?" he said as he wrapped his arms around Laura.

A muffled cry of "Daddy!" came from her before he released her to come forward and shake Taylor's hand. "Welcome, Taylor."

"Thank you, Mr. Coll…."

"None of that, please," he interrupted. "Everyone here is friend or family or, in some cases, both. My name is Sean. Laura, have you fed this young man?"

"Not since lunch, Dad."

"Then we need to fix that. Come with me, Taylor. We'll feed you some real New Mexican food before we put you to work."

Maria watched her daughter as Taylor was led into the chaos of the kitchen. She had not looked at the other one that way, the newsman she had brought here a month ago. Her Laura's heart was in her eyes as she watched Taylor walk away.

Taylor was fed, then initiated into the intricacies of *tamale* making. Beth and her mother were there as well as a number of other neighbors as they prepared the labor-intensive delicacy. There had been much discussion before Laura and Taylor arrived about the famous young man that she had invited, but no one treated him any differently than they would have a son or brother of their own. Taylor soon relaxed and was accepting the Spanish lessons he was being offered.

*   *   *

Sean Collins poured glasses of wine for those remaining after the work had been finished. Maria curled up on the loveseat waiting for Sean. Laura and Beth shared the couch while Taylor looked out over the city. He took the offered glass of wine and joined the others. Sean sat next to his wife, taking her hand as she leaned against him. For a moment, as he watched them, the pain of losing his parents was as fresh for Taylor as the day it had happened.

"*Ay, Dios mío,*" Laura's mother said, "I am so tired."

"You say that every year, Mom, and then you bounce right up again the next morning," Laura said affectionately.

"So, Taylor," Beth said, "how are you feeling? First Laura drags you all over town, and then we put you to work."

Taylor laughed. He liked Beth and not just because she reminded him of Annie. "Actually, I've had a wonderful day, but I have to admit, I am tired."

"Then we had best get you back to Laura's so you can rest. We have a lot of work for you to do tomorrow, too," Sean said. Before anyone else could speak, he continued, "Beth, why don't you drop Taylor at Laura's?

It's silly for her to drive all that way and back when you're going that
way already."

He missed the looks his daughter and wife threw at him. Beth knew
that Laura was going to be furious, but this was simply too good a
chance to pass up so she said, "Sure, Dad, that's a great idea. I'll be glad
to." She could feel Laura glaring at her and saw the amusement in
Maria's eyes.

Laura was devastated. She knew her father was only trying to be
helpful, but she had been looking forward to a little more time with
Taylor. But there was no way to say it without making herself sound
too eager.

Taylor wasn't happy with the arrangement, either. He realized that he
had been playing a fantasy in the back of his mind all evening, a fantasy
that involved kissing Laura. It just wouldn't play out quite the same way
at her parents' door, but he smiled and said it sounded like a good idea.

*   *   *

Laura walked out with Taylor after he had said goodnight to her parents. Beth had decided she had better give them a little time alone if she
ever expected Laura to forgive her.

The night was beautiful, clear, and cold with a bright moon. "Thank
you, Laura."

"For what, Taylor? Running you ragged?"

He took one of her hands in his, "For giving me a day I will always
treasure," he said quietly as he looked into her eyes. Silence grew
between them, and he began to think that his earlier fantasy might just
be possible. As he finally decided to kiss her, Beth called goodnight to
Laura's parents and Taylor reluctantly released Laura's hand.

"Laura, I'm coming out in the morning. Would you like me to bring
Taylor with me or do you want to go in and pick him up?"

"It's up to Taylor. Why don't you two work it out? If you decide I should pick you up, just call me in the morning. The number is there by the phone."

"Just don't call her too early, Taylor. Our Laura is not a morning person."

Beth hugged Laura and whispered, "I promise, I'll behave."

Laura whispered back, "You'd better! *You* aren't going away in two days!"

*   *   *

As Taylor opened the door to Laura's apartment, he realized how much of its warmth had come from her presence. It seemed much emptier without her.

Beth had grilled him on the ride home. He shook his head and smiled as he remembered. She wanted to know what he did in his off time, if he was seeing anyone, and subtly warned him that he would have to deal with her if he hurt Laura in any way.

He'd wanted to find a way to ask her if Laura was seeing someone, but the opportunity never presented itself. Instead, he had answered Beth's questions, and they made arrangements for her to pick him up in the morning. Then she dropped him off at the apartment complex and drove away, leaving his questions unasked.

Now, alone in Laura's space, he had a moment to examine his feelings about her. Pouring a glass of the wine she had left for him, he settled onto the couch and, surrounded by the things that helped make her who she was, let his thoughts roam.

He had never felt this way about anyone. He and Annie had been a failed experiment. He had never really loved Janis and had just let her convince him that he did. There had been others, but no one who affected him as deeply as Laura did. A series of pictures from the day played through his mind, and he smiled at the new memories and anticipated the ones to be made tomorrow. If Beth had not come out when she did....

The phone interrupted his thoughts. Glancing at his watch, he realized it was late. He thought it might be Laura with something she had forgotten to tell him, so he answered.

"Hello?"

There was a moment of silence; then a male voice said, "I'm sorry. I must have the wrong number."

"Wait! Who were you trying to reach?"

"Laura Collins?"

"This is Laura's. May I take a message?"

In Taos, Cary said, "No...thanks. I'll call her later."

Taylor hung up the phone. He had probably just screwed up Laura's relationship with someone. And he wasn't sure if he should be pleased or feel contrite about it. One thing for certain, he had better give up answering her phone!

Realizing the time difference made it early morning for him, he decided to head for bed. Tonight he would take advice from Scarlett O'Hara. Tomorrow was another day.

*   *   *

Hanging up the phone, Cary tried to catch what it was about that voice. It sounded familiar, but the reason was just out of reach. What the hell was a man doing in her apartment, anyway? It certainly hadn't taken the little bitch long to get over him.

Regretting the impulse that had made him call, Cary headed downstairs to the lounge and the numerous snowbunnies who would be happy to keep him warm tonight. Never mind Laura. He would call her when he got back from Atlanta and the final interview with TNC—if he had the time.

*   *   *

"Sean Patrick, what were you thinking?" Maria Collins sat on the edge of the bed and looked at her husband.

"What?"

"Sending Taylor home with Beth? Didn't you see that Laura wanted to spend more time with him without us around?"

"Then why didn't she say so?"

"Because you made it impossible. You had already pointed out how inconvenient it would be."

Sean looked bewildered, "I didn't know!"

Maria stood and put her arms around him. "Have you forgotten what it's like to be in love? I don't think she knows it yet, but our Laura's in love with this one."

Sean held her close for a minute, then tilted her head so he could look into her eyes. "You're sure?"

"Positive. And, I think he's in love with her."

"Then I guess I really screwed up, didn't I?"

She laughed softly at his confusion. "They'll survive. Now, come prove to me you haven't forgotten what love is."

*   *   *

Laura sat in the darkened sunroom, surrounded by stars in the cool light of the moon. She thought back on those few minutes she'd had with Taylor before Beth had come out. He had been going to kiss her, she was sure of it. And she had wanted that more than she would have thought possible this morning when she met him at the airport.

She had spent less than two days with this man. It was too soon to feel this way, wasn't it? And, even if he had kissed her, that didn't mean he felt this way, too. She was reading way too much into things.

She saw the light go out in her parents' room. From the stories they'd told her, it had been love at first sight for them. It was hard not to believe in fairy tales and happily-ever-after with her parents as an example.

2 O

Maria was not really surprised when Laura joined them early in the morning. She was fairly sure that her daughter had not slept much the night before. She smiled as Laura looked at her watch every few minutes as if willing the time to pass faster.

"Laura, come help me with the tortillas." Her mother handed her a rolling pin and began to make the dough into small balls that Laura ruthlessly spread flat, her impatience adding weight to the rolling pin.

Finally, they heard a knock at the door and Beth's cheery voice calling "good morning." It was only with great effort that Laura restrained herself from running out to make sure he was there. Instead, she stayed at her task, absently rolling the tortilla flatter and wider until it was little more than a whisper of dough on the counter.

"Good morning, Laura." She turned at the sound of his voice, and her mother and Beth saw the joy that filled her eyes.

"Hello, Taylor. Did you sleep well?"

"Yes, thanks." The awkwardness of the day before returned, and Maria stepped in.

"And did my daughter think to leave you something for breakfast? At least some coffee?"

Sheepishly, Taylor admitted he hadn't wakened in time to eat and would probably kill for a cup of coffee. Laura reached up for a mug, filled it with coffee, and handed it to him. His hand brushed hers, and she nearly dropped the mug before it was safely in his hand.

"Sit down, Taylor. And you girls, too. Even if you've eaten, Beth, I know you never turn down a fresh tortilla. Laura, you haven't eaten anything either. You'll all need energy for today."

She peeled the mangled tortilla from the counter and efficiently patted out three new ones and dropped them on the griddle. She scrambled eggs and served them with the fresh tortillas. Beth began to tell outrageous stories about Laura, which she denied and soon the three young people were laughing. As Sean came into the kitchen, Maria met his eyes over the head of their daughter and they both smiled. It had been a long time since they had seen Laura so happy.

*   *   *

After breakfast, Sean put them to work making the *farolitos*, the simple lanterns that would shed a soft glow to bring the Christ Child home. "Most people call them *luminarias*," Sean explained as he worked, "but those, technically, are the small bonfires used for the same purpose. No one knows for sure when they began to use the *farolitos*, but the intent was the same and it didn't matter."

Taylor and Laura had not had any time to be alone together, but they were happy to be working in the other's presence. Laura had pulled her long hair back into a ponytail, and Taylor was distracted by wisps of hair that had escaped to brush against her cheek. He longed to reach out and tuck them back behind her ears, but was reluctant to do so with her father around.

Neighbors were out, involved in the same task, and there was a lot of visiting back and forth. Taylor was introduced again and again, but there was no fuss made over who he was. He rather got the feeling that they weren't impressed, anyway, and he was relieved.

After a lunch break, Sean declared it was time for a siesta, and it seemed that much of the neighborhood would be following his example. Beth had left to help at her parents' house and Laura and Taylor finally found themselves alone.

The two of them were sitting in the sunroom, jeans rolled up to hang their feet in the water of the pool. "Meg would love this. She's really a landlocked mermaid, I think. She would rather be in the water than anywhere else."

"Maybe you could bring her with you to visit next time," Laura answered.

"I'd like that. She would, too." Taylor was very aware of how close Laura was. Her hair was still escaping from the ponytail and, without stopping to think, he reached out and tucked one strand behind her ear. "You look like a little girl with your bare feet and ponytail," he said quietly, his eyes gazing into hers before he bent his head and kissed her.

Time seemed to stop for both of them. Laura was aware of feelings that Cary's kisses had never stirred, and her hand came up to touch Taylor's cheek. His senses reeled from the closeness of her. He wanted to gather her into his arms and make love to her, but settled for pulling her hair loose from the band that held it, burying his hands in the mass of glorious, silken color.

The sound of her father's voice in the hallway caused them to break apart like guilty teenagers. There were no words between them, but the promise of later was in their eyes.

2 1

The preparations were finally finished. Taylor showered and changed in the guest bathroom, his thoughts on Laura and the promise of her kiss. Tonight, being near to her, would be torture, but he consoled himself with the promise that it wouldn't be Beth who took him back to the apartment.

Laura, in her parents' shower, was thinking much the same thing. For the first time in ages, she found herself interested enough in a man to want to go to bed with him. She was fairly sure that Taylor felt the same way, and she looked forward to the end of the evening and to what she hoped would happen.

*   *   *

Taylor and Laura helped Sean light the *farolitos* that now lined the driveway and the roof of the house. As darkness fell, Taylor stopped working to just watch the dance of light that turned such ordinary ingredients to magic. The look on his face was one of total awe, and Laura felt pleased she could share this with him.

From the roof, Sean called down, "We're almost done here. You two had better head on over if you want to be in on the beginning of the procession." His shadowy figure waved as they walked away.

Taylor took Laura's hand as they walked to the starting point. "*Posada* means inn," Laura explained. "The procession will follow Mary and Joseph from house to house as they seek a place to stay. There is a traditional song, sung in Spanish, that tells of their need to find shelter. At the first eight houses they will be turned away. Finally, at the ninth house, they will be given shelter, the Christ Child will appear, and the celebrations begin. Maybe if you're very good, we'll let you have a try at the *piñata* with the other children!" She laughed at him as they arrived.

The yard where the procession would begin was a scene of chaos. The teenager chosen to play Mary was suddenly shy at the importance of her role. Joseph, older and wiser, talked quietly with his friends as children ran around in an overexcited state. In the center of it all, a donkey stood placidly, waiting for whatever the humans had planned, secure that she would be fed and warm at evening's end.

Someone gave the signal that it was time. Joseph lifted Mary up on the donkey as candles were handed out and the flame passed from one to another. As Laura's candle burst into flame, Taylor thought her face in its glow was the loveliest sight he had ever seen. She held her candle to his, the flame shared for a moment, before he had to turn away to pass it on to someone else.

The procession started, and the neighborhood began to follow, softly singing Christmas carols from house to house, singing the traditional plea for shelter at each house on the route. As Laura had told him, they were turned away at each house until, finally, they wound down the drive to Sean and Maria's where Joseph knocked at the door and told his story of pregnant wife and no room to be found. Sean opened the door wide and welcomed them in, and Taylor's eyes filled with tears at the simple beauty of it all. Laura, watching him, knew in that moment that she had fallen in love with him.

The house filled with neighbors and friends. Long tables had been set up to accommodate the food and drink, coats were piled high on the beds, and the fiesta began. Taylor found himself separated from Laura, just as they had been at that first party when they had met. But, he wasn't alone this time. He had found shelter in the home of the woman he loved.

     *   *   *

 Taylor saw Beth whispering to Laura before the two women turned away down the hall. He decided to go see what they were up to and made his way slowly through the crowd.

 Beth pulled Laura into the bedroom. "He is so gorgeous!" she said.

 "Shh! Beth, he might hear you!" she said as she pushed the door almost closed.

 "What? You don't think he already knows he's good looking?"

 "Of course he knows. But we don't have to be discussing him that way."

 Outside, in the hall, Taylor heard their voices. As he lifted his hand to knock, Beth's next words caused him to pause.

 "Well, he's a lot better looking than Mr. Newscast."

 "Stop it, Beth. We're just friends."

 "Friends? Are you crazy? Don't you see the way Taylor's been looking at you? The only time the talking head looks that way is when he's preening in the mirror."

 "Beth, I know you don't like him, but don't start seeing something with Taylor that isn't there."

 "You're the one who's blind, Laura Collins."

 "No, you're the one who's wearing rose-colored glasses."

 "Laura!"

 "Beth!" Laura mimicked her friend's exasperated tone, and the two women dissolved into laughter.

 Taylor went on down the hall and closed the door of the bathroom behind him. What he had suspected was true. She was seeing someone. He had been foolish to think otherwise. He had only been seeing what he wanted to see. Staring at his face in the mirror, he said, "You're a fool, Taylor Morgan." Then, he opened the door to return to the party where he would have to give the most difficult performance of his life. The door to the bedroom was open; Laura and Beth were gone, back into the crowd he would have to face.

As he came back into the crowded family room, he stood by the door to the kitchen. Two women were talking just inside the door, and Taylor couldn't help overhearing.

"I thought Laura was seeing that handsome newsman. She did bring him here for Thanksgiving, didn't she?"

"*Sí*, and Maria seemed to be very pleased with him. I think they had given up hope that Laura would settle down and give them grandchildren. With Tomás gone, she's their only hope of that."

"Then she thinks they'll marry? It's that serious?"

"From everything I've heard, it seems to be."

Taylor closed his eyes as if he could shut out the sounds as well as the sights. He felt someone touch his arm, and he opened his eyes to see Laura's face, her eyes filled with concern.

"Are you all right, Taylor?"

Summoning up all his acting skills, Taylor smiled at her, "I'm fine, Laura. All the noise is just a little overwhelming."

"It can be. Find your coat and we'll go out on the patio."

The last thing he could handle right now was being alone with her. "No, I think I've had enough of the cold. The tour will start again in February, and I start rehearsals again right after the first of the year, so I'd best not risk catching a cold."

Laura heard a tone in his voice that hadn't been there before. She wasn't sure why, but his words sounded strained somehow. Before she could pursue it further, Beth came and pulled him away. "Taylor Morgan, I think you should sing for your supper," she said. "We can't have a voice like yours here and not take advantage of it."

Laura watched as he laughed at Beth, protesting to no avail that they didn't need him to sing. Beth was not taking "no" for an answer, and they were swallowed by the crowd. Cries of "Quiet" could be heard before someone began to play the piano— "Ave Maria", her mother's favorite. Beth must have told him. She listened as he began to sing softly. She couldn't see him, but instead, saw the look on his face before he kissed her this afternoon. What had changed since then? Her eyes filled with tears that were not a response to the beauty of the song.

After the applause for Taylor's song died down, the children began to cry that it was time for the *piñata*. As Laura had threatened, Taylor was blindfolded and given a chance to break the papier-mâché star to release the treasures inside. He didn't succeed, but stayed to cheer on the children until one of them connected with it and it broke open, spilling candy and toys. Soon after, people began to leave, a few at a time. Finally, just after midnight, the house had emptied of all except the Collins family, Beth, and Taylor.

"Did you enjoy *Las Posadas*, Taylor?" Maria asked as she began to gather up a few scattered plates and cups.

He took them from her and said, "Very much, Maria. I thank you for sharing it with me."

"*De nada*," she said. She liked this young man, and if what she thought was really true, she would see more of him.

"Laura should take you home now. Your plane is early tomorrow?"

Laura's heart shattered as he said, "It is. Very early, actually. Beth, would you mind dropping me at Laura's again? It's a long drive, and there's no reason for Laura to do it. I can take a cab to the airport in the morning so no one has to be bothered."

As she started to protest, he said, "No, Laura, this would be easier for everyone. I'll get my things if you're ready, Beth."

Beth met Laura's eyes and saw the devastation there. Why was Taylor doing this? What had happened in the last few hours to have changed him so? Beth was as confused as Laura was.

"Thank you, again. This was a wonderful experience, and I'll always remember it." Both Sean and Maria heard the finality in his words before he turned to Laura.

"Laura, I've had a great time. I hope someday I can return the favor if you come to Florida. Take care, and I'll talk to you soon." He hastily kissed her cheek and turned away. "Ready, Beth?" he asked before he started to the door, opening it for Beth, then closing it softly behind them.

*   *   *

In the car, Beth didn't know what to say or do. Taylor solved her dilemma by saying, "Beth, I'm sorry. I seem to have developed a terrible headache. Would you mind if I just closed my eyes for a few minutes?"

The few minutes proved to be the entire trip across town. When they got to the complex, Taylor kissed Beth's cheek, a kiss no different than the farewell one he had given Laura earlier. "Thanks, Beth. Take care of yourself," he said before he turned away. She watched, bewildered, as he climbed the stairs to Laura's apartment and closed the door behind him.

*   *   *

Laura told her mother to go on to bed. "I'll finish cleaning things up. You've done enough. Go get some rest." Reluctantly, because there was nothing else she could do, Maria kissed her daughter, then hugged her fiercely before she did as Laura asked.

Laura gathered up the last of the plates and napkins and threw them away. The house didn't look like it had been filled with people and laughter only a short while ago. It looked empty and cold—exactly the way she felt right now.

Turning off the lights, she sat in the darkened sunroom where she had dreamed of Taylor's kiss just last night, had shared that kiss this afternoon. What could have gone so wrong so quickly, she thought, searching her mind for an answer that wasn't there. Then she gave in to the tears that she had held back as long as she could, crying for all the dreams that she had so foolishly allowed herself to have.

*   *   *

Taylor stood at the glass door of Laura's small balcony, looking out across the town, across the distance that separated them. In the morning, he would go back to Florida, back to Annie and Meg, and try to forget how he felt about the copper-haired woman he was leaving behind.

*   *   *

Cary, the inadvertent cause of all of Taylor and Laura's pain, wasn't thinking of her at all. The waitress he had picked up in the bar was distracting him quite nicely as she shared his bed this early Christmas Eve morning.

*   *   *

Taylor never went to bed. He had stayed awake trying to find the right words to write in a note to leave for her. Finally, he finished and packed, called a cab, and left for the airport. He might as well be awake there as here, he thought, as he closed and locked the door, sliding the key under it before he walked away.

*   *   *

Laura came back to her apartment midmorning. She had finally gone to bed just before dawn. Her mother let her sleep late; then Laura had insisted she still had some errands to run. The excuse bought her what she desperately needed, a little time to be alone.

He had left his note on the table, propped up against a small package. She opened the note and read:

Laura-

> It was wonderful to see you again and share part of
> the holiday with you. Please tell your mother and father
> how much I appreciated it.

This is just a little something I brought for you to say
thank you and Merry Christmas.
        See you on the 'net.

                                            Taylor

   Opening the package, she found a pair of carved jade earrings. She
had no way of knowing that they had belonged to his mother, no way of
knowing he had brought them for her because he was sure his mother
would have loved her as much as he did.

22

Taylor had a lot of time to think on the three-hour flight to Tampa. He would have preferred thinking about something else, but his mind kept circling on the events of the past two days.

He realized his own expectations for this visit had colored everything. He had read too much into Laura's invitation. Friendship was all she had been offering and he had pushed past that. Now he would have to decide if he wanted to continue the friendship. Could he put his own feelings aside? Could he handle it if she married this other man?

Even three hours of thinking didn't resolve his dilemma. As he opened the door to the condo, he was struck again by the contrast between his living space and Laura's. The only things remotely personal in this place he called home were a couple of Meg's drawings on the refrigerator and the seashells on the windowsill. Because he spent Christmas with Annie and Meg, he never bothered with decorating, so there was not even a tree. The packages he would be delivering were stacked at the top of the stairs, waiting to be packed up.

Dropping his bag by the stairs, he hit the message button on the machine. A message from his agent asking him to call after the holiday, a message from Annie reminding him of the time for tonight, and a message from the employment agency that they had lined up some interviews for him for Christine's replacement. He still had to face that task.

As he turned away from the machine, he saw the computer silently waiting in the corner. Did he even want to check? Reluctantly, he turned it on and started the log-on sequence anyway.

He had forgotten to unsubscribe from the list, and his mail was full of nonsense from his fans...something about pickles this time! Skimming down the list, he deleted all of them until he came to the one he had been looking for, a message from Laura. He looked at the screen for a long time before he finally selected and opened it.

> Hi, Taylor-
>
> I hope your trip back was not too tiring. You'll probably need all your energy for Meg this evening.
>
> I'm glad you enjoyed your visit. Mom and Dad really liked you, which doesn't surprise me. You also have Beth's seal of approval. All of this is to say you're welcome back anytime.
>
> Thank you for the earrings. They're really lovely. I'll wear them to church tonight.
>
> Merry Christmas, Taylor.
>
> Laura

She had agonized over the note for an hour. No matter what she wrote, it sounded wrong. The blessing of e-mail, she thought, was that there was no paper to get tear-stained.

She had made up the bed with fresh sheets and returned the clutter she had hidden to the bathroom counter. After a long shower and a longer nap, she was now ready to leave to meet her parents.

As she picked up her coat and a few last-minute packages, she stopped, looking at the computer sitting silently on the desk. She should go, but she found herself putting things down to turn it on. Logging on, she scanned the list of messages until she found Taylor's reply.

Laura-

The trip was no problem. Just long. The lack of sleep caught up with me, and I slept most of the way.

I'm leaving in a few minutes for Annie's, and I'll be staying there tonight so we can all be together for Christmas morning. I'm looking forward to giving Annie and Meg the gifts you helped me pick out.

I'm glad you like the earrings. It seemed like you should have them.

Feliz Navidad—(thank heavens e-mail doesn't have an accent!)

Taylor

Driving to Annie's, he wondered what to tell her about Laura and the weekend. When they had talked about her, he had tried not to let Annie know the depth of his feelings, but considering her past performances, she undoubtedly already knew. He just hoped she would realize that he didn't want to—couldn't talk about it yet.

23

Somehow, they both made it through the holiday.

For Laura, it had been almost as awful as the first one after Tomás' death. She and her parents tried to ignore the one topic they all wanted to discuss, and she was relieved when the day was over and she could return to her apartment. She was even more relieved that they would be leaving on January 2nd for an extended trip to Ireland and Europe. They would be gone a month and, by the time they came back, she hoped she would have herself back together again.

Taylor had felt like there was something missing all day. He had tried to be as normal as possible. He knew Annie would have noticed if she had been feeling all right, but she'd finally given in to a headache on Christmas afternoon, going to bed, leaving Taylor and Meg to keep each other entertained. She had emerged late in the evening, saying she felt better. She certainly didn't look better, but she assured Taylor she would be fine. The studio was closed for the holiday week, so she would have time to rest.

Now, finally, he was home and had some time alone. Pouring a glass of wine, he went out onto the deck. He could hear the music from somewhere in the complex and an occasional burst of laughter. The sounds seemed to intensify his loneliness, so he went back inside, shutting them out. More from habit than anything else, he turned on the computer and logged on. As he had expected, there was very little traffic; everyone was celebrating with family or friends. He began to compose a letter to Laura.

Darling Laura-

My visit went so terribly wrong. That wasn't at all the way I had wanted it to be.

By the middle of the morning on the first day, I realized I was in love with you. I was so terribly disappointed when your father sent me home with Beth! Like an awkward teenager, I couldn't even get up enough courage to kiss you goodnight.

But our kiss the second day more than made up for it. If we had been alone, not at your parents', I would have taken you to bed and made love to you right then. I can still feel the softness of your mouth, the silk of your hair.

It was what I heard later that made it all change. You and Beth talking about the man you're dating. Then two of the neighbors gossiping in the kitchen about how you'd brought him home for Thanksgiving...how much your parents like him...how the two of you are practically engaged.

I didn't tell you that you'd had a phone call the night before—a male voice seemed very surprised to find me there. I hadn't thought about it much, but I realized later that it had to have been him—the guy you're probably going to marry.

I felt like I would ruin your life if I pursued you. With me you would be leading a gypsy life or waiting around for me to return from a tour or appearance. You're much too good a journalist to be dragged away from what you love and do so well. Sounds like this guy is a better match for you.

I wish it were different, Laura. I wish you were in love
with me instead of him. I wish I had let you know how I
felt while I was there. I wish so many things....
Most of all, I wish you were mine to love.

                                     Taylor

Shaking his head, Taylor got up from the chair, leaving the blank
computer screen patiently waiting for him to actually put his thoughts
into tangible form. He took his wineglass into the kitchen, rinsed it,
then came back and turned off the computer before he wearily climbed
the stairs to his lonely bed.

24

Laura was back at work the day after Christmas. The leftover holiday decorations looked out of place, and she removed as many as she could from around her desk. They were running on a skeleton crew; the staffers who could were taking the time off to spend the holiday week with their families. Robert had been pleased when she volunteered to work this week in exchange for the time off while Taylor was visiting.

Beth came by to see if Laura wanted to take a break. The two women walked downstairs to the coffee shop where Laura played with a piece of pastry.

"Why did you even bother to order that?" Beth asked.

"What?" Laura came back from whatever place she had been. "Oh, I guess I'm just not hungry."

Beth reached out and covered her friend's hand with her own. "Laura, it's not the end of the world. Who knows what was going through his head? Something scared him off, but that doesn't mean you have to quit living."

"I *know* that, Beth," Laura snapped. Immediately contrite, she continued, "Sorry, I didn't mean to take it out on you. I just wish I knew what happened."

"Have you thought about asking him?"

"Oh, sure, Beth. Hey, Taylor, why did you kiss me and make me think you were interested when you obviously weren't? I didn't even get far enough with him to qualify as a one-night stand!"

"That would have been better?"

"Yes…no…I don't know, Beth. And I don't want to talk about it anymore. I need to get back to work."

Laura would have to get over this in her own good time, Beth thought. But she wished Taylor were close enough that she could tell him off for what he had done to Laura. What a jerk he had turned out to be—almost as bad as Cary!

                    *   *   *

Taylor spent the day in his agent's office interviewing candidates for his assistant. They had narrowed the pool down to five likely candidates, but they were all unsuitable as far as Taylor was concerned. He felt no connection with any of them.

His agent, a man Taylor liked and trusted, tried to remind him that he needed to find someone soon. Taylor had snapped at him, "Maybe I should find a new agent while I'm at it," before he slammed out of the office and roared off in the Jag. Before he was halfway home, he had cooled down enough to know he had been way out of line. All of this with Laura was eating at him. He had to find a way to come to terms with what had happened.

Arriving home, he called his agent and apologized. "Let's leave this for a little while, Tom. I'm just not ready to deal with it yet, and we don't have anything coming up right away. We'll find someone before we pick up the tour again." His agent agreed, not that he had any real choice about it, and told Taylor to get some rest, they would try again after the New Year.

That taken care of, Taylor changed into shorts and tee shirt and took his skates for a long session along Bayshore. If he did it right, he would be too tired to lay awake tonight brooding about what might have been.

25

Laura struggled to open the door of the apartment, a take-out bag in one hand, her briefcase falling over at her feet. She dropped her keys, then the bag, and muttering a string of curses under her breath, gave up the battle. She picked up the keys, inserted them in the lock, then pushing her briefcase through the open door with her foot, she retrieved the take-out bag and slammed the door behind her.

It had already been one hell of a day. Already tired from celebrating New Year's, she had been up early this morning to take her parents to the airport. And to make the day just about perfect, she had been assigned to cover the opening of the new high school and had ended up, instead, covering the gang fight that had erupted at the ceremonies. Two teenage boys had pulled knives, and it had quickly escalated into a full-scale riot. Ten kids, including the two boys, had been arrested, six more were taken to the hospital, and the pristine campus had been left in shambles. It would be a week, at least, before it could reopen. If Robert thought she was going to cover the reopening, he was sadly mistaken.

Kicking off her shoes, Laura hit the button on the answering machine. Two hang-ups, then Taylor's voice. "Hi, Laura, it's Taylor. Sorry I missed you. It's nothing important. Call me if you have time."

His call was a surprise. They had barely been speaking to each other since his visit; you couldn't have found notes more polite if you'd checked Martha Stewart's e-mail. She had figured his messages would taper off and then stop coming at all before long.

"Taylor?"

Laura whirled around at the sound of a voice in her supposedly empty apartment. "Cary! What the hell are you doing here?" she gasped. "You scared me to death! And how did you get in here, anyway?"

"Hello to you too, Laura," Cary said as he walked over to her. He reached out to put his hands on her shoulders and give her a kiss, but she twisted away.

"Cary, you didn't answer me. What are you doing here, and how did you get in?"

"I heard about what happened at the school. I thought you could use some TLC after that, so I sweet-talked Mrs. Nieto into letting me in. Dinner's cooking, so you won't need this," he said as he picked up the takeout bag. "How do you eat this stuff, anyway?"

Laura was torn between being furious and pleased. She would have to talk to Mrs. Nieto, but she decided that, for now, pleased was the better reaction. "Cary, couldn't you at least have said something as I came in instead of sneaking up on me?"

He saw the anger fading from her eyes and stepped close enough to give her a kiss. "I'm sorry, Laura. I didn't hear you at first. I would have called you, but I was afraid you would hang up on me after the last time we were together." He looked into her eyes and said softly, "I missed you, Laura. Go sit down, and I'll bring you a glass of wine."

Laura watched him as he moved familiarly around her apartment. In the time they had been dating, he'd made himself a big part of her life. She hadn't realized just how much until now. She admired the way he looked in his perfectly fitted jeans and neatly pressed shirt and firmly suppressed the image of Taylor that appeared in her head.

As he poured the wine, Cary made the connection between the voice on the phone last week and the voice on the answering machine. Taylor Morgan had been here in Laura's apartment and, undoubtedly, her bed.

With amazing self-control, he covered up his anger until it could be put to good use.

"Here, darling." Cary handed her a glass of her favorite white Zinfandel. "I'm making green chile fettuccine for dinner."

"Thanks—for all of this. I'm sorry I snapped at you. But you did scare me half to death."

"I'm sorry," he said as he sat next to her, casually draping his arm around her shoulders. "We have about half an hour before dinner. Why don't you put your head down and close your eyes." He gently pulled her closer in his embrace and she gratefully did as he suggested. It was nice to have someone care.

*   *   *

Taylor had spent another day interviewing candidates to take Christine's place. Most of them could walk and chew gum at the same time, but that was about as far as their talents went. He made arrangements with the agency to try again next week even though he knew the problem wasn't with the applicants, it was with him.

Driving home, he was aware he was depressed—and lonely. Annie and Meg had gone to visit her parents before school started next week. He really felt like talking to someone, and Laura came to mind. Maybe it was time to try to build a new, more realistic relationship with her.

Letting himself into the silent condo, he picked up the phone and dialed her number. When the machine picked up, he glanced at his watch and realized she was probably still at work. He left his message, then tried to figure out something to do with the rest of the empty evening that loomed ahead.

*   *   *

Laura woke when he tried to retrieve his arm. "Oh, God, Cary, I'm sorry! I was just so tired."

He smiled at her and said, "No harm, Laura. I wouldn't have wakened you if I didn't have to go rescue dinner. Why don't you go splash some cold water on your face while I get dinner on the table?"

Laura was appalled when she saw herself in the mirror. She looked a million times worse than she had imagined. Quickly, she washed her face and reapplied her make-up. She slipped into the bedroom and changed into her favorite oversized shirt and leggings before returning to the living room.

From the doorway, she watched him and wondered why she didn't feel more for him. He was great looking, kind, considerate—probably brave, loyal, and trustworthy, too! Other than pressuring her to sleep with him, he was perfect. But he wasn't Taylor.

He saw her standing there. "Dinner's ready," he said as he pulled out her chair for her. The table was set with her good dishes—the ones that weren't paper—and he'd added candles and the champagne flutes he had given her at Christmas.

Over dinner, he asked, "The man on the answering machine? That was Taylor Morgan, wasn't it? I thought he was just an interview subject for you."

Laura was cautious. She knew Cary disliked Taylor intensely. "We've been corresponding for awhile now. I'm working on a freelance article about him, and we seem to have a lot in common."

"Pretty fancy company for a small-town reporter."

Laura bristled at his implied criticism. "I know you don't like him, Cary, but it has been a long time. I think he's probably changed. He's just a regular person, a little lonely inside all that fame."

"Lonely? I doubt it. He must have a girl in every city he visits, probably a whole harem full wherever he lives. He still seems to be plenty attractive to women from what I've read."

"Cary, drop it, please. We're friends—and even that may be too strong a word. Right now, he's an interesting subject for an article, that's all!"

Thankfully, he did drop it, and they moved on to dessert; chocolate-dipped strawberries that he knew were her favorites. He insisted she put her feet up while he cleaned up the kitchen. She thought, "What is wrong with me? The man is gorgeous, considerate, cooks, and does dishes! What more could I want?"

In the kitchen, Cary was thinking that there was obviously much more to Laura's relationship with Morgan. She was trying much too hard to convince him there was nothing there. He knew Morgan had been here and she had never mentioned it. He couldn't believe he had been so patient when she was obviously involved with his old nemesis. His anger grew as he thought about it, and he snapped the stem of the glass he was holding.

He joined her on the couch a little later and drew her into his arms and gently kissed her. "Better now?" he whispered. "Mmm, much better," she murmured before he kissed her again.

His kisses began to grow in intensity. Uncomfortably remembering the last time, Laura tried to move away. "No, Laura, not tonight," he said as he moved his hands up and tangled them in her thick, copper colored hair. "Not tonight," he said again as he pulled her face to his.

Laura was startled by his aggressive behavior. She thought she had made her feelings clear the last time, and she didn't want to play that scene again. As she brought her hands up and placed them against his chest to push him away, he removed his hands from her hair and roughly imprisoned her wrists. "No more games, Laura," he said, his dark eyes glittering in the dim light. Holding both her wrists in one hand, he pushed her back against the cushions and brought his other hand to her breast. His mouth descended to her throat as she struggled to free herself.

"Cary! Stop! Now! I want you to stop!" Laura tried to twist away from him, but he imprisoned her with the weight of his body. She could feel his erection as he pushed his hips against her.

"Stop, Laura?" He laughed softly. "I don't think so. Let me show you what you *really* want." He hooked the fingers of his free hand in the neckline of her shirt and, with one motion, pulled all the buttons from it, then buried his face in the hollow of her breasts.

Laura wanted to cry as she felt his breath against her bared skin, but she refused to give him the satisfaction of her tears. She tried to free herself and did manage to free one hand, which she used to push his head up and away from her. Quietly, furiously, she said, "Get off of me now, Cary." She pushed at him with her free hand, but she hadn't figured on his strength. His slim figure gave no indication of the iron-hard muscles it concealed, muscles he used now to take her hand and imprison it again. With barely a pause, his free hand moved back to her breast. Roughly freeing it from her bra, he took the nipple into his mouth with a low moan of pleasure.

Laura was genuinely frightened. This was someone she didn't know, someone she couldn't control. "Cary...please!"

"Please, what, my darling Laura? Are you finally asking for more?"

"God...Cary, stop, now. This can't be what you want." She tried to keep the tears from her voice as he looked down at her.

"Not what I want, Laura? I haven't wanted anything else since the minute I saw you. I've been damned patient with you, but no more. If you can screw that two-bit singer of yours, then you can damn well fuck me, too." Laura saw the anger in his eyes and realized she was powerless to stop him.

Powerless or not, she continued to fight, but she was helpless as he stripped off her leggings and panties and roughly took her in his hand, his fingers digging deep inside of her in an effort to dispel the dryness of her terror.

Suddenly, he released her wrists and knelt above her. For a moment she thought he had come to his senses, until he imprisoned her again with the weight of one knee on her chest as he unbuttoned his jeans and freed his erection. Moving back, he roughly parted her legs and plunged into her.

Laura continued to struggle, turning her face from his as he tried to kiss her, trying to escape from the pain inside. Then, suddenly, he cried out and collapsed onto her, breathing hard, as he spasmodically clutched at her breast. Finally, she cried as he pulled out of her, calmly buttoning his jeans as he stared down at her. He turned and looked in the mirror, finger-combing his hair, before he walked out of her apartment without a word.

*   *   *

Taylor looked at his watch again. He had spent the last hour watching a documentary on sea life and didn't know anything more about it than he had when he tuned in. It was late. Laura probably wasn't going to call. He logged on one more time—still nothing on-line, either. He turned off the computer and headed for bed trying to ignore all the reasons she wouldn't have called.

*   *   *

Laura lay on the couch, sobbing, unable to move, the horror of the last hour immobilizing her. A small, still-sane part of her brain begged her to call for help, but she couldn't will herself to move. Finally, as tremors shook her, she pulled herself from the couch, desperately clutching the remains of her shirt around her. She groped her way to the bathroom and, looking into the mirror, let out a small cry, hardly recognizing the ravaged creature that stared back at her.

Her make-up had smeared across her face; the tear-diluted mascara puddled under her eyes. Her mouth was swollen, and there was a cut at the corner. Her face and throat were red from the sandpaper of his beard stubble. Mesmerized, she let her gaze travel further down to the bruises beginning to show on her breasts and arms. And, though the mirror did not reflect that far down, she could feel the bruises beginning to form on her thighs, the stickiness of his assault seeping out of her.

She had covered rape cases before. She knew all the things a victim should do, the evidence that was needed. But all she could think of was washing it all away, washing his smell from her skin, his taste from her mouth. With shaking hands, she turned on the shower, pulled the remnants of her clothing from her body, and stepped under the hot, stinging spray.

She didn't know how long she had been in there. Suddenly she realized she had used the entire bottle of shampoo she had opened—oh, God, was it only that morning? An empty bottle of body wash lay at her feet, and the water was growing tepid. Automatically she looked at her watch and realized that, not being waterproof, it had stopped, ruined like the rest of her life.

She turned off the water and stepped out, grateful for the steam that clouded the mirror. She wrapped a towel around her head, pulled her old chenille robe from its hook behind the door, shakily made her way to the bed, and wept.

*   *   *

When the alarm when off, she was surprised that she had slept. For a moment she lay very still, willing it all to have been a bad dream. But the ache between her legs and the bruises that ringed her wrists told her it was all horribly true. She drifted back to sleep, hiding there, only to be wakened by the phone, followed by Beth's voice on the machine.

"Laura? Laura? Pick up if you're there, girl. Robert's on a rampage because you're not here and haven't called in."

Carefully, she reached out one hand and picked up the phone, "Beth?"

"Laura! You sound awful. Are you all right?"

"No…yes…Beth, tell them I'm sick. The flu or something.…"

"Laura, you don't sound right. What is it? Do you want me to come over?"

"No, I'm just...sick. I need to sleep. Tell Robert, ok?" She gently hung up the receiver before her friend could say another word. Then she drifted back to the safety of sleep.

*   *   *

She didn't know how long she had slept. There had been a noise...dear God, it was the door! Someone was opening the door! Cary! Wildly she looked for someplace to hide as she heard the door open, then close.

"Laura?" Beth's voice, filled with worry, called out softly. "Laura, it's me. I came to see how you were." Beth had a key to the apartment and had used it to let herself in.

Laura struggled to sit up, to call out, to stop her from coming in, but she was too muddled, too slow. Beth appeared in the bedroom doorway. "Laura, I was worried so I came over to check on you...." Her voice trailed off as she caught sight of Laura's face.

"Oh, my God! Laura? What happened?" Beth came to sit on the side of the bed, horrified at the appearance of her friend. She reached out to take Laura's hands, then began to cry as she saw the bruises and felt Laura wince from the pain. "Laura? Who did this to you?"

Laura couldn't answer, couldn't speak, but Beth saw the need in her eyes and held her while they both cried.

*   *   *

When their tears had finally slowed, Beth had helped Laura into the living room. After settling her on the couch and covering her with an afghan, she called the paper and told them Laura was very ill and that she would be staying with her. Then, Beth went into the kitchen and made a pot of hot, sweet tea. She was grateful for the brief interlude of solitude. As long as she lived, she knew she would never forget her first sight of Laura's sweet face, battered and bruised. The memory now caused her to shake so hard that she spilled sugar across the countertop. Gripping the edge of the sink and closing her eyes, she forced herself to breathe deeply until she felt a measure of control return.

Laura listened to the small sounds Beth was making in the kitchen. It reminded her all too clearly of last night and Cary moving around in there. She wrapped her arms around herself and forced the memories away. She was grateful when Beth emerged, carrying a tray with the teapot and two mugs. She took the mug Beth handed her and curled both hands around it, sipping the warmth gratefully, feeling some strength returning. Beth sat across from her, watching her warily, sharing her silence until she finally asked, "It was Cary, wasn't it?"

Laura nodded. "He was here when I got home last night. Mrs. Nieto had let him in."

"Stupid woman! Why in the world did she do that!"

"Beth, you've met Cary. He could charm his way around anybody. He told her that he had come to take care of me...." Her voice broke, and she took a ragged breath before continuing. "She had seen him around here often enough. She meant no harm."

"Laura, you know you have to report this. You should have reported it last night." Beth's voice was gentle.

Laura shook her head. "No, Beth. You know as well as I do what would happen. We've been in the news business long enough."

"Laura, you can't let him get away with this!"

Laura showed the first spark of her usual strength. "Beth, what am I going to tell them? My boyfriend was waiting in my apartment, fixed me a lovely dinner, was here for hours, and *now* I'm crying rape? Look at me, Beth. I've reported on enough of these things to know that I look a little roughed up, but not as if I've been attacked. Even if they would believe me, Cary's story would be that it was consensual. Sure, he'd gotten a little rough, but that's how we like it. The D.A. would never take the case." Laura shook her head. "And even if he did, I'd never win and it would kill my parents. I'll have to find my own way to get Cary."

Beth was shocked. It wasn't like Laura to give in so easily. Laura had always had such a strong sense of justice. It had gotten her in trouble in school often enough when she defended someone on the playground or stood up to a teacher she thought was treating her unfairly. Beth took a breath to launch into an argument, but was interrupted by the phone.

"Do you want me to answer it?"

"No, let the machine get it. You can always pick up if it's important." Laura looked suddenly tired and leaned her head against the cushions, closing her eyes and listening.

"Laura, I tried you at work, but they said you were sick." Worry filled Taylor's voice. "I hope it's not too serious. Call me when you feel up to it. I need to talk to you." The connection was broken, and the machine reset itself, red light blinking.

"He called last night, Beth. The message he left seemed to set something off in Cary. Cary said if I could screw Taylor, then I could...then he raped me. Oh, God, Beth, he *raped* me." Laura dissolved into tears again, racking sobs that shook her slender body.

*   *   *

"Laura." Beth sat next to her and looked into her eyes. "I can't make you report this even though I think you should. But I am going to make you go to the doctor. No arguments. I'm calling Dr. Remington now, and I'm telling her it's an emergency. I want you to go get dressed so we can leave right away."

Beth gave her no time to answer, but went straight to the phone. Laura knew she was right, so she started for the bedroom, aware that there was not a part of her body that didn't ache. She took a black shirt and leggings from the closet and pulled them on. Carefully avoiding the mirror, she ran a brush through her hair and pulled it back into a ponytail. She almost cried again when she remembered Taylor and the way he had teased her about wearing a ponytail before he kissed her.

"Laura?" Beth's face was filled with concern. "Are you ready?"

"Let's go get this over with," Laura said as she slipped on her shoes, and the two of them left the apartment and drove to the doctor's office in Beth's car.

Laura was silent all the way to the doctor's office. Dr. Remington had been gynecologist to both girls since their first exams, and she had stayed late after Beth's call. She had seen it all before, but never got used to the physical marks that rape left on the victim. The bruises were bad enough, but the utter devastation in Laura's eyes was what concerned her most. She took her back into the examining room while Beth waited, staring at the waiting room television that was muttering in the corner.

When the doctor finally came out, she said, "Laura's getting dressed. I didn't find any major damage although she's going to be sore for awhile. I gave her the 'morning-after' pill and I'm testing for AIDS. Beth, she shouldn't be alone, and she said her parents were out of the country?"

"I'll stay with her. Is there anything I should watch for?"

"She's very depressed. I want her to go into counseling, but she's fighting it. I'll check with her in a few days. I want you to take my home number and call me if I'm needed. And see if you can get her to press charges."

Laura came down the hallway and into the waiting room. The television was tuned to the news, and the anchor was saying just as she walked in:

"We have good news and bad news tonight of a personal nature. Bad news for us, good news for our colleague, Cary Edwards. He will be leaving us for the 'big time' next week when he begins a reporting job with The News Channel. We wish him well and want him to know he will be sorely missed."

Neither Beth nor the doctor was fast enough to catch Laura when she fainted.

*   *   *

She had come around pretty quickly, and Dr. Remington suggested she check into the hospital, "Just for overnight, Laura, for observation."

"No, please, I just want to go home." Laura sounded completely exhausted.

The doctor looked questioningly at Beth before continuing. "All right, Laura. But Beth is staying with you. I don't want you to be alone right now. And I want you to think seriously about the counseling."

Watching the two women leave, she felt helpless. From Laura's reaction to the news report on the television, she was fairly sure who the rapist was. But there wasn't a damned thing she could do about it.

*   *   *

When they were halfway back to Laura's apartment, she suddenly said, "Beth? I want to go out to Mom and Dad's. I don't want to go back to the apartment except long enough to get some clothes."

"Of course, Laura. We'll need to stop by my place, too."

"Beth, you don't have to stay with me."

Beth looked at her briefly, then turning her eyes back to the road, said, "How do you think you'll stop me, Laura?"

Laura did something she thought she'd never do again—she laughed, and a tiny bit of Beth's anxiety faded.

*   *   *

As they left Laura's apartment, the phone began to ring, but Laura pulled the door closed and locked the deadbolt. Neither of them heard the message.

"Laura? It's Taylor again. I'm worried about you. Please call and let me know you're all right, or have Beth or your mother call if you're still too sick. Please...."

2 6

When Laura opened the front door of her parents' house, she could still smell the ghostly scent of the *piñon* that had served as a Christmas tree and would eventually be used for firewood. Just being there eased some of Laura's pain. It was familiar. It was safe. It was home.

"I'm starving, Laura. And I know you haven't eaten all day. I'm going to go raid the freezer and see what I can find."

Laura took her bag and put it in her old bedroom. It hadn't changed much. The posters of rock stars were gone, but the furniture was still the same, the bedspread and curtains with their familiar pattern. She should have felt safe here, but she realized that while the room had remained unchanged, she had changed too much to go back to being the carefree girl who had once dreamed there.

She wandered back into the kitchen where Beth was putting a bowl into the microwave. "Mom had frozen some of the *posole* from *Posadas*. It's not chicken soup, but probably the next best thing. Why don't you get some bowls out so we can eat when this is hot?"

It was easier to do as she was told than to argue. She wasn't hungry, but she knew Beth wouldn't give up until she ate at least a little bit. Then she just wanted to go to bed, to return to the safety of sleep.

*　　　　　*　　　　　*

Taylor sat at the piano, picking out the melody line of a song he was considering adding for the next leg of the tour. He wasn't concentrating on the music, but was listening for the phone to ring. Laura must be really angry with him to be this silent. He preferred to believe that than to think she was seriously ill.

Taylor left the piano to turn on the computer. Laura checked her e-mail everyday. She should have been home by now. Maybe she had sent a message. But, there was nothing from her. He knew he was obsessing, but he needed to know how she was. If he didn't hear by tomorrow morning, he would try her parents.

*　　　　　　*　　　　　　*

Laura pretended to eat the *posole*. She was so tired that the spoon seemed to weigh pounds instead of ounces, and the mere thought of eating made her stomach clench. Beth was wise enough not to try to push her. When she had finished her own meal, she took the bowls to the kitchen and rinsed them before putting them in the dishwasher. She came back to find that Laura had pillowed her head on her arms, leaning on the now empty table.

"Laura?" Beth knelt beside her chair. "Do you want to go on to bed? It's all right if you do. I want you to take one of the sedatives the doctor gave you. It will help you sleep."

She got a glass of water and took out one of the pills. Beth waited while Laura obediently swallowed it and handed the glass back.

When Laura was ready for bed, Beth gently pulled the blankets up and smiled at her. "I feel like I'm playing 'house,'" she said, and was rewarded with a small smile from Laura.

"Beth? Stay until I fall asleep, please."

"Of course." Beth pulled a chair beside the bed and sat where they could see each other.

"Do you remember all those nights we spent in this room?" Laura asked.

"Sure, here or at my house. I don't think there was a weekend that went by without a sleepover one place or the other."

"Mm-hmm. We planned out our whole lives. Me, the great reporter; you, the artist. You were going to marry Tomás and have lots of kids, and I was going to be their eccentric aunt."

"I remember," Beth said softly.

"How come nobody ever told us it could be like this?" Laura murmured before her eyes closed and she slept.

Beside the bed, watching her sleeping friend, Beth whispered, "We wouldn't have believed them if they had."

When she was sure that Laura was asleep, she went back out into the living room and finally gave in to the tears she'd had to keep under control all day. She cried until there were no tears left, then made her own way to an early bed.

27

Taylor swept Laura into his arms and kissed her as they stood on the deserted beach. The ocean matched her eyes; the sunrise was the color of her hair. She seemed to be made of morning light, and he realized how very much he loved her. He took his lips from hers to tell her, and she pulled away from him, running to the edge of the beach, playing tag with the waves. She was laughing and held out her hand to him as she waded out further. Without warning, the water and sky turned dark, and she was pulled away from him. He tried to reach her, but she was too far away, her brightness obscured by the darkness of the sea.

"Laura!"

The sound of his own voice woke Taylor, and he found he was sitting up, reaching out, heart pounding, still lost in the terror of the dream.

A dream. Thank God, it had only been a dream. He ran his hands through his hair, then got out of bed. He was awake now; there was no chance he would fall asleep again. Shakily, he made his way downstairs, and after fixing a cup of coffee, he sat out on the deck and watched the morning arrive.

*   *   *

Laura was jolted from sleep by the sound of Taylor's voice calling her name. Disoriented, she stared wildly about the room before she recognized the familiar place. With that recognition came the memory of why she was there instead of in her own place.

She didn't remember dreaming, yet she had heard his voice so clearly. Slowly, she lay back down, pulling the covers tightly around her as she recognized that no dream could be worse than the waking nightmare she was living. It was still dark outside. The sun hadn't even begun its long climb over the mountains, and she drifted off again to the relative safety of sleep.

*   *   *

He had stayed on the deck until the sun was up, as if its rising depended on his presence. He couldn't shake the dream and remembered it with total clarity.

He had been a fool! He shouldn't have given up on Laura so easily. The old biddies said she was "practically" engaged. There was still time to change her mind, time until she actually married this man.

Going inside, he checked the computer. Still nothing from Laura. If he didn't reach her today, he would be on a plane tomorrow. He wasn't going to lose her without a fight.

*   *   *

Laura lost her argument with Beth. "Go on to work. I'll be fine."

"Absolutely not, Laura Collins. I'm calling in sick for both of us. I promise not to be in your face, but I won't leave you here alone."

"Fine. Tell Robert I won't be in the rest of this week. You, however, will be in to work tomorrow."

"Stop bossing me around, Laura. It won't do any good. See if you can stay out of trouble while I go shower!"

Laura took a cup of coffee out onto the patio. The winter haze that usually hung over the city seemed to be lighter this morning. She watched distant planes taking off from the airport and found herself wishing she was on any one of them as long as it was taking her away from here. Cary had taken so much more than her body. She had always felt safe here, in this house, this city. This morning she looked on it without the rose tinting that had always colored her life. That was completely gone, headed for Atlanta with Cary.

*   *   *

The phone rang in her empty apartment. One…two…three rings. The answering machine finally picked up on the fourth. Not wanting to leave yet another message, Taylor hung up, then dialed her parents' number.

*   *   *

Laura heard the phone ringing. No one knew she was here except Beth. It was probably for her parents, and she let it ring, their voice messaging picking it up. She couldn't hear Taylor's voice as he said, "Sean? Maria? It's Taylor. I'm sorry to bother you. I've been trying to reach Laura. The *Herald* said she was sick. I've been trying for two days now and haven't heard from her. Would you give me a call, please, or ask her to call me?"

Taylor hung up the phone. It was still fairly early in New Mexico, and the University was on break. It was unlikely they would have left for their offices. The dream still hovered in the back of his mind, and he was filled with a sense of foreboding.

*   *   *

"Did I hear the phone?" Beth was brushing her hair as she came back into the living room.

"Yes, but I let the voice messaging pick up. I figured it was for Mom and Dad."

"Could be, but it could have been Robert. I had to leave a message for him. Do you have the access code?"

"I can't remember it right now. I must have it written down somewhere...."

"Never mind. I'll just call and see if it was him," she said as she turned and walked back down the hall.

Laura sat in the living room, watching the sun rise higher and the city come to life. She could see the Pyramid in the distance and knew that the *Herald* building was in its shadow. She had a job; she should get back to it. But she couldn't—not yet.

28

Rehearsals had started for the second part of the tour. There were a few new people, and everyone was rusty from the time off, so rehearsal went in fits and starts. By midday, Taylor was pretty close to the end of his patience. In all fairness, he knew most of the problems were coming from him. Finally, when the director called a lunch break, Taylor told everyone to take the afternoon off. "We'll try again tomorrow. We've got time, so let's not push ourselves too hard in the beginning."

Leaving the Performing Arts Center where they had taken rehearsal space, Taylor put the top down on the convertible and went for a long drive. He ended up in St. Pete just before sunset. Impulsively, he pulled into the parking lot for Hurricane's. They still had a table on the balcony, and he had a beer while he watched the same sun set that he had helped to rise that morning.

As soon as he came into the condo, he knew there was no phone message from Laura. There was no light blinking on the machine, so he turned on the computer to check there. Still nothing. Looking at his watch, he realized she should be home, so he dialed the number he now knew by heart. He listened to it ring half a continent away, then hung up when the machine kicked in. Then he dialed her parents' number again with the same results.

Calmly, he dialed a third number.

"Kathy? It's Taylor Morgan. I'm sorry to bother you at home, but I need a flight to Albuquerque tomorrow…No, leave the return date open. I don't know how long I'll be gone. Give me a call back when you get everything arranged."

Hanging up, he took the stairs two at a time and pulled down a suitcase. Even as he began to gather clothes, he used the cordless phone to call his director.

"Hi, it's Taylor. You're going to have to run rehearsals without me for a few days…I don't know how long. It's a personal thing and an emergency. I'll be out of town. There's plenty for you to work on without me. You know what to do…Thanks. I'll let you know as soon as I'm back."

An hour later he was packed. Kathy had called him with the flight plans, and he was ready to leave in the morning. He thought about trying Laura again, but decided enough was enough. He would be a lot harder to brush off in person.

*   *   *

True to her word, Beth had left Laura time to think. Using the computer in Sean's study, she connected to the computer at the paper and worked on a layout that had been giving her trouble. Just knowing Beth was there was a comfort to Laura, she wasn't sure she could have handled being alone.

She had spent much of the day on the living room couch, staring out the window at the river and the trees. She'd lost count of the planes she had seen taking off and had imagined all the places they could be going, all the places she had never seen.

She had never touched her college fund. With a scholarship and student employment, she'd never had to. Her parents had given the account to her when she graduated to do with as she pleased. She had always thought about traveling, but the time had never been right. All day she'd thought of leaving—running away, she supposed. But maybe now was the right time.

Finally, late afternoon, she appeared in the doorway and interrupted Beth.

"Hey…"

Beth looked up from the computer. "Hey, yourself."

"Are you at a stopping place?"

"Sure, hang on a minute." Beth saved her work and logged off. Then she stood and stretched. "I spent too much time on that anyway. Do we need to be in here to talk, or can we use the living room?"

She stopped in the kitchen and got a soda, offering one to Laura. They sat in companionable silence for a few minutes before Laura said, "I've been thinking, Beth. It's time for me to try something different. I want to quit the *Herald*, travel, do some freelance work."

Beth was surprised. Laura had always been such a homebody. "Are you sure, Laura? Now is probably not the right time to be making major decisions."

"No, I think now is exactly the right time. I don't want to be here in the news community until Cary is just a memory for people. I need to get away, to start over. I've thought this through, and I'm sure it's what I want to do."

"Robert and Henry are going to have a cow, you know," Beth grinned at her, then sobered. "What are you going to tell Mom and Dad?"

"Henry and Robert will get over it. Mom and Dad don't have to know why. You know they'll be supportive of my decision. Money's not a problem. Want to quit and run away with me?"

"No, if you do this, you need to do it on your own. You don't need me along."

"I know, you're right. I just can't imagine doing it without you. You've always been there. We've done everything together." She reached out and took Beth's hand.

"I'll still be here, Laura, " Beth replied. "You can't get rid of me by running away. You're stuck with me for life." Raising her soda can in salute, Beth continued, "Here's to a new beginning, Laura."

Laura returned her salute, then picked up the phone.

"Hello, Henry, it's Laura Collins...I'm better, thanks, but I have a favor to ask. I'm at Mom and Dad's house. Could you stop by on your way home this evening? I need to talk to you, and I can't come into the office right now...Thanks, Henry. I appreciate it. See you soon."

29

Henry Alaniz had not been Laura's direct supervisor for a long time. He had been her boss when she was an intern, but he'd known her since she was a little girl, and he was "Uncle Henry." He was far from happy at her news.

Beth had met him at the door and filled him in briefly on what had happened so that he was better prepared not to show his surprise at her appearance. Controlling his anger at the man who had done this to her was a different matter.

"Laura, you have to report this!"

"Henry, please understand. I can't. You know as well as I do that it would never hold up in court."

He turned away and looked out the window. He had a daughter the same age as Laura. If something like this happened to Cindy....

"Henry? Sit down. It gets worse."

"Worse, Laura?"

She handed him an envelope. "It's my resignation, Henry," she said quietly before she went on to tell him what her plans were. "I don't want to go back at all, and I need you to tell Robert for me."

"Absolutely not, Laura! You can't make a decision this important right now."

"I can, Henry, and I have." He saw the determination in her eyes and knew he would never win this argument.

"I won't accept your resignation, Laura." He raised his hand to stop her as she started to protest. "I will give you a six-month leave of absence. If, at the end of that time, you still want to resign, I'll accept it."

Laura's eyes filled with tears at the kindness of this man who had been her mentor for so many years.

"But, it comes with strings attached, Collins." His voice resumed its customary gruffness. "Those freelance articles you're going to write? The *Herald* better have first crack at them. Deal?"

She held out her hand and shook his as she replied, "Deal."

   *   *   *

After Henry left, the two women made a meal out of the treasures in the well-stocked freezer. Beth was pleased to note that Laura actually ate and there was some color in her face other than the bruising.

"I think I'm going to log on for a few minutes, Beth."

"Go ahead. I'll put this stuff away, then watch some television. Take your time."

Laura went to her father's home office and booted up the computer, configuring the modem to dial her access number. It had been several days now since she had checked in. As she scanned the list of messages, she knew she was looking for one in particular—and it wasn't there. Vaguely, she remembered Taylor had called that night when Cary…but she couldn't examine that memory without looking at others, too, so she shut them all out.

She went through and deleted all but a few of the messages. They would keep for answering later. Suddenly she was so tired…She logged off, took a pill, said goodnight to Beth, and was asleep almost immediately.

   *   *   *

Laura slept through the night. No nightmares. No voices calling her awake. She heard Beth moving around, but couldn't quite make herself wake up. Beth knocked at the door to wake her, then said, "Hey, sleepy-head. I'm leaving for work now—on one condition. You have to prom-ise to answer the phone so I can call and check on you. If you don't, I'm coming back here!"

"I promise. Go on, already, so I can go back to sleep."

Beth looked back from the doorway. It was good that she was sleep-ing. She needed rest to heal physically. If only everything else could be healed as easily.

*   *   *

Taylor had slept well, too. Now that he had made up his mind, he could relax. No matter what happened, at least he would be doing something. His flight was due to leave midmorning. With the time gain, he would be in New Mexico by noon. With luck, in a few short hours, he would be telling Laura the truth about his feelings.

Whistling, he carried his case down the stairs. He picked up the phone and left a message for Annie. His agent had a number where he could be reached, but no one else knew where he was going—and no one knew why.

*   *   *

Laura slept until ten and woke up hungry. After eating an enormous portion of eggs and tortillas, she showered. The soreness was fading, as were some of the bruises. She still avoided looking in the mirror any more than necessary as she dressed in a turtleneck and jeans. As she fin-ished drying her hair, she heard the phone ringing and ran to answer it.

"Collins."

"Wilkins."

"Morning, Beth." She sounded so much better that Beth regretted that what she had to tell her would bring it all back.

"Morning, yourself. I just called to tell you to avoid reading the paper this morning—at least the arts and entertainment section. I'm sorry, Laura, but there's an article about *him*, and I didn't want you to come across it with without warning."

Silence stretched across the line as Laura's tenuous serenity vanished. Finally, she said, "Does it say when he's leaving?"

"Today, actually. He's leaving today. It's not too late…."

"No, Beth," Laura said firmly. "I'm not pressing charges."

"Laura? Are you sure? Once he's out of state it will be almost impossible."

"I'm sure, Beth."

Beth sighed. "OK, then. Have you eaten this morning?"

The conversation turned to everyday things, and Beth promised to call back in the afternoon to see what she could bring home for dinner.

Laura hung up the phone and picked up her hairbrush. Absently brushing her hair, she examined her feelings. Relief that he was gone, anger that she couldn't do something about him, excitement at the new possibilities she faced, embarrassment at letting it happen at all. Why hadn't she been able to see through his veneer of charm and caring? Dr. Remington was right. She was going to need some help to get her feelings sorted out.

Twisting her hair back into a ponytail, she picked up the phone and dialed her own number to check messages. It was time to try to get back to her life.

30

As the plane taxied to the gate at Albuquerque's Sunport, Taylor couldn't help wishing she would be there to meet him. He could see her so clearly in his mind that he was a little surprised when she wasn't waiting.

Hailing a taxi, he got in and told the driver to take him to the Hyatt. He planned on checking in, sending his bag upstairs, and immediately leaving for the *Herald*. Asking the driver to wait, he took care of the registration and came back out. As the taxi pulled into traffic, he suddenly told the driver to pull over. Jumping out of the cab, he checked the hand of the boy on the skateboard that was part of *Sidewalk Society*. It was empty, and he put a quarter on it. "Wish me luck," he said to the bronze boy before he went back to the cab. The driver was sure he had a lunatic on his hands—but this lunatic had tipped well for him to wait.

When they arrived at Herald Center, Taylor paid him off with an even more generous tip, then went into the reception area. One of the receptionists greeted him with a cheery smile that he matched with one of his own.

"Laura Collins, please."

"I'm sorry, sir. Ms. Collins began an extended leave of absence just today. Perhaps there's someone else who could help you?"

Taylor couldn't believe what he was hearing. Today? A leave of absence? Where had she gone? And why? Please God, she didn't marry him! Please, don't let it be that she had married him.

"Sir? Is there someone else who could help?"

"What? Oh, I'm sorry. I was just surprised. Is Beth Wilkins in?"

"Let me ring upstairs for you. Who may I say is here?"

"Taylor Morgan."

The receptionist's eyes widened at his name. No wonder he looked so familiar! After speaking with Beth, she said, "Take the second elevator to the third floor, Mr. Morgan. She'll meet you there."

Thanking her, Taylor walked to the elevator that was, thankfully, empty. It bought him a few moments to compose himself. Considering what Beth must think of him, he didn't think getting any information out of her would be easy.

She was standing there as the door opened. "Hello, Taylor." Her voice was cool, her eyes like stone.

"Hello, Beth."

"We can use one of the conference rooms to talk," she said as she turned and walked away. Taylor followed docilely along. Beth was his only chance of finding Laura, and if it meant listening to her tell him off, then that's what he would do.

She waited until he went into the small room, then came in, closing the door behind her. She took a seat on one side of the small table; he took the other one facing her. For a moment, he had a vision of an old prison movie, the wrongly convicted man facing the cop who had helped convict him.

"Taylor, what are you doing here?"

"I've been trying to reach Laura for days, Beth. There's been no answer at her apartment, none at her parents, nothing in e-mail. I decided that if she was avoiding me, it would be harder to do in person. And, now, they tell me she's on an extended leave of absence." He stopped and took a deep shuddering breath before he reached one hand across the table to her, "Please, Beth, tell me she didn't marry him."

Marry him? Marry who? Suddenly, she had a sinking feeling that she knew why Taylor had changed his attitude toward Laura so suddenly.

"Why would you think she got married, Taylor?"

"Beth, I heard you and Laura talking during the party. You were talking about some newsman she was dating, and she kept saying that we were just friends. Then, I overheard two of the women talking, and they said she was practically engaged. So, like an idiot, I removed myself from the picture. And now I have a horrible feeling that I'm too late."

"Oh, Taylor," Beth whispered, "why did you leave her? Why didn't you stay? Then none of this would have happened," Taylor was even more worried as she began to cry.

"Beth, you're scaring me. What is going on with Laura? Tell me, please!"

Beth brushed the tears away. "Taylor, I have to know why you're here first."

"Because I love her."

It was clear to Beth that he was telling the truth. Now she had a choice to make. Keep Laura's secret and send him away, or tell him the truth and hope he was the person she believed him to be. She looked into his eyes for a long moment, and he never looked away.

"Taylor, you can't ever tell her I told you or that you even know any of this. Promise me?"

"I promise," he said as he took her hands in his.

"Laura was raped two days ago by the man you heard us talking about." She watched as his face went ashen and felt his hands clutching hers painfully as she told him the rest of the story.

*   *   *

There had been two messages from Taylor on her machine and a number of hang-ups that she suspected were from him as well. She had no idea what he could want, and she couldn't deal with his feelings right now. For a moment she could see his face as he had kissed her, but it was quickly replaced by a nightmare vision of Cary's. The two of them were so tangled in her mind that she couldn't think of one without the other appearing, too. Shaking her head, she pushed them both away and tried to think of what she needed do next.

*   *   *

Annie pulled into her driveway, grateful that the long trip was over. It had been wonderful to spend time with her parents and watch them spoil Meg. But the trip had been far from easy.

Her mother had immediately noticed she had lost weight and begun to fuss at her about it. Annie tried to blame it on a case of the flu, but her mother wasn't buying it. She set out to make all of Annie's favorite childhood foods, but truth was, Annie had very little appetite these days. They had even had a fight about it one day.

Then, she'd had a day with one of her headaches. As usual, it had left her drained and sick. She went to the clinic at her mother's insistence. The doctor diagnosed it as a bad case of flu, prescribing bed rest and liquids. Annie was only too happy to follow his orders and let her mother take care of her. Meg was happy and safe, and Annie didn't have to worry about anything. So, she gave in to being ill and slept for two days, feeling remarkably better when she finally got up. Even her appetite had returned, much to her mother's satisfaction.

It hadn't lasted. Today, on the drive home, she felt the beginning of a headache and spent much of the drive praying that it would hold off until she could get Meg safely home.

She helped Meg bring in everything, then sent her off to take a bath before an early bedtime. She had school tomorrow, and Annie had classes starting up at the studio.

While Meg was in the bath, Annie checked her messages. Taylor had gone off on some mysterious errand. She was sure he had started rehearsals this week so it was very strange for him to leave like this. She wondered briefly if it had something to do with that woman in

New Mexico. He had been very quiet about his visit out there. But her head hurt too much to think about it much. Taylor would have to take care of himself.

31

Taylor had listened with growing anger as Beth told him what had happened to Laura. When she finished, he sat in silence for a moment, then pushed away from the table and walked to the window. Finally, he turned and looked at Beth.

"The bastard left town?"

"Today," Beth confirmed.

"Who is he, Beth?"

"Taylor, it's not important. It would be if she would press charges, but she won't. I'm not going to tell you so you can go off on some vigilante mission. Laura should be who we're thinking about right now."

There had only been two other times in his life when he had felt this helpless. The first time had been when his parents died. The second had been the night Annie had shown up on his doorstep, battered and pregnant. At least then he'd had the satisfaction of confronting her husband. Both times he had felt responsible in some way. He should have made his parents fly instead of letting them take that train; he should have talked Annie out of marrying that man. The logical part of him knew that he couldn't have done anything, but he had never quite convinced his heart.

Now, this with Laura. If he had let things take their course that night, she probably never would have seen the other man again. Once again, he had failed someone he loved.

"This leave of absence, Beth? What's she planning?"

"She suddenly decided that this was the time to make a change in her life. She wants to travel and do some freelance work. She tried to resign, but Henry would only agree to a six-month leave of absence. He's hoping she'll change her mind and come back here."

"So, what do I do now, Beth? I don't think that now is the right time for me to appear on her doorstep and offer her my heart."

Beth felt sorry for him. He looked so completely defeated. The timing in all of this was so wrong.

"I guess you go back to Florida. Keep trying to reach her, and I'll keep you posted on her plans. I don't think she'll take off until after her parents are home at the end of the month."

"Beth, thanks for telling me all of this, for not shutting me out. I'll find a way to let her know that I love her, but I promise I'll be careful."

Beth walked him to the elevator. Before it came, she stopped him. "Taylor, she's at her parents' house. If you think you can, why don't you call her there? I made her promise to answer the phone today so I could check up on her. Just don't let her know that you're here instead of in Florida."

"Thanks, Beth. I may try later." He leaned down and kissed her cheek. "She's lucky to have you for a friend." Then he stepped into the elevator and was gone.

*   *   *

As luck would have it, the same driver arrived to take Taylor back to the hotel. He was amazed at the change in the man he had delivered just an hour or so ago. He seemed to have aged in that time, his eyes haunted now by whatever had happened.

When he arrived back at the hotel, Taylor went straight up to his room. He tossed his coat on the bed, then sat in the armchair, gloomily staring out of the window, his thoughts jumbled.

Now was not the time to tell Laura how he felt. He didn't want her to come to him as a lifeline out of this nightmare or, worse, reject him because of it. He had to find a way to win back her friendship before he could try to win her love. Where to begin, though?

After an hour of fruitlessly chasing his thoughts in circles, Taylor decided to go up to the pool and see if he could work some of this anger out. Maybe then his thoughts would be clearer.

As he began to swim laps in the deserted pool, the repetitive action helped settle his mind, and he felt more at peace. He mentally began arranging his life, giving priority to Laura, the tour, and finding a new assistant. At least the tour and assistant question were interrelated.

Suddenly, the answers were clear! Clinging to the side of the pool, he realized that he could offer the assistant job to Laura. She could travel, have time to do her writing, and he would have her near enough to begin an old-fashioned courtship. He pulled himself out of the pool, smiling for the first time since Beth had told him.

*   *   *

Laura called Dr. Remington and arranged to begin counseling. The doctor had been relieved. It was a good sign that Laura was beginning to take control of her life again.

After setting up her first appointment with the therapist, Laura took a notepad and settled in on the couch to begin to make a list of things she needed to do and when they would need to be done. Absently, she pushed the play button on her mother's CD player. She was surprised when Taylor's voice surrounded her, and she let the music wash over her, listening with her eyes closed before she picked up the notepad and got to work.

*   *   *

"Art department. This is Beth."

"Beth!" Taylor said, "I'm glad I caught you. I have an idea, and I wanted to see what you think of it."

Beth listened silently as Taylor outlined his plan to ask Laura to take the assistant's job. She could hear the excitement in his voice, and his enthusiasm began to win her over. "Is there any chance this will work, Beth?"

"Taylor, a week ago I would have told you there wasn't any way she would even consider it. But, I never thought she would quit the *Herald*, either. All you can do is ask her. Then I can try to encourage her to do it."

"I'll call her then."

"Taylor? "

"What, Beth?"

"Have you really thought this through? Can you manage to hide your feelings until she's ready?"

"I'll manage somehow."

"When you call her, don't forget you can't tell her you're here. Tell her you called me at work and I told you how to reach her."

"Beth, I won't do anything to jeopardize your friendship."

"It will be all right. Don't worry, Taylor."

As she hung up, Beth hoped she was right, that Laura would forgive her. There was always a chance that she wouldn't.

*   *   *

The first thing to be accomplished, Laura decided, was to find a new apartment. Even though she planned on traveling, she wanted a home base to come back to. What had happened had made it impossible for her to return to her old place—she would never feel safe there again.

When the phone rang, she picked it up, still lost in her list.

"Hello?"

"Laura? It's Taylor."

She was so surprised, she nearly dropped the phone, before asking, "Taylor? How did you find me?"

She sounded less than thrilled to hear from him, and for a moment, he regretted calling.

"I've been trying to reach you for the last couple of days. You're pretty elusive."

"You didn't answer my question. How did you find me?"

"I called the *Herald* again today and they told me you were starting an extended leave of absence. Since the last thing I had heard from them was that you were ill, I got worried. So, I asked to talk to Beth and she told me where you were. Are you feeling better?"

Laura was torn between being furious at Beth and being grateful.

"I'm fine, Taylor. How are things with you?"

Taylor could hear the wariness in her voice.

"Actually, that's why I've been calling. I had an idea and, considering you're on leave from the *Herald*, it might really work out."

Laura listened as he outlined his need for an assistant. "We'll be traveling, mostly here in the east then a session in California. The first concert is in New York City on Valentine's Day. We'll finish up in April on Catalina Island. It's not a real taxing job, Laura. It would leave you time to do your writing and maybe give you some things to write about. I've been interviewing for weeks now and can't find anyone I feel like I can work with. So, finally, I thought I would see if I could talk you into it."

There. It was out on the table, and the next move was hers. He wished he could see her face so he had some idea of what she was thinking. The silence seemed to stretch on forever before she said, "I don't know, Taylor. I have to think about it. When do you need an answer?"

He breathed a silent sigh of relief. As long as she wasn't rejecting the idea outright, there was reason to hope.

"I'd like for you to come down to Florida by the end of the month, sooner if possible, so we could get used to working together before we actually leave on the tour."

"Why don't you fax me the itinerary, Taylor? Give me a few days to think about it, and we can discuss details by e-mail."

"Great! I'm really hoping you'll say 'yes', Laura."

They talked for a few more minutes about little things. Before they said goodbye, they had agreed that Laura would let him know about the job within a week.

*   *   *

Taylor hung up the phone and felt suddenly drained of energy. When they had begun to talk, she had been reserved and polite, but she seemed to have lost that wariness by the time they had hung up. Hearing her voice had made him long to hold her, to chase her nightmares away. If this was the way he felt just talking to her, how was he going to survive being near her everyday?

Picking up the phone again, he called the airline to make arrangements to leave. It turned out there was a flight scheduled in a couple of hours, or he could wait until morning. He chose to take the evening flight. There was no reason to stay.

*   *   *

It all seemed too convenient. Had Beth called him and told him what had happened? No, she wouldn't have done that. Besides, he had been calling before.

Laura looked at the list she had been working on. Most of it would be unnecessary if she took this job. She realized that there were a number of questions she still needed answered. Was this job just for the tour? If not, for how long? What exactly would she be doing, anyway? With the questions came a tiny inner spark of excitement at the possibilities.

Some of her questions could be easily answered by Christine. She picked up the phone to call Taylor back for Christine's phone number and was surprised when his machine picked up. Leaving a message, she realized he must have left immediately after he called her. She would check in with him by e-mail later.

*   *   *

Beth brought pizza home for dinner. As she filled Laura in on all the gossip from the *Herald*, she tried to control her curiosity. Laura hadn't said anything about hearing from Taylor, so Beth wasn't even sure if he had called. She had to wait until Laura finally said, "So, Beth, any interesting calls today?"

"Then he did call you!"

"Couldn't you have called and warned me?"

"I'm sorry, Laura. I never even thought about it."

"Did he tell you what he was calling about?"

"A little bit. Why don't you fill me in?"

Beth knew Laura well enough to recognize that she was seriously thinking about the opportunities this might offer. There was a shine in her green eyes that hadn't been there for days.

"You sound like you're really considering this."

"I am. It would be a good place to start on this journey I've set for myself. At least, by the end of the tour, I should know if I can handle living out of a suitcase. There's still a lot I want to know, and I figure that Christine would know the answers. She was his assistant when he was here." Beth's heart nearly stopped when Laura continued, "I tried to call him back right after he called here. He must have left right away." She didn't seem to be really concerned about his absence, and Beth breathed a sigh of relief as Laura went on. "I'll try to get in touch by e-mail tonight. I really would like to talk to her before I decide."

"I think it sounds like a good thing, Laura. It would be worth trying. It's only for a couple of months to begin with."

"I think I'll go try logging on now," Laura said as she got up from the table.

Beth was relieved to see her go. Lying to Laura wasn't something she'd ever tried before, and it wasn't something she wanted to do now. But, if it helped Laura to recover from all of this, the risk would be worth it.

*   *   *

Taylor got home a little after midnight. It had been a long day. Closing the door behind him, he dropped his bag by the stairs. The message light was blinking, probably Annie, he thought. She was due back today. He poured himself a glass of wine, then listened to the message.

He was startled to hear Laura's voice instead of Annie's. She must have called right after he had spoken to her. Hopefully she hadn't put things together and figured out that he had been there. She wanted Christine's number, a good sign that she was seriously thinking about accepting the job. He went to the computer and logged on.

Laura-

> Sorry I missed you. I just got in, and I don't want to call and wake you, so I thought I'd send you Christine's number this way. Since I'll be at rehearsal tomorrow by the time you get up, I thought this would be better than playing phone tag.
>
> I hope this means you're seriously thinking about taking this on. I need you.

Taylor

He added Christine's phone number and address, then logged off. He was suddenly tired and wanted nothing more than to sleep.

32

Laura looked at her watch; the plane would be landing in Tampa in less than an hour, and she would be beginning a new phase of her life. She could hardly believe it was happening. So much of the last month was a blur in her mind. A few things stood out with clarity, but everything had happened so quickly. At Christmas, just a month ago today, she would have laughed at anyone who told her she would be leaving the *Herald* and taking on the job of Taylor Morgan's assistant. Yet, here she was.

After Taylor had asked her to take the job, she had called and talked to Christine, who had been delighted that Laura was considering taking her place.

"Taylor can be a bit difficult if things aren't up to his standards, Laura, but most of the time that has to do with problems that crop up with the venues or with someone in the ensemble not carrying their weight. Those wouldn't have much to do with you. Most of the job requires acting as receptionist like I did when you interviewed him. I also took care of keeping him caught up on his correspondence, making sure he remembered birthdays and special occasions for the cast, occasionally running out to find a new shirt or the like. There was some public relations stuff, but you'll be perfect at that. Really, Laura, it can be a lot of fun if you don't mind living out of a suitcase."

She had asked Taylor numerous questions by e-mail, talked with him by phone, and finally, at the end of that week, accepted the job for the length of the tour.

As she had planned, she found a new apartment in a high-security complex. She had seen a therapist twice a week for the last three weeks until they had mutually agreed that Laura would have to do the rest of her healing on her own.

The morning her period had started was the roughest day since she had been raped. Until that moment, she hadn't realized how scared she had been that she might be pregnant, despite her doctor's assurance that the "morning-after" pill had taken care of any risk. If she had been pregnant, an abortion would have been the only answer. But, as a practicing Catholic, it would have gone against everything she had been raised to believe. With the threat of pregnancy removed, she finally had let herself rage at Cary, screaming at him in the empty apartment, telling him all the things she needed to say. When she had screamed herself hoarse, she cried for all he had taken from her. Finally, she had pulled herself together, and promised that he would pay someday. Then she put her anger aside and never looked back.

Her parents had been surprised at her decision. Calling them in Ireland, she told them what she was doing, never mentioning why. They were supportive, as always, torn between pride in her decision and grief that she would be away from them so much. She had promised to wait to leave until they came home. She smiled at the thought of the farewell dinner her mother had fixed last night—all of her favorite foods, from green chile stew to chocolate cake with mocha icing.

The pilot announced they would be landing in Tampa in ten minutes. All of her hard-won confidence that she was doing the right thing disappeared as panic moved in to take its place.

*   *   *

Taylor had decided to meet her himself, leaving rehearsal in the hands of the director. As he drove to the airport, he felt a rising sense of excitement. He knew he couldn't let her know his true feelings yet. Just having her near would have to be enough for now.

Beth had kept him posted on Laura's progress. He knew it had been hard for her, feeling like she was betraying Laura. She swore it hadn't affected their friendship, but he still wondered if it had in some way, or might in the future.

When he told Annie that Laura would be taking the job as his assistant, she had given him one of her looks, the ones she saved for when she was wondering if he had lost his mind. The last time he had seen one was when he'd asked Janis to marry him. Then it had been deserved. This time it wasn't. Annie hadn't pursued it, and he certainly wasn't going to bring it up.

As her flight arrival was announced he suddenly wondered if, maybe, Annie was right, that this was a stupid idea. Maybe he should have left her alone. Then, all of his doubts disappeared as she came through the gate. She looked thinner, more fragile, than he remembered, but he wasn't sure if it were true or if it was because he knew what had happened to her.

"Laura!" Taylor waved at her, then stepped forward. Taking her carry-on bag from her, he gave her a hug. He was momentarily surprised when she seemed to pull back from him, but he released her and smiled. "I don't think I really believed you were coming until you came through that door."

"That's all right, Taylor. I didn't believe it either."

"Let's go find your luggage and get you settled," Taylor said. "I'll need to head back to rehearsal, but I thought I would take you to dinner tonight, and we can begin to figure out where we go from here."

*   *   *

As her class ended, Annie realized Taylor must be at the airport picking up Laura. They hadn't talked about her much, and that worried Annie. Taylor wasn't usually this reserved unless it was something terribly important to him. Then he liked to have all the pieces in place before he let people know about his plans.

She was worried because it was obvious to her that Laura was very important to him. He had been too quiet after his trip to New Mexico at Christmas, changing the subject whenever the questions were specifically about Laura. Something had happened between them, Annie was sure of it. She just wasn't sure it had been something good.

Picking up the phone, she called Taylor's number and left a message inviting him to come and bring Laura for brunch on Sunday. He would be leaving again soon, and this might be their only chance to get together. And it would give her a chance to see if she could figure out what it was with Taylor and Laura.

*   *   *

Laura looked out the window of the suite that overlooked Tampa Bay. The view was beautiful, the suite equally so.

Taylor had brought her to the hotel and, true to his word, left her to get settled. They had decided that he would be back at six to pick her up for dinner. That would give her enough time, she decided, to get unpacked, and take a walk before she had to be ready.

Being with Taylor again had been easier than she had expected. The only difficult part was when he had hugged her at the airport. She still had trouble dealing with being touched. Even when her father had embraced her at the airport before she left, she found herself tensing up. Her therapist had promised her that would go away someday, but nobody seemed to be able to tell her exactly when "someday" would come. Sighing, she shook her head, then turned to the task of getting settled in her new "home."

*   *   *

Taylor arrived back at the hotel a few minutes before six. Afternoon rehearsal had gone remarkably well, and he was feeling upbeat about everything, including Laura. It was beginning to look like everything was going to work out.

Laura, wearing leggings and a lightweight sweater that matched her eyes, opened the door. He was pleased to see she was wearing the earrings he had given her for Christmas. She also appeared to be less stressed than when he picked her up at the airport. Remembering her withdrawal when he hugged her, he made no attempt to touch her as he came into the sitting room of the suite.

"Everything's all right, Laura? With the suite?"

She laughed. "It's wonderful, Taylor. Quit worrying. How was rehearsal?"

"Today, things seem to really be coming together. You wouldn't think that a month off would mean starting over again, but it does. And I'm starving! Are you ready to go?"

They went down to The Colonnade where he had arranged for one of the back corner tables. While the location didn't offer a view, it would provide some privacy and a quieter place to talk.

"I'm glad you're here, Laura." Taylor said as he met her eyes. There were shadows there where none had been a month ago.

She smiled at him and asked, "So, is it to be Mr. Morgan now that you're my boss?"

Taylor laughed, "Absolutely not! I don't think I will ever be 'Mister' material. That would mean being a grownup, something I'm not terribly good at. You'll have to live with calling me Taylor, and the truth is, you're the one who's going to have all the power."

"So, where *do* we go from here?"

"Well, to begin with, I'd like you to be at rehearsal the rest of this week, at least the ensemble rehearsals. You need to meet and get to know everyone. There will be at least a couple of afternoons that I'll be doing some solo work, which gives everyone, you included, time off.

Then, Sunday, if you want to, Annie has invited us to brunch. I would like you to meet her and Meg, not as my assistant, but as my friend."

Annie. Laura hadn't given much thought to Annie. Carefully, she probed that part of her mind that had been jealous of her, but those feelings were no longer there. They had been carefully shut away with her feelings about Taylor.

"I'd like to meet them, Taylor, but shouldn't you spend some time with them without me there since you'll be gone for awhile?"

"This was Annie's idea—not that I don't think it's a good one! I may go off with Meg for awhile if you and Annie are comfortable with the idea. Meg and I usually have a little bit of private time."

After their meal was served, Taylor turned the conversation back to what her duties would be. "At rehearsal, I'll need you to make note of any changes or new ideas. I can't remember everything that goes on, and after rehearsal, Daniel, our director, and I usually try to go over what has come up during the day. He's busy trying to juggle things too, so your notes will be a big help. I'd like your opinion on how things look from the audience point of view; what's not working, what is."

"But, Taylor, you know I have no theatre background."

"Which is why you're the perfect person to do it. The rest of us are too close to it. We need someone with a fresh viewpoint. You can give me that feedback privately if it will make it easier for you, but I really do need it, Laura."

"Then there's the fan mail. I have an arrangement with the president of the fan club. She forwards everything to me at particular stops on the tour. I'll need you to look through it and give me anything you think needs answering right away. I don't think it will take you long to recognize what's important and what isn't."

As the waiter cleared their plates before bringing dessert, Taylor looked across the table and said, "I know all this sounds overwhelming, Laura. It will be a learning experience for us both. I'll be honest with you; the next two weeks will be very busy, and you won't have a lot of free time. Once we leave on tour, it will settle into a rhythm, and you'll have a lot of down time, time to work on your own things. And I hope you'll enjoy being part of it."

"I'm sure I will, Taylor. If I didn't think so, I would never have said 'yes'. So, quit worrying so much. I promise, I'll let you know when you're becoming a slave driver."

         *   *   *

After dinner, Taylor drove her back to the hotel. As they walked down the hall to the suite, Taylor said, "I want to try to get you oriented a little to Tampa tomorrow, at least so you can find your way back and forth to the Performing Arts Center from here. I'm borrowing a car from my agent and leaving you the Jag starting tomorrow evening."

Laura stopped as she was opening the door. "Taylor, I cannot drive your car! That thing's worth a fortune."

Taylor reached past her and pushed open the door. "It's a car, Laura. A thing. There's nothing you can do to it that's going to upset me unless you get yourself hurt." He stayed in the hall as she went into the room. "Get some rest, Laura. I'll pick you up about 8:30 tomorrow." He waved as he turned and headed back down the hallway as she closed the door behind her.

33

Laura had slept better than she had expected. Her internal clock tried to tell her it was too early when the alarm went off and she realized that making time adjustments might be the hardest part of this. Still, she was excited about the day and was ready long before Taylor arrived to pick her up.

On the way, he pointed out various landmarks until he pulled into the vast complex that made up the Tampa Performing Arts Center. Taking Laura to the security desk, he introduced her, got her a security pass, and then led her through a series of hallways that seemed to twist and turn and go on forever. Within minutes, she was thoroughly lost. Finally, they came into a large, mirrored rehearsal hall. Clustered around a piano was a group doing vocal exercises. A couple of the vocalists waved at Taylor as he led the way toward a man seated in a corner, bent over a sheaf of papers.

"Daniel?"

The man looked up and got to his feet, "Morning, Taylor. This must be Laura," He held out his hand to shake hers as he continued, "I'm Daniel Li, Taylor's director and ringmaster of this circus." A shrill whistle near her ear pierced the air; startled, she looked at Taylor, realizing it had come from him. The room went quiet, and Taylor said, "Good morning, everyone, I want you to meet Laura Collins, my new assistant.

She's in charge of my life now, so you can take all your problems to her, but please not too soon! I want to keep her around."

Taylor turned back to her as everyone returned to what they had been doing. "Why don't you sit here with Daniel? Don't worry too much about taking notes this morning. Just try to get a feel for this." Flashing her a smile, he went and joined the group warming-up.

Daniel smiled at her, "He's right, Laura. Just hang out here for this morning. I think you'll quickly get an idea of what's happening. Don't be afraid to stop me and ask if something isn't making sense. I'm glad you're here. Taylor is in desperate need of a keeper!"

As Laura sat down and got out a notebook from her bag, Daniel raised his voice, "All right, people. Playtime's over. Let's get to work!"

*   *   *

The morning passed quickly, and Laura was surprised when Daniel called a lunch break. She had a page full of notes, most of which she didn't remember writing down. Taylor stayed behind with the pianist as the others left the area they had designated as "stage." The three female vocalists came over to Laura and one of them said, "I'm Maggie; this is Judy and Lois. Would you like to come to lunch with us, Laura?"

"Thanks, but I'd best check with Taylor. I'm not sure what he needs me to do."

Maggie turned and called to Taylor, "Taylor! We're taking Laura with us for lunch, ok?"

He glanced up briefly, nodded and waved, and then turned back to the discussion he was having with the pianist.

She turned back to Laura, "There. That's settled. Let's go."

They walked to a nearby restaurant, and once they had ordered, they began to get to know each other.

"Where did Taylor find you, Laura?" Maggie asked.

"Actually, I interviewed him when the tour was in Albuquerque a few months ago."

"That's why you look familiar!" Lois exclaimed. "You went to that fund-raiser party with him. But, how did you end up here?"

"Taylor and I hit it off and have been corresponding since then. I was ready to take a leave from the paper, and Taylor offered me this chance, so I took it. I'll be doing some freelance writing on my own while we travel."

Judy said, "Taylor's been doing a lot of traveling lately. He disappeared right after rehearsals started. He was gone a couple of days with no warning or explanation. That's not like him at all."

"He must have had his reasons. He's certainly been working hard enough to make up for it," Maggie said.

The conversation turned towards general get-acquainted topics. By the time lunch was over, Laura felt very much like she was a part of the group instead of an outsider.

*   *   *

The afternoon rehearsal flew by as quickly as the morning had. Daniel called a halt at four and reminded everyone to be back in at nine tomorrow. They drifted out a few at a time, and Taylor came over to sit next to Laura as Daniel conferred with the accompanist for a few minutes. The energy that had surrounded Taylor all day was suddenly gone, and he looked exhausted. Still, he smiled at her and said, "So, Laura, are you going to stay, or have we driven you away already?"

"I think I can tough it out for awhile longer, Taylor."

Taylor noticed the page of notes in front of her and reached out and took it, reading them as Daniel, carrying his ever-present notebook, came back to join them. Laura felt slightly panicked as Taylor read the notes. She would have preferred to organize them a little and make sure she had a clear idea of what she had been trying to say.

"Laura, these are good. Daniel, take a look," he said as he handed the page to the director. Daniel skimmed over the notes, referring back to his in a couple of places before he said, "Taylor's right, Laura. These are good. You have a good eye and a good feel for what works. It's going to be a big help having a fresh viewpoint while we're doing the fine-tuning. Let's go over these so we can get out of here for today."

Their discussion took another hour. At first, Laura had merely listened until they brought up a point she felt strongly about. As she explained her opinion, both men heard her out, and she finally won her point. With that, she became a full member of the team that was running the show.

*   *   *

"Can you stand having dinner with me again, Laura?" Taylor asked as they left the center for the car.

"I think I can manage it, Taylor, but you must be exhausted. Why don't you just drop me at the hotel, and I can fend for myself."

"I have to eat something, so we might as well be together. Besides, we have to go pick up the car I'm borrowing."

"Taylor, I told you...."

"No argument, Laura. You need to have transportation."

"Fine, Taylor, but I want it in writing that I'm not responsible for damage to the Jag."

Taylor laughed as he opened the door for her. As his eyes met hers, he had an overwhelming need to kiss her. This wasn't going to be easy, he thought, as he got into the car and pulled out of the parking lot.

The rest of the week passed quickly. As he had promised, Taylor had a couple of solo sessions, giving Laura time to explore the city a little. After one of those rehearsals, Taylor and Daniel had gone out for a drink.

"You should be sending up burnt offerings to the gods, Taylor," Daniel said.

"Really? I thought things were going better than that."

"Things are going very well. I meant you should be offering thanks for Laura. She's been amazing."

Taylor smiled in satisfaction. "She has, hasn't she?" he said a trifle smugly.

Daniel hesitated, then asked, "Was she the reason you took off a few weeks ago?"

Taylor played with his glass before answering. "Yes. She was going through some real changes in her life—not all of them good. I went to see if I could help, and it turned out this was the best way to do it. Lucky for us."

Daniel thought about their conversation on his way home. He would bet anything that Taylor was in love with Laura. He wasn't sure if Laura felt the same, although he had caught her staring at Taylor more than once, with a faraway look in her eyes. He hoped whatever was between them continued to work, because the last thing he needed was a star that was unhappy.

*   *   *

After Friday's rehearsal, Daniel gave them Saturday off. "You've all been working hard and it's going well. You deserve a break. Just don't be late on Monday!"

As had become their routine, Taylor and Laura stayed behind to meet with Daniel. Considering that they would be moving into the Center's Jaeb Theatre on Monday, and be adding lights and orchestra, they had a lot of notes to cover. It was after seven by the time they finished. Daniel wished them a good weekend and told them to call him "only on pain of death."

Taylor walked with Laura out to the parking lot that was beginning to fill with the evening's theatergoers. As he opened the car door for her, he said, "Dinner?"

"Taylor, I'm too tired. I just want to go back, take a shower, and crawl into bed. I'm sorry."

"Nothing to be sorry for, Laura. I'm pretty beat, too, and would have been poor company."

"We should get together tomorrow sometime. I have your mail ready for you, and I need to discuss a couple of other things about the tour."

"Why don't you come to my place in the morning? I would warn you not to come too early, but I know that won't be a problem," Taylor teased her gently.

"If you're asking if I'm sleeping late in the morning, then the answer is 'yes'. I have no intention of getting up early, but I should be awake and ready to go by eleven or so. How's that?"

"Sounds perfect. I'll see you then. Good night, Laura." He closed the door to the Jag and watched as she drove away before he left in his borrowed vehicle.

34

Taylor had stopped the night before and picked up the makings for omelets, then called and left a message for Laura that he would fix brunch for them whenever she got there. Since he was home so seldom, it required only a quick picking up to make the condo presentable.

As he waited for her to arrive, Taylor sat out on the deck. He had been able to see changes in her already this week. The haunted look in her eyes was fading, and she had begun to laugh more. When she had arrived, she had taken to wearing her hair in a tight braid. Yesterday was the first time he had seen it loosely pulled back into a ponytail, a much more relaxed style that seemed to reflect her changing feelings.

He heard the sound of the Jag pulling into the drive and went through the house and opened the front door.

"You and the Jag look like you belong together."

Laura laughed as she got out of the car. "I'm glad you feel that way. I'm just about ready to take you up on the offer to trade for my Opel."

To keep the light that was shining in her eyes, Taylor would have given her the car without another thought. "Do you always take polite conversation so seriously?" he asked.

"Only when it's to my advantage." Laura picked up a pile of folders from the passenger seat and came to the door. She was acutely aware of Taylor standing in the doorway wearing a light sweater and khaki slacks, his bare feet in loafers, the sun shining on his hair. She was surprised to find that she was still attracted to him; that she could be attracted to anyone after what Cary had done.

"Here, give me those," Taylor said as he took the folders out of her arms. "I thought we were supposed to have today off."

"The rest of them do. You and I have to make some order out of this chaos."

"Can it wait until after we eat?"

"I think we're going to need the energy! And, besides, I'm starving."

Taylor dropped the folders on the coffee table, then poured two glasses of fresh orange juice. Handing her one, he led the way to the deck. The light breeze caught her hair and teased tendrils loose, and he had to fight to keep himself from reaching out to touch them.

"It's a beautiful view, Taylor."

"That's the main reason I bought it. The rest of the place is pretty nondescript, but the view makes up for it. Are you finally getting used to Florida?"

"Everything except the humidity. Sometimes I feel like I'm trying to breathe underwater, but I talked to Mom and Dad last night, and they were having a late snowstorm. I certainly didn't envy them."

They moved back into the condo where Taylor put her to work slicing ingredients to fill the omelets. They found that they worked well together, and Taylor was amazed at how much her presence changed the feel of the condo. For the first time, it felt like a home.

*   *   *

After brunch, Laura made him sit down and look at the various folders. "The top one is the letters I think you should take time to answer. The others are in varying degrees of importance.

Taylor finished leafing through the first file, then quickly scanned the others. "It looks to me like you have a really good feel for how all of this should be handled. I'll try to get these answered tonight so we can send them out before we leave Tampa. You'll take care of the others?"

"If you're happy with that, I can. Are you sure you don't want to look at them more closely, Taylor?"

He closed the folders and put them on the table. "I trust your judgment, Laura. You should, too. You said there were some tour things you wanted to discuss?"

Laura took a notebook out of her bag. Taylor was surprised to realize it was an organized plan for the tour. "Good Lord, Laura! When did you have time to do this?" He took the notebook from her and looked through it. She had sections for everything from the itinerary to the emergency contacts for the entire cast, musicians, and crew.

"It really didn't take very long. There are a lot of details, Taylor. I decided that getting it organized from the start would be the most help." Taking the notebook back from him, she turned to a section labeled "Publicity."

"This is probably well outside the realm of my responsibilities, but who is handling your publicity?"

"Actually, my agent's office handles all of that."

"You don't have a separate publicist?"

"No. It didn't seem like there was a need. Why, Laura?"

"Taylor, when you came to Albuquerque, we received very little advance information. And I had a devil of a time trying to set up an interview with you. I think you're being terribly under-publicized, and I'd like to do some advance work with the media in the towns where we will be stopping."

"Laura, I hate interviews."

"Then get over it, Taylor! It's part of your job!"

Laura heard herself and realized she had probably just crossed a line. He had said she was in charge of his life. Now was the time to see how much he was willing to relinquish to her.

Suddenly, Taylor laughed—great, loud, whoops of laughter. "Oh, Laura, what have I gotten myself into with you? Fine. Set up the publicity you think I need. I'll notify my agent's office that all publicity requests need to be routed through you. We'll try it your way for awhile."

*   *   *

It had been a good day—an extremely good day—Taylor thought as he waved to Laura and came back inside. Once they had finished with the business she had brought, he proposed driving over to St. Petersburg and the beaches. They had taken the Jag and Laura teased him about giving him the keys to "her" car. They had a wonderful time walking along the beaches and talking. The ease that they'd felt with each other at their first meeting was still evident, and they had never run out of things to talk about. When his hand had brushed hers as they walked, she hadn't pulled away. They'd ended up at Hurricane's for dinner, watching the sunset over the Gulf. A perfect day as far as he was concerned.

She would pick him up in the morning to go to brunch with Annie and Meg. He knew if he showed up without the convertible, Meg would be very unhappy with him. If all was well between Annie and Laura, then he planned on taking Meg out for awhile.

Annie and Laura. He admitted to himself that he was nervous about this meeting. When Annie had met Janis, it had been only one step short of a catfight. They had hated each other on sight, and he was still at a loss to explain what had set them off. Janis' attitude towards Meg had been particularly condescending. He couldn't believe he had been so blind.

Laura was a world apart from Janis. Annie would like her. At least he fervently hoped she would.

Taylor noticed a folder still on the coffee table. Laura must have missed one when she left. He picked it up and opened it to find a note from her.

Taylor,

> Here are the first of what I hope will be a series of arti-
> cles. My old editor is interested in buying them for the
> *Herald*. I want you to read them. Let me know if you're
> comfortable with the idea. If you're not, I put them in my
> practice files. After all, you are the main subject.
>
> Laura

He put the folder down and poured a glass of wine. Taking a chair near the window, he turned on the lamp and sat down to read.

> How did I end up traveling with a superstar's road show?
> Like many of you, I have wondered what it must be
> like to be on the road, living out of a suitcase, a new
> hotel every night. Through an amazing series of coinci-
> dences, I now have the chance to find out, and I thought
> I would take you along for the trip.

Taylor smiled as he read the rest of the article and the following two that she had already written. She had caught the essence of what had been happening and had packaged it neatly into words that made the reader feel a part of it all. There were even a few things he hadn't known about. Laura was about to take her readers on the trip of a lifetime.

35

Laura was nervous about meeting Annie. This woman was so important to Taylor. What if Annie didn't like her? What if she didn't like Annie? And then there was Meg. Taylor was the only father Meg had ever known. She would have to resent anyone who might be coming between them.

"Get a grip, Laura!" she muttered to herself as she pulled her favorite green outfit out of the closet. Talking to herself again—not a good sign. Suddenly, she was terribly homesick for Beth. She had been Laura's sounding board for so long. She promised herself that, if she survived today, she would call Beth tonight.

Besides worrying about Annie, Laura wondered how Taylor had felt about the articles she had left for him to read. She had been pleased, but wasn't sure how he would feel about them. And she wasn't sure how she would handle it if he didn't like them.

As she put on the earrings Taylor had given her, she looked at her reflection in the mirror. The circles that had ringed her eyes for the last month had disappeared. The bruising was gone from her wrists and there were no outward signs of the devastation she had felt such a short time ago. Now if only the nightmares would go away. Shaking her head at her reflection, Laura headed out the door. Whatever was going to happen today was going to happen. There was no sense in worrying about it.

*   *   *

Annie was watching from a window as Taylor pulled into the driveway. For a moment, she stayed hidden instead of going to the door, watching as a tall, beautiful, redhead got out of the car when Taylor opened the door for her. Annie recognized the strained lines on Laura's face, the nervousness in her eyes, the light flush on her face…recognized them because she had seen the same signs on her own face when she had checked the mirror a few minutes ago. Laura was as nervous as she was about this meeting. Taylor said something to Laura that made her smile. He seemed to be the only one who was taking this meeting in stride.

As she left her room and headed for the door, she called to Meg. "They're here." No dark-haired figure came bolting out the way she usually did when Taylor was expected. Annie sighed. Meg had been in a snit ever since Annie had told her that Taylor was bringing Laura. She had been sulking in her room all morning.

There was no time to go argue with her again. Taylor knocked on the door and opened it as Annie came across the room. Taylor hugged her, then turned and introduced Laura. As the two women greeted each other, he looked for Meg.

"Annie?"

"She's in her room, Taylor. She's not very happy with you right now."

"Because of Laura?" Taylor was genuinely astonished. It had never occurred to him that Meg might not welcome her.

"Taylor!" Annie's tone scolded him. "Don't do this to Laura. Meg will come out when her curiosity gets the best of her."

Laura was intensely uncomfortable. "Taylor, why don't I just go and come back and pick you up later? You need this time with Meg."

Annie answered her. "Absolutely not, Laura! My daughter needs to learn some manners. Despite her behavior, I'm happy to meet you and am glad you're here."

Taylor, his eyes stormy, said, "Annie's right. And I'm going to go talk to Meg right now." Before either of them could say anything, he strode down the hall, knocked on Meg's door, then went in, closing the door behind him.

Annie looked at Laura who looked back at her helplessly. At the same moment, the two of them said, "I'm so sorry!"

"There's nothing for you to be sorry for, Laura. Taylor and Meg will work it out."

"Still, I feel badly that she's unhappy. I tried to convince Taylor that he needed to come alone."

"And he's not easy to convince, is he?" Annie's face was illuminated by her grin.

"Not at all," Laura replied, recognizing a friend in Annie. "Maybe you can give me some pointers to help keep him in line the next few weeks."

Laughing, the two women moved out to the deck, at ease with each other.

*   *   *

"Megan…"

Meg knew Taylor was mad. He never called her Megan unless he was. But she didn't care. He was leaving town in a few days, he would be gone forever, and he had brought this stranger into what should have been their time.

Taylor stood at the door for a moment. Meg was studiously ignoring him, her head bent over a notebook on her desk, a book propped up in front of her. He walked over to the desk, picked up the book and turned it right side up. "This would be a lot more effective, Meg, if you looked like you could really be using it." He took the pen from her hand, closed the notebook, and turned her around on her swivel chair so she was facing him as he sat on the edge of her bed.

"What's this all about, Meg?"

"If you don't know, Taylor, then there's no point in telling you."

"Oh, I know all right. I just wanted to hear you say it. But I'll do it for you since you insist. You're angry with me because I brought Laura along today. You're jealous of someone you don't even know."

"I am not jealous."

"Yes, you are, Megan Elizabeth. And I'm really disappointed in you."

Meg looked at him from beneath her bangs. He was really angry with her. "Taylor! Why did you have to bring her? You're supposed to be spending time with me and with Mom. We don't need to have to share you with her!"

"Meg, how many times have I taken your friends along with us on some outing? Remember the last time I took you to the stables? You simply had to have Emily and Dante go with you. And I didn't object because I didn't mind. I was taking you there in the first place because it made you happy. If having them along made you happier, that was fine with me."

He reached out and lifted her chin so she was looking into his eyes. "Meg, Laura is my friend. You're my friend. Is it so terrible to want my friends to like each other? Besides, she's moved all the way here and has no one else. All of her family and friends are back in New Mexico. And I care about her enough to want to make her feel welcome. Something that you're really not helping with, Meg."

She knew he was right, but admitting it wasn't something she wanted to do. Instead, she twisted her head away, freeing her chin from his hand, then turned her back on him.

"Meg, don't be this way. I can care about Laura, and I can care about you. Neither takes away from the other. I'm going back out there now, and I hope you'll come join us. But, if you don't, Meg, it's your decision and your responsibility."

She listened to the sound of his footsteps crossing the room. The door opened, then closed, and his footsteps faded away while tears ran soundlessly down her cheeks.

*   *   *

Taylor stopped in the kitchen and fixed himself a glass of lemonade. It bought him a few minutes to compose himself. He really hadn't anticipated Meg would react this way. If she were this upset because he had brought Laura today, what would Meg do when he married her?

Annie and Laura's mingled laughter drew him to the door. Annie saw him and put a finger to her lips to hush Laura. Laura turned, and the two of them tried to look innocent. "Why do I get the feeling this was a total mistake?" he asked as he pushed open the door and joined them. His question just sent them off into laughter again. He tried to look stern, but it was hard when he was so pleased to see that they liked each other.

*　　　　*　　　　*

Meg listened to the distant sound of their voices and laughter. Taylor was right, of course, he usually was. She *was* jealous of Laura. He had rushed off to see her in December and, now, he'd brought her here and was taking her on the tour with him. If he liked her enough—if he loved her—they'd get married and *she* probably wouldn't want Taylor to see them again. It would be like a divorce. Enough of her friends had that problem with their stepmothers. If only Taylor and her mother…sighing tragically, Meg went and washed her face, then went out to meet her enemy.

*　　　　*　　　　*

Taylor saw her first. "There you are, Meg. Come out and join us." As she came out on the deck, Taylor held out his hand to her. "Meg, I'd like you to meet Laura. Laura, this is Meg."

Laura was beautiful! She looked perfectly matched to Taylor as she rose to meet Meg. All of Meg's fantasies about Taylor and her mother crumbled, and she politely said, "It's nice to meet you, Laura. Taylor said you helped pick out my bracelet. It's lovely. Thank you."

Taylor met Annie's eyes. This wasn't their Meg. She was too reserved and grown-up.

"Hello, Meg. I'm glad to finally get to meet you. Taylor talks about you all the time. I was beginning to get jealous."

Jealous? This incredibly beautiful woman was jealous of her? Meg took a seat at the end of the chaise lounge that her mother occupied and listened while the grown-ups talked.

She noticed that, even though Laura was in the love seat, Taylor had taken another chair across from her. And he seemed to be paying equal attention to both of the women. Maybe all her worrying had been for nothing.

*   *   *

Over brunch, Taylor told Annie that Laura was going to be writing a series of articles about the tour. "I've read the first three, and they're really good. I had no idea that some of that stuff was going on behind my back."

"Then you need to pay more attention, Taylor," Laura said. "None of it is a big secret—except how the cast feels about you, of course. Wait until I get to that subject!"

By the time brunch was over, Meg had to admit that Laura wasn't as bad as she'd expected. At least she didn't talk to her like she was a baby the way that Janis-woman had. Laura seemed to be genuinely interested in what she had to say. And she didn't act like she was in love with Taylor. When Laura teased him, it was pretty much the same way her mother treated him. Maybe it would be all right after all.

As they began to clear the table, Laura said, "Taylor? Why don't you and Meg go on and do whatever it is you have planned. I'll help Annie with the dishes."

Taylor looked at Annie for permission. "Go on. Not too late, Taylor. School tomorrow."

Meg and Taylor solemnly chorused, "Yes, ma'am," before Meg ran off to get ready. As Annie went back out to bring in more dishes, Taylor stopped Laura and said, "Thanks."

"She's just worried about losing you, Taylor. I'd be jealous, too, if someone tried to steal my father away from me."

Annie caught the look that passed between them as she came back into the kitchen. If Taylor wasn't already in love with Laura, he was heading that way fast, and it looked as if Laura felt the same way. Annie was pleased. She'd never liked Taylor being so much alone.

Meg reappeared in the doorway. "Taylor! Are we going or not?"

"We're going, Meg. We should be back by five, ladies. Annie, please don't tell Laura too many of my secrets while I'm gone!"

36

Annie and Laura finished the dishes, then moved back out onto the deck.

"I still can't get used to how warm it is here. I spoke to my parents last night and it was snowing there. That's unusual for this time of year, but it's still heavy sweater weather, at least!"

"I hated New York for that very reason. I never could get used to the cold. When Meg was born, I just wanted to come home and raise her here. I'm sorry you had such a rude introduction to her."

"Annie, stop apologizing. Meg's great. I can remember being much the same way when I was her age. Taylor obviously adores her and she returns it."

"I don't know what we would have done without him all this time. He's been more of a father to her than her blood parent would have been."

"Taylor told me some of what happened."

"Did he tell you he saw through Cary? I was the only one blind enough to miss all his imperfections."

Laura's face went white. Cary? Oh, God, no!

"Laura? Are you all right?" Annie's face was filled with concern.

"I'm fine, Annie. I just knew someone named Cary. He was a news anchor in Albuquerque."

"I've lost track of him, but he started in the news business in New York. It's all he ever wanted, so I imagine that's what he's still doing. His name was Cary Edwards."

Laura willed her voice not to shake as she replied, "That's him then. Meg has his coloring and those same blue eyes."

Annie could see that Laura was shaken. "Yes, it would have been easier if she had looked like me. She doesn't know any of the truth about him. She just knows he left before she was born." Concerned about Laura, Annie changed the subject. "Those years in New York weren't all bad. They were incredibly good for Taylor. I began a scrapbook of our notices then and continued it for Taylor. Would you like to see it—well, them, actually. He's long since filled up that first book and several others."

"Yes, I'd like that," Laura said, her mind whirling. *Annie* was Cary's ex-wife? The one he had beaten while she was pregnant if she believed Taylor. The wife that Taylor had stolen if she believed Cary. But she *didn't* believe Cary. She realized now that he had made all of it up about Taylor and Annie to keep her from getting involved with Taylor. Dazed, she followed Annie into the house.

* * *

Meg had asked if they could just go for a drive today. Taylor was happy to oblige and put a classical CD into the player. They let the music and the sunshine and fresh air wash over them. He could see Meg relaxing next to him. After a little while, Taylor pulled into a beach parking lot. "C'mon, Meg, I feel like walking awhile."

She wandered along a few steps behind or in front of him, picking up seashells here and there. Finally, he said, "Meg, come sit down. We need to talk."

Reluctantly, she came over and sat next to him. He took her hand in his before he said, "Meg? Do you want to tell me what's really bothering you about Laura?"

She was quiet for a long time before she finally asked, "Are you in love with her, Taylor?"

"I don't know, Meg. I might be, but we haven't known each other very long. We need more time to get to know each other. Does it worry you that I might be?"

"What if you marry her and she doesn't want you to see us anymore?"

"She's not like that, Meg."

"But a lot of my friends…their dads stopped seeing them because their new wives didn't want the kids around."

"I can see that it could worry you. I promise, Meg, if I ever do marry someone, she won't be someone who would stop me from seeing you. You're my family, and she'd have to accept you as part of the deal."

"Taylor? Why aren't we enough family for you?"

"Oh, Meg, that's so hard to answer. Love is a difficult thing to explain."

"It's stupid, too. I swear, Taylor, I'm never going to fall in love with anyone!"

"I'll remind you of that, Meg, just before I walk you down the aisle," he said as he stood and extended a hand to her. "How about right now, I walk you down the beach and we'll eat enough ice cream to spoil our dinner?"

Meg giggled at him. "Taylor, you are so silly."

"I am that, Miss Meg. And I probably always will be."

*   *   *

Taylor watched as Laura drove away from the condo. Something had been wrong when he and Meg had returned to the house. Laura had seemed withdrawn and distracted, so he had suggested they leave soon after. He had the feeling Laura was very relieved when he had suggested it.

There had been no chance to question Annie, and he decided to call her now. He needed to talk to her about what had happened while he was gone, and he needed to talk to her about these mysterious headaches Meg had mentioned on their way home from the beach.

She had told him that her mother hadn't been feeling well. "She's having terrible headaches, Taylor. I don't know if she's seen the doctor yet, but I'm really worried about her. You know she won't tell me if something's wrong. Maybe she'll tell you."

He poured a glass of wine and opened the doors to the deck. Sitting where he could enjoy the view, he dialed Annie's number.

"Hi, Annie, it's me."

"Taylor! I'm glad you called. Is Laura all right?"

"I was going to ask you the same thing. What happened while we were gone? You two were on your way to being best friends when I left, but Laura had turned into a stranger when I came back."

"Taylor, I don't know! We were talking about you and Meg and the subject of Cary came up. When I mentioned his name, she went white. It turned out she knew him in New Mexico! He was a news anchor there. At least I think it was him. There can't more than one Cary Edwards in the news business."

Taylor was silent long enough that Annie began to wonder if he had hung up. Finally she heard a whispered "Bastard," so she knew he was still there.

"Taylor?"

"Annie, Laura was dating some news guy. When I went out there for Christmas, I overheard people talking about her and him and the general consensus was that they were practically engaged. So, I left. Then, right after the first of the year, she disappeared. No phone, no e-mail. She quit her job. That was where I went last month." Annie could hear the anger in his voice as he went on. "She had disappeared because this man she'd been seeing had raped her."

It was Annie's turn to be silent.

"Laura's friend, Beth, was the one who told me. Laura doesn't know that I know. Beth wouldn't tell me his name. Annie, I never thought it could be *him*."

"Oh, God, Taylor! No wonder she reacted the way she did. She didn't press charges against him?"

"Laura told Beth it would never hold up in court, and she refused to put her parents through the trauma of a trial."

"Is he still there? In Albuquerque?" Taylor could hear a note of panic in her voice.

"No, Annie. Beth said he had left. Some big-time news job."

"He hasn't changed. I wonder how many other women besides Laura he's hurt."

"Annie, stop it. It's not your fault. Even if you had brought charges against him, he would have gotten a slap on the wrist. You are not responsible for what he was then or what he is now!"

"I know, Taylor. I just wish…" Annie's voice trailed off.

"I know, Annie, I know. I'll call you tomorrow to let you know how she is."

"Taylor?"

"What, Annie?"

"You're in love with her, aren't you?"

"I have been from the minute I met her, I think. That's really why I went back out there. I'd decided not to give her up gracefully. But, instead of being able to tell her how I feel, I have to help her put the pieces of her life back together first."

"Well, she couldn't have found anyone better to help her do that. It will be all right, Taylor. Don't give up on her."

"Thanks, Annie. Goodnight."

He hung up the phone and walked out onto the deck. The sun was gone, and there was a chill in the air, but Taylor didn't feel it. All he could think of was that the same man had hurt both of the women he loved. And he was powerless to do anything about it. It wasn't until much later that he realized he hadn't asked Annie about the headaches.

*   *   *

"Hi, Beth. It's me."

"Laura! How are you? What's happening? How's the show? You're still in Florida, right?"

Laura couldn't help laughing. "Slow down, Beth! I can't answer everything at once. Tell me what's happening there first."

As Beth filled her in, Laura was grateful for the normalcy of her report; the gossip about people they both knew, new stories of Henry's curmudgeon act. The afternoon with Annie had been surreal. She kept thinking she must have dreamed it, but she knew better.

"Laura?" Suddenly she became aware that Beth had asked her a question.

"Beth, I'm sorry, what did you ask?"

"Never mind, Laura. What's wrong?"

"Nothing, Beth."

"Laura Collins, don't even try lying to me. You know you can't get away with it." Beth's voice went from lecture to concern as she continued, "There's something wrong. Tell me."

*　　　　　*　　　　　*

Annie went in to say goodnight to Meg. She was suddenly aware of how much her daughter looked like Cary with her coal black hair and midnight blue eyes. She really hadn't thought about him in years. He had never been a part of their lives. All she wanted to do was forget about him. Why she had come up with his name this afternoon was something she couldn't explain.

"Mom? Why are you staring at me?"

Annie shook off the memories. "I was just noticing how tall you're getting. By next year, you'll be taller than me, I bet."

"Well, Mom," Meg said with an impish grin, "being taller than you isn't going to be hard."

"Oh, yeah? I may be small, but I still know everything there is to know about you. Don't get too smart, miss. I have videotapes of you as a baby that I'm just saving to show your first boyfriend."

"Mom!" It was amazing how a three-letter word could be stretched out into multisyllables.

"Meg!" Annie answered in the same drawn-out tone. "Into bed, miss."

Annie pulled the light blanket up over her daughter and sat beside her on the bed. "Are you okay about Laura, now?"

Meg made a face, then said, "I guess so. Taylor thinks he might be in love with her."

"Did he tell you that?"

"Well, I asked, and then he told me."

"It's not a bad thing, Meg."

"I know. But I don't want things to change. If he marries her...."

"If he marries her, you and I will dance at their wedding and be happy for them."

"I just wish...."

"I know, Meg." Annie smoothed the hair away from Meg's face and kissed her. "Goodnight."

"'Night, Mom."

Annie closed Meg's door and went to her own room. Standing on a chair, she reached far back into the closet, to a top shelf, and pulled down a box. Sitting on the bed, she opened it and took out the tangible proof of her life with Cary. There wasn't much; their marriage license and divorce papers, her wedding ring, and a few newspaper clippings. She had kept these things because someday Meg would ask about him, and she had a right to know what her father looked like even if Annie hoped she never found out what he had been like.

In the bottom of the box was their wedding picture. They couldn't afford a professional photographer, so Taylor had taken it. She no longer recognized herself in the free-spirited girl who was gazing adoringly at the almost sullen groom. As she looked at him, she felt the beginnings of a headache, and she hated it that he still could affect her this way.

        *   *   *

Beth had listened silently as Laura told her of the incredible connection between Cary and Taylor.

"Beth, I barely could get through the rest of the afternoon. I kept thinking about the things Cary had done to his pregnant wife. Annie is small like you, Beth. He could have easily made her lose the baby or seriously hurt her. And the things he did to me. Why is he still being allowed to walk the streets?"

Beth refrained from pointing out that Laura had helped contribute to his freedom by not pressing charges. Annie had, too, and so had Taylor back then.

"Laura? Are you going to be all right?"

"I will be, Beth. This week is going to be very busy. And we leave next weekend for New York. There's not going to be much time to think about it. It's just it was all such a shock!"

"Laura? Have you thought about telling Taylor the truth?"

"No, Beth. He doesn't need to know. Thanks for listening. I really wish you weren't so far away."

"I'm always just as far away as your phone, Laura. You know that."

"I know, Beth, and it helps. Goodnight."

Hanging up the phone, Laura sat silent for a few minutes, then said, aloud, "Damn you, Cary. You're not going to wreck my life." Resolutely, she picked up her notebook, and turning to the section for publicity, she began to make plans for the calls she would make tomorrow.

37

Laura seemed to be fine the next morning when they met at the center. In fact, she was an oasis of calm in the center of the storm that was happening with their move from the rehearsal hall to the theatre. Taylor had no time to worry further about her as they dealt with one crisis after another.

She spent a good part of the day in the control booth at the rear of the theatre. She could watch and make her notes from there while she was using the phone to beef up his publicity appearances. When the end of the day finally came, it was an exhausted trio that met to go over their notes.

"Taylor, I don't know about you and Laura, but I am simply too tired to think right now. How would you feel about meeting early tomorrow before rehearsal?"

"I think it sounds like a good idea, Daniel. It's been way too long a day already."

"Fine, let's pack it in then," Daniel said as he closed his notebook. "I'll see you two in the morning."

Taylor and Laura walked out together. "How are you, Laura? I feel like I haven't seen you all day."

"I'm fine, Taylor. I was able to schedule some interviews, and we'll need to go over them as well. Can we try for dinner tomorrow? That way I can make any changes you want."

"Tomorrow should be better. We'll plan on it. Goodnight, Laura."

As he drove home, he realized he needed to call Annie. She was expecting a report on Laura. But, after a shower, the temptation to lie down for awhile proved to be too much. He closed his eyes and was asleep almost instantly, not waking until morning, never hearing the phone when Annie tried to reach him.

*   *   *

The next day was almost as chaotic as the one before. Starting earlier had only served to make the day longer, and the last thing Taylor wanted to discuss was the new publicity schedule. As Laura set it out for him over dinner, he finally just closed the folder she had given him.

"Laura, I'm sorry. Just set up whatever you think is best. I'll do them all. Right now, I just want to stop thinking about the tour in any form."

They finished their dinner in silence, then went their separate ways.

*   *   *

The third time proved to be the proverbial charm. Rehearsal ran like clockwork, music, lights, costumes all finally coming together. By the end of Friday's rehearsal, everyone was feeling good about the imminent tour.

"That's it then, people. I think we have a show," Daniel said as he dismissed them on Friday afternoon. "I will see all of you bright and early on Monday morning in New York."

As the others left, Daniel turned to Taylor. "So, what are you doing for your last day of freedom, Taylor?"

"Same thing you are, Daniel—packing! I'll see you Monday morning. Thanks for pulling this all together."

Daniel waved away the thanks as he headed out the door. Taylor glanced up at the control booth and caught a glimpse of Laura's bright hair. He produced a piercing whistle that brought her to the door. "The day's over, Laura. Let's go!"

She waved at him and then returned to gather up her notebook and folders. Coming down the aisle to him, she said, "Sorry. I just got off the phone. I really wish you would take a serious look at the publicity schedule I've put together, especially the New York segment."

"I will tomorrow, I promise. I plan on going to Annie's for awhile, but there should still be time to look at it."

"Have fun. I need to do some shopping before we leave on Sunday. How do you want to handle getting to the airport?"

"Arrange a car and driver, Laura. You can bring the car over, and they can pick us both up at my place.

"I'll see you then, Taylor. Have a good Saturday."

*   *   *

There was a message from Annie waiting when he got home. When he called her back, she said, "Taylor, Meg's sick. She has this flu that all the kids are passing around. You'd best not come out tomorrow."

"Annie, that's my last chance to see you for awhile."

"I know, but you don't want to be around Meg to catch this stuff. It's not going to go over well with your audience to have you barf on stage."

"Lovely image, Annie! But, you're right. Tell Meg I'll call her tomorrow." Remembering that he had not yet asked about her headaches, Taylor went on, "Annie?"

"Oh, no! Taylor, she's getting sick again. I have to go."

Taylor hung up the phone. While he was truly disappointed that he wouldn't be able to spend any time with them before he left, a day of peace and quiet certainly had its advantages.

38

Valentine's Day. Opening night in New York. As he dressed for the concert, Taylor thought back over the last few days.

The trip to New York had been uneventful. He had finally gone over the publicity schedule on the plane. It was more than he was used to doing, but Laura had planned out a balance of television and print interviews starting with the morning shows this week. She was doing an excellent job weeding out the requests and had worked with the president of his fan club to make sure all of their needs were addressed. She had even talked him into making a short appearance at the fan club's post-concert party tonight. As he tied his bow tie, he glanced down at the picture of his parents. "You would like her, Mom. You told me I would know when I found the right one, and you were right. I just wish you could be here for our wedding."

There was a knock at the door. "Five minutes, Taylor." Laura looked wonderful. She was wearing the same copper-colored outfit she had worn to the charity party in Albuquerque. "Is there anything you need?"

"I'm fine, Laura. How does it look out there?"

"Everyone seems to be ready to go. It's a full house. Your fan club is in the first five orchestra rows and they are beyond excited. So, be prepared!"

"Thanks, Laura." He turned away from the mirror and came over and put his hands lightly on her shoulders. He felt her tense at his touch, but didn't remove his hands. "I don't think I could have done this without you." He leaned down and lightly kissed her cheek as they heard the opening music begin. Smiling at her, he said, "They're playing my song. See you after the concert, Laura."

She watched him as he ran down the hall and up the stairs to the wings of the stage. She could still feel the gentle pressure of his hands and of his lips as she heard the audience erupt into frenzied applause as he made his entrance.

*   *   *

Laura watched the concert from the wings, amazed all over again at the tremendous presence that Taylor projected from the stage. No wonder his fans loved him. He had the perfect balance of flirting and story-telling and talent.

As he came offstage for the intermission, Laura handed him a bottle of water and followed him back to his dressing room. "It's going well, Laura, don't you think?"

"It couldn't be going any better, Taylor. It's perfect."

"Thanks," he said as he smiled at her. "I like knowing you're there. I can feel you watching."

She blushed, then said, "Is there anything you need, Taylor?"

To take you in my arms...to kiss away your fears...to make love to you 'til morning...All of those answers occurred to Taylor, but he only said, "No, I'll just rest for a minute."

"I'll call you when it's time," she said as she closed the door behind her.

*   *   *

It didn't seem possible, but the second half of the concert was even better than the first. Taylor was riding high on the enthusiasm of the audience. After his "final" number, Taylor came offstage and, without thinking, picked Laura off her feet and whirled her around before he kissed her. "This has been an incredible evening!" he said as he put her down and returned to the stage for the first of his encores.

Laura retreated to his dressing room where she tried to stop the shaking that his exuberance had begun. A part of her was thrilled with his kiss, but the larger part of her feelings had to do with being imprisoned in his arms, the helpless feeling as he kissed her. Looking into the mirror at the white face her makeup couldn't hide, Laura's eyes filled with tears. "Damn! Why can't I forget what happened and get on with my life?" she said to her reflection. "Why is it so hard?"

She heard the growing swell of applause and realized that Taylor was finished. He would be back here in a moment. Taking a tissue she carefully wiped the tears from her eyes and pulled herself together. It was a smiling Laura that greeted Taylor and Daniel as they came laughing into the dressing room.

"Congratulations, gentlemen!"

"Thank you, Laura," Daniel said as he swept her a bow. "We couldn't have done it without you."

"Nonsense, Daniel."

"No, Laura, Daniel's right. You were a big part of this. Welcome to show business."

"Taylor, you need to get changed so we can head over to the fan party. I promise, you don't have to stay there more than fifteen minutes."

"See what a slave driver she really is, Daniel?"

"Which is the main reason I'm glad she's your assistant, not mine," Daniel said as he ducked out the door.

*   *   *

As they came through the hallway to the rear entrance of the ballroom where the fan club was meeting, Taylor pulled off his overcoat and handed it to Laura. He was wearing jeans and a blazer with a turquoise shirt that matched his eyes. Before she went through the door to let the club president know that they were there, Laura stood on her toes to whisper in his ear, "If you're trying to impress them, Taylor, be sure you turn around at least once." Startled, he looked at her as she waved to him before going through the door. If he didn't know better, he would swear she was flirting with him. Consequently, his smile was even brighter than usual as he came through the door and greeted the crowd that was responsible for his success.

The reviews of the concerts in New York, combined with Laura's publicity schedule, resulted in sold-out concerts for the entire tour. Everything ran smoothly for Taylor, and he knew that was completely due to Laura. He'd had no idea what an incredible job she would do when he decided to ask her to take the job.

Most of the concerts had been in the East, but as they traveled to the final concerts in California, they stopped in Denver for two nights. As a surprise, Taylor flew Laura's parents and Beth from Albuquerque to join them. She had been thrilled, and the spontaneous hug she gave him was more than sufficient thanks.

Slowly, she had begun to relax, no longer jumping when someone touched her. At a run-through to get familiar with one of the theatres, he noticed her when they were taking a break. She was talking with some of the vocalists when one of them said something that set the whole group off in laughter. One of the male members of the orchestra put his arm around her as they stood there, and she didn't move away or seem to be uncomfortable. The healing process was slow, but he could see it happening.

The tour officially ended with a concert in Los Angeles, but it wasn't really over. After a week off, they would move to Catalina Island where there would be two more concerts that would be filmed and edited into a television special to be shown in the fall.

39

The various members of the ensemble had been full of their plans for the break. Some were flying home for a quick visit; others were planning on playing tourist. Laura had waited for Taylor to give her some idea of his plans. Since their break was falling as her parents were in Europe for a conference, she had made no plans to go back to Albuquerque. Beth was going to be gone, too, so she had no reason to make the trip.

Not only had Taylor not said anything, but he had been uncharacteristically withdrawn. The night before they began the final week of concerts, Laura had asked for some of his time, and they met for dinner in his suite.

"Taylor? What are your plans for the break?"

"I guess I should make some, shouldn't I? Are you going home?"

"No, Mom and Dad are in Europe. Beth has to go to her cousin's wedding in Ohio. I thought I would just find someplace out here and do nothing for a few days."

"Sounds pretty good to me. Any particular place in mind?"

"Not really. Taylor? Are you all right?" Laura's voice was concerned.

"I'm fine, Laura." He walked to the window before he continued. "The town I was born in is within a day's drive from here. I haven't been back since my parents' funeral."

Laura waited for him to continue, but it was a long time before he did. Turning to face her, he said, "I've been thinking about going back there, Laura, but I really don't want to do it alone. Could you give up a couple of your days of nothing to come with me?"

Laura hesitated. She had known for weeks now that she was in love with Taylor. What Cary had done hadn't changed that. The nightmares were gone, her body seemed to be coming alive again, but she wasn't ready to risk her feelings. Going with Taylor would be a definite risk.

She also knew that if she chose to let him know her feelings, she would have to tell the truth about what had happened to her. The thought still frightened her.

"Laura, it's all right if you say 'no,'" Taylor said gently.

"I don't know what to say, Taylor. It's not something I'd thought about."

"Then, please, think about it. I'll probably go either way, but it would be a help to have a friend with me." Suppressing his somber mood, he said, "I think I'm going to go for a swim. Want to come along?"

Begging off, she returned to her room where she called Beth.

                    *   *   *

"Hi, Beth, it's me!"

"Laura, I was just thinking about you! How are things in the jet set?"

"Pretty slow, actually. We start the last week of concerts tomorrow. Then a week off before we go film the special on Catalina. I was going to come home, but Mom and Dad are gone, and you're going to the wedding."

"Don't even mention the wedding to me! I don't know how I got roped into being a bridesmaid. She's chosen *bubblegum-pink* satin dresses, Laura! With big bows across the rump! I'm going to look like a giant wad of chewing gum!"

Laura laughed. "Be sure and send me pictures. I can't wait to see this outfit."

"Thanks so much for your support!" Beth was laughing, too. "Promise me that you'll chose something decent for me when you get married."

"I'll give some thought to it." Married. Not anytime soon, Laura thought.

"How are you, Laura?"

"I'm better, Beth."

"And Taylor?"

"Actually, he's why I'm calling. He asked me to spend part of the break with him, to go back to his hometown."

"Just the two of you?"

"Yes. Beth, I don't know what to do. I'm still in love with him. I figured that out almost right away. And I want to be with him, but…"

"But what, Laura?"

"Before I can make any kind of relationship with him, I'll have to tell him about Cary. And I'm afraid to."

"Afraid, Laura? What do you think he's going to do?"

"I don't know. It could go almost any way. He could be supportive. He could blame me. Beth, I don't know! I've never had to do anything like this before."

"He'll understand, Laura." Beth was tempted to tell her that he already knew, but that was Taylor's choice to make, not hers. "I know he'll understand."

"I wish I could be as sure as you are," she said quietly before changing the subject. "Enough of that. Tell me what's going on at home."

*   *   *

Taylor didn't understand why he felt so compelled to go back to Woodland. He had never really missed it before. He hadn't stayed in touch with most of his friends. The house had been sold long ago. He had never planned on going there again.

All of this could be traced back to Laura. Seeing her with her parents in Denver and listening to her relate small tidbits from their phone calls had made him acutely aware of the absence of family in his life. He called Annie and Meg at least once a week, but lately, that hadn't been enough.

Now that he had asked Laura to go with him, he was already beginning to regret it. Maybe she would turn him down.

*   *   *

She didn't turn him down, and a week later he found himself waiting for her in front of the hotel. As she came out and handed her case to the valet to place in the car, his heart lifted at the sight of her. She suddenly looked like the same woman he had spent the day with in Albuquerque what seemed like a lifetime ago.

"Taylor, what is it with you and sports cars?" Laura asked as she looked at the ice blue BMW roadster he had rented.

He opened the door for her, then came around to the driver's side before answering. "It's a guy thing, Laura. Bigger, better, stronger, faster...although bigger doesn't really work for this, does it?"

Laughing, she pulled a scarf from her purse and tied back her hair as he pulled out into the California sunshine.

*   *   *

Woodland hadn't changed much in the years he had been gone. It was still a small community in the middle of the farmlands around it. There were a few more fast-food restaurants than he remembered, but it was mostly the same. He was surprised at the sense of homecoming he felt as he drove into town. He pointed out various landmarks to Laura as he drove.

"That's the high school up ahead. It looks smaller than I remember it," he said, sounding surprised.

"I know the feeling. I had to do a report about my old high school shortly after I started with the *Herald*. I couldn't believe how much smaller it seemed, how young the students looked."

The sign in front of the school announced that *Our Town* would be playing that night. "I wonder who's teaching drama here now," Taylor said as they drove by.

A few blocks later, he turned down a quiet, tree-lined residential street and came to a stop in front of a two-story, wood-framed house. The yellow paint had faded, and the white trim was beginning to peel. The grass was too long, and the gardens were overgrown. There was a "For Sale" sign in the front yard. Instinctively, Laura knew this was the house where he had grown up.

He sat there for a few minutes, the car still running, as he was deluged by memories. Finally, he turned off the engine and got out of the car, slowly opening the gate and walking halfway up the front walk.

Laura got out of the car and stood beside it, watching Taylor, not wanting to intrude on his memories. She saw him walk slowly up onto the wide, shady front porch, his hands unconsciously caressing the post at the bottom of the steps. He automatically reached for the doorknob before he caught himself and, instead, cupped his hands against the window to peer inside.

He turned around then and was almost surprised to see Laura waiting for him. She wasn't a part of the time he had just been in, wasn't a part of this place. She could have been, should have been, if his parents had lived. He should have been bringing her home to meet them, the girl he was going to marry, and he glanced back over his shoulder at the door that should have been opening to frame his mother welcoming them home. For a moment, the grief was as fresh as the day he had lost them as he slowly walked down steps that he used to take two at a time.

"It's a beautiful house, Taylor," Laura said as he came to stand beside her.

"It was once. My mother would be furious to see her gardens so neg-
lected. She had the proverbial green thumb. Dad and I could kill a plant
just by looking at it."

Laura reached out and took his hand, wanting to let him know he was
not as alone as he felt in this moment. He didn't seem to notice at first but
then gently squeezed her hand to let her know he knew she was there.

"See that tree?" he said, pointing with his free hand. "My room was
right beside it. I used it on more than one occasion to sneak out late at
night to meet my friends. One morning, after I had used that route, Dad
greeted me at breakfast and handed me a key to the front door, suggest-
ing I might want to use it instead." Taylor laughed softly. "I never could
get much past him. I think it was why he was such a good principal."

Suddenly, his eyes lit up and he said, "C'mon, Laura," as he went
around to the driver's side of the car. He didn't bother with the door,
swinging himself up and in before she had even moved. "Move it, girl,"
he said, starting the car.

"Taylor? What are you up to?"

"You'll see," he said as he pulled away from the curb.

*   *   *

An hour later they were back with the key to the house. Taylor had
driven to the realtor's office, prepared to explain that he used to live
there, but it hadn't been necessary. The realtor was an old classmate of
his—Marsha something—and she had been thrilled to see him and
more than happy to trust him with the key.

He opened the door and stood aside to let Laura go in first. It was
empty of furniture, holding only the waiting silence of a long-empty
house. Their heels sounded uncommonly loud as they walked across
the hardwood floors.

Memories rushed at him. His father's voice as he came in the door in
the afternoons. His mother's exasperated voice as she told him again to

"*quit sliding down the banister, Taylor!*" The house was full of ghosts, but they weren't the ones he had feared. It was good to be back, and he walked through the house accepting the gifts it offered to him.

He was surprised when he looked at his watch and realized it had been two hours that they had been there. Two hours that he had ignored Laura! He came back down the stairs and found her sitting in the bay window that had been his mother's favorite place. The late afternoon sun was glinting off her hair and he realized she looked like she belonged there.

"Still here, Laura?" he said quietly as he came to sit beside her. "I'm sorry. I didn't mean to have taken so long."

"It's all right, Taylor. Did you find what you were looking for?"

He took her hand and said, "I think I did. I'm glad I came, and I'm glad you were here with me."

He stood and pulled her to her feet. In the shadows he studied her face, then brushed his hand across her cheek. "Thank you for being here."

He locked the door behind them and walked with her to the car. Looking back at the house once more, he could see how the light streaming in the windows on the other side of the house made it look as if lights were on and someone was waiting. He smiled as he got in the car and drove away.

*   *   *

The distance made it difficult to make the trip in one day so they had planned on staying over. Dinner, then maybe a walk around the park—Taylor really wasn't quite sure how they would spend the evening. It was still too soon to let Laura know his feelings—he wouldn't risk frightening her away. As he drove back past the high school, he suddenly had an idea.

"Laura? What would you think about going to a play tonight?"

"What, Taylor?"

"A play. I feel like seeing *Our Town*. What do you think?"

Not knowing how they were to fill the long evening ahead, Laura clutched at the lifeline he was throwing her way. "It sounds like fun, Taylor. Let's do it."

*   *   *

When he returned the key, he mentioned they were planning on seeing the high school production that evening. When he left, Marsha picked up the phone and made a few calls. Taylor Morgan, back here in Woodland—it was the best gossip she'd had to spread for a long time!

*   *   *

When he pulled up in front of the high school's Little Theatre, he was embarrassed to see a banner that said, "Welcome Home, Taylor Morgan" draped across the front of the building. And it looked like half the town was waiting for them. "Marsha always was a terrible gossip," Taylor muttered as he turned off the engine. "If I'd known it would turn out like this, I would never have come, Laura."

"They're proud of you, Taylor. That's all."

As he opened Laura's door, he saw a woman coming down the steps to greet him, and a smile lit up his face as they walked to meet her.

"Hey, Lady…" he said softly before he hugged her. Stepping back he drew Laura forward. "Laura, this is Lady—Mrs. Carroll, I mean. She was my drama teacher."

"I'm glad to meet you," Laura said as she shook her hand. "I'm Laura Collins, Taylor's assistant."

"I'm so glad you're both here. The kids are beyond excited, Taylor. You're legendary around here, and they can't believe you'd come to see one of their plays."

"Lady, I'm sorry. I hadn't planned on any of this fuss."

"Don't be sorry, Taylor. This is the biggest house we've had in a long time."

*   *   *

It was closing night, and the cast party afterwards had two extra guests. Taylor had been reluctant to go, but finally gave in when he went backstage to congratulate the cast. They had been the ones to finally break down the barrier and convince him to come.

It had been a great party. He had quickly put them at ease when they realized he might be famous, but was really just a regular guy who had taken the same classes they had and eaten the same bad cafeteria food. He'd won them over with stories of Lady and some of the things they'd done when he had been a student there. "Do you realize this woman," he said looking at Lady with the devil in his eyes, "actually turned me down on my first two auditions? It wasn't until Simon Stinson came along," Taylor said gesturing to his counterpart in this production, "that she let me on the stage." Before he could finish the story, Lady had chimed in, "And I couldn't get him off of it after that!" and the whole group had dissolved into laughter.

It was in the early morning hours when the party finally broke up. Taylor had talked with them about the real life of a theatre gypsy, had posed for photographs and signed autographs, and altogether had a wonderful time. Laura had enjoyed watching it, realizing that this is what her life would be if she stayed involved with him—always in the shadow of his celebrity. She didn't mind.

The sun was just coming up as he walked her to the door of her room.

"I hope this wasn't too hard on you, Laura. I really hadn't planned on all of this happening."

"Don't be silly, Taylor. I had a good time. You know, you would have been a great teacher if New York hadn't worked out for you."

"Maybe—I'm glad I didn't have to find out."

"Goodnight, Taylor, or should that be good morning? Either way, I'll see you after I've had a few hours sleep. How about we meet around noon to go back?"

"That should work, Laura." He took both her hands and held her eyes with his. "Thank you for being here," he said. "Sleep well," he whispered before he turned away to go to his own room.

*   *   *

He woke earlier than he expected. Looking at the clock, he realized it was only ten. Laura would kill him if he woke her this early, he thought with a smile.

There was a new feeling of peace in his heart this morning, and he knew that coming here had been the right thing to do. There really was only one other place he should visit before they left. He got up and showered and dressed, leaving a message for Laura that he would be back by noon.

*   *   *

The cemetery was quiet, only a few people here and there visiting the graves of their loved ones. He knew it would get busier after church and was glad he had this quiet time.

He found his way to the dual stone that marked the resting-place of his parents. He took the wilting flowers out of the vase on the stone and replaced them with the yellow roses he carried. Sitting on the grass, reading the simple words on the stone, he knew that they weren't here. All that they had been—all the love and joy his parents had shared— they had left with him. Only now, with Laura, had he found a way to use that gift. He sat in the sun, feeling their love surround him once again.

40

The group reconvened on Catalina Island for the taping of two concerts that would be edited together for an upcoming television special. The beautiful and historic Casino building that dominated the harbor would host the performances. Built by William Wrigley as a "meeting place," the original meaning of the word "casino," the three-story round building housed an art deco theatre, the island museum, and the impressive ballroom where the concerts would take place.

During rehearsals, they were interrupted once an hour during the day when tour groups were brought by to peer in the doorways at the chaos that marred the normally serene beauty of the historic ballroom. No one seemed to mind. The tour guides kept the crowds at a distance, and the cast and crew learned to ignore them. All too quickly, the rehearsal week had passed, and the concert nights had arrived.

As he dressed for the second concert, Taylor knew this was his last chance to get it all right. A hopeless perfectionist when it came to his performance, Taylor wanted the finished program to include only the best. Laura and Daniel had assured him that last night's concert was perfect, and he should stop worrying. He had laughed with them as they had laughed at him, but he was still nervous about this first foray into television.

Looking out the window high above the harbor, he could see the boats docking from the mainland and the glittering audience members disembarking and walking up Casino Way, much as the crowds had done when William Wrigley first built it. Then, the crowds had come to dance and be entertained by the legendary big bands. It was a pretty heady legacy to live up to.

The knock at the door came at precisely five minutes before performance. Laura opened the door and said, "Taylor, you ready?"

"I think so, a little stage fright. Was that really Charlton Heston I saw coming in awhile ago?"

"It was. I think anyone who is anyone is here tonight!" He could hear the suppressed wonder in her voice.

"Oh, good. If I screw up, all of Hollywood will witness it."

"Most of America, too, since 'Entertainment Tonight' is here as well. You promised them a post-concert sound bite," she said as she smiled at him.

"No, Laura Collins, you promised it to them. I'm just the one who has to deliver!" He tried to sound stern, but it didn't work.

Her smile softened as she came over to him. "Here. I brought you something." Her hands trembled as she pinned a yellow rosebud to the lapel of his tux, and she kept her eyes lowered as she said, "Thank you, Taylor, for letting me be a part of this." She looked up at him and smiled, "It's been wonderful." She stood on tiptoe and kissed his cheek. "Now, go out there and show them who Taylor Morgan is."

As he heard the opening music starting, he took her hands in his, gazing into her green eyes. "I can't tell you how glad I am that you were along. I couldn't have done it without you." He brushed his lips across her cheek and then turned to head toward the door. He looked back at her and said, "See you after the concert," while his eyes told her he loved her.

Laura straightened up his dressing room, killing time while she tried to get her thoughts under control. She had seen the message in his eyes, and she knew he had been able to see the same in hers. The rest of the cast and crew were leaving in the morning after the post-concert party tonight. Taylor had asked her to stay here on Catalina with him for another day—and night. And she had said "yes." Looking at herself in the mirror, she realized that the frightened girl who had taken this job as an escape had made it past the need to be rescued. She was on firm ground again and knew exactly where she was heading.

             *   *   *

Laura woke slowly the next morning. She knew from the light streaming in the windows that it was late. She squinted at the bedside clock. Almost eleven. Taylor was probably having fits even though he had promised to let her sleep in.

Last night's concert had been a resounding success. The rich and famous had been as appreciative as Taylor's regular fans always were. "Entertainment Tonight" had done interviews with his fans before and after the concert and their brief interview with Taylor after the show had caught his elation. Once the interviews were over, he had showered and changed clothes before he and Laura headed for the Inn on Mt. Ada where the closing night party would take place.

Taylor had been touched by the cast's heartfelt applause as he entered the room. They had become a family over the last few months, and there were more than a few tears at the thought of breaking up the group. There had also been more than a few whispered comments at the way Taylor had watched Laura all evening. Most of them expected wedding bells before long and were genuinely happy for them.

The party had gone on until the early hours of the morning, when good-byes were said and plans made for the morning departure. Daniel had been one of the last to leave. He drew Laura to one side as the others were saying good-bye to Taylor.

"What are your plans now, Laura? Taylor said you had only agreed to do this on a trial basis for the tour. Are you going back to your newspaper? Or are you planning on staying on with Taylor?"

"I really don't know yet, Daniel. I'm going home for a few days to try to figure out exactly what it is I want to do." And a lot depends on what happens in the next forty-eight hours, she thought.

"Whatever you decide, Laura, I wish you the best. I've enjoyed working with you. Personally, I hope you decide to stay on with Taylor. He needs you." More than you know, he added silently. "Be well, Laura," he said before he kissed her cheek and walked away.

With everyone gone, Taylor walked Laura down the hall to her room, across from his. That was when she had made him promise to let her sleep in.

The others would be gone by now, leaving her alone with Taylor. She thought again about the look in his eyes last night. There had been no mistaking it, and she knew she was hoping tonight would lead to its logical conclusion. The smile that crossed her lips at the thought quickly disappeared as she also realized she had to tell him about Cary before they could go any further.

The phone rang, and she smiled again, knowing who it had to be. "Good morning, Taylor."

"Laura, the *morning* is almost gone. You have one half hour to get down here because we have a snorkeling appointment. So, get up now, miss!"

Laura laughed at the barely disguised annoyance in his voice. "Hey, I thought today was a day off. I shouldn't have to answer to you if I'm not working."

"Then you're working until you get down here, Ms. Collins. I'll meet you in the dining room."

                    *   *   *

Laura took his breath away as she came into the dining room. Her hair was caught back into a ponytail, and the green outfit she wore intensified the color of her eyes. She looked rested and, most importantly, happy.

"It's about time you got here," he growled with a frown that didn't reach his eyes.

"What is this about snorkeling, Taylor?"

"Lover's Cove. We're going snorkeling in an hour, which gives you barely enough time to eat so you can go into the water."

"I've never been snorkeling."

"I figured you hadn't. No offense, but it does require a little more and a little clearer water than the Rio Grande has to offer."

"I still need to get the last of the stuff from the dressing room."

"Already taken care of. Normally, my assistant would have done it, but she has the day off."

"Smart woman," Laura commented as they were interrupted by the server waiting to take their order.

4 I

It had been a magical day. After the snorkeling, which she had loved, they had gone on a tour of Holly Hill House, the Queen Anne-style house that sat on a hill overlooking the harbor. Laura had fallen in love with it instantly when they arrived. Taylor had made some inquiries, found that the owner's wife was a fan, and sent them tickets to last night's concert with a request for a private tour. They had been delighted and received Laura and Taylor for afternoon tea. He hadn't paid a lot of attention to the spectacular view from the beautiful cupola that topped the house; he preferred to keep his eyes on Laura.

Leaving Holly Hill in the late afternoon, they wandered through the shops that ringed the harbor. Laura helped Taylor pick out some gifts for Meg, and they returned to The Inn in time to change for dinner.

Laura wore a dress she had bought before Christmas, but had never worn. Pale green with a sweetheart neckline it boasted a mid-calf skirt of layers of chiffon in varying colors of blues and greens. The earrings Taylor had given her were the only jewelry she wore. As she pinned her hair up, she looked with approval at the woman who confidently met her gaze in the mirror.

Taylor knocked, and as she opened the door, she was struck again by how good-looking he was. His reddish hair and turquoise eyes were such an unusual combination. In black slacks and turquoise shirt with a black blazer, he looked wonderful.

Over dinner, they talked and laughed. Laura realized he was flirting with her and she with him, and it felt so right. The ghosts that had haunted her were safely tucked away, and she really believed she could be happy again.

*   *   *

After dinner, Taylor and Laura returned to his suite. The balcony doors were open, letting in a gentle sea breeze. While Laura stood on the balcony watching the lights of Avalon and the small boats in the harbor, Taylor poured two glasses of wine and joined her.

"Thanks, Taylor," she said as she took a glass. "This has to be the most perfect place on earth."

"I've always liked it here," he said, his eyes on her, not the harbor. "I've thought about moving here on more than one occasion. If it weren't for Annie and Meg, I might have by now."

"Mmm…living here would be wonderful. I never thought I could love someplace as much as I do Albuquerque, but if I were ever tempted to leave permanently, I think Catalina would be the place I would come."

Taylor put down the glass and took a deep breath. Now was the time to tell her. He wouldn't go on pretending anymore that he wasn't in love with her, but before he could speak, the phone rang. The switchboard usually put all his calls through to Laura, and she ran interference for him. There hadn't been many. A couple from Meg…but it was awfully late for Meg to be calling. He hesitated for a moment before answering the phone, suddenly filled with a certainty that this was bad news.

"Hello?"

"May I speak with Taylor Morgan, please."

Taylor didn't recognize the voice and cautiously asked who was calling.

"This is Dr. Pearson in Tampa. Annie Miller has listed his name as next of kin."

Laura watched as the blood drained from Taylor's face and he groped for the chair behind him.

"I'm Taylor Morgan, Doctor. What's happened to Annie?" he asked, his voice curiously flat.

"Mr. Morgan, Annie was brought into the hospital today after she collapsed at her studio. She asked that we call you to return as soon as possible."

"As soon as I can get a plane, I'll be there." From the corner of his eye, Taylor saw Laura open the door and go across the hall to her room. "But, Annie? Is she all right? What's wrong with her?"

"Mr. Morgan, I really don't want to discuss it with you over the phone. Annie is stable, for the moment, and we will be running tests that will probably keep her in the hospital for a few days. She is very concerned about her daughter."

"Megan. Where is she?"

"We were able to contact her regular caregiver who is staying with her at their home."

"Tell Annie I'm on my way, Doctor. I'll be there as soon as I can."

He broke the connection and went to the open door. Across the hall-way, Taylor heard Laura saying, "Thank you. I'll have him at the airport within half an hour."

She hung up the phone then turned to look at him. "Taylor?"

"Annie's in the hospital. The doctor wouldn't tell me what was wrong, only that she's stable and they're doing tests. I need to get back there right away."

"I've already called the Catalina airport. They'll have someone take you back to the mainland as soon as you can get there. The next question is, do you want me to arrange a commercial flight or charter a plane for you?"

"Whichever is faster, Laura. Thanks. I need to call Meg. It sounds as if Susan is with her, but I need to know. I'll pack while I call." He went back across the hall as Laura once again picked up her phone.

As he threw clothes into his suitcase, Taylor listened to phone ringing a continent away.

"Miller residence." It was Susan's voice.

"Susan, it's Taylor. The hospital just called. What happened?"

"Oh, Taylor, I'm so glad they found you. Megan is about out of her mind with worry. Annie complained of having a headache during her advanced class this afternoon and turned it over to her assistant. When class was over, Jane went into her office and found Annie unconscious on the floor. She called an ambulance and had the presence of mind to call me."

"The doctor wouldn't tell me anything. What do they think it is?"

"They're not giving out much information, Taylor, but they have a 'cat' scan scheduled for morning. She's admitted that she's been having these headaches off and on for awhile now, but she attributed it to stress."

Taylor was overwhelmed by guilt. Meg had tried to tell him, but he had never found time to ask Annie.

"What about Meg?"

"She's been crying almost nonstop all evening. Annie is in intensive care, so they wouldn't let Meg in to see her. I think she may finally have fallen asleep."

"Susan, if she has, wake her. I need to talk to her."

"Taylor, shouldn't we let her sleep?"

"Please, Susan."

He waited while she went to wake Meg. Tonight was turning out so differently from what he'd had planned.

"Taylor?" Meg's tear-filled voice filled his ear.

"It's me, Meg."

"Taylor, where are you? Mommy's sick. I'm so scared." She started to cry and Taylor's eyes filled with tears.

"Meg, I'm in California, but I'm leaving in a few minutes to start back. It will take a little while, but I'll be there as quickly as I can. I'll go straight to the hospital to see your mom, and I'll call you as soon as I know something. You're going to have to be strong for a little while longer, Meg. Can you do that?" Taylor could hear her sobbing. "Megan? Sweetheart, talk to me."

"Please hurry, Taylor."

"I will, Meg. Try to go to sleep now. It will make the time go quickly. I love you, Meg."

"I love you, too, Taylor."

As Taylor broke the connection, Laura knocked at the door.

"How's Meg?"

"Absolutely shattered."

"There will be a private jet waiting when you get to L.A. You should be back there four or five hours from now. Are you ready to go?"

"Ready as I'm going to be, I guess. Laura—thanks for taking care of all of that."

"You're welcome, Taylor. I'll finish things here in the morning, then head back to Albuquerque. Please call and let me know as soon as you know something."

He nodded, then picked up his suitcase. They went downstairs where one of the hotel staff was waiting to take them to the airport. When they arrived, Laura walked with Taylor to the small plane that was waiting. He handed his case to the pilot, then turned back to Laura.

"Laura, this wasn't at all the way I had hoped tonight would turn out. There's so much I need to say to you, but it will have to wait." He reached out and gently touched her cheek, his heart in his eyes as he looked at her. He kissed her lightly, then turned away, boarding the plane that would take him away from her with so much left unsaid.

4 2

Laura was in his arms by the edge of the water, and he was lost in the joy of her kiss when he heard Annie's voice calling him. He broke away from Laura. Laughing, she began to walk away from him, beckoning him to come with her. He turned to the water and saw Annie being pulled out to sea and he knew he could only chose one of them. Laura had already faded into the distance and Annie's cries were growing weaker as Taylor stood mired in indecision, knowing that choosing one would cause him to lose the other.

He awoke with a start, disoriented until he realized he was on a plane on his way back to Tampa. The nightmare was real.

The copilot came in. "Mr. Morgan, we'll be landing in Tampa in about half an hour. Would you like to me to radio ahead for a car for you?"

"Thanks, but no. I'll probably just grab a cab." He watched the man go back into the cockpit, then made his way to the bathroom. The man looking back at him from the mirror was haggard and old, not at all the person he had been less than forty-eight hours ago. Coming off a successful concert tour, sure of his love for Laura and hers for him, he had been on top of the world…but he couldn't allow himself to think about that now. Getting a razor from his carry-on, he tried to make himself presentable.

*   *   *

He arrived in Tampa at five a.m. Since the condo was on the way to the hospital, he had the cab drop him there, so he could take his own car. It was almost six when the elevator opened on the intensive care waiting room. There were several people there, all of them looking as worn as he felt.

"I'm here for Annie Miller. My name is Taylor Morgan," he said to the nurse on duty.

"Mr. Morgan, Annie's been asking for you. It will be a few minutes, but I'll call you."

Nodding silently, he turned away and walked to the window, not seeing anything but pictures of Annie in his mind. The only other time he had been at a hospital for any length of time was when Meg was born. That had been a time of joy, not like now. What if Annie….

"Mr. Morgan," the nurse said his name softly so as not to disturb the others in the waiting room. "You can see Annie now."

He was ushered into a large room lined with separate cubicles and a dazzling array of monitors and equipment. The nurse led him to one at the far end and stood back to let him go through the door. "Mr. Morgan, I'm going to stretch the rules since you just got here, but only to ten minutes."

Taylor nodded absently as he entered the small space and saw Annie in the high bed. A number of monitors, each with a different pattern, surrounded her. She had an I.V. in her arm and an oxygen tube ringed her face; she looked totally vulnerable as Taylor took her hand and her eyes opened

"Taylor—I'm so glad you're here."

"Where else could I be, Annie? I got here as quickly as I could." His eyes filled with tears as he pulled a chair beside the bed.

"No tears, Taylor. Have you seen Meg?"

"Not yet. I came straight here from the airport, but I talked to her last night. Susan's with her and she's safe. You don't need to worry about her."

She smiled at him. "Good. But she needs you, Taylor. Promise you'll go out there soon."

"Soon, Annie, but not until I talk to your doctor. Annie, Meg told me you were having these headaches, and I didn't pay enough attention. Why didn't you go to the doctor sooner?"

"I did. When I was at Mom's. He told me I had the flu."

"He was obviously an idiot," Taylor said fiercely. He couldn't bear seeing Annie this helpless.

"Taylor, hush. We'll get through this. I want you to go to Meg."

Taylor opened his mouth to argue, but was interrupted by the nurse. "Mr. Morgan. I'm sorry, but you'll have to leave."

"Go on, Taylor. I'll see you in a little while."

He leaned down and kissed her forehead then whispered, "I love you, Annie." He felt her return the pressure of his hand before he let go and reluctantly left the room.

Back in the waiting room, the nurse handed him a list of rules for the ICU. He would only be allowed to see her for five minutes every hour.

"Can you tell me when Dr. Pearson will be in?" he asked.

"He usually checks on his patients around seven. I'll let him know you're here."

Taylor resumed his vigil at the window. The sun had come up while he was with Annie. It was going to be another picture-perfect Florida day, but he never even noticed.

*　　　　　*　　　　　*

About 7:30, the nurse called him. "Mr. Morgan, the doctor is just finishing up and would like to see you. There's a conference room just down the hall; he's waiting for you there."

As Taylor opened the door, a tall, thin man wearing a doctor's white coat looked up from the papers he was studying. "Mr. Morgan?"

"Yes. You must be Annie's doctor."

"Jared Pearson." He shook Taylor's hand, then indicated a chair across the table. "Annie asked that you be given any information she was given, so I wanted to bring you up to date on where we are. Annie was brought in yesterday after losing consciousness at work. By the time she was brought in, she was alert again, but in considerable pain, complaining of a headache. We've done a number of tests already, but we have a CT scan scheduled for later this morning. I should have the results back by one. I'll meet with you and Annie then."

"Doctor? What is it?"

"Mr. Morgan, I don't want to speculate. Wait until I have some real answers to give you." He stood, effectively dismissing Taylor. "I'll see you this afternoon."

Taylor returned to the waiting room and was told he could have another 5 minutes with Annie.

"Hello, beautiful," he said as he sat beside her bed again.

"Taylor, have you called Meg?"

"Annie, I'm going out there as soon as they kick me out of here again. I met with your doctor, and he said he would meet with both of us this afternoon, hopefully with some answers. That gives me time to go to Meg." He brushed her hair away from her face. "Stop bossing me around, Annie Miller."

"Not a chance, Taylor! How did the concerts go on Catalina?"

He laughed softly, "Annie, that's not important."

"It's important to me, Taylor. Tell me."

"They were a success, Annie. I think the television special is going to be really good." He went on and told her about the glittering audience and the cast party.

"I'm so proud of you, Taylor," Annie said with a smile. "Not bad for a small-town boy."

"Mr. Morgan."

"I'll be right there." Taylor held Annie's hand for a moment longer. "I'll go see Meg now, Annie. I'll bring you a report this afternoon."

*   *   *

Taylor pulled into the driveway of Annie's house a little before nine. Other than his nightmare-plagued nap on the plane, he had been awake for more than 24 hours and was beginning to feel it.

As he got out of the car, he saw Meg standing at the door. She looked so lost and vulnerable that it broke his heart. He ran up the steps and took her in his arms and held her while she cried. When she quieted, he took her hand and led her back into the house where Susan was waiting.

"Meg, I saw Annie this morning. She's terribly worried about you and practically threw me out so I'd come here. She has some more tests this morning, but I'll go back this afternoon to talk with her and the doctor."

"What's wrong with her?" Meg's voice was still thick with tears.

"They don't know yet, Meg. That's what the tests are for. We should know more this afternoon. When I go back, I have to be able to tell her you're all right. You're going to have to be strong for a little longer, Meg. I want you to go get dressed while I talk to Susan. I need to take a walk and thought you might go with me. Would you?"

She nodded silently before padding off to her room.

"Taylor?"

"What I told Meg is all I know, Susan. I wish it were more. Can you stay awhile longer?"

"Whatever it takes, Taylor. I'll run home for some clothes and things while you're out with Meg. What time should I be back?"

"Make it noon, Susan. I'll need to leave for the hospital shortly after that."

                    *   *   *

Taylor drove to their favorite beach, and he and Meg began to walk along the shore. Meg was quiet, walking beside him, holding his hand. Normally she would have been darting here and there and talking a mile a minute.

"Meg, let's sit here for awhile." He drew her down beside him on the sand, and they silently watched the endless surge of the sea. Finally, Meg said, "Taylor, thanks for coming back."

"Of course, Munchkin." He hadn't called her that since she was a little girl. One day she'd put her hands on her hips and informed him she was too old to have such a ridiculous nickname. She had been all of six years old then, but Taylor had not used it since. It somehow slipped out now, but Meg didn't notice.

"I want to see her, Taylor."

"Meg, I know, but they won't even let me in for more than five minutes every hour. Until she's out of intensive care, they won't let you in at all."

"It's not fair!"

"No, Meg, it's not, but that's the way it is. As soon as possible, I'll get you there. If we're lucky, she'll be home soon and we won't have to worry about it."

Meg angrily brushed tears from her face, but didn't say anything. He left her alone until she was more composed. Then he said, "Meg? What about school?"

"I don't care about school, Taylor!"

"Meg, I know that, but the law says you have to go to school. Susan must have called in for you this morning, but we have to decide what to do from here."

"Taylor, I can't go back. Not yet. Please, let me stay home this week. I'll call some friends to get my assignments, and I won't get behind, I promise."

"That sounds fair, Meg. I'll call the school when we get back and explain it all to them. We better go now, sweetheart. I'll need to make those calls, then get back to the hospital."

He took her hand, pulling her up from the sand. "Meg, you're not alone in this. I'm here, and I won't leave you." She wrapped her arms around him and hugged him fiercely, clinging to him as the only anchor she had.

*   *   *

When they returned to the house, he called the school as he had promised. Then he dialed Laura's Albuquerque number. He wasn't surprised when the machine picked up. She probably wasn't back from California yet.

"Laura, it's Taylor. Annie's still in the hospital, and they're running tests. We should know something more later today. Meg is hanging on, at least for now. I'll call you when I know more."

Hanging up the phone, he realized how much he missed her. She'd become such a part of his life that not having her around left him feeling lost. He didn't plan on letting her be away from him for long.

*　　　　　*　　　　　*

Annie had been moved from ICU to a private room by the time Taylor got back to the hospital. As he ran to her new location, Taylor tried to believe that this was a good sign. He nearly ran into the doctor as he came around the corner in her hallway.

"Slow down, Mr. Morgan."

"I'm sorry, I didn't know she had been moved and I was afraid I'd be late."

He opened the door for the doctor and followed him in. Taylor went to the head of the bed and kissed Annie. "Meg's doing fine. She misses you and is worried, of course, but she's strong like her mother." Annie gave him a grateful smile as they turned their attention to the doctor. Taylor could feel her tension as she gripped his hand.

"I wish this were better news, Annie. And there's no easy way to tell you. The CT scan revealed what I had been afraid of. You have a brain tumor, very large—and inoperable."

43

Taylor stood by the sunroom window at the end of the hall. Annie had asked for some time alone. Since he had no comfort to offer her, he had kissed her gently and come down here to wait.

The doctor had explained at length that there was nothing they could really do. Chemotherapy might retard the growth of the tumor. At best, it might extend her time for a month or two, but would probably leave her feeling worse than she did now. He assured Annie that even had she come in when the headaches had started, the prognosis would have been the same. The tumor was simply too deep and too involved for them to reach.

"I would like to keep you another night, Annie. I'll be sending a counselor up to talk to you. If you decide you want to try the chemotherapy, we can do your first treatment tomorrow before we send you home. Either way, I'll dismiss you tomorrow if there's someone at home to help."

Taylor had managed to speak. "I'll be there with her, Doctor."

"Good. Annie—Mr. Morgan—if you think of any questions, have them page me. I'll be here at the hospital until late this evening." He turned and walked to the door, then looked back. "I'm truly sorry that there's nothing I can do," he said quietly before he left the room.

*   *   *

They had been silent for a long time after the doctor had left. Taylor had sunk into the chair beside Annie's bed, struggling to make sense of what they had just been told. Annie was dying. Taylor tried the phrase in his mind. Dying. Oh, God, no, not Annie! Meg needed her. He needed her. Stunned, he looked up and met Annie's eyes, their clear blue shimmering with unshed tears. Silently, he moved from the chair and sat facing her on the bed. Her eyes never left his until, suddenly, she said, "Megan. How are we going to tell Meg?" The tears had come then, and he held her until she asked him to leave.

He looked at his watch; three o'clock. Two hours had passed since their meeting with the doctor, more than an hour since she had asked him to leave. Turning from the window, he went back to her room. After knocking softly, he opened the door and found her out of bed, standing by the window.

"Annie?"

Without turning, she said, "Taylor, do you remember, about a year after your parents died, you came to talk to me because you said you couldn't remember what your mother looked like?"

He remembered all too clearly. It had been the first anniversary of their deaths. He had made it through all the milestones of that year, the birthdays and holidays, but he hadn't been able to handle that they'd been gone for a year. He had shown up on Annie's doorstep, drunk and in tears because he couldn't remember his mother's face without a picture to prompt him.

"I remember."

She turned to look at him then. "You were twenty-one when they died. You'd had twenty-one years to memorize her face and you still forgot. Meg's only eleven, Taylor."

He crossed the room and caught her as she crumpled into tears. He couldn't tell her that Meg wouldn't forget. He couldn't tell her that Meg would be all right. All he could do was hold her while she cried.

Finally, her tears had slowed, and she looked up at Taylor. "I want to see her, Taylor."

"Tomorrow, Annie, when we take you home."

"No, Taylor, tonight. I have to see her tonight."

"Annie, are you sure?"

She laughed a little wildly. "Of course I'm not sure, Taylor. I'll never be sure of anything again. But I know I need to see her."

"Then I'll go bring her to you. Will you be all right while I'm gone?"

Mutely she nodded, and he helped her back to the bed before he left.

*   *   *

Taylor didn't know how he was going to get Meg to the hospital without her noticing that something was terribly wrong. He was a pretty good actor, but this…. As he pulled into Annie's driveway, he was almost overwhelmed by grief, but managed to pull himself together. He was a little surprised that Meg didn't come out to meet him.

He entered the quiet house. "Meg? Susan?"

He heard Susan's voice from the kitchen, "In here, Taylor."

The kitchen was filled with light and the smells of baking. He was suddenly aware he hadn't eaten all day. Meg said, as she took a tray of cookies out of the oven, "We've made Mom's favorite, Taylor. Will you take some to her tonight?"

"I think she would like it more if you delivered them, Meg."

"Really?" She threw her arms around him. "I can go see her tonight? Honest?"

"Honest, Meg. They've moved her to another room, and she can have visitors now. I was ordered by the Queen herself to fetch the Princess."

"I'll go change. I'll be right back." The elated girl ran out of the room.

Susan looked at him, shaking her head as she said "Taylor, you look terrible. When was the last time you ate?"

"Dinner last night, I guess." It seemed much longer than 24 hours ago that he'd been flirting with Laura over dinner. In his mind he could see her laughing.

"Then you're going to eat now, Taylor. Don't argue. We already have Annie sick. We can't do without you, too." She opened a pot on the stove and ladled out a bowl of soup. "Eat this. My Jewish mother swears it will cure anything."

"Thanks, Susan." He sat at the table and picked up a spoon. "Can you come to the hospital later to pick up Meg? I want to stay awhile with Annie."

"Of course I can, Taylor. Visiting hours end at eight, right?"

"I'm not sure, but that sounds about right. And can you stay with her tonight? I'll be going back to the hospital early, and my place is a lot closer."

"I'll be here as long as Annie needs me, Taylor. Now, eat that soup. You're not leaving until you do."

Dutifully, Taylor ate the soup and felt some energy come back into his tired body. Susan packaged up the cookies, and by the time Meg came back, he was ready to leave again.

*   *   *

Meg was quiet as they waited for the elevator. "Meg? Are you all right?" She took a deep breath, then nodded. "It's a pretty scary place."

"Scary because you're worried about someone. There's some good stuff happening here too, like babies being born. That can be pretty scary, come to think of it. I remember how scared I was while you were being born, but it all went away when you wrapped your fingers around mine about five minutes after you arrived." He smiled at her. "That was an amazing moment, Meg." He put his arm around her and gave her shoulders a squeeze as the elevator doors opened.

Taylor knocked lightly on Annie's door and pushed it open, letting Meg step in before him. She stopped just inside the door, unsure of

what to do until her mother opened her arms and simply said, "Meg!"
Her paralysis vanished, and she launched herself across the room and
into those waiting arms. Taylor closed the door and walked down the
hall to the increasingly familiar waiting room.

He had been sitting there for half an hour when he saw Dr. Pearson
heading down the hall. "Doctor, wait!"

Pearson turned around. "Mr. Morgan. I was just on my way to see
Annie."

"Can it wait a little? I know you're busy, but her daughter's here
and…" Taylor's voice trailed off.

"It can wait. What about you, Mr. Morgan? You look like you could
use some serious sleep."

"You're right, and I'll try for that later. Right now, I have a question.
Do you have a minute to answer it?"

"Sure, let's use the conference room."

When they were settled, Taylor was suddenly at a loss for words. "I'm
sorry. I…I wanted to know…"

"You wanted to know how long Annie has?" Taylor nodded, grateful
that the doctor had not made him say the words. Hearing the answer
would be hard enough.

"It's hard to say, Taylor. I don't want to give you false hopes. A tumor
of the type that Annie has moves at its own speed. With chemotherapy,
we can slow its growth a little, but it could happen as quickly as a couple
of months, as long as six, if we're lucky."

Taylor buried his face in his hands. So little time!

"Taylor, I'm going to leave now. Use this room as long as you need it."
He touched Taylor's shoulder in mute sympathy before he left the room.

                    *   *   *

Susan was getting off the elevator as Taylor came out of the conference room. He had no time to compose his features, and she caught her

breath at the desolation she saw in his eyes. She sat across from him in the waiting room and quietly said, "It's bad news, isn't it, Taylor?"

"The worst," he said. "But we have to keep it from Meg until Annie decides it's time to tell her. Susan, you're going to be with her a lot. Can you keep it from her?"

Susan's eyes were filled with tears that she blinked away. "I will somehow, Taylor."

"Annie can come home tomorrow. There's nothing they can do here that we can't do for her at home." Taylor saw Meg emerge from Annie's room and signaled Susan to be quiet.

"A good visit, Meg?" Taylor stood and gave her a hug.

"Uh-huh. Mom says she can come home tomorrow."

"That's good news. I'll call you in the morning as soon as I know when I can bring her."

Taylor chuckled as Meg tried to stifle an enormous yawn. "I bet you don't make it home before you fall asleep. It's a good thing Susan is driving! Goodnight, Meg. Try to get some rest."

"'Night, Taylor." She waved sleepily as Susan led her to the elevator, and Taylor started down the hallway to Annie's room.

*   *   *

The first thing Taylor noticed as he came into the room was an air of serenity that surrounded Annie. She seemed to have reached some place in herself that let her find some peace, and she smiled at him as he came in.

"Thanks for bringing her, Taylor. She's better than any medicine."

"For both of you. That was a different child who came out of here than the one I brought."

Annie reached out and caught his hand in hers. "And you, Taylor? When was the last time you slept?"

"Good Lord, Annie, after today, how the hell can you be worrying about me?"

Annie's eyes grew solemn as she pulled his hand to have him sit on the bed beside her. "Because, Taylor, I need you now more than I ever have. So, you have to be all right."

Taylor picked up her hand and kissed it. "I'm fine, Annie. A little punchy from lack of sleep, but basically ok."

"I need to talk to you for a minute, Taylor, then I want you to go home and sleep."

He nodded, and she searched his eyes as if she could find the answer she was seeking hidden there. "Taylor, it's about Meg. You know I named you her guardian right after she was born." Taylor nodded before she went on. "But that was a long time ago. Neither of us ever thought something like this would happen. I need to know now, Taylor, if you're still willing to take on that responsibility."

"Annie, how can you even ask? I promised you then I would always be there for Meg."

"Taylor, it won't be the same. You'll have to be the grownup, and preteen girls are only marginally easier than the teenager she will become. It's a tremendous responsibility."

"Annie, I won't let you give her to someone else. Meg's my daughter in all the ways that count."

Annie smiled at him as her eyes filled with tears. "Thank you, Taylor. I know she could have gone to my parents, but they're too old to take her on. She'd be miserable. This will all be hard enough…" her voice trailed off.

"Annie, remember when Meg was baptized? I wasn't just mouthing the words when I made those promises as her godfather. I meant every one of them. I'll do my best to help her to become the woman you dream her to be." He gathered Annie into his arms, and they sat in silence for a long while.

Finally, Annie pushed away from him. "It's time for you to go home, Taylor. Get some rest. I've asked my lawyer to be here in the morning so we can make sure your guardianship is assured. You'll need to be here at ten."

"I'll be here, Annie," he promised as he leaned down to kiss her. "Goodnight."

"Goodnight, Taylor."

As the door closed behind him, Annie had never felt more alone.

*   *   *

He opened the door to the condo. It was only 10:00, more than early enough to call Laura, but he couldn't do it. To hear her voice would have broken down every barrier he had spent the day building around his emotions. Instead he turned on the computer and logged on to his e-mail. There was a brief message from her letting him know that she had arrived home safely. He began to compose a message to her.

Laura-

> I'm sorry. I know I should have called, and I hope you'll check in tonight to read this. I just can't bear the thought of hearing these words said again.
>
> Annie is dying.
>
> God, how it hurts to even type that!
>
> It's a brain tumor, and she doesn't have very much time. I'll be canceling everything until further notice. I have to be here for Annie and Meg.
>
> I'm Meg's guardian, Laura. After this is all over, she'll be my responsibility, a constant part of my life. I've not had a lot of time to think, but I know that my lifestyle will have to change. Luckily, I have more than enough money put away so that I shouldn't have to work for awhile.
>
> Annie hasn't told Meg yet. I don't know when she will. They're releasing her from the hospital tomorrow. She has to make a decision about chemotherapy, but I'm

pretty sure that she's going to opt for quality instead of quantity for what time remains.

I'll try to check in when I can, but things will be crazy around here. I'm moving out to Annie's tomorrow. You can reach me there if you need me.

Taylor

He glanced back over what he had written and sent it out. He climbed the stairs to his bedroom, threw himself on the bed, and lay there staring into the dark until the weariness won and he slept.

*   *   *

Laura checked the answering machine when she got back from dinner with her parents. The apartment still felt strange. She had only lived here a few days before leaving for Florida, and there were still boxes to be unpacked. When she realized that Taylor had not called, she logged on and found his message.

She remembered how she had felt when they were told that Tomás was dying. Her world had narrowed until there was only room for Tomás and her parents. She had done what work she had to and spent the rest of the time with him. They had talked for hours, night after night, and it had been Tomás that helped her in those nightmare days.

Now, Taylor was doing the same thing, focussing on what was necessary to get by. She wept as she sent him an answer.

Taylor-

I wish there were something I could say to help you through this. Unfortunately, you have to find your own way. Just remember I'm here if you need someone to talk to, someone who has been there.

My heart is with you and Annie and Meg.

Love-

Laura

44

When Taylor came into Annie's hospital room, a woman rose from her seat at the side of the bed. Annie said, "Taylor, you remember Jude MacMurray, my lawyer?"

"Of course. Jude, it's good to see you again."

"I just wish it were in other circumstances, Taylor. Annie's filled me in." He could see the sorrow in her eyes before she brusquely said, "About this guardian thing. I don't know. I'm going to have to do some research, but I'm pretty sure that whatever you put in your will, Annie, if Meg's birth father wants her, the courts will look favorably on him."

"What?" Taylor nearly shouted at her. "That is so damned stupid! That bastard walked out on Annie before Meg was even born! He's never sent one penny to help. I doubt he even remembers he has a child!"

A nurse pushed open the door. "Ms. Miller? Is everything all right in here?"

Annie told her it was, and the nurse looked sternly at Taylor. "Please, keep your voice down, sir, or I'll have to ask you to leave."

Instead of apologizing, Taylor turned his back on her and walked to the window, fighting for control. His hands clenched at the idea that the courts could even consider giving Megan to Edwards!

"Taylor..." Annie spoke softly from her bed. "Taylor, we have to hear the rest of what Jude has to say."

He turned and looked at them. How could they be so calm about this? He sank into a chair by the window and tried to focus on what the lawyer was saying.

"Annie, Taylor, I'm sorry. I'm not sure of any of this. If you were married, then the courts might look more favorably on you, Taylor. But, as a friend of the family, you're just not as important as a blood tie. The law is wrong, but it *is* the law. Unless we can get a signature from him relinquishing his parental rights or find some way to prove him unfit, he still has first rights to his daughter."

"She's not his daughter, damn it. She's mine." Taylor's voice broke as he said it.

"Taylor, I know that. I'll be here to help, but I still think we have to find him and get him to give up his rights. Even then, Taylor, you'll have to prove you're a fit parent. And, face it, your life as it is now, isn't going to make you a real viable possibility."

Annie spoke. "We'll worry about Taylor's lifestyle later. Right now, we have to locate Cary. I'll go…."

"No, Annie, I'll go," Taylor interrupted. "You're not going to have to suffer that, too."

Jude looked from one to the other of them. "Let's just find him first. Then we'll figure out the next step. I'll call you at home as soon as I have a more definitive answer."

She leaned down and hugged Annie, then waved to Taylor as she left the room. They stared at each other in silence until Taylor said, "What time can I take you out of here, Annie?"

"The doctor should be along soon. He's waiting for my decision about the chemotherapy."

"You've decided against it, haven't you?"

"I have, Taylor. They can't offer me any hope that it will prolong my life—just the agony. I want to be as well as possible for the time I have left with Meg."

Taylor ran his hands through his hair. "Annie, I need to get out of here for awhile. Can you handle this with the doctor, or do you need me here?"

Her eyes softened as she looked at the man who had been so much more than her best friend. "Go on, Taylor. I'll be here waiting when you get back."

He stopped and kissed her before he left the room. She knew the demons chasing him—they had left their twins with her.

*   *   *

Taylor walked across the bridge to where the path began along the bay. It was filled with runners and walkers, people on skates or bicycles, all without a care in the world. He walked quickly, his mind in turmoil, until he had no energy left and collapsed on a bench, leaning his head on the railing that lined the path.

Losing Annie was already too much to handle. He couldn't lose Meg, too. More importantly, he couldn't let Cary have any chance at taking her. Judging by his attack on Laura, Cary hadn't changed. The idea of a helpless child in the hands of that monster was more than he could bear. There had to be an answer, a way to protect Meg. Staring out at the ocean, he replayed the lawyer's comments in his head until the answer he had been avoiding became the only option they had left.

45

"With this ring, I thee wed." Taylor's voice was strong and sure as he placed the plain gold band on his bride's finger and smiled at her. The presiding judge said, "I now pronounce you husband and wife. You may kiss your bride, Taylor."

He kissed Annie as their friends surrounded them. Annie's parents were beaming as they welcomed him into their family. Daniel Li, acting as best man, shook Taylor's hand even as he tried to figure out how all this had happened. He had been sure that Taylor was in love with Laura, yet, here he was, less than a week later, married to Annie. Megan was almost beside herself with joy. She had been her mother's maid of honor as her secret wish finally came true.

The party moved inside the condo. The sun had been setting as they said their vows on the deck overlooking the bay. Now, the living room was alight with candles as the caterers served champagne. Daniel tapped on his glass to get everyone's attention, then said, "I was honored when Taylor asked me to stand up with him today and be a witness to the beginning of his new life. I wish Annie and Taylor much happiness and long life. May they have triple the years together than the years it took them to reach this place. To Taylor and Annie."

As the guests echoed Daniel's toast, Taylor pretended to drink. Long-life. Someday, Daniel would regret those words and resent that Taylor had let him say them. He felt Annie squeeze his hand and he smiled at her, every inch the joyous bridegroom, as long as no one looked too closely into his eyes.

As Daniel lifted Megan on to a chair, Taylor met Susan's eyes and smiled at her. Of all the people here, only Susan and Jude knew the truth about Annie. His attention returned to Meg as she tapped on her own glass for attention. "My turn," she said in a shaky voice. "My turn to wish Taylor and my mother happiness. Taylor's been the only father I ever had, and it's nice to have it made official." Affectionate laughter surrounded her. "So, to Taylor and Mom—and our new family."

Even as they were surrounded by well-wishers, Taylor felt as if it were all a dream that he might yet wake from. Only a week since he had been on Catalina with Laura. Only a week...

*   *   *

When Taylor had returned to the hospital, the papers had been signed to release Annie. She looked so well that Taylor found himself almost believing that the diagnosis had been a mistake. As they drove away from the hospital, his heart was heavy with the knowledge that they would eventually be back here.

Meg had come running out of the house to greet her mother. She helped Annie up the steps—not that Annie really needed any help—and settled her on the couch in the living room before running off to bring her cookies and juice. Taylor and Annie had looked at each other and burst into muffled laughter at her gravity.

"I might have been better off in the hospital," Annie whispered.

"Except they didn't bake you cookies," Taylor answered as he went out the door. He came back a few minutes later with Annie's things and a small suitcase. Annie raised her eyebrow in question and Taylor answered, "I'm moving in, Annie."

"Taylor! Don't be ridiculous. I'm fine. You don't need to be here."

"Actually, Annie, I do need to be here. You were sent home with the understanding that we would be here to take care of you. I can't do that if I'm across town." When their debate was interrupted by Meg bringing in the treat for her mother, Taylor picked up his suitcase and went down the hall to the guestroom. He would be staying, no matter what Annie said.

Susan had joined Annie when Taylor came back into the room. "Susan, I can't thank you enough for being here for Meg," Annie was saying.

"That's what friends are for, Annie."

Taylor said, "She's right, Annie, you're just going to have to put up with people caring about you. Susan, I'm sure you're ready for a rest. I'll be staying here, so why don't you take some time off."

"There's a casserole ready to be heated for dinner and a salad in the fridge. I'll go do some grocery shopping tomorrow, but I'll check with you first to see what you need." She hugged Annie. "I'm glad you're home. Call me if you need me."

As he walked out with Susan to her car, she asked, "Taylor, what's going to happen?"

"I don't know for sure yet. Annie and I need to talk tonight. The most important thing is to get back to some semblance of normalcy for Meg's sake. I'll keep you posted."

*   *   *

Meg had tucked her mother into bed before she would even consider going to her own. Taylor finished cleaning up the kitchen, trying to stay out of the way, giving them time together. Meg came to the door, "Mom's in bed. She says she's going to read for awhile. I just wanted to say goodnight, Taylor." She gave him a fierce hug. "I'm glad you're staying here. Thank you."

"I'll be here as long as you need me, Meg. Go on to bed now. You need to get some rest so you don't get sick." He kissed the top of her head. "Sweet dreams."

When he was sure Meg was settled for the night, he knocked at the door of Annie's room.

"Come in, Taylor."

Annie was propped up in bed, a number of ledgers and papers scattered around her.

"Annie, what are you doing?"

"Taylor, I still have a business to run. I've got to make some decisions on this."

Taylor sat beside her on the bed and took the book out of her hands. Gathering it up with all the other things, he stacked them on the floor. "Not tonight, Annie. The business can wait. You and I need to talk about Meg."

"I thought we'd settled that this morning. We're going to find Cary..."

"Annie—please, just listen to me." He took her hands in his as he continued. "I want to start adoption proceedings for Megan right away. That means we do have to find Cary and get him to give her up officially. But, adopting her will legally make her my daughter."

Annie looked confused. "But, Taylor, I'd have to sign away my rights as well."

"Not if you marry me, Annie." Taylor's eyes never looked away from hers. "If we're married, it will make all of this easier. So, Anne Elizabeth Miller, will you marry me?"

Annie's eyes filled with tears. She knew exactly what Taylor was doing, and she knew he was right. But he would be giving up so much.

"Taylor, there must be some other way. What about you? What about Laura?"

She saw the pain that flashed in his eyes at the mention of Laura's name. "Laura will understand, Annie. I never got a chance to tell her how I felt, so I'm not breaking any promises to her. Right now, Megan is my first priority." He'd smiled at her as he wiped away her tears. "So, Annie...will you marry me?"

They had argued about it for another hour before he finally won and Annie agreed to marry him.

"You are a stubborn woman, Annie Miller soon-to-be Morgan. Now, is day after tomorrow too soon?"

"What? Taylor, there are a few practicalities here. Like a marriage license?"

"That's where money and influence come in. There will be a clerk here in the morning to witness our signatures and issue the license. A judge friend of Jude's will preside; the wedding will be at the condo at sunset. The caterers are already at work on the reception. All that's left is to call and invite the people we want to be there. I suggest we start with your parents since they need to know their flight time."

"Pretty sure of yourself, weren't you, Taylor?"

He touched her cheek gently. "Pretty sure that you would see this was our best hope of protecting Meg."

"Don't you ever get tired of rescuing me, Taylor?"

"Annie, I only wish I could."

*   *   *

A burst of laughter brought him out of his reverie. Some of the guests were getting ready to leave. Meg was bossily lining up all the women so that Annie could throw the bouquet. She never noticed that no one else tried to catch it as it landed safe in her own hands. Then she told Taylor and Annie to wait as she shooed everyone outside, finally calling to them that they could come out. As they did, they were met with a shower of rice and good wishes as they ran for the Jag. Taylor helped Annie in, then picked up Meg and whispered in her ear, "Just remember, you're the one who will clean every grain of rice out of this car, miss." She just giggled and kissed his cheek as he put her down. As they drove away, Taylor was startled at a terrible rattling in the usually quiet car until he realized that Meg had tied tin cans to the bumper.

Neighbors he had never seen before came out to stare at the racket in the normally staid neighborhood.

He stopped outside the security gate and detached them so the rest of their trip home was much quieter. Meg was staying with her grandparents at the condo so that he and Annie would have the house to themselves for their "wedding night." It wouldn't be what everyone was imagining. They had agreed that theirs was to be a marriage in name only, its purpose to provide strength for Annie and safety for Meg.

*   *   *

As the other guests departed, Taylor's agent made a decision. This was a publicity gold mine. Taylor and that chit who had taken over his publicity were missing an incredible opportunity. As soon as he was in his car, he pulled out his cell phone and made a few select calls, leaking the news for the morning papers.

*   *   *

Before Annie could step through the door, Taylor surprised her by picking her up and carrying her across the threshold. "No sense in tempting fate," he said as he put her down, his arms still around her. "Did I remember to tell you that you're a beautiful bride, Annie?"

"Thank you, Taylor. It was a wonderful wedding."

"Meg certainly enjoyed it," he said as he released her and closed the door behind them.

"Just think what she might have come up with if she'd had time to plan," Annie said as she pulled off her shoes.

Taylor could see she was tired. Today—the last few days—had been so stressful. It was fairly early yet, but he suggested she go on to bed. For now, he would be staying in the guestroom. They hadn't quite worked out how to explain that to Meg yet, but they would think of something. He kissed her forehead and said he'd check in on her before he went to bed.

When she had disappeared into her room, Taylor poured himself a glass of wine and went out on the deck. He'd already lied to Annie today. What a great way to start a marriage…

*   *   *

Annie found him just before the ceremony was to start. Meg had been determined that they not see each other so Annie had sent her off on an errand in order to sneak down the hall to Taylor's room.

"Taylor?"

He had been surprised to see her. "Annie? Is everything all right?"

"I'm fine, if that's what you're asking, Taylor. I just wanted to give you one more chance to back out of this. It's not fair to you. You're in love with Laura…"

"Annie," he'd said, placing his fingers across her lips. "Stop. I know what I'm doing."

"And Laura?"

"Laura understands."

"You talked to her, then?"

"Annie, stop worrying so much. Go, before Meg catches us."

She laughed at him and hurried back down the hall as they heard Meg coming up the stairs.

It hadn't been the truth. He hadn't talked to Laura. He hadn't been able to bring himself to tell her. He hoped she would understand, but this would be the second time he had walked out of her life. He wasn't sure she would give him a third chance.

Now, in the darkness of his "wedding night," he sat alone, waiting for his wife to be asleep so he could call the woman he loved and break her heart.

46

It was only six a.m. when the phone rang. Laura reached out and picked it up, swearing to kill whatever idiot was calling this early.

"Hello?"

"Laura, this is Elodie Nee." The president of Taylor's fan club sounded indignant as she demanded, "What's going on with Taylor?" Laura had found the woman to be very possessive of Taylor and any information about him. She seemed to believe that only she had the right to release any details of Taylor's life and career and she'd made it very clear that she didn't like Laura. The feeling was mutual.

"Elodie, I don't know what you're asking. Taylor is away on personal business."

"Personal? It certainly looks that way from the item in the *Times* this morning."

Laura sat up in bed and leaned against the headboard, trying to get her brain to take in what Elodie was saying. "Item? What item? We haven't released anything."

"Let me read it to you." Laura could hear paper rustling before she began to read. "Here it is,

> Sources close to superstar Taylor Morgan have let us
> know that entertainment's most eligible bachelor has
> finally tied the knot. Morgan was married late yesterday
> at his home in Florida to his long-time friend, Annie

Miller. Not only is the handsome bachelor now a married man, but he is a father as well, since his new bride brings with her an eleven-year-old daughter.

Laura, why didn't you let us know? News of this sort should appear on our information line as soon as you've released it to the papers."

Laura was stunned. It couldn't be true. Taylor had said he was moving out to Annie's. Some idiot reporter hadn't checked the facts and had jumped to the wrong conclusion.

"Elodie, calm down. Taylor didn't release this information. It sounds to me like someone was desperate for something to fill space in the gossip column."

"The Internet is already going nuts with it."

"Try to keep them calm. I'll get hold of Taylor and get an official announcement to release. I'll call you as soon as I know something."

All thoughts of sleep gone, Laura hung up the phone. It was still early in Florida. Taylor was probably awake, but Annie might be resting. She decided to wait another hour before calling. In the meantime, she would check out the news on the web and see what was being said on the list. She had the feeling she would be doing a lot of damage control later.

*　　　　　*　　　　　*

As Laura suspected, Taylor was awake. In fact, he had never been to sleep at all. He'd sat out on the deck for a long while last night, running every possible scene he could think of for telling Laura. No matter how he approached it, every one of them had ended with her walking out of his life. Finally, exhausted, he had gone back into the quiet house. As he had started for the guestroom, he'd been surprised to see Annie's light on. Knocking softly, he opened the door and found Annie standing by the window.

"Annie? It's late. You should be resting."

She'd turned and he could see she had been crying—was still crying. "Taylor, we've made a terrible mistake." She sank into the armchair by the window and buried her face in her hands, crying as if her heart was broken.

Taylor crossed the room and kneeled beside her. "Annie, what is it? What's wrong?"

"What isn't wrong, Taylor? This is our wedding night! I can remember a time that I would have been thrilled to say that. Now, all I know is that I've let you screw up your life by marrying me. I should never have agreed to this. Your life should be with Laura."

Taylor put his arms around her and let her cry. He wasn't going to argue with her. She was in no shape to listen to reason—and he was in no shape to offer it even though she was only partially right. He should have been married to Laura. But, he was the one who had screwed that up by leaving her at Christmas. If Laura loved him, she would find a way to understand why he had to be here with Annie for now.

When her tears had ceased, Taylor carried her to the bed and tucked her in. Taking a tissue, he gently wiped the tears from her face before offering it to her to blow her nose. That made her laugh.

Taking her hand and touching the gold band he had placed there, he looked into her eyes and said, "Annie, you have to stop beating yourself up over this. I did what I wanted to do. When have you ever known me to do something because I had to? This wasn't your idea, it was mine and I *do not* regret it. Annie, darling Annie, marrying you was as much for myself as for you and Meg. I want to be here for you. I want to spend as much time as I possibly can with you. I married you because I love you, Annie Morgan, so stop feeling guilty about it."

He leaned down and kissed her and felt her return his kiss as her arms came around his neck. For a moment, they were both still, their lips barely touching, waiting, exploring the emotions that surrounded them.

Taylor remembered the young woman who had shared his bed in New York all those years ago and how much he had loved her, how much he had loved making love to her. Even after they broke it off, through all these years of friendship, he had never forgotten what it was like to make love to Annie Miller.

Without taking his lips from hers, he breathed her name in question; her answering kiss was invitation enough, and he stretched out beside her, caressing her, murmuring her name as he unbuttoned the night-gown she wore.

*   *   *

Afterwards, in the darkness, he held Annie and tried to make sense of what had happened. He didn't know if their lovemaking was a product of her need or his, but the fact that it had happened had changed everything.

He had planned on telling Laura the truth about his marriage—that it was a means to protect Meg—a marriage of convenience. But what had happened tonight had changed all that. If he told Laura what he had planned to tell her, it would be a lie. If he told her what was now the truth, he would lose her forever.

Shortly before dawn, he untangled himself from his sleeping bride. Looking down at her, he realized the love he felt for her was much more complicated than he had thought, and he knew he couldn't promise Laura that he and Annie would never be together like this again. Picking up his clothes, he headed for a shower, hoping it would help clear his fuzzy brain. Afterwards, he would have to call Laura. It couldn't be put off any longer.

47

Taylor was waiting for a reasonable hour to call, reluctant to wake Laura with the news. When the phone rang at nine, he picked it up, never thinking it could be her.

"Good morning, Taylor."

"Laura! I was going to call you a little later. What are you doing awake this early?"

"Well, it certainly wasn't my idea." She laughed, and his heart lightened at the sound. "I got a phone call from Elodie at six this morning."

"What? Why would she be calling you so early? Why would she be calling you at all?"

"There's a report in the *Times* this morning that you and Annie were married yesterday, Taylor." His heart sank as he heard the words. "She's been besieged by phone calls, and the list is going nuts. I think you need to release an official statement to the fan club, at least, and I would recommend that you release one to the media as well."

He was appalled. Laura wasn't supposed to have found out this way. It was something he had needed to tell her himself. How had the papers gotten hold of the information?

"Taylor?"

"Laura...it's true." He could hear how emotionless he sounded. It was as if someone else was reading lines for him. "I never got to call you last night to tell you. I also never released the information, so I'll have to find out who did."

Laura felt her dreams shatter as he coldly said the words that destroyed all her hopes. She had been so sure after the tour, after that day on Catalina. How could she have misjudged his feelings so completely?

"Laura?"

"I guess congratulations are in order then, Taylor." He could hear the reserve in her voice as she shut him out. "I'm very happy for you both."

The phone had wakened Annie, and she had gotten up to see who had called. She stepped out in the hall just in time to hear Taylor plead, "Laura, please! You don't understand." Annie could hear the heartbreak in his voice, and she realized he hadn't told Laura. She must be devastated. Quietly, she retreated to the bedroom so he wouldn't know that she had heard.

"Taylor," Laura said, her voice all business," we need to release something to the media and to your fans. How would you like it phrased?"

"Laura…"

"I would like to get it out as soon as possible. I know you must have wanted it to remain private for awhile, but it's out now and you need to comment."

"Laura, just write up whatever you think is best. Just please don't mention Annie's illness." Laura could hear the defeat in his voice and knew that he had given up trying to justify it to her.

"Fine, Taylor. I had better go call Elodie before she loses it completely. Give my love to Annie and Meg, please."

He heard the click as she broke the connection between them. He silently replaced the phone. One by one, all of his nightmares were coming true.

*　　　　　*　　　　　*

Hanging up the phone, Laura was numb. First Cary, now Taylor. She had trusted them both. She had to be the most incredible idiot on the face of the earth!

She had seen Taylor with Annie the day they had spent with her. He hadn't acted like a man in love. He obviously adored Meg, and he cared for deeply for Annie. But to suddenly marry her? She knew that news of Annie's illness had hit him hard. Maybe it had brought out feelings he didn't realize he had.

Even if that were true, it didn't change the fact that he had said nothing to her, that he had let her find out through a carefully-placed leak. She wasn't sure what hurt more, misjudging his intentions or realizing her feelings were so completely unimportant to him.

As her anger grew, she made no attempt to keep it under control. It was easier to be angry with him than to try to understand what had happened. Resolutely, she turned to drafting a press release—the last one she planned on writing for him.

*   *   *

Taylor had no idea what to do now. Annie and Meg were still his first priority. They had to be. Yet all he wanted to do was get on a plane to Albuquerque and try to explain it all to Laura before he lost her for good. He picked up the glass he had been drinking from when the phone rang and threw it as hard as he could against the wall. As the glass shattered, he saw his dreams shattering, too.

"Taylor?" Annie spoke softly from the doorway of the bedroom.

"I'm sorry, Annie. I didn't mean to wake you. Don't come out here yet. I broke a glass and need to clean it up."

He went to the kitchen, coming back with a broom and dustpan. As he began to sweep up the glass, Annie said, "I heard the phone. Was it Meg?"

Taylor stopped and looked at her. "No, it was Laura. The news of our wedding was leaked to the papers. She wanted to know how to handle damage control." His voice was tight, and she knew him well enough to know he was hiding his true feelings.

"Is she all right, Taylor?"

He returned to his task so he didn't have to meet her eyes. "Laura is fine, Annie. Please stop worrying about it." Sweeping up the last of the glass, he continued, "There, I think it's safe to come out now, but make sure you're wearing shoes."

She watched as he walked back to the kitchen. After a few moments, she followed him. "Taylor," she said as she poured a glass of juice, "you've been so busy with all of the preparations for the wedding that you haven't been out on your skates in days. Why don't you go out for awhile? Surely, you need it by now."

Taylor looked at her as she busied herself with taking out bread and putting it in the toaster. Annie knew something was wrong. She had always been able see through him. He would have given anything to be able to talk to her about it.

"Will you be all right here, Annie?"

She turned around and met his eyes. "Let's get something straight, Taylor Morgan! I will not be watched all the time. I won't be coddled. I am still here and I intend to live my life without you or anyone telling me what I should and shouldn't be doing. So, go! Now!"

"Fine, Annie," Taylor said with a smile that didn't reach his eyes. "But the tabloids are going to have a field day with it when they see me out the morning after my wedding!"

Laughing, she threw a towel at him. "They're going to have a field day no matter what, Taylor. You might as well give them something to work with."

*   *   *

Cary sat at his desk looking over the morning papers. As he turned a page of the *Times*, Taylor's name practically leaped off the page at him.

He read the brief note and smiled to himself. So, Taylor Morgan had finally married Annie. He was probably the only reader who wasn't surprised at the news, although he did briefly wonder what had happened to Taylor's budding relationship with Laura. He had seen her articles about the tour and had assumed they were lovers.

He stood and walked to the window of his TNC office. Already he had been given a couple of plum assignments and was pretty sure he was being groomed to take one of the anchor slots. Things were going well for him. He wasn't going to let news about Taylor and Annie bother him. He really didn't care what either of them did anymore. They were the past. The world outside this window was the future.

*   *   *

The commercial ended, and the camera came in on a close-up of the "Entertainment Tonight" anchor's face as she said, "Congratulations and Best Wishes are in order for Taylor Morgan, who has released the news that he was married in a private ceremony last night. Morgan, seen here after his triumphant Catalina concert last week, confirmed the news through his spokeswoman this morning. According to Morgan, his bride is a long-time friend from his Broadway days and the mother of Morgan's goddaughter, Megan."

The camera cut back to the anchor who smiled brightly and said, "We should note that the woman in that clip is not Taylor's new bride. That was his assistant, Laura Collins, who sent us the story this morning. We wish Taylor and his bride all the best."

As soon as they were safely into the next tape, the woman turned to her partner and said, "I was there the night we shot that clip. I would have bet money that Taylor was going to be married soon, but to his assistant, not to someone we've never heard of. Goes to show that appearances can be deceiving."

*   *   *

Taylor watched the "E.T." story. Laura had done a good job with the announcement but he knew it must have caused her tremendous pain. Annie and Meg were doing homework in Meg's room, so Taylor picked up the phone to see if Laura had calmed down enough to speak to him.

*   *   *

Laura was at the computer, composing her letter of resignation when the phone rang. She didn't want to talk to anyone right now, so she let it ring until the machine picked up.

"Laura? It's Taylor. I just watched the piece on 'E.T.'—you did a great job. I just wanted to tell you." His voice trailed off but he didn't break the connection. Laura waited to see what he would say. "Laura...I really would like to talk to you about all of this. There's a lot I need to explain. Please, give me a chance to tell you how this happened. Call me at Annie's."

She listened as the machine reset itself after he hung up and then returned to her letter.

*   *   *

In Florida, Taylor hung up the phone. He was sure she had been there, listening to him. He had to find a way to talk to her.

As Annie had suggested this morning, he had gone out for awhile. His in-line skates were still at the condo, so he chose to go for a run instead. It felt good to push himself and he ran further than he usually would have before he turned and began a slow jog back to Annie's—back "home." The exercise had helped clear his head and had given him some time to think things through, to get his priorities straight.

After he showered, he found Annie at her desk in the family room. "Annie, are you working on that again?"

She looked up from the ledger in front of her. He looked better than when he had left. "I have to get this all together, Taylor, if I'm going to sell the studio."

"Is that what you've decided to do, Annie?"

"Eventually. I want to keep teaching for now. If I don't, Meg will know there's something seriously wrong. But I want to talk to Jane to see if she wants to keep it. She's good with the kids and has a good feel for running the studio. I'd like her to have it."

"Why sell it to her, Annie? Why don't you just give it to her, or sell it for some minimal amount to satisfy the IRS? If it's for money for Meg, she's never going to want for anything, Annie, you know that."

"Taylor, I have never taken money from you before and I'm not about to start now!"

"Annie! We were never married before. You don't have much choice."

She glared at him for a moment until she gave in to the smile that had spread across his face. "Damn it, Taylor. You always win."

The smile faded, and shadows filled his eyes. "Not always, Annie."

She looked away from his grief and said, "I'll think about the studio a little longer. Right now, we better come up with an explanation for our separate bedrooms before Miss Eleven-going-on-thirty gets home."

"After last night, Annie, is there any point in keeping separate bedrooms?"

"Taylor, it shouldn't have happened. I'm sorry...."

"No, Annie, don't!" She was surprised by his anger. "Don't you dare apologize for that. What happened between us should be something we're celebrating. Can you honestly tell me that you don't want me there?"

"Taylor, I don't know what to say." Annie came over and kneeled beside his chair. "Last night was wonderful. But we agreed that wasn't what we were going to be."

Cradling her face in his hands, he looked into her eyes. "We were wrong, Annie. I think we both need this marriage. I love you, Annie, more than I realized."

He kissed her gently. Annie wanted to remind him about Laura, but she couldn't. She needed him to be there for her, and right or wrong, she wanted to be his wife.

*   *   *

Before Meg had come home, he moved his things into Annie's bedroom. He had no doubts that this was the right thing for them. He had made a commitment to Annie, a commitment that he planned to honor. He shut Laura out of his mind and heart, safely locking the memories away with all the others of his past.

He spent the day installing his computer in the guestroom that Annie insisted he take as his own space. He had done some research and found listservs for children with critically ill parents, listservs for children who had lost parents. He wanted Meg to have as much support ready for her as possible when the time came.

Annie's parents and Megan arrived in the afternoon, and they had dinner together before Annie took her parents to the airport. She had made the decision not to tell them, or Meg, about the tumor until it was absolutely necessary. She and Taylor had also agreed that, if Meg asked, whichever one of them she questioned, she would have to be told the truth.

Annie had gone to bed long before him and had been asleep when he finally joined her. She murmured his name sleepily as he slipped in beside her, and he took her in his arms, holding her as she slept, wondering late into the night how it was possible to love two women as deeply as he did.

*   *   *

He received Laura's resignation the next morning. He had been up early and out for a run before either Annie or Meg woke. He had just been returning to the house when a delivery truck pulled into the driveway. Taylor had intercepted him before he could ring the door-bell, signing for the package addressed to "Barnum." It had come overnight express from Albuquerque and he knew before he opened it what it would contain.

He threw it, unopened, onto his computer desk and gone to take a shower. Irrationally, he was hoping it would be gone by the time he came back to it, but it was there waiting for him, and he knew he could-n't put off opening it any longer.

Taylor-

It is with regret that I tender my immediate resigna-tion as your assistant/publicist. Now that the tour is over, I have requested to end my leave of absence early and will be returning to the *Herald*.

I have enjoyed my time as your assistant and am grateful for the opportunities it offered. Please let me know if there is any way that I can help with your search and training for my replacement.

Sincerely-

Laura Collins

Gently, he placed the single sheet of paper back in the envelope. That was it, then. Laura was out of his life. He couldn't have expected any-thing else, but he had hoped.

*   *   *

Taylor told Annie that Laura had resigned. "She's decided she really wants to go back to the paper."

"Are you going to try to change her mind, Taylor?"

"No, Annie. She made it clear that this is what she wants to do. I don't really have much for her to do anyway. I've already instructed my agent's office to cancel anything I was scheduled for. They can handle any publicity I might need, and I've asked Elodie to send out a message to the fans that I need a little time with my new family. It's better this way."

Annie knew it wasn't better for him at all. She could hear it in his voice, see it in his eyes, and she was powerless to do anything to change it.

*   *   *

They quickly settled into a routine. Meg returned to school, a mini-celebrity because of the news she brought with her. Annie returned to the studio part-time, teaching only her advanced classes. Only Taylor was left with nothing to keep him busy. He had kept the condo as a rehearsal space rather than moving the piano to Annie's. It was too big to really fit in her house, anyway. Most days he took Annie to the studio, then went to the condo to "work" before picking Annie up when her classes were over.

He didn't get much work done. He couldn't find the joy within himself anymore to sing. Mostly he just did exercises to keep his voice in shape and spent the rest of the time reading or staring off into space.

*   *   *

Laura hadn't told Taylor the truth. She hadn't asked to return to the *Herald*, not yet anyway. She still intended to try to make a go of it as a free-lance writer. She resumed her counseling sessions and began to build a new life—again.

*   *   *

Annie tried to carry on with her life in as normal a fashion as possible. She was actually able to forget for long periods of time that she carried a time bomb in her head. She was grateful to Taylor for his love and support but never ceased to feel guilty that she was the obstacle that was keeping him from Laura.

While Taylor worked on the computer in the evenings or watched television with Meg, Annie worked on getting her affairs in order.

*   *   *

Two weeks after their wedding, Annie returned to the hospital for another CT scan. According to the doctor, the news was "good"—the tumor didn't appear to be growing, and the medication was managing the pain.

That was the night that her lawyer called with the news that she had located Cary.

48

"I actually found him almost right away, but I decided to try to obtain his signature without either of you having to have anything to do with him."

Taylor took Annie's hand, then said, "I assume he wouldn't cooperate."

"Not a chance. I received this from his lawyer yesterday."

She handed them a letter. It was written in formal "legalese," but they were able to get through enough of it to know that Cary wouldn't sign the papers without meeting personally with Taylor to "assure himself that the petitioner will be an appropriate guardian for his daughter."

Annie was confused. "Why Taylor? Wouldn't he want to take it out on me?"

"He's been biding his time all these years, Annie, waiting to get his revenge. If I come crawling to him, wanting something he controls, then he's put back in the position of power. Power over me and over you. He doesn't give a damn about Megan. He just wants to make us grovel." Standing and moving to where he could look out the window, Taylor was silent for a minute before he turned back to them. "If groveling is what it takes to keep Meg safe, then that's what I'll do."

"Taylor, we could do this completely through the courts, you know."

"And have tabloids get hold of it? Have Meg dragged through all of that? No, I'll play his game. It will be easier in the long run. Set up the meeting as soon as possible."

Jude had called them that evening. "He's insisting on meeting with his lawyer present, Taylor. Do you want me to go with you? I would advise that you say 'yes.'"

"I suppose that makes some sense. I doubt he'll cave in at this first meeting. He's more interested in humiliating me and hurting Annie. He's not going to give up on that quickly."

"There's always the publicity angle to hold over him. From what I gather, he's a rising star at TNC. A public scandal about his abandoned child won't help his career."

"No, we can't use that unless it becomes absolutely necessary. He's liable to call our bluff on it, and then Meg would be the one who was hurt. Just set up this meeting, Jude. The sooner we start playing his game, the sooner it will be over."

*   *   *

One week later, Taylor and Jude entered the offices of a prestigious law firm in Atlanta. Identifying themselves, they were shown into a conference room and offered coffee or tea, then left alone for a few minutes.

Taylor stood at the window while Jude sat at the table and took out her files. She looked at him and could see the lines that all of this had already etched into his face. He turned as the door opened, and Cary Edwards entered the room followed by his lawyer.

Cary was at his most charming when he was introduced to Jude, and he played the "old buddy" as he said to Taylor, "It's good to see you again, Taylor. You've made quite a success of yourself since the good old days in New York. And, I think we have a friend in common. Laura Collins? I read somewhere she was your assistant. She and I were pretty heavily involved while I did my time in Albuquerque."

Jude saw the fury in Taylor's eyes and interrupted Cary's carefully scripted reunion. It was obvious that he knew exactly what to say to goad Taylor. It was her job to keep Taylor from losing it.

"My client and I have a return flight to catch. Perhaps we could get started?"

The lawyers opened the discussions with a lot of legal thrust and parry. Taylor and Cary were only observers in this opening round of negotiations.

Cary sat across the table from Taylor looking relaxed and without a care. Taylor's tension showed in the lines around his mouth and eyes. The stiffness of his posture contrasted graphically with the relaxed attitude Cary projected.

"Perhaps Mr. Edwards would care to tell us his concerns so that my client and I might address them." Jude deftly took control away from the opposing lawyer.

"Of course," Cary said as he straightened his tie. "I never had any concerns about my ex-wife's ability to care for *our* daughter." His emphasis was subtle but unmistakable. "I do have concerns now that Taylor has reentered the picture. His lifestyle is far from steady, and I have some concerns about who will be caring for my daughter while Taylor and the former Mrs. Edwards are following Taylor's 'muse.'"

Jude answered; she had cautioned Taylor not to make any statements unless she specifically asked for one. "I understand your concern, Mr. Edwards. However, the record shows that Mr. Morgan has been on the road less than six months total in the last five years. That's not a lot. I would venture to guess that your reporting duties have taken you away for equal, if not longer, periods of time."

Cary wasn't happy. He had underestimated Taylor's lawyer, dismissing her as an unimportant *woman* who would quickly fall prey to his charms. He threw a look to his own lawyer, who, taking his cue, responded, "How my client has spent his time is not relevant. Since Mr. Morgan is petitioning for custody of the minor child, he, and his lifestyle, are what are in question here."

After another hour of legal wrangling, Taylor was at the end of his rope. As he had predicted, Cary had no intention of giving in at this meeting. He couldn't understand why Jude was insisting on continuing.

Finally, Cary's lawyer said, "I can see we are making little progress here. Unless there are extenuating circumstances that make speed an important part of this process, I think we should agree to meet again in, say, another month? We can prepare a list of questions and send them to you so that we can try to cut to the heart of this in a more expedient manner."

A month? Taylor wasn't sure if Annie had a month. But the last thing they wanted was for Cary to know that Annie was dying. He heard Jude agreeing to the proposal and knew that Cary had won this round; he wasn't prepared at all for Cary's parting shot.

"I have been thinking that I would like to meet with my daughter to see how she feels about all of this. Perhaps she would prefer to come live with me?"

Jude was too slow to stop Taylor as he came to his feet so quickly he knocked over his chair. "Damn you, Edwards! You won't get anywhere near Megan. You walked out of her life before she was even born. You haven't made one attempt to see her in the eleven years she's been alive. If you make any attempt to see her now, I'll kill you!" Taylor turned and left the room before he gave in to the urge to smash Cary's self-right-eous face.

*   *   *

Jude found him fifteen minutes later in the small courtyard of the building that housed the law office. He looked completely defeated, and she wished she could say something to make him feel better. But, the truth was, his outburst had just made things worse.

He turned at the sound of her footsteps. "We'd better head back for the airport, Taylor," she said. She headed for the street, Taylor following, to the cab the receptionist had summoned for them. Giving the driver their destination, she waited until he had pulled out into traffic before she quietly said, "You know that wasn't any help, Taylor."

"I know. Even when I was yelling at him, I knew it was the wrong thing to do. The idea of his having anything to do with Megan…I'm sorry. I lost it."

"You could have gotten away with yelling at him, Taylor. Threatening to kill him was the mistake. If this, God forbid, goes to court, he can use it against us. Your outburst today and your physical attack on him before Meg was born, can be made to look as if you are unstable and unsuitable to be Meg's father. When we meet with him again, Taylor, you have to keep your personal feelings for him in check. You simply can't risk an outburst like that again."

Taylor only nodded mutely. He knew he had blown it. The thought of Cary being anywhere near Megan, hurting her as he had hurt Annie and Laura, had just been more than he could handle.

Jude reached out and put her hand on his. "Taylor. It's fixable. For what it's worth, I think you're right. He's just playing with you. He doesn't want Megan, he just wants your pride. Meg will be safe."

Taylor noticed she didn't promise. Until those papers were signed, Cary could still take Meg away from him.

*   *   *

It was late when they finally arrived back in Tampa. As Taylor was driving Jude home, she said, "Taylor, you need to let go of this afternoon. This will all work out." He nodded even though he didn't believe it.

The house was dark as he pulled into the driveway. It felt as if a lifetime had passed since he left that morning. Quietly, he opened the door and came into the silent house. He walked down the hall to Meg's room and opened the door. She was sleeping, secure in the love of her mother and the knowledge that Taylor would take care of her. He just hoped he could live up to her expectations.

"Taylor?" Annie spoke quietly from the darkened hallway behind him, and he closed the door before he turned to answer her.

"Annie, I didn't mean to wake you."

"You didn't, Taylor. I've been waiting for you to get home."

Taylor put his arm around her and walked with her back to their bedroom. "He wouldn't sign, Annie," he said with defeat in his voice.

"Then you were right. He's playing some kind of game with us."

"Don't worry, Annie. He doesn't want Meg. We just have to let him think he's winning for awhile but he'll sign the papers eventually." He kissed her forehead, then held her for a moment. "Now, back to bed with you, Annie. You need your rest."

She looked up at him. "And you, Taylor?"

"I can't sleep yet, Annie. I'm too keyed up. I think I'll stay up and read for awhile."

She brushed her fingers across his cheek. "Don't stay up too much longer, Taylor. You look worn out."

"I won't, Annie," he said as he left the room.

*   *   *

Taylor sat in the dark of the guestroom that had become his space in this house. His mind kept replaying the scene in the lawyer's office until he was sick of thinking about it. He decided to check in on his e-mail to see if that would distract him.

Logging on, he scanned the list of messages. Most of it was from the fan list. The discussions lately had been about his marriage, and he had found some of them pretty scary; a couple of them had even threatened suicide because he was no longer available. Maybe, when this was all over, he would officially retire, take Meg, and live in Europe for awhile. He was tired of the rest of the world acting like they owned him.

Almost without thinking, he found himself composing a note to Laura.

Laura-

    I hope you'll read this instead of deleting it just because it's from me. I guess I really need to talk to someone.

    Annie is doing well. If I didn't know better, I'd think she was perfectly all right. The medications seem to be handling the pain, so she's able to handle everything else. Meg is Meg. She still has no idea of what's going to happen, what is happening on her behalf now.

    Laura, I'm trying to adopt Meg. Annie's lawyer is pretty sure that just naming me Meg's guardian in her will is not going to be enough. If her birth father decides to crawl out from under a rock and take her, the courts would favor him over me because he's her birth father. It seems to make no difference that he's never seen her, never provided any support. Because she is his blood, he would be deemed more suitable.

    So, we've traced him down. He's in Atlanta, a rising star at TNC. He refused to sign the papers sent by our lawyer, insisted on meeting with me. That happened today.

    He hasn't changed. He's still smooth and charming, and if you didn't know what he was really like, you could easily be taken in by his veneer. He claims he wants to make sure I'm a fit father for Meg, and is raising all sorts of objections. Our lawyer was pretty good at taking away his excuses, but we didn't reach an agreement.

    I never thought he would agree in this round anyway. He's never forgiven me for saving Annie from him all those years ago. He has a chance now to have the upper hand, and he's taking full advantage of it, enjoying seeing me grovel. I think he'll sign eventually—he certainly doesn't want to be bothered with a little girl.

He doesn't know that Annie's dying. If he did, I'm afraid he'd just refuse to sign to make the time she has left as miserable as possible. It's all such a confusing mess.

Meg doesn't know any of this is happening. We decided not to tell her until the papers were signed.

I truly complicated it today. He threatened to demand to meet Meg before he would sign. I lost it. I came out of my chair, and if I could have reached him, I would have killed him then and there. Instead, I only threatened to—in the presence of my lawyer and his.

Laura, I'm sorry. I have no right to expect you to listen to me. If I told Annie any of this, she would only worry. No one else, besides our lawyer, knows what's happening. You are one of a handful of people who know the truth about Annie.

Don't feel like you have to answer this. It helps to clear my head just setting it all out like this. I can convince myself that you're reading it.

I miss you.

Taylor

49

Sleeping late was one of the advantages of being her own boss, Laura thought when she woke. The luxury of sleeping in after last night's late flight from California was wonderful.

On the other hand, paying the bills was one of the disadvantages. She could not afford to turn down any work right now and was forced to accept when Robert had asked her to write an article about Catalina Island for a special travel supplement that was coming up. Ironically, it had been her last article about the tour that had given him the idea, an article written before she had learned of Taylor's betrayal.

It had been hard to go back. There were memories everywhere she looked and people who had remembered her, asking endless questions about Taylor and his marriage. Kicking off the blanket, she resolved to get the article written today; then she could stop thinking about it—stop thinking about him.

*   *   *

An hour later, showered and dressed, she went to the computer and turned it on. While it was booting up, she found her book with her notes on Catalina. The article should be easy to write if she just stuck to the facts.

Before she started, she opened her e-mail and quickly scanned the list of messages, swearing she was not going to be distracted by any of them. Her resolution went out the window when she saw the message from "Barnum".

Why was he there? What could he want? Other than a formal letter from his lawyer acknowledging her letter of resignation, enclosing a final paycheck and bonus, she had heard nothing. Why now when she was trying to get on with her life? He had already broken her heart twice. She would have to be crazy to let him into her life again. Her fingers reached for the delete key, touching it gently, playing with it, before she finally pressed it and watched the "D" appear beside his message.

*   *   *

Taylor was surprised when he woke up to find it was already nine o'clock. Annie would have had to be at the studio by now. She should have wakened him, but when he looked out the window, her car was gone. She had obviously gone on without him. Still not completely awake, he opened the refrigerator and found a note from Annie leaning up against the juice bottle.

Good morning, lazy!

You were sleeping so soundly I couldn't bear to wake you. You're doing too much and getting too little rest, Taylor. It's time you quit taking care of me and took a little care of yourself.

I have some errands to do this afternoon after my class. I'll pick Meg up at school, and then we'll be home.

Enjoy the quiet!

Love,

Annie

She was right; he hadn't been sleeping well. Evidently his body had decided that he needed some rest. Opening the door to the deck, he stepped out into the tropical morning.

There were times he really missed having well-defined seasons. Spring, when he was growing up, had meant the return of real green. He could still hear his mother calling him and his father to come out and see the first daffodil of the season. They would come grumbling out to look at the flower, and the joy on her face had never failed to cheer them out of their winter doldrums.

He remembered then that he'd written to Laura last night—crying on her shoulder. How could he have done something so stupid? He missed her terribly, but he had no right to be barging back into her life. He went back inside, going to the computer and turning it on. Nothing. Of course there was nothing. He had sent the message at one a.m. Laura would have long been asleep and was probably not up yet this morning. Even then she would be rushing around to get ready to go to work. Checking his sent-mail file, he reread his message. It sounded so pathetic in the bright light of day. He would have liked to take it back, but that was impossible. He would have to wait to see if she responded—and he was not sure if he wanted her to or not.

*　　　　*　　　　*

As if pressing the delete key would instantly remove the message, Laura quickly "undeleted" it, annoyed to find her heart racing at having almost lost his words. She got up, went to the kitchen and opened her morning soda, before she slowly carried it back to the computer. She was almost surprised to find the message still there, the cursor waiting patiently for her command.

She sat down again and, taking a deep breath, opened his message.

*　　　　*　　　　*

Taylor took the car and his in-line skates to Bayshore Drive. He had been running most mornings in Annie's neighborhood. It had been more than three weeks since he had taken off on his skates beside the restless waters of the bay. He was late enough today to have missed the early-morning joggers. Instead, he encountered mothers with strollers and old couples walking slowly along. He smiled or nodded at a few of them, returning greetings when they were given, but mostly keeping to himself, lost in the rhythmic push of his wheels.

*   *   *

Sitting at her desk, Laura cried as she read his message. For the first time since Cary had raped her, she regretted not pressing charges. If she had, he wouldn't have been threatening Annie and Taylor this way. The thought of Cary with an innocent little girl filled her with horror at what he might be capable of doing.

Her desk had been a gift from her father when she left for college. He had built it for her and included an ingenious hidden drawer for her "secrets." As she pressed the catch that released it, she knew he had never dreamed that any secret it would hide would be this horrible. She took a manila envelope out of the drawer and carried it to the couch. Remembering what it contained, her hands were shaking as she opened it.

Before she left for Florida and the tour, Laura had visited her lawyer's office. She had made sure her will was in order, then asked that he bring in a stenographer to take down what she needed to say. With her lawyer as witness, she had given a verbal accounting of Cary's attack, and waited while his secretary put it in written form. Then, computer disk and hard copy, along with an audiotape of her statement, were placed in an envelope, sealed, and left with her lawyer. A second printout had been given to her, and she had brought it home and placed it in her hiding place.

She had not known why she had felt compelled to do it—insurance in case Cary ever appeared again, she guessed. Whatever had led her to do it, she had slept better and felt safer knowing there was a record.

Now this was happening. Cary was deliberately hurting someone else, someone she cared about, and here, in her hands, she held the key to stopping him. It was a risk. If he called her bluff, she would have to go through with releasing it and pressing charges. He could always claim blackmail...which it was, she acknowledged ruefully. It would be his word against hers, but she was sure he wouldn't risk it. His career was too important to him. If signing away the daughter he did not care about would buy him freedom from this threat, she was sure he would do it.

Sliding the papers back in the envelope, she went back to the computer and began a search that would lead her to Cary Edwards.

50

An elated Cary almost ran down the corridor to his office. He had just been handed his first big assignment, covering the never-ending peace talks in Northern Ireland. Sure, it was dangerous, but it was the kind of thing that could push him to the top. It was his ticket to the big time. He was smiling broadly as he came into the waiting area outside his office, but his smile quickly died as he saw who was waiting there.

"Hello, Cary." Laura showed none of the nervousness she felt. She was cool and collected and every bit as beautiful as Cary remembered.

"Laura, this is a surprise!" Conscious of the eyes of the secretary, he was careful not to show any of the dismay he felt. "What are you doing in Atlanta?"

"Research for a story on absentee fathers. I've left the *Herald,* and I'm doing freelance work now. I figured I might as well look you up while I was here. After all, we hardly got to say goodbye properly." Her voice held a hint of sensuality that his secretary was finding very interesting.

"Well, come in so we can get caught up. Joanne, hold my calls."

He led the way into his office, closing the door behind them before retreating behind the security of the desk. He did not for a moment believe that she was here just to say "hello." Laura wanted something and it frightened him to think what it was. Her timing was uncanny. Any hint of scandal right now would send him back to the bottom of the ladder, and he was prepared to do whatever it took to make her go away quietly.

"So, Laura, let's stop playing this game. What do you really want?"

She took a manila folder from her briefcase and handed it to him. "Take a look at that, Cary. I think you'll find it interesting reading." She settled back into her chair and watched as he opened the file.

It was all there, in a stack of six pages of photocopied, computer-generated text. In graphic terms she had described the events of their last meeting, leaving nothing to the imagination except the names of the parties involved—at least he assumed that was what was blacked out throughout the text. The portrait it painted was far from flattering. He carefully closed the file and folded his hands on top of it, waiting to see what she would say.

"Interesting reading, isn't it, Cary?" All hints of warmth were gone from her voice. In fact, Cary imagined that he could feel the temperature dropping in the office as she went on. "I'm sure your lawyer and your boss would find it very interesting. Don't you agree? I know my lawyer found it fascinating when I dictated it in his office. Fascinating enough that he kept a copy of the recording and the original computer disk that holds the transcription."

"What do you want, Laura?"

"I want you to quit fighting Taylor Morgan's petition to adopt Megan." Cary laughed. "So that's it. You're still carrying a torch for him."

"What I'm feeling is irrelevant, Cary. If you don't sign the papers within a week, I'll go public with this story."

"It will be my word against yours, Laura. I'm not without influence."

"Influence that would dry up the minute this hit the news, Cary. You know it, and I know it so let's stop playing games." She stood and leaned over the desk so that her face was just inches from his before she went on, "I'll release it Cary. Don't make the mistake of thinking I won't."

She picked up her briefcase and then opened the door. Turning back before she went through, she said, brightly for the audience in the outer office, "It was wonderful to see you, Cary, to talk over old times. Take care." She smiled at the secretary and left the waiting room, the perfect picture of confidence and success.

* * *

Cary sat in his office, stunned by the implications of her visit. Laura had changed, become stronger, and he had no doubt she would go to the press if necessary. Even if he were somehow not convicted, his reputation and career would be destroyed. After feeding her file through the shredder, he picked up the phone and called his lawyer.

* * *

Laura's calm and confidence lasted only until the elevator doors closed. She was alone, so there was no one to see the tremors that began to shake her as she leaned against the wall, eyes closed. When she exited the elevator on the ground floor of Cary's building, she rushed to a nearby ladies' room where she lost everything she had eaten for breakfast that morning.

* * *

It had been almost a week since he had sent his message to Laura, and there had been no answer. Taylor began to believe that she really had trashed it. He couldn't blame her, but he had hoped they could some-how salvage their friendship. Despite her silence, he refused to give up on her, checking his e-mail at least twice a day.

* * *

On the plane back to Albuquerque, Laura ran through the scene with Cary again and again in her mind, feeling sicker each time. The flight attendant, noticing her pallor and the sweat that beaded her

brow, stopped to ask if she was feeling all right and brought her tea
and crackers.

She had done what she could. She had to hope it would work and
that Taylor would let her know it had. She had not answered Taylor's
message. She wanted to wait, to see what happened. If she answered too
soon, Taylor might make a connection between her and Cary. There was
no reason now for him to ever know what had happened.

5 1

It was late when the phone rang. Annie had gone to bed, Meg was asleep, and Taylor was trying to avoid checking his e-mail for the third time today.

"Hello?"

"Taylor! It's Jude. I've been out of the office all day, in court and in meetings. I just stopped by on my way home to check the mail. You will not believe what I found!"

Taylor had never heard their normally calm lawyer sound quite so excited. "Jude? Are you all right?"

"I'm fine, Taylor, and so are you and Annie and Meg! He signed the papers, Taylor! Edwards has given up his rights to Meg!"

Taylor was numb. It was too easy. A few days ago, Cary wouldn't give Meg up for anything. What could possibly have happened in that time to change his mind?

"Taylor? Are you there?"

"I'm here, Jude. I just don't believe it. It's amazing and too easy. Are you sure?"

"Signed by Edwards, witnessed by his attorney, notarized, and sent air express. It's real, Taylor. Megan is your daughter—at least she will be as soon as we get a court date."

"Jude, thank you. I don't know what else to say."

Her voice softened. "You don't have to say anything, Taylor. Just go tell Annie the good news. I'll talk to you both tomorrow as soon as I get a date scheduled for the adoption hearing. It's over, Taylor. You and Annie can sleep well tonight."

Taylor replaced the phone, still in shock, and went to their room. Annie was already awake.

"Who was on the phone, Taylor?"

He sat beside her on the bed and took her hand in his. He looked so serious that Annie was frightened. "Taylor? What is it? Is something wrong?"

"No, Annie, something is very right. That was Jude. God knows why, but Cary's given up the fight. He signed the papers that clear the way for me to adopt Meg."

He watched as the news slowly sank in and was surprised when Annie burst into tears. He held her tightly while she cried, then brushed the tears from her face.

"Oh, Taylor, I never thought he would sign them. I've been so afraid…afraid that I would leave Meg unprotected."

"Annie, I would have fought him tooth and nail, you know that."

"I know, Taylor, but the legal system is so screwed up. I couldn't count on it recognizing what was right for Meg. But, with you, she'll be fine, and all that I've dreamed for her…" Annie's voice trailed off into tears again.

"All that you've dreamed for her, I'll do my best to make come true, Annie."

Annie placed her hand on his cheek and said, "I love you, Taylor Morgan."

He answered her with a gentle kiss that led to a physical demonstration of that love for only the second time in the month they had been married. Afterward, in the darkness of the room, his arms around Annie as she slept, Taylor went over the battle with Cary in his mind. There was some key, something that had triggered his change of heart—although heart was probably not the right word! Look at what he had done to Annie, to Laura…Laura! *She* was the key. Taylor knew it! This had happened too easily, too quickly after he had written to her. She must have used what Cary had done to her as some kind of bargaining chip. Someday, he promised himself, someday I'll find out if I'm right. For the first time in weeks, Taylor slept peacefully through the night.

52

Meg had been ecstatic when they told her Taylor wanted to adopt her. Once Cary had signed the papers, everything went smoothly. Less than two weeks later, on her twelfth birthday, a judge declared that Megan Elizabeth Miller would now be known as Megan Elizabeth Morgan. To mark the occasion, Taylor gave her his mother's locket. "She would have loved having you for her granddaughter, Meg," he said as he fastened it around her neck. "As much as I love that you're my daughter now in the eyes of the world." As Meg had thrown her arms around him, he met Annie's eyes and saw a new peace there.

Unfortunately, that peace was short-lived.

The next CT scan was bad news. The tumor was growing again, and Annie admitted she needed more of the pain medications just to get through the day. When they came home, she was so drained, physically and emotionally, she went straight to bed.

Meg had bounced in from school, her exuberance stilled when Taylor told her that Annie was resting.

"Taylor?"

"Meg, let's walk down to the duck pond for a little while." Taylor could see the question in her eyes and knew that it was time to tell her the truth. As they sat on a bench watching the ducks and the people feeding them, Meg finally asked the question he and Annie had known would come some day.

"Mom's really sick, isn't she?"

"Yes, Meg, she is." Taylor reached out and took her icy hands in his.

"Is...is she going to get better, Taylor?" Meg looked at him, fear evident in her eyes.

"No, Meg," his voice broke as he said it, "she won't be getting better."

She stared at him, her eyes wild as she tried to take in what was saying, trying to turn the truth into something she could understand and live with. Then, with a cry of "No!" she twisted away from him and took off running towards home.

Taylor ran after her, but she still beat him there. He expected to find her with Annie but the bedroom was dark, Annie asleep. As he came to Meg's door he could hear her weeping.

"Meg..."

"It's all *your* fault, Taylor! I told you she was having headaches and I asked you to talk to her, but you just went off on your tour and now she's never going to get well and it's all your fault!"

He was stunned. She was right. He had not listened, hadn't checked, had forgotten and, by forgetting, had failed Meg. It would not have changed what was happening—the doctor had already told them that—but it might have saved Meg from feeling so betrayed.

"I hate you, Taylor Morgan. I hate you and I don't want to be your daughter. I don't want my mother to die...."

"Oh, Meg..." Annie spoke softly from the doorway. Taylor turned to her, but she waved him away, going straight to Meg and pulling her into her arms. It didn't matter that Meg was nearly as tall as she was now. Annie sat in the rocker where she'd nursed her, holding her tightly, crooning to her in that language unique to mother and child. Taylor left the room, closing the door behind him.

It was a long time before Annie came out, looking as shattered as Meg had earlier. Taylor went to her, picking her up before she could collapse, and carried her to their bedroom where he held her much as she had held Meg. When Annie had finally cried herself to sleep, Taylor checked on Meg who was sleeping too. Gently he pulled the sheet up over her before he left the room.

He wanted to rage and scream at the injustice of it all, and he felt so *alone*. There was no one he could turn to. *Annie* was his best friend. She was the one who had always listened to him, always been his solace. Turning to the only one could think of, he logged on and poured his heart out to Laura.

She had finally answered him when he had written to tell her that Cary had caved in and Megan was now legally his child. Her note had been reserved, but it had been the beginning of the bridge back to their friendship. He had gotten in the habit of writing to her and she answered occasionally. It had been a help just knowing *someone* was listening.

His letter was long and rambling, filled with his grief and remorse and made little sense. But, putting it all down in writing had eased his immediate pain. It was after midnight before he finally fell asleep in the chair.

In the early hours of the morning, he was jolted awake by something—Meg covering him with a quilt. When his eyes opened, she whispered, "I'm sorry, Taylor...I didn't mean it." He picked her up and wrapped her in the quilt with him before he whispered back, "I know, Meg. It's all right. I love you." She fell asleep then, and he held her through the rest of the night.

*   *   *

Laura continued to be there for him even though each of his messages reminded her of all they had lost. She suggested to Taylor that he give Meg her e-mail address so she had someone to talk to who had been there. Meg discovered in Laura a place where she could express her fears, and the two of them forged an e-mail friendship.

*   *   *

When school was out at the end of May, Taylor took Annie and Meg to Paris and London. The doctor had raised no objections. The tumor was still growing; Annie's time was short and might as well be spent giving them happy memories for later. Annie was happy—as happy as she could be given the circumstances, but Taylor could see a steady change as her condition declined.

They had been gone three weeks and were scheduled to leave for Italy in a few days when Annie came to him. "It's time, Taylor."

For a brief moment he had seen that other time, that joyous time, when she told him it was "time" to go to the hospital for Meg's birth. This time there was no joy, only weariness as she continued, "It's time to go home."

They made love that night, gently, carefully, as if afraid to disturb the delicate balance that was their life. It was the last time. Two days after they returned home, Annie lapsed into a coma. Two days later, with Taylor by her side holding her hand, she was gone. It was the last day of June, just over three months after their wedding.

53

Laura-

The funeral is over, and now Meg and I have to figure out a way to get on with our lives.

There were a lot of people there today. Annie was loved, probably more than she ever realized. Megan did all right, considering. She's asleep now, completely worn out.

I've established a dance scholarship in Annie's name. The first recipient will be announced next week, one of her graduating students. I think she would have been pleased.

I'm not sure where we go from here. When we went to Europe, I had planned on us spending the whole summer there. I'd rented a house on the Mediterranean, and I never got around to canceling the lease. If Meg agrees, I want to go there for the rest of the summer, maybe longer.

I can barely stand to be in this house. There's so much of Annie here. I keep expecting to hear her call Meg or me, to see her in the garden. It's too much right now...but you know all of that, how awful it feels.

I don't think I've remembered to thank you for letting me use you as a sounding board. It's helped more than you can ever know.

I'll let you know what our plans are.

Taylor

He sent the message, then turned off the computer. He would sleep in here tonight as he had done the last few nights while Annie was in the hospital. At least, he would sleep if he could.

Barefoot, he went down the hall and opened Meg's door. She was sleeping, a pillow from her mother's bed clutched in her arms. Suddenly, he was overwhelmed by the responsibility. Annie had trusted him to take care of Meg, but what did he know about taking care of anyone, let alone a twelve-year-old girl?

Quietly, he closed the door. As he came back through the dining room, he saw his jacket still hanging on the chair where he had left it this afternoon.

Jude had come back to the house after the funeral with a few other friends. She stayed until almost everyone had left. Susan and Jane were in the kitchen, and Meg had long since retreated to her room.

"Taylor, I have something for you." She reached into her purse and withdrew two envelopes, handing them to him. One was addressed to him, one to Meg, in Annie's handwriting. "She left them with me to deliver after…after she was gone, Taylor. You can decide the best time to give Megan hers." She hugged him and kissed him on the cheek. "She was a very special lady, Taylor. You made her very happy."

He walked her to the door, then put the envelopes in his jacket pocket before hanging it here as he went to help Susan and Jane. He hadn't really forgotten about them; he just hadn't been ready yet.

He poured a glass of wine and, sitting at the kitchen table, opened the envelope addressed to him.

My dearest Taylor-

I want you to know how happy I've been to have you in my life. Not just these last few months but the years that you've been my best friend. I was so lucky to run into you at that audition that day. I had no idea then how important you would be to me.

I know you, Taylor. You're probably panicking right now because I've left you with someone to take care of, probably thinking you have no idea what to do. But you do, Taylor. You've always been good for Megan. I couldn't have asked for anyone better for her. There is no one who could love her more, care for her more, than you. Just take it one day at a time, Taylor. It will be fine.

I know that, despite the love we've shared these past few months, you're still in love with Laura. And I know that you probably think you've ruined that relationship for good. I think you're wrong, Taylor. You assured me time and again that Laura would understand. Believe in her, Taylor. Give yourself another chance at the happiness you deserve.

Don't wait, Taylor. Don't worry about what other people think and say. You, of all people, should know how precious and limited our time can be. Don't waste it mourning me or doing what others say is right. You'll know when it's the right time for you.

Wherever I am, Taylor, I will be dancing at your wedding. Thank you for always being there.

Be happy, my love.

                                        Annie

Carefully he refolded the pages and placed them in the envelope. Putting Meg's aside to give her in the morning, he opened the door and went out onto the deck. The night was clear, the stars shining brightly. He wanted to believe that one of those stars was Annie's spirit, but right now he was having trouble believing in anything. The emotions of the day caught up with him. He did not have to be strong any longer and was finally able to ease his heart with tears.

*   *   *

Two days after the funeral, Laura received a package from a Florida law firm. Inside was a sealed envelope, her name written in an unfamiliar hand. A cover letter was attached:

Dear Ms. Collins-

Our client, Annie Morgan, left this letter with us to be delivered to you after her death. We regret to inform you that Ms. Morgan died last week, so we are hereby honoring her instructions.

If we can be of any help, please let us know.

Jude MacMurray

Laura picked up the envelope and carefully opened it to find a few handwritten pages.

Dear Laura,

There is a lot I feel should be explained to you. I just never had the courage to do it. I apologize for that and hope you will forgive me when you've read this.

Taylor married me because it was the easiest way to make it really possible for him to adopt Megan. Our lawyer was worried that if Cary chose to pursue it, he would be granted custody. Neither Taylor nor I could bear that thought. Of our few options, this was the one that offered our best hope.

Taylor was, and is, in love with you, Laura. He told me that he has loved you from the day he met you. I realize it doesn't seem that way, but it is true. I won't explain for him why he left you the first time; I can only let you know what led him to leave this last time.

He will be hurting now, and as is typical for Taylor, he will withdraw from the world for awhile. But I am sure that once he has had some time, he will come back to you. I'm hoping that knowing the truth will allow you to give him another chance. I don't know how long it will take him, but I hope you still think he's worth waiting for.

I realize that Meg has complicated your relationship as well. Being involved with someone with an almost-teenage daughter will be hard. I know that you've been writing to her, and I thank you for helping her through this time. Having women like you in her life will help her fill the gap I am leaving.

There will be those who will criticize Taylor for coming back to you, especially if it's what they consider too soon. Don't listen to them, Laura. Follow your heart and don't waste a moment of the time you might have together.

                         Annie Miller Morgan

Laura put the pages down on the table and went out onto the balcony that looked out over the city. It must have been hard for Annie to write that letter, giving a blessing to her and Taylor, she thought as she wiped away tears.

The thought that Taylor hadn't left her because he didn't care sang in her mind. In that moment, with Annie's help, Laura was finally able to forgive him. She still loved him—and would wait until he was ready to love again.

54

Having given up Meg and knowing that Laura would keep her word, Cary threw himself into preparations for his move to Ireland, arriving there one week after Laura's visit. There had been another bombing that morning, so he was on-air within two hours of his arrival.

He quickly found a niche in the press corps. Most of them were housed in the same hotel and were in the habit of meeting in the hotel bar at the end of the day to compare notes. His good looks brought him the female attention he felt was his due, and he was turning in brilliant reports. He was TNC's rapidly rising star, rumored to be in the running for an anchor position. His life was right on track and Cary was as close to happy as he had ever been.

Not too long after his arrival, he noticed the barmaid, a leggy, red-headed local girl named Shannon Eileen O'Hearn. "Shaleen" was the only girl and the youngest child of a large Catholic family. Sheltered all of her life, her family was only allowing her to work at the bar because her brother, Jamie, was the bartender.

Jamie had liked the new TNC reporter right away, and was pleased when Cary turned his eye to Shaleen. The girl could do worse than a fine American reporter, he thought, and in the guise of friendly interest, he learned that Cary was Catholic, lapsed mind you, but raised in the church. He had come from a large family who still lived in the States and seemed to have a bright future ahead of him. Jamie had no way of knowing that Cary was lying to him, making up a background to suit his own purposes, as usual.

At first, it was just a little friendly flirting as Shaleen served the evening's beers. All of the male reporters flirted with her and the women, not totally in jest, warned her away from the guys. She enjoyed the attention and was attracted to the dark-haired, blue-eyed reporter from America. Soon, Cary was hanging around after the bar had closed, sharing a drink with Jamie and Shaleen.

Finally, one Sunday, he was invited home for dinner. Gritting his teeth and turning on his considerable charm, he won over the whole O'Hearn clan and earned the approval of the patriarch.

He was at the bar, the ever-present television tuned to the news, when he heard of Annie's death. Taylor's name had caught his attention, and he looked up in time to see Annie's face as the announcer offered condolences to Taylor and "his daughter." There was a brief glimpse of the funeral with Taylor standing next to a girl with long dark hair, his arm around her as she leaned against him.

The news hit him harder than he would ever have expected. Annie? Dead? She was so young! His face must have changed, because both Jamie and Shaleen had come to see if he was all right. He was surprised to find his hand shaking as he set down the glass he was holding.

"That story? Annie Morgan, Taylor Morgan's wife? We were all friends long ago in New York when Taylor was getting started in theatre and me in broadcasting. I can't believe she's dead."

Shaleen's hand had covered his as her brother poured something a little stronger than what Cary had been drinking. Some of the others in the bar heard his announcement as well. None of them had ever seen Cary Edwards shaken by anything, but he quickly threw it off, asking them all to raise their glasses in a toast to the memory of Annie, even as his mind calculated how to use this to his advantage.

*   *   *

When the bar closed that night, Jamie left Shaleen and Cary there with a bottle of his finest. "You'll see she gets home safely?" he asked Cary as he prepared to lock up. Cary assured him he would, and they both waved at him as he walked out the door.

"Your friend? Annie? You were close to her?" Shaleen's eyes were full of sympathy.

"Yes, we even thought about getting married once, but her career was more important to her then. Still, I've always had a soft spot in my heart for her." Shaleen reached her hand out to him, and he took it, crocodile tears in his eyes.

"I'd best be getting you home," Cary said in his best Irish accent. It wasn't bad, but it made Shaleen giggle. "Where's your coat, darlin'?" He started to help her on with the coat when he stopped and said, "My coat. I must have left it in my room. It looks a little cold outside. I think I should go get it."

Shaleen wanted to wait for him there, but he talked her into coming upstairs to his room with him. "I can't leave you down here alone, Shaleen. What if you were carried off by a leprechaun? How would I ever explain it to Jamie or your father? It will only take a minute; then we'll go."

Taking her hand, he led her to the elevator, then down the hallway to his room. He opened the door, letting her step in ahead of him, then closing it behind them. "I'll get my coat," he said as he touched her cheek. "Unless...."

He drew her into his arms and kissed her then. Shaleen felt her knees go weak and hardly recognized the girl who was kissing him back with an urgent passion. He slid her coat from her arms and let his hands wander up beneath her sweater, stroking the smooth skin of her back, as he whispered her name. He let go of her only long enough to lead her to the couch where they sat so closely together that they might as well have been one person.

Shaleen had never been with a man before. There had been sweaty-palmed, pimple-faced boys before, but she'd never felt this way with them, never let them get as close to her as she was letting Cary. She gasped as his hands came up to her breasts, cradling them in his hands as he rained kisses on her face and throat. She was surprised, but didn't fight him, as he began to unbutton her sweater until he reached the swell of her breasts and undid the clasp of her bra to set her breasts free for his roaming mouth and hands. She knew she shouldn't be doing this, knew it was wrong, but couldn't bring herself to ask him to stop.

Cary pulled back and looked at her. "Ah, Shaleen, you're so beautiful," he whispered, then stood, pulling her from the couch into his arms. She was surprised when he picked her up and walked with her through another door, gently placing her on his bed.

"Cary...no, this is...I need to leave," she said, trying to get up and cover her bared breasts, suddenly shy and embarrassed.

"Shh, Shaleen. Stay here. Let me love you. Don't leave me alone tonight." Cary placed his hands on her shoulders and pushed her back against the bed, his eyes devouring her with a look that frightened her.

"No, Cary, please..."

But there had been no stopping him. He held her down as he stripped off the rest of her clothing, ignoring her tears. When she tried to scream for help, he hit her, snarling at her to be quiet as he stood long enough to shed the rest of his clothes.

Then he raped her.

*   *   *

When it was over, as she lay sobbing on the bed, Cary got dressed. He gathered up her clothing and tossed it to her. "Get dressed, Shaleen. I promised Jamie I'd see you safely home."

She dressed, shaking, too afraid not to do as she was told, while he watched her dispassionately from a chair by the door. As she put on her shoes, he came to her, raising his hands to her breasts, laughing as she turned away. "Your sweater's buttoned wrong, darlin'," he said, his accent no longer funny to her. She stood still as he unbuttoned it before, slowly, doing up the buttons again. Then he looked at her, assessing her, before saying, "You're going to have a nasty bruise on your cheek, Shaleen. It's really too bad that had to happen—falling against the bar like that when you slipped on that puddle of melted ice." He smiled at her confusion. "We can't be telling them the truth, now, can we?" and she mutely shook her head.

No one saw them when he walked her out of the hotel as if nothing had happened. She was acutely aware of him beside her and kept seeing glimpses in her mind of what had happened. When they came to her house, he stopped and lifted her chin to look into her eyes.

"Sweet Shaleen. I'm sorry your first time had to be so rough. We'll do better tomorrow," he said as he kissed her gently before giving her a little push toward the stairs and door. He watched her go in before turning away, heading back toward the hotel, whistling, a man well-pleased with his life.

*   *   *

He was awakened the next morning by a pounding on his door. Muttering a string of curses, sure that it was his cameraman ready to leave on some hot tip, he pulled the door open, "Tim, you bastard, this had better..." His voice had trailed off as he saw it was the hotel manager, with a couple of policemen and Jamie O'Hearn.

"Mr. Edwards, I'm sorry to be bothering you so early, but these gentlemen insisted they had to see you." Cary could see the murder in Jamie's eyes and knew he would have to do some quick talking to get out of this one.

"That's fine, come in. Could you see that some coffee is sent up, please?" he asked the manager before closing the door. Turning to face the trio who waited for him, he realized that both of the police officers were O'Hearn brothers as well.

"Sit down, please."

None of them made any move as Jamie asked in a deadly quiet voice, "What the bloody hell did you do to our Shaleen last night?"

Cary sat down, looking cool and composed. "Me do to Shaleen? I assure you it was the other way around, boys."

He then spun them a tale of getting drunk and Shaleen insisting on seeing him up to his room. "I was still upset over the death of my friend. Shaleen seemed determined to comfort me, and Jamie, I'm sorry, but I was in no shape to say no."

"Then why did she try to kill herself last night?" Jamie asked as he threw a piece of paper at Cary. "Why did she leave this note for our mother to find this morning when she didn't come down for church?"

Cary was genuinely surprised. It had never occurred to him that she might react this way. "I'm shocked. The poor girl must have been so ashamed of her behavior…" His sentence was cut off as Jamie's massive fist made connection with his face.

*   *   *

He spent most of the day in a filthy jail cell, the brothers having arrested him for rape and assault. They hadn't even allowed him to dress, dragging him out of the hotel barefoot and wearing only his robe, his nose still bleeding from the blow that Jamie had landed.

Luckily, his cameraman had seen what had happened and called TNC. The network contacted a lawyer who arrived just at the end of his initial hearing. His objections and the network's personal assurance had gotten Cary released on bail, confined to the hotel suite until a trial date was set.

His lawyer had found him there two hours later, packing.

"Going somewhere, Mr. Edwards?" he asked as he looked at the partially packed suitcases.

"Hell, yes! You don't think I'm going to hang around here while some Irish whore makes up lies about me?"

"That's precisely what I think you're going to do, Mr. Edwards. The 'whore', as you so graciously put it, is in the hospital. She regained consciousness a little while ago. She's given a statement to the police, and I think they'll be here as soon as they get the judge to revoke your bail."

"Then I had better get moving," Cary said as he closed a suitcase. "You'll take me to the airport, won't you?"

The lawyer was saved from answering by a loud knocking at the door. Before they could answer, it was opened with a passkey. Cary was once again led out of the hotel, better dressed this time, but with the same accessory handcuffs.

*   *   *

This time he spent two days in jail before he received word that a deal had been struck. He was being deported, the network would be paying a bundle to Shaleen, and he was fired as soon as he stepped foot on American soil.

He was released and returned to the hotel. The first flight out was not until morning, so Cary spent the night in the hotel room, an O'Hearn guard outside his door. He consoled himself for the loss of his career with a bottle of the finest Irish whiskey. In a brilliant display of convoluted logic, he blamed it all on Annie. If she hadn't died…if he hadn't seen that report…if Shaleen had not been so concerned…He drank himself into a stupor, never hearing the door when it opened.

55

"*Signor?*" Taylor looked up from the book he was reading to see their housekeeper, Rosina, standing in the doorway.

"*Sí*, Rosina?"

"*Scusi*, but the little one—Meg—she is too much alone. It is not good for her. If you will permit, I have a niece of the same age. I could bring her with me. She could be company, a friend?"

Taylor looked out the open doors that led to the swimming pool. As usual, Meg was in the water, this time with her arms and chin propped up on the side of the pool, her eyes closed, lost in her own world. Rosina was right; she did need someone else around.

"That's very kind, Rosina. Thank you for thinking of it. She could perhaps come with you tomorrow?"

"*Sí*, she will be with me in the morning." Rosina was all smiles as she left the room.

Taylor turned back to look at Meg. They had been here two weeks already, and he felt like it had been good for both of them. At least here they had some privacy.

A few days after the funeral, Meg had gone out to get the mail. A photographer had jumped out from his hiding place and frightened her to tears. It had been the last straw; they had been plagued by the media ever since it was announced that Taylor Morgan's bride was dead less than four months after their wedding. The speculation in the media was rampant; some of the tabloids even suggested that Annie's death was *mysterious*! He released a statement through his agent's office, but it hadn't satisfied them. The day after the incident with the photographer, Taylor and Meg had left the country, coming here to the quiet villa by the Mediterranean.

The peace had been welcomed by Taylor. He had assumed that Meg felt the same way. Obviously, Rosina had been paying more attention than he had. Hired by the leasing agency, she had been doing her best to "mother" both of them since their arrival.

Putting down his book, Taylor walked out into the late morning sunlight. In the distance, he could see the sea, the pool designed to blend in with it. Meg heard his footsteps and opened her eyes.

"Have you grown fins and a tail yet, Meg?" He kicked off his sandals and sat on the edge of the pool with his feet in the water.

"Not yet, Taylor, although I think I may have seen some webbing between my toes this morning."

Taylor laughed as he said, "I don't doubt it, Meg," and he kicked his feet to splash her. He watched as she dove under the surface and swam to the end of the pool and back without coming up for air. When she surfaced again, he said, "Come sit with me a minute, Meg. Rosina made some lemonade."

When they were seated under the table umbrella, Taylor took a good look at her. Her fair skin had darkened to a golden shade from the sun. The circles that had been under her eyes for so long were fading, and she looked more like the Meg he was used to.

"How are you doing, Meg?" They hadn't talked much in their time here, each of them needing space and recognizing that need in the other.

"I'm better, Taylor."

"I can see that. Are you getting bored just hanging around here with me and Rosina?"

She thought for a moment before she admitted, "A little..."

"Rosina has a niece who's your age. She thought she might bring her tomorrow."

"Does she swim?"

"I don't know, Meg. You'll have to ask Rosina."

"It would be nice to have someone around," she said before her eyes widened. "I didn't mean...."

"I know, Meg, it's all right."

"I'm going to go talk to Rosina, okay?"

"Go on. Then, later, if you'd like we can take a walk down to the village."

"Great!"

Taylor shook his head and smiled as she disappeared through the open door. She was beginning to sound like the old Meg, and he was grateful that Rosina had come to him. It would be nice to hear Meg laughing again.

*   *   *

When Taylor came down to breakfast the next morning, laughter, or giggling to be more exact, was just what he did hear. As he came out onto the pool deck where the table was set for breakfast, he suddenly wondered if Meg had been cloned during the night. Instead of one dark-haired girl child, there were two.

"Taylor! This is Elisabetta. Rosina is her aunt. She's twelve, too, but I'm a week older, and she loves to swim and says her uncle has horses that we can ride!"

"Good morning to you, too, Meg," Taylor said with a smile as he sat at the table with the two girls. "I'm happy to meet you, Elisabetta. I'm Meg's father."

"Sí, *Signor* Morgan, I am happy to meet you, too."

"If it is all right with Rosina, you may call me Taylor. I'd like that better than *Signor* Morgan. What are the two of you going to do today?"

As Megan talked about their plans, Taylor studied them. They were pretty much the same size. Elisabetta's hair was longer and her eyes a deep brown, but it would have been easy to mistake them for sisters.

"Taylor, I'm taking Betta upstairs. See you later." He could hear their laughter as they ran up the stairs to the corner room that Meg had claimed. For the first time since he'd told her about her mother's illness, Taylor felt like she was going to be all right. He poured a cup of coffee and looked out over the endless sea, the constant ache in his heart eased for the moment.

*   *   *

Laura-

It appears that I now have two daughters instead of the one I brought with me. Betta, short for Elisabetta, is the niece of our housekeeper. She suggested a couple of weeks ago that she could bring her along because Meg needed someone. I'm so glad she did.

In a sad coincidence, Betta lost her parents two years ago in a car accident. She's been living with her aunt and uncle ever since. The girls hit it off right away, and I think it has helped Meg to know she's not the only one who has lost a parent. Rosina hadn't told me that detail, but Meg did the first night after Betta had gone home with her aunt. When I asked Rosina about it the next day, she smiled and said that wasn't the way the girls should meet. Friends first—stories later. She was right. The two of them have become inseparable. Betta is here with us almost more than she is at her own home.

The most important thing is that Meg is laughing again. I still hear her crying some nights, but I think she has begun to live again.

And, I guess I am, too. The morning Betta came into
our lives, I finally was able to begin singing again. Or at
least, I'm trying to get my voice back into a reasonable
shape. Months now without practice, and I sound like it!
That first morning, I was interrupted by a knock on the
door. It was Rosina, with a wide-eyed Betta behind her,
asking if I was all right! I think I better work hard!

Taylor

Laura had already heard all about Betta from Meg. They were still
corresponding by e-mail and Meg had written the evening of her first
day with Betta. She had been so full of joy about her newfound friend
but was worried that she shouldn't be so happy. Laura had assured her
that it was fine, that her mother would have wanted her to laugh and
have friends. After that, Meg had written less often. While she missed
her messages, Laura was glad that Meg was going on with her life.

Taylor was a different problem. He had only written a few times since
he and Meg had returned to Europe, always polite, friendly notes with
nothing of substance. As Annie had predicted, he had withdrawn. This
message was a good sign that he was beginning to think about living
again—and she could begin to hope.

*   *   *

Laura-

It doesn't seem possible that the summer is gone. I've
decided to stay here for awhile longer. Meg has been
enrolled in the convent school that Betta attends. She's
so happy here that I hate the thought of uprooting her.

I'm still studying with the voice teacher I found. He's
a terrible slave driver and has been furious that I let my
voice go without exercise for so long. He's right, of

course, and I have finally begun to feel like I might make it back to where I was.

My agent has been after me to think about a new CD and, amazingly enough, I am. I've begun to play with some ideas and some new music. Any requests?

Taylor

     *   *   *

Laura-

You should hear Meg chattering away in Italian! It's as if she was born to it. She and Betta love to use it to tease me since I am nowhere near as fluent as they are. Betta has made equal progress in English, and the Sisters of the convent school seem pleased with the advances that both of them have made.

Now, if only my voice teacher were as pleased!

I've signed a contract with the recording company. I'll start on the new CD in the spring or summer, to be released next fall. I'm still sorting through music, trying to decide what to include. They've given me free reign with this one so the responsibility is all mine.

Taylor

     *   *   *

Laura-

What a pleasant surprise to open my weeks-late Smithsonian this morning and find your article on Holly Hill House! Why didn't you tell me? You more than did it justice, and I'm sure the owners (and the Chamber of Commerce!) were pleased. I remember how taken you were with the house and am glad you went back to visit it.

All of that seems so long ago—a lifetime, really. It will soon be five months since Annie died. I still see things every day that I want to tell her about, but it's getting easier to bear.

Meg and I are hosting a dinner party for Thanksgiving. Of course, it's just another day here, but we decided it was a good day to thank all of our new friends. Betta's other family is coming, as are my voice teacher, and Meg's teacher and principal from the school. We plan on doing an old-fashioned, traditional dinner. Meg even convinced her teacher that it's going to be an educational experience, so both she and Betta are off for the day to help on the condition they turn in reports about the holiday.

I wish you could join us.

Taylor

*   *   *

The Thanksgiving dinner was a great success, once they got Rosina to give up her kitchen to them! Finding all the ingredients had been an adventure in itself, but everything had come together and seemed to be appreciated by their guests.

It was late by the time everyone had left. Rosina had wanted to stay and clean up the kitchen, but Taylor had forbidden it and made her leave with the rest of her family. Betta had gone home with them, and Taylor had sent Meg on up to bed. She still had to go to school tomorrow.

With everyone gone and the house quiet, Taylor finished up in the kitchen. All day, he'd been haunted by memories of last year. Annie had always teased him about his lack of cooking skills—she would have been astounded at the dinner he and Meg had managed. For the first time in a long while, he felt an overwhelming grief for the loss of Annie. He was standing at the sink, his head bowed and eyes closed, the pain of losing her as fresh as it had been the first day, when he felt Meg's arms go around him. Turning, he looked down at her and could see the same pain in her eyes.

"Missing her, Meg?" She nodded soundlessly, her eyes welling with tears and he picked her up and carried her into the living room. He sat down in an oversized chair and wrapped an afghan around them both. "I miss her, too," he whispered as her tears soaked the front of his shirt, his getting lost in her hair.

56

Laura stood by the postal drop-box with a manila envelope in her hand. It contained the contract she had just signed to write an article about the Mediterranean countryside. She had enough of a freelance reputation now that most of her proposals were getting picked up. But this one—this one was different.

It was six months now since Annie had died. Six months that Taylor had been dropping in on her cyberlife. Six months of not knowing how he really felt. And she was tired of waiting. This time she was going after what she wanted. In this case, what—who—she wanted was Taylor.

She didn't have a lot to go on. Taylor had never told her exactly where he and Meg were living. All she knew was it was a villa on the Mediterranean. This envelope was her financing to get her there.

"Lady? You gonna stand there all day?" Laura turned to find an impatient line forming behind her.

"Sorry," she said, then dropped the envelope in the slot.

It was done. There was no turning back. Laura left the post office with a new spring in her step as she thought about the possibilities.

*　　　　　*　　　　　*

"You did what?" Beth was sure that she hadn't heard Laura correctly.

"I signed a contract to go to Italy right after the first of the year—specifically the Mediterranean where Taylor is."

"Have you lost your mind, Laura? He's broken your heart twice now. You're giving him a chance to do it again?"

Laura got up from the couch and picked up the wine bottle on the table. She was grateful she'd had the foresight to invite Beth here to tell her instead of some place public. Refilling Beth's glass, she said, "You don't know all of it, Beth."

"I know enough, Laura, to know that I don't want you hurt again." Beth had never forgiven herself for her part in Taylor's second try at Laura.

"I need to tell you the parts you don't know. Annie was dying, Beth. That's why he went back to Tampa at the end of the tour. He didn't go back to marry Annie, but that's what happened."

Beth was silent—stunned—as Laura told her the rest of the story.

"I didn't know any of it until after Annie died. I wouldn't speak to Taylor and I never let him explain his side of it. I jumped to all the same conclusions that everyone else did. Annie's letter changed all that. I'm still in love with him, Beth, and I'm tired of waiting to see if he feels the same. For once in my life, I'm going after what I want. No one, including you, is going to change my mind."

Beth reached out and took Laura's hand. "What if Annie was wrong? What if he doesn't care about you? Can you handle being hurt again?"

"There are no guarantees in life, Beth. I've quit looking for them. All I know is that I love Taylor Morgan, and I'm not willing to let him go without a fight."

Beth could see she was determined. Laura had survived so much this year, and she was stronger for it. Still, Beth knew there was one more piece of information that Laura needed as she began her search.

"Laura…I have to tell you something." Laura was surprised at Beth's tension. What could she possibly have to say that put such fear in her eyes?

"Beth? It can't be that bad, whatever it is!"

"Taylor knows what Cary did to you." There was no way to sugar-coat it, so Beth blurted it out all at once. "He came out here looking for you the day after Cary...He had heard you and me talking about Cary at *Posadas*. To make it worse, he heard two of Mom's friends talking about how you were going to marry Cary. So, he removed himself from the picture."

"How do you know all of this?" Laura asked quietly.

"Taylor told me," she said as she went on to tell her the details of Taylor's visit that had come just a few days too late. "Laura, I told him about Cary. I know I shouldn't have. It wasn't my right but I was so worried about you..." Beth began to cry.

He had known. All those weeks on the tour, he had *known*. Looking back, she could see that he used the information to make things easier for them. He had courted her, giving her the space and time to heal and learn to love again.

"Laura? Please, say something! Are we still friends or not?" Beth's tearstained face looked at her pleadingly.

"I love you, Beth Wilkins!" she said as she folded her best friend in an enormous hug.

57

Laura-

Meg is an angel. At least she is in the pageant that the school is presenting next week. And she's the only angel to have a line. She's the one who speaks to the shepherds, then to Mary and Joseph. And she will be doing it in Italian, too. I'm rather proud of her. Of course, Betta is also an angel, which is lucky for me since Rosina has taken on the job of making their costumes.

I've found myself thinking a lot about last Christmas as this one approaches. I really had a wonderful time. I think I may have talked Mother Superior into letting me do farolitos for the church entrance on the night of the pageant. She seemed rather intrigued by the description I gave her. The chapel at the convent is at least a century old, and I think the farolitos will give it a special charm.

Please, wish your parents and Beth a Merry Christmas for me. We will be thinking of you here.

Taylor

*   *   *

Taylor finished lighting the last *farolito* as the last of the sunset glow faded. The simple little lanterns stretched from the chapel door down the walk and across the front of the fence that framed the church. They looked like they belonged here, and he was pleased he had been able to talk Mother Caterina into letting him do it. As if summoned by his thoughts, she spoke from behind him. "They are lovely, Mr. Morgan. I can see why you wanted to have them. They were a tradition for you and your family?"

"No, Mother, I only saw them for the first time last year when I was visiting a friend in New Mexico. They have been a tradition there for many years."

"How are you and our Megan doing this holiday? It must be very hard for you, all of these first holidays without your wife."

"It is, Mother. Annie and I were only married for a few months, but we had been best friends for years. I miss her every day, but it's harder at all of these special times."

"The friend you visited last year? She's someone special to you?"

"Yes—but how did you know my friend was a 'she'?"

"It was in your voice and in your eyes, Mr. Morgan," she said with a gentle smile.

"You must think I'm terrible—to be interested in someone so soon after losing my wife?"

"No," she smiled as she gently shook her head, "I think it's a good sign that you are ready to get on with living. Your Annie would have wanted that, I imagine."

"You're very wise, Mother."

She came over and took his hand in hers. "If you go, we will miss Megan terribly. Betta will be lost, but maybe it's time you and Megan went home." She made the sign of the cross on his forehead. "Bless you, my son."

As she faded into the night, Taylor realized she was right. It was time to go home—wherever that was. It didn't mean they would never come back here, but it was time to get on with their lives. He saw Betta's family, including Meg, coming down the walk, the girls faintly luminous in their white robes, and he hurried to greet them.

The pageant was a success. Meg delivered her line in flawless Italian much to the delight of her surrogate family. With no school tomorrow, actually no school for the next month, Meg was staying the night with Betta.

Taylor had been distracted through most of it. Before the play had started, he'd had a long conversation with Rosina and Matteo. Receiving their approval for his plan, he now had one phone call to make. After figuring the time difference, he picked up the phone and dialed.

*   *   *

Laura had been busy all day with preparations for *Las Posadas*. She couldn't help thinking about last year and what almost happened. She hadn't heard from Taylor in more than a week. She was beginning to think that he was going to stay in Europe forever, and she was starting to get cold feet about her plans to find him. It was all so depressing. If all of this didn't mean so much to her parents, she would just go home and sulk all evening, she thought, as she filled the last of the brown paper bags with sand.

Her mother had been distracted all day, her thoughts far away. Laura, sure she was thinking of Tomás, didn't question her. She was having enough trouble already with her own emotions this year.

As she straightened up and stretched, her father came out and said, "Go on over to the beginning, Laura. I'll finish up here."

"Oh, Dad, I think I just want to stay here tonight."

"Nonsense! You haven't missed a procession in years. Besides, there's Beth waiting for you."

Waving at her friend, Laura got her heavy coat and pulled it on over her sweater and jeans. Picking up her gloves, she called 'goodbye' to her mother, kissed her father, and walked over to Beth.

The two women started over to the house where the procession would begin. This year the procession would end at Beth's, so she had been working with her mother all day to prepare.

"I don't know about you, girlfriend," Beth said, "but I'm getting too old to do all of this!"

Laura laughed. "Me, too! But it would be a strange Christmas without it, don't you think?"

"How are you doing, Laura?" Beth thought of what a rough year it had been. Laura had always had trouble with change, and there had certainly been a lot of that in her life this year.

"I'm okay, Beth. I'll be glad when this year is finally over. It's not been one of the best."

"You've made it through it, though—and in one piece! I probably haven't told you, but I am very proud of you. Someone else would have crumbled under all of this."

Laura stopped and said quietly, "I couldn't have done it without you, Beth. Thank you for taking care of me."

*   *   *

Laura was soon caught up in the magic of *Las Posadas*. Even with Taylor's memory beside her, she still loved the tradition of the ages-old story and music. When they came to her own house, Laura watched as her father turned Joseph away. As the procession continued their journey, she blew her father a kiss that he caught as he had when she was a little girl, tucking it into his pocket for "later." Hurrying to catch up with Beth, she didn't see a figure come out of the house to join the procession.

The next house was the last one. Joseph sang the traditional words a final time:

"From a very long journey"
Laura was startled to hear a familiar voice join in behind her.
"we've arrived and are weary"
She turned and met the eyes and smile of the man who held out his hands to her as he sang
"and come to implore you
for shelter this night."
Her eyes filled with tears, and as the traditional welcome was being sung all around them, she stepped into his arms and welcomed him back to her life with a kiss.

58

Slowly, Taylor became aware of the silence around them and broke their embrace. They were alone in the yard; everyone had gone into the house, leaving them behind.

"Taylor, what are you doing here? When? Where?" she laughed as she finally said, "I don't care. I'm just glad you're here."

"So am I, Laura. We need to go somewhere where we can talk." He took her hand and began to walk away from the house.

"Taylor, wait! We can't just leave. My parents will worry."

He turned back and grinned at her, "No, they won't. They already know I'm kidnapping you. Actually, I traded them my two daughters for their one."

"My parents knew? And you brought Meg and Betta?"

"Yes, your mother was in the procession with both girls. Your mother didn't want them to miss it, and they found it a great game to stay out of your sight. I stayed at your house with your dad—who, by the way, had quite a bit to say to me! When the procession left there, I joined it." She looked bewildered by the convoluted plot to get him to her. "Laura, darling, I'll explain it later. Please, just come with me now."

*   *   *

When they got into his car, he started it and pulled out of the farolito-lined neighborhood streets. "Taylor, where are we going?"

"At the risk of being trite, your place or mine?"

Her apartment had become her sanctuary. She rarely had friends over, preferring to meet them at some neutral spot. It was easier having a space without extra memories. Still, a hotel would be so impersonal.

"Laura?"

"My place, I guess, Taylor. Turn left and catch the freeway."

As they drove across town, Taylor was silent, almost grim. Laura studied him surreptitiously. The last few months had obviously been rough on him. There were lines around his eyes and mouth that hadn't been there before, and the boyish look had vanished.

As they drove into the gated community, Laura leaned across to identify herself to the guard. Recognizing her, he opened the gate and Laura directed Taylor to the building where she lived.

As she opened the door, she was conscious of him beside her. He had not said one word on the way here, and his intensity was a little frightening.

"Come in, Taylor," she said as she turned on a lamp and took off her coat. For the first time she got a really good look at him and was surprised to find that he had begun graying at the temples. It didn't mar his good looks but gave them an added dimension. Still, it was another indication of how the last year had left its mark on him.

He took off his coat and watched her as she went about getting wine-glasses and opening a bottle of wine. He recognized little in her apartment. She had evidently gotten rid of anything that could remind her of Cary—and of him? Wordlessly, she handed him a glass of wine and took a seat at one end of the couch, turning to lean against the arm so she could look at him. Taking his cue, he sat at the other end, but still neither of them spoke until they both did at once.

"Laura" "Taylor" They both stopped, then laughed. She gestured to him to go on.

"I don't know where to begin, Laura. I guess I'm surprised to find us here. I didn't expect you to welcome me back with open arms. I think I was expecting you to slap me and tell me you never wanted to see me again."

Laura seemed genuinely surprised. "Why, Taylor? We're still friends—aren't we?"

"Only because you must have the most generous heart on the planet. I screwed up big time last Christmas when I left you. I heard you and Beth talking about the man you were dating and others saying you were practically engaged. I gave up instead of trying to win you away from him."

Laura's face was white, and her hands were shaking as she carefully put her glass of wine on the table. "Why didn't you ask me, Taylor?"

"I don't know. I guess I thought I was doing the noble thing by stepping out of your life and leaving you to him."

"His name was Cary Edwards—Annie's ex-husband." Her voice was flat as she said it, holding herself still as if any movement would crack the fragile shell around her. "And I know that you know what he did to me. Beth finally told me that it was no coincidence that you offered me the job."

"I had come out here because you wouldn't return my calls or messages. I thought if I appeared on your doorstep you'd have to listen. Since I didn't know where you were, I went to Beth. She told me because she was so terribly worried about you. That was when I had the idea of offering you the job. I wanted you where I could try to help you through it and where I could try to win your heart again. It didn't change how I felt about you, Laura. It only changed how I could show you. It wasn't until the end of the tour that I felt you were ready to hear me. If I hadn't gotten that call on Catalina...."

"But, you did. And you married Annie."

"I will never forgive myself for the way you found out. I never intended to hurt you that way. I married Annie because it was the only way we felt that we could guarantee the courts would let me adopt Meg. I had to put her safety first, Laura."

Laura leaned forward and placed her fingers across his lips. "I know, Taylor. Annie told me."

"Annie? When?"

"Actually, she left a letter for me, and it was delivered after she died. She told me why you had married her—and that you were in love with me."

Taylor closed his eyes for a moment. Even then, Annie had been protecting him, and he sent a silent thank-you to her. Opening his eyes, he met Laura's. "Annie was right, Laura. I've loved you from that first day you came to interview me. The timing was never right to tell you. But, I have to tell you something more before we go any further. I don't want secrets between us. My marriage to Annie became more than the marriage of convenience we had intended that it be. I loved her, Laura, and she needed me. And, I discovered I needed her, too. We had been lovers years ago, before Cary came into the picture, before Meg was born. We'd called it off then because it didn't work. Our friendship was more important. But we rediscovered each other. I know this isn't going to make sense, but it didn't change how I felt about you. I had put you in a place in my heart and my mind where I didn't have to deal with you on a daily basis. It was the only way I could survive."

Laura saw the pain in his eyes and reached out a hand to him as she said, "I never stopped loving you, Taylor. Even when I was so angry with you after you married Annie, I never stopped loving you. I think Annie knew that. She told me you would come back eventually."

"Then it's not too late, Laura?"

"I don't know, Taylor. I'm not the same person I was a year ago. Recovering from what happened was hard. It still is."

"It was you, wasn't it? You used what he did to you to make him change his mind about Meg."

Silently, she nodded her head. He could see the shadows in her eyes. He had seen those same shadows in Annie's when she left Edwards. His voice was hard as he said, "Laura, the world catches up with people like him. Someday, he'll get what he deserves."

Laura's eyes widened and she whispered, "Oh my God! You don't know? He went on assignment to Ireland, and he never came back, Taylor. The story going around in the local media circles said that he'd raped some young girl in Ireland. TNC managed to get him off, but his career was over. Nobody knows what happened, at least nobody's telling, but he disappeared from his hotel before he was deported. A week later they found his body outside of town. The rumor mill said there was not a bone in his body that hadn't been broken. Someone had beaten him to death."

"And you had to deal with all of that alone? Why didn't you say something, Laura?"

"What could I have said, Taylor? I didn't find out that you knew what he'd done to me until a couple of weeks ago. You had been so formal, so distant, that I had almost given up hope you'd ever come back to me!"

Taylor stood and pulled her up from the couch into his arms. "Laura, I'm sorry—so sorry. I have been such an idiot, but I'm here now, and I love you. I *love* you."

Holding her face in his hands, Taylor looked into her eyes, and then kissed her gently. He felt her arms come up around him, pulling him closer. "Laura?" he whispered and looked into her eyes for the answer he was seeking. Finding it there, he lowered his mouth to hers again, kissing her deeply as he pulled her close to him.

Laura was overwhelmed with the closeness of him, the feel of him in her arms, his mouth covering hers. Almost as if they had a life of their own, her hands crept under his sweater, caressing him. A low moan came from him as he pulled her even closer. She brought her hands around to his chest and pushed him gently away. Instantly, he broke the contact, his breathing ragged, his eyes full of questions, unwilling to hurt her in any way.

Smiling, she caressed his cheek before she took his hand and led him to her bedroom. They stood beside the bed, the light from the living room providing just enough illumination for him to see her before she put her arms around him again and rested her head on his shoulder. For a long moment, that was enough, to be holding her, smelling the scent of her hair, feeling her softness as she leaned against him. Then, sliding her hands once again beneath his sweater, her trailing fingers leaving paths of heat along his bare skin, she kissed him deeply, a kiss full of promise.

He met her passion with his own, his hands finding their way to her breasts beneath her sweater. Insistently, she pulled his sweater up and over his head, tossing it into a corner before she pulled off her own.

Gently brushing his hands over the fragile fabric that covered them, he felt her nipples harden beneath his touch as he lowered his mouth to her throat and then followed with his lips the path his hands had taken. Sliding the straps from her shoulders, he found the clasp and released her breasts to be cupped by his hands.

Forcing himself to take it slowly, he stepped back from her and found the snap on her jeans, his fingers brushing lightly inside her waistband before he opened the snap and slid them, with her panties, to the floor. His arms came around her, and he caressed the length of her back as he felt her arch against him.

Trembling, Laura unbuckled his belt and let his jeans fall to the floor where he impatiently kicked them away, his body on fire where it contacted hers. Releasing her, he pulled the covers back from her bed and tumbled her onto the sheets, laughing as he covered her body with his own.

"What's so funny, Taylor Morgan?" she whispered.

"Not funny, my darling Laura. Just happy," he said as he turned to the serious business of loving her.

*   *   *

It was a long time later when, their passion spent for the moment, Taylor said, "Laura?"

She stretched like a cat waking from a well-deserved nap. "What, Taylor?" she asked as she turned to cross her arms on his chest, lifting her head to look at him.

"How long would you have waited for me?" he asked as he traced her mouth with his finger.

"Another week," she said, then laughed when she saw his face. "Truly, Taylor! Another week, then that was it…" she kissed him softly, "…then I was coming to look for you."

"I love you," he said as he tangled his fingers into her hair.

She laughed softly, "You said that already."

"I know, but I don't think I'll get tired of saying it." Then, he twisted away from her and got out of the bed. Startled, she sat up and watched as he searched the floor for his discarded jeans.

"You could turn on a light, Taylor."

"Never mind. I found what I was looking for."

As he came back to her bed, Laura realized she wanted him again. All of her fears of intimacy were proving to be groundless. Sitting beside her, he let his fingers trail down her cheek and throat, brushing across her breast before coming to rest on her hip. Then he took her hand in his and said, "Will you marry me, Laura?" as he slipped a ring onto her finger.

*   *   *

"Am I to take that as a 'yes'?" Taylor said some time later.

"Yes," she said as she kissed his mouth. "Yes, Yes, Yes," she whispered as she kissed his eyes and nose, returning to his mouth for a kiss that took his breath away.

"Tomorrow?"

"What?" Laura sat up and pushed the hair back from her face. "You're crazy, Taylor!"

"I have to go back to Europe tomorrow, Laura. I promised Betta's family she would be home for Christmas. We have reservations, four of them, on a flight out at six tomorrow evening."

"Taylor. It's too soon. People will talk. We should wait."

He sat up and took her by the shoulders. "No, Laura. No more waiting. I don't give a damn what the world thinks. I love you, and I won't wait any longer to spend my life with you."

"Taylor, we have time. What if I marry you on New Year's Day? It's just a little over a week."

"You are a cruel woman, Laura...I don't even know your middle name!" He seemed genuinely astonished at the discovery.

Laughing, she said, "It's Elizabeth, the same as both your daughters."

"All right, Laura Elizabeth Collins. I'll wait until New Year's day but no longer. In the meantime, will you come back with me so we can have Christmas together?"

He looked so much like a little boy, she couldn't help laughing. "Yes, Taylor, I'll go back with you. Although how we're going to pull a wedding together is beyond me."

*   *   *

Laura woke early for a change. Taylor was still asleep, and she took a moment to study his face in the morning light and smiled. The lines around his eyes and mouth seemed less deeply etched this morning. She stretched her arms out and the morning light caught the ring she had not had a chance to really see yet. Holding her hand in a sunbeam, she admired the simple beauty of the emerald framed in diamonds on a gold band.

"Do you like it?" His voice was sleepy as she felt his fingers trace a pattern down her spine. "I carried it every day of the tour, waiting for a chance to give it to you."

"It's beautiful, Taylor," she said as she kissed him.

"You're beautiful," he said as he pulled her to him once again.

59

It was midmorning before they finally got up. A shared shower delayed them further, and it was almost noon before they started back to her parents' house.

Laura was withdrawn and Taylor, worried, asked, "Laura? Is something wrong?"

She turned to him. "Taylor, what about Meg?"

"She'll be fine, Laura."

"Are you sure, Taylor? It hasn't been that long."

"Laura, Meg knew I was coming here to ask you to marry me."

"Still, before we tell my parents, let me talk to her."

"You're worrying for nothing, Laura, but I'll send her out."

Laura wandered around to the front of the house that overlooked the river. She hadn't known it was possible to love someone this way, and she finally understood what had been between her parents all these years. For the first time in what seemed like forever, she was at peace.

*   *   *

Once Taylor had sent Meg out to meet Laura, he asked Maria to call Beth to come over. He knew he had better do some fence-mending with the best friend of his bride-to-be.

Beth had lost track of Laura last night as everyone had crowded into their house. She had been surprised that Laura hadn't come to help her in the kitchen but didn't have time to check. It wasn't until later that she saw Maria and Sean to ask.

"Where'd Laura get to?"

"She's with Taylor, Beth," Sean had replied.

"Taylor! He's here?"

"He called and wanted to see her. He was at our house during the procession and joined it then. He and Laura have gone off together," Maria's voice was gentle as she looked at her almost daughter. "He loves her, Beth."

"That's what he told me last year before Laura went to work for him. And look what happened!"

"Beth, you can't live her life for her or protect her from everything," Sean had said as he put his arm around her shoulders. "Besides, I had a long talk with Mr. Morgan while we waited for the procession. It will be all right, Beth, you'll see." He kissed her forehead as she muttered, "It had better be."

*   *   *

He was waiting for her as she came down the driveway.

"Hello, Beth."

"Taylor. Breaking her heart twice wasn't enough? Are you counting on the third time being the charm?"

"Beth, can we sit down and talk for a minute?"

She nodded then followed him to the low wall that framed the garden.

"You have every right to be mad at me, Beth. I know that you think I used you to get back to Laura and, I guess, in a way, I did. But everything I told you that day was true. I love Laura. I have from the moment I met her. You know why I left last year, but what you don't know is why I married Annie."

"But I do, Taylor. Laura finally told me a couple of weeks ago. She had made up her mind..." Beth stopped before telling him that Laura had planned to go searching for him. This time she wasn't volunteering any information. "Why are you back this time, Taylor? How can I be sure you're not going to hurt her again?"

"Beth, I promise you, I'll do my best never to hurt her again. And, one of the things that would hurt her terribly would be if you and I couldn't get along. Can you at least find it in your heart to give me a chance to prove to you that I can be trusted with your best friend?"

As Beth looked at him, he was struck again by how much she reminded him of Annie. It was more than the physical resemblance. Beth had Annie's fiercely loyal spirit and he hoped they could be friends before this was all done.

"All right, Taylor. But God help you if you screw up this time."

He laughed and held out his hand to her. "Then come inside. Laura and Meg will be back soon, and I think she'll have something to tell you."

*   *   *

"Laura?"

She turned and saw Meg coming down the steps from the deck. She hadn't seen her since before the tour began, and Meg had changed quite a bit. Taylor probably hadn't noticed since he had been around her daily, but Laura could see the changes. She was taller and had lost much of that little-girl innocence. The past year had left its mark on her as well.

"Meg! You're so tan!" Laura gave her a hug.

"I spend a lot of time in the pool. Taylor is sure I'm going to grow fins soon."

"Taylor said that Betta is with you. I want to meet her, but I wanted a few minutes with you first. I'd like to show you something."

Laura led the way down the cliff path to the river. When they came to "her" rock, she climbed up on it and sat in the sun. Meg followed her and waited for Laura to speak. She had checked earlier to see if Laura was wearing the ring Taylor had shown her and had been pleased to see that she was.

"This is the place I've always come to when I need to think things through," Laura said as she gazed across the river. "Meg, Taylor says you know that he's asked me to marry him. I guess I need to know how you feel about it."

Meg knew that Laura was serious and wanted to give her the best answer that she could. "I guess I'm happy for Taylor—and for you, too! I think Taylor needs you."

"What about you, Meg? You and Taylor have made yourselves a family. Will you mind terribly that I'll be moving into your life?"

"Mom left me a letter. She told me then that Taylor was in love with you and would come back for you when it was the right time. She told me that it wouldn't make Taylor love me any less, and I know she was right."

"Meg, I don't know anything about being a mother, and I know I could never replace your mother. Do you think being a friend would be enough? I think I could handle that."

"I think that would be great, Laura. I'm glad you're coming to live with us. Taylor's been too sad."

"Well, now that I know this is all okay with you, I guess we should go tell my parents. They are going to be so excited to have an instant granddaughter."

Hand in hand, they walked back up the trail.

*　　　　　*　　　　　*

Taylor was waiting for them on the deck. He kissed Meg and sent her inside.

"So?"

"So, you were right, Taylor. She's an extraordinary girl."

"So are you," he said as he kissed her in a far-from-fatherly manner. "I called Beth and told her to come over. I knew you would want her here, and maybe now she'll forgive me for deserting you."

Laughing they went to share the news that no one was really surprised to hear.

60

As the bell tower on the Italian chapel chimed the twelve strokes of noon, Taylor turned to the doorway and waited for Laura to appear.

It had been a scramble to put it all together. They had flown back to Europe and had Christmas with Betta and her family. He had lost track of how many phone calls it had taken to get everything arranged before everyone had arrived here two days ago.

Now, with a violinist softly playing, he saw her come to the doorway. Sean was holding her hand on his arm, less to support her than to support himself. Maria had come in a few minutes before and given Taylor a kiss before she took her place in the front row. Meg and Betta, looking more alike than ever in their matching dresses, were solemn, and Beth was fighting tears as everyone turned to Laura. The only other guests were Rosina and Matteo, Beth's parents, and Mother Caterina. She was smiling with satisfaction as Taylor Morgan watched his bride.

Laura was radiant. Her long dress was the palest shade of green, and she carried a simple bouquet of mixed white flowers with trailing ivy. Other than her engagement ring, the only jewelry she wore were the earrings Taylor had given her that ill-fated Christmas that nearly cost them each other. She chose to not wear a veil, letting her hair provide a frame for the cameo of her face.

She kissed her father, then took her place beside Taylor, ready to begin again.

EPILOGUE

Taylor, co-host of the Tony awards, watched from the wings as the number from the last nominated musical was performed. Next up was his category, Best Actor in a Musical. He could see Laura from where he was standing. She was still the most beautiful woman in the place. Meg and Betta were seated next to her, and she didn't look much older than their now-grown daughters. All three of them looked much more nervous than he felt.

Tomorrow, Meg would be married. He looked forward to reminding her that she had said she would never fall in love. He knew Annie would have been proud of her…and of him, he hoped. Betta, home from Milan, had designed Meg's wedding dress and would serve as her sister's maid of honor.

He listened as veteran star, Michael Crawford, read the names of the nominees. This role had brought him full circle. He was doing a revival of the show that had given him his start. Only, this time, he was playing the older husband instead of the young singing master. It seemed appropriate somehow.

Then Crawford announced, "The Tony goes to—Taylor Morgan!" He watched as the women in his life came to their feet applauding and cheering. He could see the tears in Laura's eyes from here.

Taking the stage, and his award, Taylor. stepped to the microphone. "They say that behind every successful man is a woman. In my case, it's taken six of them to get me where I am today. The first was my mother, who gave me the key to the magic. The second was Annie Miller, my friend and support through the hungry years. The third and fourth are my elder daughters, Megan and Elisabetta, who have kept me on my toes. Fifth is my youngest daughter, Annie, who should be in bed by now but probably isn't. She keeps me young when she isn't taking years off my life." Taylor met Laura's eyes as he finished, "And, finally, my beautiful wife, Laura, who taught me the most important lesson of all...*timing is everything.*"

ABOUT THE AUTHOR

Sabra Brown Steinsiek is a native-born New Mexican who lives in Albuquerque with her husband, Will, and son, Jared, and their two cats, Vincent Vanilla and Hobbes America. An information specialist with the UNM Law Library, she is, in her "real life," a calligrapher, professional storyteller, and active e-mailer (wordesmythe@hotmail.com).